Live And Let Spy

(The King's Rogues Book 1)

Elizabeth Ellen Carter

Print Edition

Published by Dragonblade Publishing, an imprint of Kathryn Le Veque Novels, Inc

By Elizabeth Ellen Carter
Captive of the Corsairs, *Heart of the Corsairs Series*
Revenge of the Corsairs, *Heart of the Corsairs Series*
Shadow of the Corsairs, *Heart of the Corsairs Series*
Dark Heart
Live and Let Spy, *King's Rogues Series*

Knight Everlasting Series by Cassidy Cayman
Endearing
Enchanted
Evermore

Midnight Meetings Series by Gina Conkle
Meet a Rogue at Midnight, book 4

Second Chance Series by Jessica Jefferson
Second Chance Marquess

Imperial Season Series by Mary Lancaster
Vienna Waltz
Vienna Woods
Vienna Dawn

Blackhaven Brides Series by Mary Lancaster
The Wicked Baron
The Wicked Lady
The Wicked Rebel
The Wicked Husband
The Wicked Marquis
The Wicked Governess
The Wicked Spy
The Wicked Gypsy
The Wicked Wife

Books from Dragonblade Publishing

Dangerous Lords Series by Maggi Andersen
The Baron's Betrothal
Seducing the Earl
The Viscount's Widowed Lady

Also from Maggi Andersen
The Marquess Meets His Match

Knights of Honor Series by Alexa Aston
Word of Honor
Marked by Honor
Code of Honor
Journey to Honor
Heart of Honor
Bold in Honor
Love and Honor
Gift of Honor
Path to Honor
Return to Honor

Beastly Lords Series by Sydney Jane Baily
Lord Despair

Legends of Love Series by Avril Borthiry
The Wishing Well
Isolated Hearts
Sentinel

The Lost Lords Series by Chasity Bowlin
The Lost Lord of Castle Black
The Vanishing of Lord Vale
The Missing Marquess of Althorn
The Resurrection of Lady Ramsleigh
The Mystery of Miss Mason

Highland Loves Series by Melissa Limoges
My Reckless Love
My Steadfast Love
My Passionate Love

Clash of the Tartans Series by Anna Markland
Kilty Secrets
Kilted at the Altar
Kilty Pleasures

Queen of Thieves Series by Andy Peloquin
Child of the Night Guild
Thief of the Night Guild
Queen of the Night Guild

Dark Gardens Series by Meara Platt
Garden of Shadows
Garden of Light
Garden of Dragons
Garden of Destiny

Rulers of the Sky Series by Paula Quinn
Scorched
Ember
White Hot

Highlands Forever Series by Violetta Rand
Unbreakable
Undeniable

Viking's Fury Series by Violetta Rand
Love's Fury
Desire's Fury
Passion's Fury

Also from Violetta Rand
Viking Hearts

The Sins and Scoundrels Series by Scarlett Scott
Duke of Depravity

The Sons of Scotland Series by Victoria Vane
Virtue
Valor

Dry Bayou Brides Series by Lynn Winchester
The Shepherd's Daughter
The Seamstress
The Widow

Men of Blood Series by Rosamund Winchester
The Blood & The Bloom

Dedication

I'd like to thank my long-suffering husband, Duncan, who can tell at a glance when I'm plotting – and who helps keep me honest when I try to get away with unworkable macguffins. A big thank you to my queen, Kathryn Le Veque and the rest of the wonderful Dragonblade Publishing authors who are so generous and inspirational. And to my amazing editor, Scott, who provides such insightful observations.

Table of Contents

Chapter One 1
Chapter Two 12
Chapter Three 22
Chapter Four 31
Chapter Five 40
Chapter Six 49
Chapter Seven 58
Chapter Eight 68
Chapter Nine 77
Chapter Ten 86
Chapter Eleven 97
Chapter Twelve 107
Chapter Thirteen 116
Chapter Fourteen 125
Chapter Fifteen 135
Chapter Sixteen 145
Chapter Seventeen 155
Chapter Eighteen 164
Chapter Nineteen 174
Chapter Twenty 183
Chapter Twenty-One 191
Chapter Twenty-Two 204
Chapter Twenty-Three 214
Chapter Twenty-Four 224

Chapter Twenty-Five..233
Chapter Twenty-Six..243
Chapter Twenty-Seven..252
Chapter Twenty-Eight..264
Chapter Twenty-Nine..273
Chapter Thirty..283
Chapter Thirty-One..291
Chapter Thirty-Two..299
Epilogue..305
Author's Note..309

To old friends and new.

There is a tide in the affairs of men, which taken at the flood, leads on to fortune. Omitted, all the voyage of their life is bound in shallows and in miseries. On such a full sea are we now afloat. And we must take the current when it serves, or lose our ventures.

– William Shakespeare (Julius Caesar)

Chapter One

Admiralty House, London
May 1804

ADAM HARDACRE HAD long passed the sailors practicing the drills on the parade ground, yet the regimented strike of the marshal's drum vibrated through the very core of his being.

One, two, dru-um, dru-um, three, four, dru-um, dru-um…

He marched down the magnificent halls of Admiralty House in time to the beat only he could hear.

Attired in boatswain's dress uniform, he cut an impressive figure.

Six foot tall, clean shaven, sandy hair lightened further still by the sun, face lightly lined by the weather, Hardacre's quick, thoughtful manner had propelled him from the ranks of able seaman to one of the leading petty officers aboard his ship and, indeed, in the entire service.

Rising to the rank of a petty officer in the Royal Navy would be enough for many men – particularly for ones of uninspiring birth, such as the son of a carpenter from Ponsnowyth in Cornwall – but the world of a petty officer was not enough for Adam Christopher Hardacre.

One, two, dru-um, dru-um, three, four, dru-um, dru-um…

He had passed his examinations, so there could be no possible reason why he should not be elevated to the ranks of the senior officers as lieutenant.

Without conceit, Adam knew he was an exceptional sailor, respected by his bosun's mates as well as the officers above him. At thirty-six, he was one of the oldest officers to sit for the lieutenant's examination. That, in and of itself, caused a great deal of stir.

He did not walk alone today. At his side marched his friend and advocate, Lieutenant Harold Bickmore. The fact the twenty-eight year old outranked him, not only on ship, but also in social convention, didn't matter a bit.

Adam was glad to have Harold at his side. He was nervous. But he'd sooner spit at the devil than admit it.

One, two, dru-um, dru-um, three, four, dru-um, dru-um...

The two men rounded a corner to the final long corridor that would take them to the boardroom.

"Now, remember," said Harold in a whisper. "This is the final interview before Admiral Stroughton; remember what we rehearsed."

All Adam could manage was a curt nod. He knew very well it was the final interview. He'd run through it ten times with Harold and he'd run it through his mind a hundred times more. He stretched the fingers that had been gripping the brim of his bosun's hat, its tall crown painted with the symbol of his ship, the *Andromeda*.

He marched to a stop before the big, heavy oak doors. Harold watched him intently. Adam ignored him and took a deep breath before raising his gloved hand. He rapped on the door twice before taking half a step back.

The door was opened by another lieutenant, not someone Adam knew.

"Petty Officer Adam Hardacre?"

Adam snapped to attention and crisply saluted.

"Yes, sir!"

The lieutenant glanced away and acknowledged Bickmore with a nod befitting their equal rank.

"Follow me gentlemen. The Board will see you now."

They crossed an anteroom where a dozen other officers worked at desks or pored over maps. Adam didn't look to the left or to the right, but caught several of the men glancing up at their party out of the corner of his eye.

The escort knocked at the inner door. The hubbub of voices from inside ceased.

"Enter."

The door opened.

Adam waited two beats before complying. It was his habit to do a visual reconnoiter of his surroundings before blundering into *anything*.

The boardroom was modern, as was Admiralty House itself – just ten years old. The south-facing windows were deeply recessed and flooded the room with natural light. The coffered ceiling above added to the impressive height that such an auspicious space demanded.

The wall facing the windows was lined with books and charts.

But by far, the most impressive feature was at the far end of the room. Dominating the wall was a large clock, about three feet in diameter by Adam's estimation. It showed the time to be a quarter after two. Below it, fluted Corinthian columns flanked two glass-fronted bookcases and, in the center, stood two large globes, one shelf above another.

Finally, Adam turned his attention to the table in the center of the room, inset with green baize, large enough to seat ten men with ease.

Today there were five. Four Royal Navy officers comprised the board – Admiral Stroughton, two vice-admirals, and a captain. The fifth was a civilian, a man in his late forties, judging by his face.

Adam caught Harold's eye and detected a slight furrow between his eyes. His friend had obviously had the same thought as he did.

What the hell is a civilian doing here?

"Petty Officer Adam Christopher Hardacre," the lieutenant announced to the gathering. "Currently serving on the third class frigate, *Andromeda*."

Adam smartly stood to attention and kept his eyes on the minute hand slowly making its way down the clock face.

"At ease, Petty Officer Hardacre," said Admiral Stroughton.

Adam stood with his feet apart.

"Won't you and your second take a seat?"

"Thank you, sir."

Adam sat at the end of the table, placing the hat to his left, while Harold took the seat at his right.

The naval officers looked down at the papers before them. Adam could no longer see the civilian. He was at the far end of the table, obscured by the two rear admirals.

Adam squared his shoulders. His life was before each man in those papers. In them, he was certain he would be judged worthy of joining the highest ranks of the Royal Navy.

"You have been with the Royal Navy for twenty years," continued Admiral Stroughton. "Is that correct, Mr. Hardacre?"

"It is, sir."

"And before that you were apprenticed to your father as a carpenter. What caused you to enlist at the age of sixteen?"

"I was..."

Adam didn't want to say he was *pressed* into the Royal Navy, although forced he most certainly was.

The civilian, who had yet to be introduced, leaned forward. "...Carried away by patriotic fervor?" he offered.

Adam met the man's look and acknowledged it with one of his own. There was something leonine about the man, predatory – and it wasn't just his reddish hair, glinting with a few strands of silver that did it either.

"You could say that, sir."

The admiral riffled through his notes once more. "You worked as a ship's carpenter apprentice, then promoted to able seaman, leading hand, bosun's mate, and now bosun. For a man in your situation, you should be very proud of your accomplishments."

Adam raised his chin.

Yes, he knew what *that* was code for. Few men outside the noble or moneyed classes aspired to reach beyond what fate had allotted them.

"I *am* proud, sir. But I know I can offer my country more."

The civilian leaned in once again. "No wife? No family?"

"None to speak of, sir. I am wedded to the Navy."

And at that, the man made a note on his report with a pencil and sat back with an air of finality.

This time, Adam *did* exchange a glance with Bickmore, and it was enough to tell him this was an unusual procedure, indeed.

"I understand, Mr. Hardacre," said Admiral Stroughton, "that this is not the first time you have sat for the Executive Officer's examinations."

Aye, there was the rub.

"Twice prior to this, sir. Each with more than a passing grade. The second result better than the first."

Again, there was more shuffling of paper at the table.

"In fact," Adam continued, "last time, I finished second in a class of two hundred officers."

"Well," announced one of the vice-admirals, "I'm pleased to inform you, this time, you have finished top of your class. Our congratulations to you, Mr. Hardacre."

Warmth and pride bloomed in his chest. These men couldn't possibly refuse his promotion now. He controlled the outward expression of his emotion, a slight flex of his right hand, the one that carried his tattoo, was his only "tell."

"Thank you, sir," he answered.

"Indeed, of this year's crop of candidates, you are certainly among the most outstanding…"

It was subtle, so subtle he almost missed it.

It was a change in the atmosphere as though the barometric pressure had just dropped a couple of bars. At sea, Adam would identify the signs of impending gloom – rain or a storm. The ability ran through his core like a sixth sense. He didn't need an instrument to tell him what his body told him was true.

He had once saved an entire flotilla of ships off the coast of Barbados with his instinct. He had assumed the role of post-captain and ordered the fleet of British vessels out to sea to ride out a fierce storm that had taken everyone else by surprise. Two days later, only the *Andromeda* and the two schooners that followed his order were undamaged.

His right hand flexed once more.

Admiral Stroughton sat up straight, pulling his papers together. He gave the civilian a direct look, and closed the cardboard cover. Stroughton looked Adam directly in the eye.

"It is with profound regret that we advise we will not be promoting you to lieutenant."

"What?"

The outburst came, fortunately, from Harold, the heat of anger turning the man's face florid. Adam felt the same emotion, but he pushed it down, down, down until he'd submerged it, mindful of the powder keg of fury in his soul.

The voice of his sixteen-year-old self screamed in his ear.

No! It's not fair! It's not right!

"Might I know the reason, sir?" To his own ears, the question had the grumble of distant thunder.

"Your age is a factor for one," said the vice-admiral.

"And your unfortunate background means you are unlikely to be…" the other vice-admiral looked to his compatriots around the table as if to ask for help in searching for the right word, "…the right fit."

Now the fuse had been lit. Adam could feel it burning in his gut.

"What my colleague is saying," added the first vice-admiral, "is that some of the senior officers might find it difficult to accept taking orders from someone who is not their social equal."

Adam pushed back his chair and rose to his feet.

He would *not* lose his temper. To do so would only prove the point in their eyes. But by God, it was a struggle.

"Twenty years..." he said through gritted teeth "Twenty years, I've willingly given in the service of my country, and now I am to be spat at?"

"Calm down, Mr. Hardacre," said Admiral Stroughton with a level of indignation as if Adam had thrust himself angrily forward across the table. "Lieutenant Bickmore, as Hardacre's second, please speak sense to the man—"

Adam sensed rather than saw Harold stand up beside him. But his second said nothing. His silent show of support was welcome right now.

"More than half my life, gentlemen," Adam continued, "and you all but tell me it is worthless? I risk my life to defend English interests, English principles of justice against the forces of tyranny, and all I ask in return is every Englishman's right – equality under the law. I do not demand more than I have earned from my own effort, effort which, I might add, appears to have outranked every other officer candidate for lieutenant."

A hubbub arose of protesting, indignant murmurs from the officers at the table. Of all the men before him, only the civilian did not look offended. Indeed, he looked almost disinterested.

Adam raised his voice but only enough to be heard.

"I will no longer play in a rigged game, *sirs*! I hereby resign from the Royal Navy, commencing from this very moment."

He turned on his heel and pushed away his chair with one sweeping motion. The chair teetered unsteadily a moment before righting on its four legs.

Without looking to the left or right, Adam marched out of the door, past the adjutants and down the hall he had strode along filled with hope not twenty minutes before.

He was vaguely aware of Harold behind him, calling his name, but the red mist at the corners of his vision allowed him to only see what was ahead. He was only aware he'd held his breath when he emerged into London's late afternoon and onto Whitehall.

He crossed the street into Horse Guards Parade, looking for some kind of sanctuary in the gardens of St. James' Park.

He made it within sight of Buckingham Palace before Harold caught up enough to clamp a hand on his shoulder.

"Let it be, Adam, as a friend."

Adam slowed and came to a stop.

"There are days when I wonder if it has all been worth it."

Adam spied a bench being vacated by two pretty young ladies out for a stroll. He made his way toward it and set himself down heavily. Fury roiled in him, so he kept his eyes on two swans gliding serenely on the lake.

"They've treated you shabbily, man," said Harold. "There's no doubt about that."

"It's for the last time," Adam warned.

Silence stretched out between the two for a length of time until the spell was broken by the peal of bells from Westminster Abbey.

"What are you going to do?"

"Get drunk?" Adam offered and, even as he did so, shook his head.

Harold took the comment as the jest it was intended and grinned. "So what *will* you do?"

"I don't know. Go back to Cornwall perhaps."

"I can't see you rusticating."

Adam let out a long sigh and stretched his legs. "Neither can I. I just need time to think."

Harold got to his feet, fiddling with the hat in his hand. "I'm still your friend, Adam. Anything you need…you only have to ask."

Adam held out his hand. Harold stopped playing with the hat brim and accepted the firm handshake.

"Thank you."

Adam counted to three hundred to ensure Harold had long gone before he allowed his shoulders to slump. He needed something physical to do. The brisk stride across the park had not been enough. His body clamored for motion, manifesting itself in shaking hands which he had concealed as clenched fists.

He recalled his sixteen-year-old self, terrified of this new life he had no memory of signing up for. He had been young then with no experience, but a whole world of opportunity ahead of him. Now, he was a man with experience, but no opportunity.

Shadows lengthened as the sun began to fall. He couldn't just sit like a lumpen until the end of time. He got to his feet.

"I hope you're not leaving on my account."

He swiftly turned. It was the civilian from Admiralty House. He hadn't even heard the man approach.

"No, by *all* means," said Adam, giving a sweeping bow. "Take the bench, take the park, take the devil, too, for all I care. I'm leaving."

The stranger grinned, clearly amused. Adam's hands turned into fists once again.

"I wanted to see you before I left London," the man said. "And I'm very much obliged to you for making it easy. I thought it would take me days to track down whatever tavern you were drowning your sorrows in."

"Go to hell! Who the devil do you think you are?"

The man didn't react at all to the invective. He reached into his dark blue coat and withdrew a thick white card. He held it out.

"My name is Sir Daniel Ridgeway, and I have a proposition for you."

Adam accepted the proffered card with reluctance and looked at it.

Charteris House
Truro, Cornwall

"And what *is* your proposition?"

Ridgeway shook his head, giving Adam a chance to look the man up and down more thoroughly. He was solidly built. Perhaps he'd been a boxer in his day, but unlike others long retired from the ring, this one had not gone to fat. Oddly, the silver that glinted in his dark reddish hair made the man look younger, rather than aging him.

He was forced to acknowledge Ridgeway exuded physical power as well as aristocratic confidence.

"No. Not here," said Ridgeway. "Come to Charteris House three weeks from now."

"Why?"

"I'm not prepared to discuss it here."

Adam sneered contemptuously.

"I've been pushed around and humiliated quite enough," he said, lifting up the calling card. "You either tell me what all this is about, or I tear this into pieces and lay you out on your pompous, aristocratic arse."

Ridgeway weathered Adam's rage with equanimity – in fact, with too much calm.

Adam's eyes narrowed.

"Did *you* have anything to do with me not making lieutenant?"

"Look at your right hand, man!" said Ridgeway. "They were *never* going to give you that promotion. No matter how much you deserved it."

Adam's eyes were drawn back to his right hand and the crossed anchors tattoo. The mark of Cain.

"And you *do* deserve better than that. *That's* what I'm offering you Mr. Hardacre, *if* you're willing to take a chance offered by a pompous, aristocratic arse."

Before Adam could draw breath to refuse, the man reached back into his coat pocket and pulled out a thickly wadded envelope.

"Fifty pounds. Consider it a signing bounty."

Adam regarded the envelope in Ridgeway's hands.

"I could walk away now and be fifty pounds the richer with no obligation to you."

"You could. But you won't."

Adam snorted and took the envelope.

"You seem very sure of yourself."

Ridgeway grinned in response.

"I know what sort of man I'm dealing with."

"Do you now?"

"A man with curiosity, and that's good enough to begin with. I'll be expecting you in early June, Mr. Hardacre."

Ridgeway tipped his hat and started back in the direction of Whitehall before halting and half-turning back to look at Adam.

"Whatever you decide to do, Mr. Hardacre, I'd be most obliged if you spoke to no one about this conversation. Not even your friends."

Chapter Two

Kenstec House
Cornwall
June 1804

"GOODBYE! YOU *WILL* write to me, won't you, Miss Collins?"

Olivia accepted the brief and enthusiastic farewell embrace of Lydia Denton.

"Of course I will," she assured the girl – correction – young woman. "It has been an honor to be your governess for the past ten years. I'm sure you made your late father proud."

Mercifully, Olivia considered, Lydia favored her mother in looks – both the Denton women boasted fair hair and skin, as well as pretty blue eyes. Lydia would not want for suitors. She was as perfect as any sixteen-year-old could boast of being. And her mother, Caroline, was still a very handsome widow of not yet forty, so she, too, would not lack male attention if she wished it.

And, in that case, their permanent relocation to London, following a summer in Bath, was a shrewd decision, Olivia thought, although it wasn't her place to remark on such a thing.

She bobbed a curtsy to the squire's widow. How was it that, dressed in lavender, in deference to her half-mourning, Caroline Denton looked younger than she had eight months prior, just before her husband's death?

"Thank you for staying on and helping Mr. Fitzgerald settle the estate," the widow said. "I'm sure you will not be waiting long for a new situation."

"Your letter of recommendation was most generous, Madam, thank you."

Mistress Caroline inclined her head graciously in response before the groomsmen aided her into the carriage.

Olivia waved as the vehicle made its way down the drive and watched as it disappeared through the copse of trees that lined the border of the estate on three sides.

An afternoon breeze from the Carrick Roads, just a short distance away, tugged at Olivia's skirts. She headed back into the house the long way around, via the kitchen where Polly Trellow bustled about. Polly was a plump and jolly woman, the wife of Jory Trellow, owner of the Angler's Arms. She had taken on the role of temporary cook and housekeeper for the family after Cook left on the news that the new widow was to sell Kenstec House.

In fact, all the servants had either found new positions or had gone on ahead to London to set up a new household for their mistress and her daughter. Only Olivia, caught in the strange social status of a governess – neither servant nor family – now remained.

"I don't like the idea of a young girl such as ye stayin' in the big house here alone," said Polly – and not for the first time this week. "Ye be a sensible lass. Why don't ye come and stay with Jory and me at the Arms?"

Olivia lifted up the cloth covering the wicker basket and saw game pie. She sniffed. It was still warm and smelled delicious. Despite Polly's attempts at persuasion over the past week, she knew Olivia was not going to change her mind.

"Tosh! I'll only be alone overnight," she answered. "Mr. Fitzgerald is arriving first thing tomorrow morning. Then I shall be too busy and too exhausted helping him to sort out the squire's papers to traipse back and forth.

"Besides, I have plenty else to do. Miss Lydia's room for one. The gowns she's discarded need sorting, and I also have free rein in the squire's library. I'm sure I can find a book or two to read and pass the hours when I'm not busy."

Olivia glanced over at the woman. Polly's ample posterior was the only view as she bent nearly double to blow more life into the coals in the kitchen fireplace.

"Well, as ye say, Miss," Polly said, adding more wood to the fire to build up its heat, "but if there is anythin' ye be needin' then take the short path through to the woods – we're less than a mile away."

"Thank you, Polly."

"Hrumph! Ye can thank me tomorrow when I find ye're still alive and not had yer throat slit or worse by some footpad."

Olivia laughed. "You can be as gruesome as you wish. If someone did have a mind to murder, then the ghost of Kenstec House will have me as an eternal companion."

"There's no such thing as—" Polly caught herself. But Olivia pounced on the admission.

"—Ah-ha! That's not what you told me two nights ago. Your spectral spook is no more real than *Jenny Greenteeth!*"

Polly screwed her nose up at Olivia. She gathered up two baskets, holding one in each hand. "Well, don't ye come complainin' to me, Missy, that's all I'll say on the matter."

Olivia approached and gave the big woman a hug.

"Thank you, Polly. You and Jory have been so kind to us all. I shall miss this place when I leave."

She endured the woman's censorious look with good humor and escorted her to the door.

"Be sure to lock the door behind me."

"Yes, Polly. I'll be quite all right, you know."

"Hrumph!"

Despite her brave words, Olivia spent the next hour after Polly's departure going around the ground floor of the three-story manor house checking that all the windows were, indeed, locked. The house already had the air of desertion. Many of the finest pieces of furniture, including the carpets, had already been shipped off to London to adorn the new townhouse. Olivia's footsteps echoed throughout the rooms and the passageways.

It would be easy to imagine herself a ghost here…

"Don't be silly, girl," she told herself out loud. "You'll give yourself the *heebie-jeebies* if you keep on like that."

She returned to the kitchen and filled a coalscuttle to carry to her own bedroom that adjoined Miss Lydia's on the second floor. She made up a fire but didn't light it yet. She made more trips back and forth to return with several buckets of water, then, lastly, the pie and a bottle of cider.

It was tempting to light the fire and settle down a while. But, no, she had herself a job of work to do before nightfall, and she would do it.

She went to Lydia's room. It was on the southwest corner of the house, and featured corner windows that, on a clear day like today, gave a view of the sea beyond. Olivia felt it was a pity she possessed only the most middling talent for painting. A view like this was worth remembering.

Perhaps she should try to do it justice before she left and create a keepsake of her very first posting as governess as an untried eighteen-year-old young lady.

How naive she was then…

Kenstec House may not have ghosts, but it *did* have secrets. She knew that from the very first morning she arrived.

Her mind turned to the embarrassment she felt that day at getting off on the wrong foot with her employer. She had made the mistake of thinking Miss Lydia's father was actually the girl's grandfather.

Mortified she was at the time.

Olivia shook her head now with wry amusement and began sorting through the half-dozen dresses Lydia had carelessly thrown over a chair, one of only two pieces of furniture left in the room.

The other was a large oak wardrobe taking up half the length of one wall, apparently deemed too heavy to move, and so abandoned.

All Olivia had known from the advertisement she'd answered was that "a young lady of good skills and refinement" was required as governess to a girl of six years old. The slightly-hunched man who addressed her on arrival was clearly well into his sixth decade. He looked as though the burden of the world had been put on his shoulders, weighing him down and spreading out across his middle.

She was not afraid to admit the man had terrified her at first. One did not so much have a *conversation* with Squire Denton as much as respond quickly to his grumped questions. The mystery of it had been how he had wooed and won his wife, Caroline, who was startling in her youth and beauty.

She was the squire's second wife, Olivia learned as time went by, but no one ever spoke about her predecessor. *That* was the true mystery. No signs of the first mistress of Kenstec remained in the house, and if not for the headstone in the churchyard, there would have been no reminder of her at all.

Of the daughter from that first marriage, Olivia knew even less. Once a year, on All Souls' Day, several of the old family servants would make a private pilgrimage to the village church and pray for the girl they called Constance. But unlike her mother, there was no grave marker, and the servants would not be drawn on her.

It was as though Constance Denton had disappeared from the face of the earth.

Olivia held up the first dress. It was a lovely evening gown in silk taffeta, a sea green shot with blue and bore scalloped lace trim over the bust and sleeves. She had handled the garment a number of times when she acted as Lydia's lady's maid but never dreamed of owning something as beautiful herself.

It would make a lovely wedding dress...

If she ever married.

There was no other sound in the house other than the muted rushing of the wind, the rustling leaves outside, and the steady tick of the long case clock in the hall, which Olivia keep wound for familiarity and comfort.

She ran her hand over the beautiful fabric – a gift from her former charge. *Try it on,* a little voice whispered. *There is no one to see.*

After a moment's hesitation, Olivia unfastened the buttons of her dark blue cotton day dress. It slipped to the floor. Out of habit, she picked it up and lay it over the other cast-off garments Lydia had left behind – a raspberry red day dress with brown velvet trim, a linen nightshift – unworn and still in its paper packaging – another day dress in cream, decorated with exotic flowers of turquoise blue, cyclamen pink, and grass green.

She slipped into the evening gown. It fit, but only just. At twenty-eight, her figure was more mature than Lydia's. Olivia started for the wardrobe. Inside the door was a full-length mirror. She hesitated.

Did she want to see her reflection? The gown was oh-so-beautiful. She wanted it to fit, and she wanted to look beautiful, but what if the whole thing was ridiculous – like casting pearls before swine?

Before she could second guess herself, she reached forward and pulled open the wardrobe door.

The squeak of the hinge hid her own gasp of surprise. She barely recognized the woman in the mirror. She loosened the knot of brown hair at the nape and piled it high on her head, letting small tendrils fall about her neck.

The neckline of the dress stretched across her bust, lifting the breasts slightly so the tops of them were just in view over the lace.

She turned this way and that, examining the fall of the gown and the figure beneath.

"Vanity thy name is woman," she muttered.

Where on earth would she ever wear such a thing? She removed the gown and put her comfortable, familiar day dress back on. She carried the gown and the rest of Lydia's largess into her own room and packed them away.

When she returned to Lydia's room, she found it warm from the afternoon sun streaming through the uncurtained windows. She opened one. Eddies of salt-tinged air swept through the room.

Since she was alone in the house and the owners would never return, Olivia was – at least for tonight – mistress of Kenstec. Just as she had tried on the green evening gown a short while ago, now she did something she would never have dreamed of doing while she was in service.

She approached and touched Lydia's wardrobe, sweeping a hand across the doors, feeling the fine joins where foliate marquetry had been cut into the oak. She was familiar with the piece and yet it was strange how it overpowered the room now in a way it hadn't when the space was filled other furniture.

It was an old piece; it might have always been with the house. Had it been there when the first Mistress Denton and her daughter lived? Perhaps this had been Constance's room…

She explored the old wardrobe systematically, starting with the center doors and their hanging spaces. Empty. No treasures, no secrets, no long-forgotten pieces of jewelry that Olivia would be obliged to post on to their rightful owner.

The compartment on the left with pull out shelves and drawers was also empty, apart from the faded rose-colored linen paper that still faintly smelled of the distilled essence of that flower. The compartment on the far right of the wardrobe was similarly appointed, except it contained two large drawers at the bottom.

Olivia pulled out one drawer and then the other. Both empty. But on closing the bottom drawer, she felt resistance and found it refused to close fully again. She withdrew the drawer completely and bent down to peer inside the void. That's when she spotted it, a desiccated bundle of paper held together by a black ribbon. It looked as if it had fallen back there and been compressed against the backboard of the compartment for years. She reached in and pulled it out.

The breeze from the window lifted one yellowed corner of paper. She saw a name written with an unschooled hand – *Constance.*

Bang!

Olivia jumped and dropped the papers. A door had slammed somewhere within the house. It took a moment to still her racing heart.

Wind. It is only the wind. There must have been an open window somewhere else in the house she had overlooked. She went in search of it.

By the time she returned to Lydia's old bedroom, the sun had moved fully to the western part of the sky and the glare from the undraped windows was nearly unbearable. She retrieved the letters and retreated to her own room which was cooler and where the sunlight was less intense.

She sat at her small writing desk and worked the knot of old ribbon that held the papers together. They were letters and, in the end, only six pieces of paper – little more than notes really. All were written by the same hand which she concluded was that of a male with only a modest education.

My darling Constance,

My words cannot do justice to what my heart said to me when I received your letter. It was as though you had reached into my very soul to see what was written there.

I love you.

Knowing that you share my desire makes our fleeting times together all the more precious to me.

Meet me by the old ruins in the woods this Wednesday at noon.

Your beloved Adam.

The other notes expressed the same ardor and invitation to an assignation.

Olivia smiled to herself as she wrapped up the letters and folded them into her own diary for safekeeping.

Perhaps Constance and her lover had eloped.

She liked that idea. Her own experience of romance was limited to reading novels. Few opportunities for flirtations came to a governess in this part of Cornwall.

An elopement…perhaps, that was why Constance's name was never spoken, although it was odd that some of the servants would hold a vigil for her on All Souls' Day if she were *not* dead.

A darker thought emerged. What if she *was* dead? Why and how? What if the thwarted lovers died together in a suicide pact? That could be the reason why Constance was not buried in the churchyard.

She could go and ask Reverend Fuller if she could search the parish records. It was a pity the old priest and his curate had long since passed away. They would have known Constance's story.

The late squire would have known…

Beaufort Denton had been a hard man, not given to sentiment or emotion, but surely he didn't completely expunge his daughter from his life.

The study. It might tell…

Olivia could count on one hand the number of times she had set foot inside the room. It was Squire Denton's domain; no one entered without permission. And when he was absent, the room was locked.

The light in Olivia's room turned gold and then pink, as the sun descended toward the sea. But late spring evening light meant she still had a little time left to explore.

She made her way down the stairs but hesitated at the entrance to the study, even though the door was ajar and in the coming days she was to assist with the papers in here. The habit of a decade was hard to break.

There were ghosts here, too. Their voices were heard in her memory – violent outbursts, tears, oppressive silences to which all the servants had been mute witnesses.

"Pull yourself together!"

It seemed to help to say the words aloud.

"Mistress Caroline and Mr. Fitzgerald asked you especially to help set the estate papers in order. You have the run of the house. You *have* permission to enter."

On hearing no dissenting voices, Olivia stepped across the threshold.

Chapter Three

Truro
Early June 1804

ADAM EXAMINED THE card given to him by the mysterious Sir Daniel Ridgeway.

Charteris House stood in the middle of a whitewashed terrace row of shops. Unlike the ironmongers to one side and the bank on the other, there was no indication what business might be transacted behind the bright red door. It carried no shingle and no awning outside under which a passerby might linger.

He had positioned himself in sight of it an hour ago and perused at his leisure over a pint and a meal at the pub on an opposite street corner. In all that time, no one went in and no one came out.

It would be just his luck for the place to be deserted.

Well, if nothing else, he still had forty pounds in his pocket and that might give him a chance to start life over somewhere.

He wiped his mouth and rose from the seat. He dropped some coins on the table, left the tavern and crossed the street.

He opened the red door and a bell over it tinkled brightly. The place seemed to be some kind of chandlery or perhaps a cartographer's. Large maps of the Cornish coast lined the walls, showing Portsmouth to Bristol and every town and hamlet in between, right down to every islet that made up the Scilly Islands.

Every conceivable surface was occupied by navigation equipment of various types – sextants, magnetic compasses, mapping compasses, a bell, deck pumps, cleats and chocks, chains and anchors. And on one wall, an eccentric set of ship's clocks – all accurately keeping the time. When he entered, he noted every single one read ten after ten.

He politely and disinterestedly examined the navigation items, waiting for the shopkeeper to emerge. At the sound of the quarter chime on two of the clocks, he decided he had been patient enough.

"Hello?" he called.

There was no response other than the metronomic ticking of the timepieces.

He walked behind the shop's counter and called again. Still no response.

He squatted and rummaged the shelf underneath the counter. No strongbox, no ledgers. Odd…

"May I *help* you?"

Adam raised his head slowly and somewhat sheepishly. Across the other side of the counter where *he* should have been, was a small man – just five-foot-two by his reckoning. He had appeared there silently and from nowhere. His black hair was slicked back revealing a pronounced widow's peak. Owlish eyes peered out from thick, round glasses.

Adam decided charm would be his best defense. He stood to his full height and moved around to the correct side of the counter.

"Forgive me, good fellow," he said. "I came in and I didn't see anyone here so I thought…"

"…You thought you'd steal my till."

"No!"

"Then state your name and business, sir," the little man demanded matter-of-factly.

"I'm here to see Sir Daniel Ridgeway."

The shopkeeper looked about as though searching for a peer of the realm amongst the flotsam.

"Well, he's not here."

Adam closed his eyes and counted to ten, feeling sick to the gut. He'd been made a fool of once more.

"Then I am mistaken," he ground out. "Good day, sir."

He surged forward, almost colliding with the man on his way to the door.

"Did you have an *invitation*?"

Adam's hand reached the door handle and stopped there. The brass was cool under the palm of his hand.

"An *invitation*," the man intoned once more.

"If you mean this," Adam said, retrieving from his pocket the plain white card with black type and holding it up, "then *yes,* I have an *invitation.*"

The little man held out his hand for it. Adam all but threw it at him. The shopkeeper examined it closely.

"We've been expecting you, Mr. Hardacre," he said with a direct look. "Return tomorrow morning at nine o'clock. Behind the map behind the counter is a door. Go upstairs and everything will be explained to you."

"You wouldn't care to explain things to me *now*, would you?"

"No, Mr. Hardacre, I would *not*. Remember, nine o'clock—"

"—The door behind the map, go upstairs…yes, I got all of that."

"In which case, we shall see you then."

IT WAS EARLY afternoon by the time the passenger coach had almost completed the twelve-mile journey from Truro to Falmouth, but Adam's foul temper had not abated one iota. In fact, a mile out from his destination, before the coach had made its descent into the town, he banged his hand on the roof of the carriage and demanded it stop.

He answered the coachman's sour look with one of his own, hoisted his pack over one shoulder, and watched the carriage trundle along the country road until it disappeared into its own dust.

From here, Adam could see the harbor below and amidst the forest of masts he picked out the vessel he knew was the *Andromeda*.

The journey here was additional insult to injury.

A letter from the Navy had found him at his temporary lodgings to say his resignation had been accepted, but he would have to see the paymaster from his own ship to collect his wages due and savings made.

Bastards.

At least a walk would burn off the some of the roiling resentment that lingered. He loved the *Andromeda*. He loved the crew on board and respected her captain, and he would miss her as much as a man would a retiring mistress, but there was a principle to stand on.

He paid for lodgings overnight at the Red Lion and booked passage on the early morning mail coach back to Truro. He would return to Charteris House simply because, if nothing else, Sir Daniel had gotten one thing right – he was a curious man.

"Adam! I didn't expect to see you here."

"Harold!"

Adam forced down the reflex to salute his senior officer. He had to remind himself that *he* was a civilian now.

"Good to see you, man. I take it you're here to see about your pay."

Adam confirmed it with nothing more than a nod and continued toward the ship. Harold Bickmore fell into step. "I should tell you your resignation has been the talk of the ship for the past fortnight, so be prepared to stand drinks at the pub tonight."

A wry smile in response was the best Adam could manage at the moment. He was conscious of how shabby he looked in his traveling clothes compared to the crisp uniform of the lieutenant.

"Officer aboard!"

Adam cast his eyes across the deck, watching the sailors as they worked, repairing parts of the rigging and polishing the brass trimmings to remove signs of corrosion. He couldn't help ask the question. "Have they replaced me as bosun?"

"There's a new man starting next week."

"Do I know him?"

Harold shook his head and escorted Adam down to the Master Secretary's room. The ship's purser, a man in his forties without a single strand of hair on his head, rose from his seat and extended his hand.

"Ye'll be missed here, Hardacre, that's for certain."

Adam shook the man's hand and thanked him quietly. The purser rummaged through his papers and found what he was looking for – a ledger account for Adam Christopher Hardacre.

"That's a decent payout, if ye don't mind me saying so Mr. Hardacre. A very tidy sum to retire on."

And, indeed, it was, nearly five hundred pounds. It was enough to buy a small working farm – which would be fine if he was a farmer, but he was not.

You could always go back to Ponsnowyth and buy back the old man's carpentry shop.

That didn't have much appeal either. Too many bittersweet memories.

"Now, I take it the captain knows ye're here? He asked me special like to let him know because he wanted to say farewell."

Adam nodded an acknowledgement, then shook his head. "I didn't write ahead, but I'm hanging around the area for a bit. I'll make sure I see Captain Sinclair before the *Andromeda* next ships out."

The purser signed several documents and then turned them around for Adam to sign. One of them was a cheque from the Bank of England – which could very well have been given to him back in London.

Bastards.

On top of the cheque was a cash amount of eleven pounds, ten shillings, and thruppence-ha'penny.

Accounted to the last ha'penny. Adam would have laughed if he wasn't still angry.

Once the business was concluded, Harold slapped him on the back. "Let's get drunk, like we were supposed to in London."

This time, Adam was hard pressed to disagree.

THREE HOURS LATER, a dozen crew from the *Andromeda* were gathered in a private room in the back of the Red Lion. Adam didn't consider himself drunk – he was far too cautious to let himself get so inebriated as to be an easy mark for some footpad – but still, the beer and rum he had consumed had left him feeling more merry than choleric.

So much so, he joined in a spontaneous chorus of Heart of Oak.

Come cheer up my Lads, 'tis to glory we steer,
To add something more to this wonderful year.
To honor we call you, as freemen, not slaves,
For who are so free as the sons of the waves?

Heart of oak are our ships, jolly tars are our men,
We always are ready, Steady, boys, steady,
We'll fight and we'll conquer again and again!

We ne'er see our foes but we wish them to stay,
They never see us but they wish us away.
If they run, why, we follow and run them ashore,
For if they won't fight us, we cannot do more.

"Damned bloody shame what the Navy did to you," said Harold for at least the tenth time this evening.

Adam's friend had been less moderate in his drinking than he. Already, Harold's face was red and his forehead drenched with sweat.

He swung an arm around Adam's shoulder and exhaled boozy breath into his face.

"If we were different sorts of people, old chum," he whispered, "we'd teach them a thing or two, wouldn't we?"

Adam threw off the arm and pushed Harold away.

"You're making no sense, you teasy git."

But the young man would not be deterred.

"That's 'cause you're not listening to me, me old mate," Harold punctuated his statement by jabbing his finger into Adam's chest, "I mean, a bit of turnabout has got to be fair play, right?"

"You've gone soft in the head."

"No, no, no, I mean it," Harold leaned in closer. Adam wrinkled his nose and pushed him an arm's length away. "There are people who think that French had it right all along."

Adam sobered right up.

"What exactly are you trying to say, Harold?"

The young lieutenant's eyes widened as though he'd suddenly become sober, too.

"What?"

Adam shook his head and shoved his friend back. Harold almost toppled off his chair. "Your head is going to rue your tongue, you daft bugger."

He got to his feet – more or less steadily – and called out to the assembled gathering.

"Next round is on me boys, but I'm off. Some of us have got to find a job in the morning."

A cheer went up. Adam threw a handful of coins on the table, bade the group goodnight and made his way out of the tavern.

Outside, he stopped and breathed in the summer night air mingled with salt from the sea and the scent of honeysuckle from one of the nearby cottages. He looked up at the near cloudless sky and examined the stars above, the constellations as familiar to him as the scars he wore, or the crossed anchors tattoo on his right hand that branded him – condemned him – to rising no higher than society allowed him.

He needed the bracing cold night air and sober, solitary reflection, not drink or company. He walked down to the water and looked across the estuary of the River Fal, fancying he could see the Ponsnowyth village church over there. He found himself a position on the sea wall and sat down to think.

Now, now, now...whatever happened to Constance Denton? It was a question he'd asked himself every so often over the years. No doubt, she'd be a grandmother by now, or nearly so. He smiled to himself trying to imagine how twenty years might have aged the fair-headed girl of eighteen he once knew.

Ah, there was no doubt *he* was nothing more than a summer fancy for the squire's daughter to console herself over her unhappy and unsuccessful first season. But, oh how he fancied himself truly in love as only a callow sixteen-year-old youth could be.

It would have been about this time of year twenty years ago that Adam first encountered her in the woods near Kenstec House. She was weeping alone by the banks of a stream that ran not far from the ruins of an old priory.

On that first occasion, he'd shared his lunch and made her laugh, cheering her up by telling funny stories about some of the villagers. When they parted, it was early evening and he summoned up the courage to tell her she was the prettiest girl he had ever seen.

The next week, she had left him a note tucked into the hollow of a tree, asking to meet the following day, and he was only too happy to oblige, once he'd been released from his duties as his father's apprentice.

Their romance had been chaste at first, both of them only too aware of the difference in their ages and stations. But after they had shared their first kiss, a passion between them burned hot.

Once he had been content to worship her from afar, but soon he worshiped her in body as they made love in the lea of the old ruins. What a wondrous experience it is when it is new, Adam thought.

By early August, he'd noticed a change. No longer would she leave notes begging to see him. Instead, it was *he* who would leave the notes. Each day, he fretted, wondering whether Constance would even turn up.

She did, but looking a little sadder each time. He was desperate to please her in whatever way he could, but Constance would refuse to tell him the cause of her sorrow. And when once she had been eager for the joining of their bodies, for his kisses and caresses, these signs of affection now came reluctantly until one day he stopped offering and she stopped asking.

Then she no longer responded to his notes.

His final plea had been in the form of a gift – a copy of his carpentry apprentice piece. Adam had made a writing box of plain mahogany on the outside but the lid was inlaid with marquetry in the shape of a star made up of little scraps of other woods.

He had included a secret message just for Constance, hidden in the back.

Behind the drawers, where only she would see, was another inlay in stained black to mimic ebony wood. It was a representation of nearby Pendennis Castle and, beneath it in maple, the letters C and A intertwined.

The gift was gone from the hollow of the tree when he checked the next day.

And standing up to walk away was the last thing he remembered until he woke miles out at sea with a split head, a clanging headache, and the master carpenter telling him he'd better shape up because he was in the Royal Navy now.

Adam slid off his stone perch and picked up a few loose pebbles from the road. He pitched them with all of his strength.

Just like the ebb and flow of the tide in the River Fal, so much water and so much time had passed.

Too much time to hang on to a first love.

Chapter Four

OLIVIA WOKE AT dawn and hurried down to the study the moment she was dressed.

She had spent four hours in Squire Denton's study last night, only stopping when the lines of ink swam before her eyes in the candlelight. At least the monumental task seemed less daunting in the light of day.

Her task was to sort papers for the solicitor's review. She had cleared the surface of the old squire's desk. All the household receipts were placed on one corner, papers that looked like business dealings on another and, finally, personal correspondence on another.

Polly and Jory arrived soon after seven o'clock, bringing breakfast and an energy that would shame people half their age.

"Don't mind us, Missy. We'll be startin' on the top floors with the cleanin'. Our Will's joinin' us today. Him and Jory'll be movin' the servants' furniture down to the lower floor so we can close the upper wing down proper."

By the time the hall clock chimed eight, Olivia had just one more cupboard and the bookcase to clear out. The latter would have to wait until she had access to the keys. She turned to the unlocked cupboard.

It was empty but for a mahogany box.

Olivia reached in and pulled it out. It was heavier than it appeared. She quickly turned and put it on a small side table. The box was a cube, about fifteen inches along all edges.

The top was inlaid with a beautiful multi-pointed marquetry star contained in a roundel, with depth and color brought to it by the choice of woods – ash and apple, beech and maple, walnut, pine, and oak.

Olivia stroked her fingertips over it. It was good work but, yet, something about it suggested it was not the work of a London cabinet maker.

She spied the small brass escutcheon. *Would it be too much to hope that it was unlocked?* Fortune favored her. The lid opened. So did the front face, which dropped to become a writing slope.

The slope was inset with a small green leather writing surface and a chiseled groove as a pen rest. Inside the box, foliage flourishes in beech decorated a shallow pen drawer at the bottom. Above the pen drawer were two square drawers with small turned knobs. She opened them and discovered the round inserts were empty where they should have contained bottles of ink.

A top drawer was decorated with two intertwined marquetry roses, the stem and thorns shaped to form a heart beneath the flower heads.

This was a *love* token!

Olivia sat back on her heels. This obviously did not belong to Lydia's mother or it would have been taken with them. The idea that the dour Squire Denton would purchase such a gift for his first wife did not at all match with her decade-long experience of her parsimonious and humorless employer.

She drew out the top drawer and discovered it contained a small diary in white calf leather – clearly a woman's accoutrement. And below it, another sheaf of letters.

Something caught her eye in the space behind the drawer. She pulled it out completely and soon all the others. She let out a gasp. There was a hidden message in the box itself!

An imposing castle in black and, beneath in pale wood, intertwined initials C and A. She thought instantly of the letters she had found last night – *Constance and Adam.*

And there was a date beneath the initials.

1783.

The diary! Olivia reinserted the drawers, but not before she retrieved the diary. She opened the cover and, in a young woman's handwriting, was the owner's name, *Constance Marie Denton.*

She stared at the name, transfixed. Then the spell was broken by the loud ringing of the front door bell.

Olivia dropped the diary, her hands shaking.

"That'll be Mr. Fitzgerald from Truro," Polly yelled. Then the old woman stuck her head in the doorway of the study. "Don't get up, dear. I'm closest to the door."

Olivia nodded mutely, hastily put the papers and diary back in the drawer, and closed the front and lid. And it was just a mahogany box once more.

She got to her feet at the sound of the front door opening and listened to the exchange of greetings between Polly and Mr. Fitzgerald. She wiped her still shaking hands on her olive green skirts.

Was this how Pandora felt?

At approaching footsteps, she went to the door of the study.

Peter Fitzgerald was aged about fifty, but he was a man who carried his years well. He was tall and his physique was still trim. His grey hair and a neatly trimmed Van Dyke beard gave an authoritative bearing. In the man's hand was a leather folio case.

"Good morning, Miss Collins," he greeted. Then he looked over her shoulder and into the study.

"My goodness, you've done a lot of work already. Thank you."

Olivia bobbed a curtsy and tried to find her tongue. Fortunately, Polly appeared.

"Now, would ye like me to bring in tea?"

"Thank you, Polly. That is most kind of you."

Olivia stood aside while Mr. Fitzgerald approached the squire's desk. She folded her hands within her skirts; a residue of guilt for putting her nose in where it didn't belong. She couldn't help a sideways glance at the mahogany box on the side table.

"I'm afraid the squire wasn't especially diligent in how he managed his documents," she said, looking back at the solicitor.

Fitzgerald flipped through one pile of papers, and then another. "You've done very well under the circumstances, my dear."

She blushed in spite of herself and it didn't go unnoticed.

Stop being a little fool. You've done nothing wrong.

She squared her shoulders and approached the desk.

"How should we proceed?"

"We're looking to establish the late squire's worth so we can finalize probate for the widow and her daughter." Fitzgerald smiled. He opened his case and pulled out two brand new ledgers. "We'll have to start with a process of elimination. If I may ask for you to run through these papers once again and summarize them in one of the ledgers? We're looking for anything that suggests Beaufort Denton might have had business interests or investments."

The day proceeded quite productively, and with the sounds of Polly and her family bustling about the cleaning, it felt as though Kenstec House lived once more. Yet soon, it would be sold.

The thought filled Olivia with sadness. She would miss this place. Ponsnowyth was a beautiful little village and the rolling green hills and the azure blue of the river that spilled into the sea just a short distance away were a delight. The climate here was the very model of *temperate* – never too hot, never too cold – and it almost never snowed in winter.

It suddenly occurred to her that she didn't even own a proper winter cloak. She would need one if she had to move up north.

That was a matter she would need to consider. There had been little need to search for a new position while the family still needed her. But over the past couple of months as her tenure was approaching its end, Olivia started going through the local papers looking for a new situation. So far, it had been to no avail.

There was nothing else for it. She would have to write to the agencies and move away from Ponsnowyth for good.

The clock struck one. Olivia heard Fitzgerald release a tired sigh and close his ledger with a thud.

"I don't know about you, Miss Collins, but I think we have worked hard enough for one day and the outdoor beckons. Will you take a turn about the garden with me?"

"That would be most agreeable, Mr. Fitzgerald."

While Fitzgerald worked the bolt to the French door that led out to the garden, Olivia went upstairs for her hat and a light shawl. As she followed the lawyer out into the garden through the study, she glanced at the mahogany box once again.

If only she'd had the forethought to put it back in the cupboard before Fitzgerald came into the study. No one else had known it was there, and though a good box, it was clearly made by a local craftsman, not one of the major cabinet makers, so it had little intrinsic value. Furthermore, the contents, such as *they* were, were unlikely to be of interest to Caroline Denton or her daughter.

Olivia worried her lip. She couldn't simply *take* it. That would be stealing. And yet the more she thought about the ill-starred lovers, the more intrigued she became.

She walked at Fitzgerald's side, letting him dictate their choice of path until they reached the part of the estate that fell toward the lowlands of Ponsnowyth and the sea beyond. Caroline Denton had the gardener place a seat there. Alone. On its own. *Lonely* – so very much like the mistress herself.

And yet from this vantage point, she could see the village beyond and the people like miniature figures. Women were hanging out washing. Young children played on the streets or were making their way to the river to fish or have some other adventure. Men were at their labors, too – milling timber in the lean-to outside the carpenter's shop, the fishmonger salting down a catch for preserving, farmers out in their fields.

And up here there was silence.

"Is aught amiss, Miss Collins? You seem very quiet."

"Forgive me, Mr. Fitzgerald. I've been woolgathering."

"You're not troubled, I hope? As a friend of the family – and of the household, I hope you will feel free to call on me if I can be of assistance."

She smiled. His attention of her was kind.

"If the truth be known," she said, "I shall be sad to leave this place. I had feared I would have to leave following the squire's death, so I am grateful for the extra six months. But I'm saddened to know I will have to leave the district, perhaps even the county."

"Must you go?"

"Mr. Fitzgerald," she said with a tinge of gentle reproof, "I *have* to earn a living."

"Will you not marry, Miss Collins? Surely during your time here, there has been a bachelor you might be content to settle down with? And, if I might be so bold, you are still a very handsome woman."

Olivia wondered whether there was supposed to be something else in those words.

"Alas, not for me," she said, moving away from him and the conversation by pretending an interest in the fruiting of a nearby Cornish Gillyflower apple. "But do not think me ungrateful for the life I have."

An uncomfortable moment's silence continued before Fitzgerald made the welcome suggestion to return to the house. This time, she set the pace – and made it a little quicker.

"I'm sorry that Beaufort Denton wasn't more generous in leaving you a bequest," he said.

"In truth, I was most surprised to have been considered," she said. "Ten pounds is not an inconsiderable sum – a pound per year of service…"

"And yet you have stayed on here and been of tremendous assistance to me. As executor of Beaufort's estate, I should be paying you, but I think, as you've gathered, there is little to spare in the estate at all."

"All of which rightfully belongs to Mistress Caroline and Miss Lydia," she observed. "No, Mr. Fitzgerald – your offer of payment is very kind, but…" A thought cut short her words.

Fitzgerald noticed her hesitation and paused. Olivia licked her lips and prepared a question. *This was an opportunity to ask for the box without revealing her true motivation.*

"What is it, my dear?" Fitzgerald prompted.

"Well, as it happened, I came across an old writing box in the back of one of the cupboards. You might have seen it on the side table." She looked up at Fitzgerald, knowing he was watching her intently.

"Uh…it's not very expensive," she went on. "In fact, it looks like something which might have been made here in the village." She was aware she was rushing her words. It took just about all of her effort to not lick her lips again. She looked and sounded guilty enough as it was. "It's little more than a trifle, a keepsake, but I'd like to have it, if I may?"

Fitzgerald inclined his head, giving her a look that seemed to waver between pity, indulgence, and condescension. Under other circumstances, Olivia would have rankled but, now, she swallowed every ounce of pride in the hopes the solicitor would not see through her ruse.

"Let's take a look when we get back, shall we?"

Not a complete victory, but not a defeat either.

Fitzgerald offered her his arm and, under the circumstances, it seemed churlish not to take it.

Perhaps flirting and playing the coquette was the way some women achieved their ends but it was not something she felt comfortable doing – not that she even had a talent for it.

When they entered the study, Polly was there with a tray of tea and light refreshments.

She bobbed a curtsy and addressed Fitzgerald.

"Jory and me have finished doin' the list of furniture from the top floor servants' quarters, and the second floor with the exception of Miss Olivia's room," she said. "I got most of the kitchen sorted, too."

"And an estimable job, too, I have no doubt," said Fitzgerald.

Polly blushed and curtsied once more. "Then there's just the ground floor to do. We can get started on that tomorrow, if it be pleasin' ye, Mr. Fitzgerald. It will take another two to three days, by our reckonin'."

"Yes, that will be fine, Mrs. Trellow, but I think I can lighten your load just a little."

Olivia held her breath as he approached the box.

"Is this the one, my dear?"

She nodded mutely.

The solicitor picked it up and gave it a cursory examination from the outside. Then, cradling it with one hand, he opened the lid and allowed the slope front to sag open while he took a quick look inside. Not concerning himself with further exploration, he closed it up again and set it back down on the table.

Olivia's heart pounded in her chest, demanding air. She compromised by letting out a small breath and taking in another.

"This is for Miss Olivia," he said to Polly, "an ex-gratia payment, because she has been such a kind and efficient *helpmeet* to me."

"Thank you very much, Mr. Fitzgerald," said Olivia, and her heart started beating again.

The solicitor smiled at her and she returned it with a mix of gratitude, delight, and relief. Then it struck her – his was not the benign smile of an acquaintance and better, but the open smile of an equal. Her face reddened and she looked away.

"Well deserved, too, if I might say," Polly agreed. "We'll be the poorer when Miss Olivia moves away."

"Well, let's hope that's not *too* soon, Mrs. Trellow."

OLIVIA CLOSED THE curtains and raised the wicks of two lamps until the bedroom filled with light. She stared at the writing box, running a hand over it, trying to imagine the hands that fashioned it and the hands that received it.

She didn't want to rush her exploration. This was a twenty-year-old mystery *and* a romance. In doing so, she wanted to honor both Constance and Adam. At length, she opened the lid and the writing slope to retrieve the diary and the letters tenderly, as if they were written to her.

Where to start?

The letters.

Olivia opened the first.

To Beaufort Denton
Esq.
Ponsnowyth, Cornwall

It is to our regret to inform you of the passing of your daughter Constance Marie Denton following a difficult birth of a son.

Olivia raised a hand to her mouth in shock.

She was struck by childbed fever and lived a full week before succumbing. Dr. Norbert attended her and I enclose to you the bill for her care.

I beg to ask of what arrangements are we to make for your daughter's interment?

Chapter Five

Charteris House
Truro

A CHORUS OF chimes from the clocks greeted Adam as he walked into the shop. Like yesterday, there was no sign of trade or of a shopkeeper, nor did he stop to look for one. As instructed, he went around the counter, pulled the hanging map aside, and with the crook of his finger, tugged a recessed ring that appeared to function as a handle. The door pivoted on its hinges to reveal a narrow staircase and faint sounds from the floor above.

Adam ascended.

The strange shopkeeper from yesterday was hunched over a desk, spectacles on his forehead, eyes just inches away from piece of paper which he was studying with great concentration. Sir Daniel had his eye glued to a telescope trained out the window to a distant hill where Adam could just make out the semaphore hut, one of many hastily erected along the length of England's southern coast over the past two years at great expense.

Speaking of which, Adam spied an absurdly expensive silver tea service on the sideboard.

"Help yourself to tea, Mr. Hardacre," said Ridgeway without once looking back. "It's freshly brewed."

Adam did so, dropping a couple of lumps of sugar into a rather dainty china cup.

"Any news from London?" he inquired casually as he poured the amber liquid. It smelled good on an empty stomach.

"Nothing of interest," Ridgeway answered, turning back to the room and collapsing the telescope.

"Then would you mind telling me why I'm here? The suspense *has* been killing me."

Ridgeway picked up on his sardonic tone and answered it with a half-grin.

"On behalf of His Majesty's Government, I have been authorized to offer you a secret commission."

Adam nearly choked on his tea but mercifully refrained from spilling any on his shirt.

"I am refused a rightful promotion in front of the Board in London but now you're willing give me my due – as long as no one knows about it? Is that how things go, Ridgeway?"

"You forget, the failure to award your promotion to lieutenant was a deliberate one."

Adam slammed the teacup down, not caring if it broke or not. "It was a humiliating one."

Ridgeway conceded the point with an incline of his head. "I regret the wound to your pride, but the public spectacle was necessary. News of your resignation in high dudgeon has been the talk of the Navy from admiral down to ordinary seaman."

"I'm *so* glad to have provided amusement."

Ridgeway gestured to a chair.

"If you've quite finished sparring, we have work to do."

Adam remained where he stood for several beats before moving. Whatever Ridgeway and his men thought, he was no one's lackey to jump when told. Finally, he sat.

"There is a group within the war office whose remit is to conduct espionage," Ridgeway began. "We answer directly to the Prime Minister and, occasionally, to the Prince of Wales himself. You will not find us mentioned in dispatches, nor will our work appear in any official war record. There are no glory hunters here, Hardacre."

"There's a war on, *obviously.*"

"Before the end of the year, there may be two – Spain is being quite bellicose. *Again.* But that's by-the-by. It's the French we're concerned about. We've received word that the self-styled Emperor Napoleon plans to invade England. We've managed to thwart one plot but, according our sources, it is not the only one."

"Then we must protect our shores."

"That's why we're putting Nelson in charge."

A shudder went down Adam's spine. Everyone knew of Lord Horatio Nelson. The man was a war hero, damned near invincible some called him. Very few men carried the injuries he wore and still lived. And yet there was more than just cannon and gun to kill a man – his own grief could do that, too.

Adam had nothing but the greatest admiration for the admiral but, even so, a man had his limits. "I hear Lord Nelson is ill and heartsick after the death of his child. Are you sure he's the right man for the job?"

"He assures us he is and, as you know, there is no better naval tactician and commander in the entire Royal Navy, but let's not get side tracked. Napoleon has called on all the resources of the state in his effort. Stopping an armada and France's march into England, let alone across Europe, will be moot if we don't first get rid of the rats in our own ranks. That's where you come in."

"I've been demoted to rat catcher?"

"More like promoted to Pied Piper."

Adam blinked. He had no comeback for that. He wasn't even sure what it meant. Ridgeway gave him a look.

"Whether you recognize it or not, a lot of people have had their eye on you. You're an impressive man, Adam Christopher Hardacre. You've risen through the ranks by your own efforts alone."

"But not good enough to be awarded a commission," Adam said bitterly.

"Then I'll come to the point," said Ridgeway. "France is recruiting spies right under our very noses, turning some of our own men into traitors to their country. They've been feeding on malcontents."

Then all the pieces fell into place. Adam closed his eyes briefly and shook his head.

"My humiliation was a set up," he said under his breath.

Ridgeway picked up his own teacup. "I did say it was deliberate, old man," he said, the barest hint of regret in his tone. He took a sip and put the cup back down. "Spies are all well and good, Hardacre, but we need counterspies. We need someone to infiltrate their ranks, identify the ringleader, and discover whether France has other secret invasion plans."

"And *that* is my commission."

"If you choose to accept it."

"Do I have a choice?"

"There's always a choice. And the fact that you're still sitting here talking to me suggests you've already made it."

Check and mate. Adam sighed and sank into the chair.

"Then what's next?"

"Your *humiliation,* as you call it, should prove irresistible. Based on past experience, you're likely to be contacted by a former associate or acquaintance who will sound you out on your loyalties. Let them cultivate you. Give them as much rope as you think necessary and report developments to either myself or to Bassett."

The half-blind shopkeeper raised his head from his work and grinned.

"Welcome aboard, Lieutenant Hardacre. Anything you need, I'm your man – equipment, weapons. Lord Ridgeway here will arrange clearance from the Admiralty for anything else you require."

"Bassett here is an excellent forger."

"Sentenced for seven years transportation to New South Wales before Lord Ridgeway employed me," the strange little man boasted.

Adam struggled to keep up with what just happened.

"*Lieutenant* Hardacre?" Adam had to admit he rather like the sound of *that* said aloud.

"It was the rank you applied for and giving it to you keeps the clerks in the Exchequer happy. Your wages will be two hundred pounds a year plus reasonable expenses which you'll run through Bassett here."

"When I do begin?"

Lord Ridgeway rose to his feet and extended his hand.

"My dear chap, you've already begun. The *Andromeda* will remain in Falmouth for another six weeks. Stay in touch with your former crewmates. You have ties in the area, don't you?"

"I used to. All of my family are dead."

"Surely there's some old sweetheart you can be down here to see."

Adam entertained the idea of calling on Constance for exactly half a second. He shook his head.

"In that case, since you've 'resigned', look as though you're planning to settle down. You come from a line of carpenters, don't you?"

"My father had the mill in Ponsnowyth."

"Perfect – right in the center. Nine miles from Truro, and five miles from Falmouth, make sure you're seen about the place. Any questions?"

Adam started to shake his head then stopped. "A disaffected bosun and a convicted forger – it's a hell of an operation you're running Ridgeway. Is this how you recruit all your spies?"

The man grinned once more. "That's nothing. Remind me to tell you one day how I came to meet my wife."

"IS ANYTHING AMISS, my dear?"

Olivia started and the ledger in front of her sharpened back into focus. She glanced up at Fitzgerald's mildly concerned face.

"My apologies, Mr. Fitzgerald," she answered. "I'm afraid to say I slept poorly last night and I'm more tired than I had realized. Where were we?"

"There's not so much to do – certainly not as much as I feared, and in light of your fatigue, I think we should finish our work tomorrow. Or perhaps, it is being cooped up in this room all day which is the cause. Would you like to accompany me back to Truro? I can attend to some neglected work at my office while you indulge yourself at the shops, then we might have supper and I can escort you back home."

"That's extraordinarily kind of you, sir, but I must decline. While a ride out sounds wonderful, I would be much better served by retiring early. Perhaps another time."

Olivia wondered whether the solicitor would press the matter but he did not.

He rose to his feet and took his hat from the coat rack. She followed him outside and held his russet horse still, stroking its neck absently while he harnessed the gig.

"You *do* ride?"

"A little. I would accompany Miss Lydia from time to time."

"Then you must ride with me before the weather turns. I see two of Beaufort's horses at the pasture. Horses need be ridden."

"Then you're very kind to offer to accompany me," she responded.

"It is you who does me the honor."

Fitzgerald reached out his hand. Olivia accepted it, expecting just a handshake. Instead, she felt a tug at her hand to draw her closer. There was a look in Fitzgerald's eyes that made her think he wanted to kiss her hand.

She withdrew it, masking her intent by stroking the horse's muzzle once more. She wondered whether she had been successful. Mr.

Fitzgerald kept his expression closed.

"Until tomorrow, Miss Collins," he said, climbing up into the gig.

She stepped away from the horse and waved him away, glad for the solitude that was hers. It allowed her to indulge the subject which had genuinely occupied her thoughts.

Oh, poor Constance.

The poor woman – *girl* – Olivia reminded herself, she lived only long enough to mark her twentieth birthday. She would be thirty-eight if she had lived – the same age as her father's second bride. She turned away from the drive and began to walk through the gardens toward the edge of the estate that overlooked Ponsnowyth.

She had read all the letters and the diary last night. Sleep had claimed her only after the sky had turned grey in the pre-dawn light. Even so, Olivia had risen early when she remembered Peter Fitzgerald's impending arrival.

Perhaps it was her exhaustion as much as her own fanciful imagination, but she was struck by a sensation, an awareness of Constance Denton. How had she never recognized it in all the years she lived at Kenstec? But now, having read the young woman's diary, she now saw her presence everywhere.

She stopped and turned back to look at Kenstec. Her description of the house, of dinner parties in the dining room, the dances in the entrance hall were brought vividly to life in the long forgotten pages of the girl's journal.

Now, the permanent pall which seemed to inhabit the place finally had a cause.

She continued her walk through the grounds, deep in thought.

The diary told of a very shy and lonely young girl, intimidated by her father – terrified of him, in fact. She would only have one debut season, and that proved to be less than successful. The only offer made for her hand came from a rather odious toad whose lascivious intent made itself known on more than one occasion.

Constance found a small wellspring of courage and refused the match. She was sent home alone in disgrace and her misery was complete, banished for the summer alone at Kenstec House while her father found his own amusement in Truro.

Little by little, page by page, the diary revealed the beginning of a friendship with a boy from the village named Adam. He was young, handsome, and treated her like a princess. His kind attentions were just the balm needed to soothe a wounded spirit. They met nearly daily by the old priory ruins at the edge of the estate.

Olivia felt the urge to go there keenly, as though Constance's spirit, rather than Olivia's own natural curiosity, drove her. She followed the path to the right, past the kitchen gardens which were already beginning to show signs of neglect following the departure of the household staff.

A large beech tree overhung the track that led into the woods. The heavy weight of still ripening beechnuts obscured the way forward, but Olivia knew the path well. She pulled some of the newest leaves from the tree and chewed on its cabbage-like texture to satiate a noon hunger. She would not go back to the house, not now as Constance called her forward.

Besides, the dappled shade of the woods was pleasant in contrast to the beating heat of a sun which had not yet passed its zenith.

Constance had such a lovely way with words. In her diary, she described the gorse and the colorful meadow flowers of whites, yellows, pinks, and blues that raised their heads above the leaf litter to turn their faces to the sun. The stream that would eventually make its way to the Carrick was still a ways ahead and the old priory another one hundred and fifty yards beyond that.

Out of the corner of her eye, Olivia spotted a wagtail, its vivid yellow breast glinting in the sunlight as it darted in and out of the leaves, hunting for insects. Overhead, somewhere beyond the canopy, she heard the petrels calling.

Nothing would have changed since the days Constance walked in these woods some twenty years ago; an enchanted wood where she found love for such a short time.

Olivia imagined herself in Constance's shoes for a moment. What must the first flush of love feel like? To look into the eyes of another and see admiration and desire reflected back in equal measure? To be held and caressed with tenderness?

Constance had described all of those feelings and more for someone who was no more than a youth and she not much older.

Snap!

The distinct sound of a twig breaking underfoot pulled Olivia from her daydreaming.

Someone else was here! *No one* should be in the woods.

She ran toward the ruins of the old stone monastery and had just managed to hide herself when she spotted the man. She peered through the windowless aperture of one of the standing end walls.

Whoever he was, he was a working man. A poacher? He carried no gun. He didn't have any traps or snares with him either. A thief? If so, then why would he linger here in the ruins and not reconnoiter the house?

The man was tall with fair hair cut neat. His clothes were not expensive, but they seemed new. Brown breeches tucked into black boots; a cream shirt worn without a jacket in deference to the warm summer's day; sleeves rolled up to the elbows. The forearms below them were tanned.

Olivia glanced through the woods toward the house. Should she break cover and make a dash back to the house? She glanced back at the man who had stopped at the edge of the stream. Curse her luck. He seemed to be in no hurry to move.

He just stood there.

Then he turned her way.

Chapter Six

ADAM FELT THE hair rise on the back of his neck.

He was not alone.

Whoever watched did not want to make themselves known. He turned slowly, looking in the shadows for a telltale figure. Nothing made itself obvious to him. The stream bubbled along merrily as it had always done; the old priory was still there. He'd played in the ruin as a child and later became a man there, in deed if not in years. In fact, it looked as though not another stone had tumbled since he first saw it. It made him feel like he was ten years old once more.

Surmising that whoever watched had slipped away, more cautious of him than he was of them, Adam started whistling a familiar tune, one they used to keep time as they brought in the halyards. He approached the standing end wall where an old window opening would have once have contained stained glass, the sill at waist height. Adam placed a palm flat on the wall to the left of the opening and closed his eyes, feeling the rough texture of stone weathered for centuries but still solid – a mute sentinel which had stood watch while two young people cautiously and tentatively explored the act of love together.

Sweet Constance.

Kenstec House was only just through the trees. Perhaps it wouldn't do any harm to venture as far as the edge of the lawns. He doubted anyone would recognize him. Squire Denton would be in his seventies now, if he lived.

Even if his presence was questioned, he could always say he was a rambler who had lost his way.

Adam took a deep breath, bringing with it the nostalgic scent of honeysuckle. It was a perfume Constance favored, and it was strong here, as though her presence lingered still. And yet…

He furrowed a brow. There was no honeysuckle covering the ruins, so where had it come from?

He opened his eyes and was face to face with a woman through the opening in the wall.

"Constance?"

The woman looked as shocked as he did.

Before he had time to compose himself, the woman fled, disappearing into the thick of the trees.

"Constance!"

He called out her name once more but had gone no further than a few steps in pursuit before his rational mind could alert him to the differences between the two women.

Constance would be nearly forty now. That woman was at least ten years younger. This woman's hair was much darker. But it was the eyes he remembered. Constance's eyes were the lightest shade of blue. His wood sprite had brown eyes – as big and as frightened as a doe's.

Adam chuckled to himself. He'd frightened a maid from Kenstec House. Or perhaps, it was *she* who startled *him*.

Either way, it wasn't an auspicious return to Ponsnowyth.

He left the woods by the same path he'd entered, one that would take him out to the main road down into the village. He had made his lodgings at the local inn owned by the Trellows and given his name to the young man behind the bar, but nothing out of the ordinary registered on his face.

It would appear the name of Hardacre in these parts died along with his father ten years ago. And he himself had been gone for twenty…perhaps Ridgeway had miscalculated. Why would anyone particularly care about him? And yet his lordship seemed certain enough.

Walking the road, he reached the entrance to the formal drive to Kenstec House and leaned against a stone pillar to relace his boot. Framed in the line of trees was the figure of the young woman in green he'd startled. Now, she made a less hurried pace back to the house.

He smiled to himself and carried on.

At least he could assure himself he hadn't seen a ghost. His own memories were enough to contend with.

THE ROUNDISH, MIDDLE-AGED woman emerged from the tap room and stood before him, her arms placed on her hips, now making her twice as wide as she was tall. She looked him up and down.

He grinned before swooping down and kissing her on the cheek.

"It never is…Adam Hardacre!" she cried. "I thought my boy Will had got it wrong when he told me who the new lodger was."

"Good day to you, Mrs. Trellow. It's good to be back."

"Well, I never thought I'd see the day – I thought ye were wedded to the sea!"

Adam turned around at the male voice and was met by Polly Trellow's husband, Jory. He shook the big, meaty hand of the tavern owner. Although he was no longer a young man, Jory had a grip that was still strong. "It was just after yer father passed when ye were last here, weren't it?"

"Aye, it was."

Jory shuffled past him and his wife to reach the bar. Without asking, he pulled three ale glasses out from under the counter and started pouring from the tapped keg. Polly herded Adam toward the bar with a pat of her hand on his arm.

"Now, are ye back for good?" asked Jory.

Adam had thought long and hard about his answer on the journey from Truro. He was not a man who complained about his lot. He preferred his actions to speak for him. It was in his nature to shrug off a setback and walk on, but now he had a new role to play.

"Maybe so. It seems the Navy has no time for men like me. Good enough to be a warrant officer, not *the right sort* to be in the upper ranks."

Polly clucked her tongue. "Well, perhaps that's the kind of trouble ye don't want," she said. "Them gentry types are peculiar – not for the likes of us to be fussin' about with."

"Perhaps you're right, Mrs. Trellow." Adam picked up one of the ales and took a long draught. He sighed with great appreciation. "Ah, the finest lager anywhere in the world. It's good to be back. Here's cheers."

They toasted with their ale glasses and Adam took another mouthful then continued. "I was going to stop by the mill. Does old man Kernow still own it?"

"He's too old to work it now," answered Jory. "He leased it to a young couple by the name of Trezise. They've not been long in the district, but they're a nice family."

"Well, I've got a little money behind me – the Navy's had to pay me out for twenty years of service. Perhaps I'll buy myself a cottage and a fishing boat, and that'll do enough for me."

Mrs. Trellow cocked an eyebrow at him. "Now ye've settled down, ye should be thinkin' of findin' yerself a wife to keep house and be a companion – ye're not as young as ye used to be!"

"Leave him be, Pol, there's plenty of time for him yet."

"I appreciate the vote of confidence." Adam grinned behind his glass and drained the rest of the beer. "I think I'll take a walk down to the fleet at Flushing and see if there's anything doing."

"Have ye been to Falmouth, lad?"

"Just once," said Adam. "The *Andromeda* is still in port and..."

He shrugged his shoulders, leaving the rest of his feelings unspoken. Jory nodded his understanding. Polly shook her head, tut-tutting her dismay once more.

"Make sure ye be back by dark," she said. "I be servin' up pie tonight and there's a fresh barrel of cider Will's bringin' back from Truro."

"Thank you."

Adam meant it sincerely. The Trellows were decent people, salt of the earth, and he wanted to lie to them as little as possible.

THE ROAD FROM the village rounded a hill over a distance of several hundred yards before it emerged onto the low lands exposed to the English Channel. Standing lookout over them all was Ponsnowyth Church, Norman in design, made of bluestone. The cemetery beside it was windswept, keeping the grass low, while both tree and headstone alike bowed to the greater power of the elements.

Adam looked up at the sky. With twilight still some time off, he figured he had time to stop. In fact, he had time to do anything he wished. He shook his head at Ridgeway's instruction to keep himself visible.

In that case, perhaps he should march up to the front door of Kenstec House and deliver a blow or three to Squire Denton in long-overdue repayment of the beating he received at the hands of Geen the overseer as a first and final warning to stay away from Kenstec, and Constance in particular.

For a long time, what happened in the wood after he found his gift to Constance gone was knocked clean out of his head. It came back to him bit by bit like a jigsaw over weeks and months. He had been in agony, Adam recalled, every inch of his body hurt from the beating when they handed him the quill. He signed what he thought was a promise to never see Constance again and another paper that Geen had told him was an apology for presuming to be familiar with someone his better.

What he hadn't known was one was a letter to his family telling them he had made the decision to go to sea, and the other was his letter of indenture. Adam had only learned about *that* when he returned to sort out his father's effects after the old man's death.

By that time, the circumstances of his enlistment had been moot because, by some strange quirk of nature, Navy life had agreed with him. He had been just promoted to bosun's mate by then and, for the most part, the resentment was as long gone as the bruises and the cuts he wore on his first voyage. He was genuinely content for a while. His old life – and Constance – just a bittersweet memory.

He glanced over the low stone wall that surrounded Ponsnowyth Church. There, among the greyed and weathered headstones flecked with moss and yellow lichen, was a clean, new gravestone, a little grander than the rest – in marble, no less.

Who was this then?

He opened the gate and entered the churchyard. The western sun shone brightly on the stone and he couldn't make out the inscription until he was almost upon it.

Beaufort Denton
Esq.
9 September 1732 – 6 January 1804
Late of Kenstec House
husband of Caroline
father of Lydia

So, the old man had kicked the bucket at last. In the mood he was in at the moment, Adam was tempted to spit on his grave, but he refrained.

Caroline and Lydia. The old man had also remarried and sired another daughter. Adam looked at the well-tended but older grave alongside the squire's.

Tressa Denton (nee Keast)
1754 – 1782
loving wife of Beaufort Denton, esq
mother of Constance
forever missed

Obviously not missed that long. But that was odd...why wasn't Constance's name on her father's grave, along with her father's widow and her half-sister?

With trepidation and increasing confusion, Adam walked along the row of graves that marked the resting places of generations of the Denton family.

Constance's name was not among them.

CONSTANCE? CONSTANCE!

The man's question lingered and his exclamation rang in Olivia's ears as she ran through the woods into the safety of the estate grounds.

Who was he? Why would this stranger mistake her for a girl who had been dead these past twenty years? She was afraid she knew the answer, but no – surely it was too much of a coincidence for it to be Adam Hardacre.

By the time Olivia had got halfway across the lawn, she had dissuaded herself from such a foolish belief. She must have misheard the man. Clearly, he had been as surprised by her appearance there as she was of his.

She let herself into the house via the kitchen and bolted the door. In the stillness, she became acutely aware of her isolation inside the manor walls. Perhaps it *wasn't* wise to stay here on her own tonight.

She wondered if it was too late to accept Polly's invitation to live at the inn for a few days. Olivia hadn't minded being on her own in the earlier part of the week when there was much to do in the house. But now, with that work nearly completed, one could almost entertain the thought of ghosts.

And while she was in the mood to contemplate such matters, it was also time to stop dwelling in the past; worse still, in *someone else's* past.

The fate of the ill-starred lovers from Constance's diary was long ago and there was nothing more she could do about it. The mystery of it had been solved.

Olivia went up to her room and packed a small valise. The afternoon sun through the window brought out the red grain of the mahogany of the writing box. Inside it, she had reunited Adam's love notes with Constance's diary as well as the letters from St. Thomas' Hospital in London which told of the young woman's untimely end.

She ran her hand over the box. Did this Adam the carpenter still live?

If she left now, she could stop by the Trezises' at the timber mill on her way to the inn and ask if they knew how to contact the former owner. She would write him a letter to explain who she was and what she had found. She would make the offer of returning the box and the papers relating to his one-time sweetheart.

Without truly knowing why she did so, Olivia shoved the writing box under her bed next to her trunk. Something that had been hidden for so long ought to be *kept* hidden until it could be returned to its *rightful* owner.

And as for the stranger, she would describe him to Polly and Jory and see if they knew him from their village or the surrounding area, or if someone new had arrived locally. If anyone would know who he was, then they would.

The sun had reached the top of the tree line by the time Olivia had bolted the kitchen door and it took another half an hour to brush down and feed the old grey gelding before it started to feel too neglected.

Perhaps she should ride him, although she would struggle to get a saddle on him without the assistance of a groomsman. Cooper, the youngster the Trellows employed as a stable boy, could look after him much better than she could. She would suggest to Mr. Fitzgerald that the horse be agisted in the paddock behind the inn until Mistress Caroline made a decision whether or not to sell the animal.

Olivia tied the green ribbon of her straw hat under her chin and picked up her bag. She followed the drive to the road and took one glance back at the imposing house.

She'd almost forgotten about the uncomfortable exchange with the solicitor earlier that morning. Mr. Fitzgerald had been about to kiss her hand and there had most definitely been a *look*, although, equally, she could have been mistaken in believing his interest in her extended beyond that of the most basic and professional sort.

But what if she wasn't wrong? Should she accept his attentions? What were his intentions? Inexperienced in these matters she may be, but she was not a naive woman. Olivia knew full well that a man may use flattery to win his way and offer a woman nothing more than words that would prove empty in the morning.

Olivia Faith Collins, you're a shilly-shally of the worst order!

And with that admonishment, she squared her shoulders and marched down the road in the late afternoon sun.

It was high time she stopped putting off a decision about her future. The next time Mr. Fitzgerald came to call, she would ask to accompany him back to Truro so she could call in on an agency and begin her search for new employment.

Chapter Seven

OLIVIA WALKED INTO the inn, hoping Polly wouldn't make a fuss. Luck wasn't with her.

"See, what did I tell ye? Feelin' lonely up at that big house by yerself? Didn't I tell her, Jory?"

"Aye, ye did," her husband answered with a smile and friendly wink in her direction.

The woman dropped her drying cloth on the bar, which her husband picked up and seamlessly added the task of drying glasses, mugs and pots to his well-practiced routine. Olivia felt sheepish, but nonetheless allowed herself to be embraced in Polly's mothering arms.

"Come with me, I have a nice little room for ye," she said, leading Olivia up the narrow stairs to the floor above. "It will be so nice to have dinner with ye again. Ye'll meet our new lodger – he's just come in and will be stayin' with us for a little while."

"A new lodger?" she asked, hoping her inquiry didn't come across as too nosy.

"Well, he's not really *new*. We've known Adam and his family for years."

Adam? Olivia nearly missed the top step and only just avoided a stumble.

She felt herself go red and it didn't go unnoticed by Polly.

"Are ye feelin' yerself, dear?" she asked, opening the door to the room. "Ye've gone quite a color. I expect the exertion in the heat's done it – and I bet ye're not eatin' proper."

"You've spoiled me for anything I might have prepared for myself," said Olivia. She placed the valise on the bed. "This Adam, he's a local man?"

Polly pulled back the curtain, spilling the room with light, before wrestling with the latch on the window.

"Oh, my word," she averred. "His family lived here for years but he up and went into the Navy. Now, he's back for good – or so he says – but ye can never tell with sailors.

The sash lifted with a squeal.

"I'll introduce the two of ye," said Polly.

"Oh no, please don't go to any bother, I'm sure Mr...." Olivia stopped herself from saying the name Hardacre aloud since Polly had never mentioned the man's surname. "Er, your *guest*, will be catching up with friends and family."

Polly patted Olivia's arm in passing. Her protest fell on deaf ears. "No trouble at all, Missy. He'll be in for tea."

Now alone, Olivia put hands to her cheeks. They still felt warm. She was drawn to the fresh air, still warm as twilight approached. The long rays of the sun painted the road in front of the inn gold, like a strip of ribbon as it curved around the hill.

The streams and tributaries that fed into the estuaries were a flat, pale, blue-grey color highlighted by the sun, brighter than the land around it – paddocks and farms dotted about, cast in heavy purple and green shadows as twilight advanced.

Below her, Will lit the lamps over the entrance of the inn. Little flickers of yellow light danced and bobbed before finally filling the glass with a cheerful buttery glow as the young man closed the front glass.

She tried to take in the name of the new lodger and wished she'd asked Polly his last name. Did she actually *want* confirmation of it?

Footsteps below heralded someone's approach but the man's features were obscured by the tricorn hat he wore.

"Evening, Will."

"Evenin' sir, fine night it is."

"Aye, fine night it is."

Was that the man she saw in the ruins? She didn't think so, but she wouldn't know for sure until she saw him. And what then? What exactly would she say? Are you the Adam who gave some measure of happiness to a sad young woman one summer twenty years ago? Did you know there were fruits of your passion? Did you know it came to such a sad end for her? And, perhaps, also for the child she carried?

Olivia closed the window part way, enough to let in a little of the breeze. She slipped off her walking shoes and lay on the bed. Over and over in her mind, she practiced the conversation.

The best and most satisfactory one to her mind was the version in which the man from the woods would frown and say, "I think you have me confused with some other fellow."

Yes, that would be the best result of them all.

THE SOUND OF a door closing startled Olivia from a doze. The room was in darkness apart from a sliver of moonlight through the window.

Heavy booted footsteps walked past her door and down the stairs. Now fully awake, she heard the sound of conversation in the dining room and kitchen below. She quickly set a lamp, then hastened to draw the curtains before freshening herself up.

Ponsnowyth itself was a little village that served the wider district. But being so early in the week, only half a dozen people were in to dine. Olivia was acquainted with all of them though not terribly well. The Denton family didn't socialize much in the village and she had been bound by the family's habits. But she knew many of the local people from church and had encouraged Lydia at least to do her social duty and call when someone was ill.

On her way to a quiet corner, she made sure to stop and greet each of the diners. Although no one here was a stranger to her, neither was she so well acquainted with any that she would be invited to join them for supper.

It didn't bother her. She frequently dined alone – it was the expectation for a governess and she had done it for years. In fact, it wasn't until after Squire Denton's death that his widow insisted she join the family for meals, saying it was good for womenfolk to stick together.

Even now, however, sharing mealtimes with others seemed strange. While she could coach young Lydia into being an informed and witty companion at the dinner table, Olivia had not the confidence, nor the opportunity to practice such lessons for herself.

Polly set a pasty before her. The aromatic filling of beef and vegetables stewed in a brown fish stock set her mouth to watering – along with the perfectly cooked buttery pastry. Soon, all the meals had been served. A few more villagers came in to spend the evening – some to drink, others to play draughts or the traditional skittles game of *scattle and smite* – but none were the mysterious man from the woods.

The evening wore on and after having thoroughly beaten Will in a game of dominoes – and to be fair, he had been distracted, only laying down a tile each time he passed her table on the way to perform chores – Olivia decided to retire to bed.

However, as she passed by the inn door, it swung open abruptly and she was nearly barreled over by a rushing man. His strong hands held her shoulders as she regained her balance.

"I beg your pardon for bumping you, Miss, I was in a hurry," a warm, pleasant voice apologized. "Polly's so strict about closing her kitchen on time."

Olivia smiled, raising her head to tell the man the offense was small and forgiven. Then she looked into his face.

The man from the woods!

She heard herself gasp. The man's expression changed from concern to surprise as he, too, remembered *her*. She had no idea how long they stared at each other, but the tension was broken by Polly's call as she approached.

"Adam! Ye're back."

He gave Olivia's shoulders a quick squeeze of reassurance and released them before sidling around her in order to greet Polly.

"I'm not too late, I hope. I just about ran all the way back from Flushing for one of your pasties."

Polly laughed and gave the man an affectionate pinch on the cheek. Olivia started for the stairs but found her hand snagged.

"Don't go away, Missy, there's someone I want ye to meet."

She allowed herself to be drawn back to the hallway.

"Adam, this is Olivia Collins. Olivia, I'd like to introduce ye to Petty Officer Adam Hardacre."

POLLY SLIPPED HER arm in his.

"Adam's retired from the Navy—"

"—In a manner of speaking—"

"—And he's come home to Ponsnowyth."

Adam watched heightened color come to the woman's cheeks and the doe-like eyes from their earlier meeting widened once more. He felt her discomfiture. She dropped a small curtsy, out of habit it would appear, although he thought under the circumstances *he* ought to bow to *her*.

"Miss Olivia was governess at Kenstec House," Polly continued without once taking a breath. "Miss Lydia and Squire Denton's widow have taken themselves off to London."

So, she was not a *maid* at Kenstec.

"I'm afraid I won't be in Ponsnowyth for much longer, Mr. Hardacre," the governess said. "I shall miss this place, but I wish you well for your homecoming. I imagine there is much you will want to catch up on."

She stepped back as though about to take her leave, but Polly wasn't having any of it.

"Ye can have a chat while I bring his supper and fetch ye a slice of apple pie with a cup of tea."

Adam met the woman's eyes once more, and they shared a mutual look of empathy – the recognition that being under Polly's roof gave her permission to order anyone about as she pleased. They followed her across the dining room.

One or two of the men – old men now who had been acquainted with his father – rose to greet him. A moment later, everyone in the inn – including people Adam wasn't sure he actually *knew*, was shaking his hand to welcome him home.

Adam hadn't expected to be recognized, but there it was. By this time tomorrow evening, his return would have been announced from Perranporth to Porthleven and all points between. Mission accomplished, even if mostly by accident.

By the time he had managed to extract a promise of a longer reunion on the morrow in exchange for a quiet supper tonight, Olivia Collins was already seated at the table. The poor thing looked like she would rather face her own execution than dine with him.

He leaned across the table.

"If you wish to be away, I can have your excuses ready by the time Polly returns."

The woman shook her head and smiled, open and unforced. It warmed something in him.

"I wouldn't want to get you into trouble, Mr. Hardacre, and besides, I do wish to speak to you..." She hesitated. "About a mutual acquaintance."

The warmth in his chest turned to stone. When Ridgeway told him to expect the traitor to make contact, he had no idea they would use a woman as a go-between and do it so soon.

"You may speak as freely as you wish," he answered. Her lovely brown eyes met his once more. He knew she had not missed his change of tone.

"No, it can't be here." She paused and swallowed, her nervousness returned. "The matter is of a delicate nature."

"Then where?" he said, his voice little more than a low grumble so as not to be overheard. The woman before him moved her arm but not before he noticed the rise of goose flesh on it. He watched her frown as if the question had not occurred to her – or perhaps she was trying to remember what she had been told.

"Tomorrow then," he said, voice decisive. "I can escort you back to Kenstec House in the morning and we'll speak on the way."

Rosy cheeks turned deathly pale. "No! Don't come to the house. Tomorrow afternoon. Meet me at two o'clock in the woods in front of the ruined monastery where we saw each other today."

Adam cursed the missed opportunity to ask her more questions as Jory and Will appeared with their food and drink. Miss Olivia Collins sat back in her seat and brought the cup of tea to her lips with the faintest of tremors.

They ate in uncomfortable silence – or rather *he* ate while she pressed a fork into the slice of pie with clotted cream to make it appear as though she had attempted a bite. She did finish her tea though.

She eyed him cautiously as he set down his fork. There remained nothing of the pasty but a few flakes of pastry on the plate.

"Is there something amiss? Do I have food on my face?" He couldn't stop his slightly peevish tone.

She shook her head and offered a tentative smile. "Here."

Adam found her plate pushed toward him.

"Do I look famished?"

The smile became a small giggle, a charming sound, like the sound of wind chimes.

"If I've offended you, Mr. Hardacre, I apologize," she said. "I suggest, if it is any consolation, that you could consider this a service to me because if Polly returned to an untouched plate I would have to answer to my appetite, and the quality of her cooking which, as you and I both well know, is without peer."

Adam felt the weight of suspicion ease a moment. He returned her smile. Olivia Collins had a very pleasant face to look at – a clear complexion, a small straight nose, and lips tinted the softest shade of rose.

"So eating a slice of delicious pie is an act of chivalry?" he asked lightly.

"It is a sacrifice to be sure – especially when I am certain you will be expected to eat a portion of your own much larger than this before the night is out."

Adam took the plate after a moment's hesitation.

"I've been told I have an appetite for danger."

"Really?"

"Indeed," he replied, and shoveled in a mouthful of pie.

HE ROSE JUST at dawn. Jory yawned a good morning in the yard and Adam raised a fishing rod in response. He settled the strap of a wicker creel across his shoulder. He looked like he was going to be out for the day – and that was exactly the impression he wanted to give.

A glance up at the second story window revealed it still curtained. A certain female was not yet up. That suited him just fine.

Adam had spent another pleasant hour of conversation with Miss Olivia Collins last night. It had been a dance of sorts. She took a step forward and spoke of her family from Yorkshire; he returned the compliment by telling her an amusing story about being accidentally locked in the cellar overnight here at the Angler's Arms. He skirted the topic of his return to town, while she danced around the issue of her current employment.

Before they parted for the night, he once again made the offer to escort her back to the house and, once again, she withdrew, adamant she required no such assistance and that she would see him at two o'clock as agreed.

He dropped the matter instantly, lest he arouse more suspicion than necessary. *So, why that hour in particular?* Was she expecting someone beforehand? Who?

Well, that's what he intended to find out.

He made his way toward one of the popular fishing spots just outside the village and ventured further into the woods, following the watercourse upstream until it crossed onto Denton land. Adam continued until he could see the house and still remain within cover.

Time to make himself comfortable, he thought. He settled himself against a tree trunk and placed the rod on the ground next to him. He unbuckled the lid of his basket, pulled out a spyglass, and trained it on the windows of the house. No discernible sign of life within presented itself.

So far, it had appeared to be exactly as he had been told; Denton's young widow and daughter had packed up, bag and baggage, to London and the house was closed up.

He set the spyglass back and looked inside his hastily prepared kit. A knife, a notebook, and pencil. Next to it, a small bottle of ale and beside that another pasty that Polly had thoughtfully left for him. Adam took out the food and settled himself against the tree.

He did not have to wait long. By the time the morning sun had lit patches of lawn, Miss Collins appeared, moving with great alacrity toward the house. He raised the glass and found her once more, head down, hurrying along as though she was late for an appointment. She crossed the front outside of the house and went down the northern side toward where the kitchen would be.

About an hour later, he spotted a figure moving in the house. One window opened, then another. Adam tried to recall what that room might be – a library or drawing room perhaps.

He had actually been inside Kenstec House several times as a young boy. The first Mistress Denton would hold a Christmas feast and pageant every year for the villagers, but he had never been any further into the house than the entrance hall.

Outside, very little appeared to have changed, except for the unusual extension built into the southwestern corner of the house. Extending above the roofline by ten feet or so was a round tower topped with a small iron railing. He could not recall it from his childhood visits. And now, as he looked carefully, he could see how the bricks of which the turret was built had not weathered the same as the centuries-old house.

He attuned himself to the sounds around him. Birds twittered in the trees, a dog barked somewhere beyond the estate, the gentle morning breeze caused leaves to clap, the stream behind chortled to itself.

He allowed his mind to wander a little. It was a perfectly *ordinary* late spring day, hardly the backdrop for spies and intrigue. The whole thing seemed rather ridiculous. *He* was beginning to feel ridiculous.

A short time later, he heard a faint rhythmic clip-clop of a horse and cart out on the road. He strained his ears to determine whether horse and rider would continue down to the village or turned into the drive. The driver turned.

Adam pulled out a pocket watch and glanced at the time, ten minutes to ten. Through the spyglass, he watched the man – older than himself, perhaps in his fifties, a distinguished manner – bring his gig to a stop by the front door. It opened with his very own Miss Collins there to greet the man.

So, who exactly was this person she hadn't wanted him to know about?

Chapter Eight

OLIVIA WAS PLEASED to have had no sight of Adam Hardacre on her walk back to the manor. She'd wondered, having refused his offer of an escort, if she would find him waiting for her and insisting on accompanying her.

With Fitzgerald coming to the house to finalize the paperwork today, she wanted her mind clear for the task. She didn't stop for breakfast, instead getting up at first light to walk "home" to Kenstec. She let herself in through the kitchen to set a fire to heat some water for tea before going upstairs. She washed and changed her dress quickly, hoping the solicitor remained his punctual self and did not arrive early.

After hanging up yesterday's dress to air, Olivia got to her knees and felt under the bed for the writing box. It was still there, and she breathed a sigh of relief. It was a silly superstitious act, but somehow she needed the reassurance of its presence for her meeting with Adam Hardacre this afternoon.

It was odd. Even without hearing the confirmation of his identity from his own lips, she somehow knew when she first saw him he *was* the man in Constance's diary.

Of course, he would have been only an adolescent then, but there was no mistaking the sandy hair and hazel eyes. Age had merely turned the youth into a man, the experience edged into the light lines around his eyes and mouth. Years at sea had added color to his skin, making the hazel eyes even more pronounced.

Adam Hardacre was one of the most striking men she had ever seen.

She hurried downstairs and opened a couple of the study windows. She wanted to be able to hear Fitzgerald arrive before he knocked at the door. Before too long, she heard his gig turn into the drive and approach the house.

Olivia opened the front door and drew near to the horse, holding its bridle as the solicitor climbed down. She felt oblige to follow him about as he unhitched the animal.

"Good morning, Miss Collins," he announced. "Such a fine morning – we ought to be well pleased if the weather stays like this for a few weeks."

"It would be a most pleasant thing indeed, sir."

Fitzgerald looked as though he was about to say something else, mayhap to advance the acquaintance beyond that of professionals as Olivia suspected he was leading to yesterday. She turned away to head back to the house while he led his horse to graze.

"I imagine you should like to get started," she said as he entered the front door. "I shall leave you to the study while I attend to the tea."

He was giving her that look again. It was not lascivious – although she had little direct experience in *that* matter – but watchful and attentive. The burden of carrying someone else's secret weighed on her. Olivia wondered whether it showed on her face.

She would have to be careful in the solicitor's company, mindful that her words and actions contained nothing to reproach her.

To her surprise, the morning continued pleasantly. They worked in efficient silence. The talk between them pertained only to the business at hand. And soon enough, that was concluded.

"My watch tells me it's nearly twelve o'clock," Fitzgerald announced. Olivia waited for a repeat of an invitation to dine with him.

She readied an excuse in her mind, but he continued, "…and so I must leave you now. I have an afternoon appointment in Falmouth."

Olivia exhaled her relief slowly as he went on, "I don't want to take these documents with me since I'm likely to be away late…"

"Then allow me to bring them to your office in Truro tomorrow, Mr. Fitzgerald," she said decisively. "I have a few appointments of my own in town."

The solicitor's face brightened. "A capital suggestion! I gladly accept on the condition that you dine with me as you promised to do yesterday."

Olivia knew she couldn't have one without the other, so she accepted. She allowed him to take her hand. He bowed over it and, for one awful moment, she was afraid he might kiss it, but he did not. Yet that peculiar *watchful* look returned.

She locked the door on his departure, but watched through the window as the gig made its way down the drive and disappeared into the trees at the front boundary. She hurried upstairs into one of the empty bedrooms and peered out through the upper story window. Fitzgerald turned left to go down toward Ponsnowyth where he would meet the main road to Falmouth.

Olivia prepared for the meeting she both anticipated and dreaded.

THE BUTTERFLIES IN her stomach returned as she carried the writing box, covered by a shawl, in both arms into the woods where she had arranged to meet Adam Hardacre. Although she was early, he was already there waiting.

All the words she had rehearsed and practiced in her mind since yesterday fled.

He watched her with the same intensity as Fitzgerald, yet somehow it was different. This man had good reason to be wary of her. She was a stranger to him who insisted in meeting under unusual conditions in a place that probably held great significance to him. *She* would be suspicious if the circumstances were turned about.

She approached one of the tumbled-down blocks from the ruin and sat down on it with the box, still covered, in her lap.

"Thank you for being punctual, Mr. Hardacre," she said.

The man shrugged his shoulders and approached, but came no closer than a yard. "You piqued my curiosity last night, Miss Collins, as does whatever you have under that shawl, I must say."

She drew breath to speak but the words disappeared.

After a moment Hardacre tilted his head.

"Are you unwell?"

She shook her head and fiddled with the shawl. A gift from Miss Lydia, it had come from Spain – large red roses painted on silk, edged with a black crocheted border and silk fringing.

Hardacre stood at ease, his arms folded.

She breathed out. "I scarce know where to begin..."

"The beginning usually works."

She gave him a sideways glance and continued to fiddle with the fringing.

"Mistress Denton asked me to stay on at Kenstec to assist the solicitor with settling the estate. I accepted, grateful for the opportunity for more time to find new employment..." Her words tapered away yet again.

"And?" he prompted.

"I found this."

She drew back the shawl to expose the writing box and watched for his reaction.

At first, there was none but slight puzzlement. Then Olivia witnessed a frown, eyebrows drawing down.

"Dear God..." he almost whispered, then a grin split his face and spilled into his voice. "Where did you find it?"

"It was in a cupboard in the study."

Hardacre reached out. She handed him the box to examine and he turned it in his hands but did not open it.

"Not bad…but my marquetry skill has dramatically improved since then," he said, more to himself than to her.

"Do you remember who you made it for?"

"I made two. One was an apprentice piece for my father to judge. That was among his belongings after he died. This one I made for—"

"—Constance," she finished.

"Yes, that's right," he smiled wistfully. "It was so long ago. In fact, the last time I saw this box was right here."

He held it out to Olivia and she accepted it from his hands. He shook his head slowly and with unmistakable affection.

"She must be a married woman with a brood of children by now. I take it she no longer lives in the district?"

Olivia's chest constricted, making it difficult to draw breath.

Oh, dear God – he doesn't know. He doesn't know any of it!

ADAM STARTED AS the woman before him suddenly burst into tears. He crouched down at her side and touched her elbow to draw her attention. Her warm brown eyes swam with tears. He took the box from her lap and placed it on the ground. She clasped her hands together, sobbing.

"What's upset you so?" he asked, deliberately keeping his voice gentle.

"Constance Denton has been dead these past twenty years…" she sobbed. Adam strained to make clear her words. "She died from childbed fever."

He bowed his head and closed his eyes a moment, desperately trying to conjure up the image of Constance in his mind's eye, but it was not there. With nothing to remind him, he had nearly forgotten what she looked like. The revelation that she had passed away was a shock to be sure, but it did not touch him as he thought it might.

He *cared*. He had carried her memory in his heart through all the years and only a short time ago thought of her so fondly while sitting on the sea wall overlooking the Fal. Hearing her name spoken again was like unexpectedly coming across a pressed rose in a book, a remembrance of an earlier happier time. But it was only an echo, a refrain.

Olivia Collins would think him a heartless individual, but he could not muster up the strength of emotion she had. Too much time had passed.

He started at a gentle touch. Adam opened his eyes and saw Olivia Collins' fine-boned hand on his, her fingers covering the purple-blue of the crossed anchors tattooed on his flesh between his index finger and thumb.

He looked up and saw the governess had recovered herself. Her eyes were clear but grave. She spoke low, ensuring the words were for his ears alone although he was certain they were alone.

"I was employed by the Dentons for ten years. I'd been here three years before I first heard Constance's name. There was nothing of her memory in the house. The servants who'd known her were afraid that speaking of her would rouse the squire's displeasure. A few days ago, I found notes she had hidden behind a wardrobe drawer. *Your* notes to her. Then I found the writing box." She glanced at it. "It contained her diary and some letters from St. Thomas' Hospital in London."

Her fingers curled around the palm of his hand and gently squeezed it.

"I have read the diary, Mr. Hardacre," she continued. "You were her one and only love. Do you understand what I'm telling you?"

"Constance died of childbed fever," he said.

Olivia nodded. "Bearing *your* child, Mr. Hardacre."

The full realization dawned on him. *Constance Denton has been dead these past* twenty *years.*

He rose to his feet slowly. The smell of Olivia's honeysuckle scent touched a once potent memory in him. Her hand fell away as he stood.

"I'm more sorry than I can say," he said. "I didn't know. How could I?"

The woman before him stood also. She picked up the writing box and shawl, placing them on the stone that had been her seat.

"Please, don't misunderstand me," she said. "No blame attaches to you. Constance felt she was being watched every time she left the house. She kept the secret of her condition to herself until it was unmistakable. By that time, the squire had had you *impressed* into the Navy."

"Well..." Adam couldn't think what to say. So many emotions roiled in him as he tried to fully process the meaning of everything he had just learned.

"Thank you for letting me know," he offered blankly, taking a step back from the woman before him. "You've told me much I'd wondered about these many years. I'll be sure to go back to the cemetery and pay my last respects..."

He got as far as three yards away when Olivia Collins called out to him. "She's not there, Mr. Hardacre. You won't find her interred at Ponsnowyth."

He spun about. "What the *hell*?"

The profanity was out of his mouth before he could censor himself – too much time at sea and not enough time in drawing rooms – yet the woman in front of him did not seem disconcerted in the slightest. Rather, he saw in her the righteous anger of an avenging angel.

At that moment, Olivia Collins was beautiful.

"Her *father*, in his deference to his own reputation," she continued, contempt clear in her voice, "refused to accept charge of her mortal remains. He also refused to let anyone else in the family aid her. There was an aunt, I believe, with whom Constance was close."

The recollection of Squire Denton's own grave marker in the church cemetery – the large and ornate marble headstone boasting his status to the world – lit the spark of Adam's anger.

Woe unto you, scribes and Pharisees, hypocrites! For ye are like unto whited sepulchers, which indeed appear beautiful outward, but are within full of dead men's bones, and of all uncleanness.

He gave vent to a volcanic rise of fury. "That vicious old *bastard* condemned his only daughter to a pauper's grave?"

Tears sprang once more to the woman's eyes.

Before he knew what he was about, Adam had advanced and has his arms around Olivia, holding her close as she wept into his chest. The force of *her* emotion, not his, touched something deep in his soul. A desire to protect, to comfort, reached in and took hold. For a moment, with the scent of honeysuckle in his nostrils and the gentle curves of a woman in his arms, Adam embraced, and accepted the embrace, of both Olivia Collins *and* Constance Denton.

When he closed his eyes, Constance's face finally appeared before him as though only twenty minutes, not twenty years had passed. He rained kisses in her hair, grateful someone as wonderful and beautiful as she would ever give him the time of day, let alone her body. Having once touched her, he wanted – *needed* – that feeling again. He kissed her with increasing passion.

Adam tasted a protest on her lips at his last open-mouthed kiss.

He stopped and opened his eyes. The lips did not belong to Constance.

Olivia pulled out of his arms, eyes wide with alarm and hand across her mouth, her neatly pinned chignon in disarray with one long lock tumbling down her shoulder. And, in a split second before she had raised the hand to her mouth, he had seen her lips, full and red with the force of his. To his shame, Adam felt his body stir.

He took a few paces back to protect himself as well as her.

"That was unforgivable. Miss Collins, Olivia, I..." He tried to fashion the words for an apology. He had none.

"That was unforgivable," he repeated. "I'm sorry…"

Olivia licked her lips to wet them – or perhaps soothe them – before taking a deep, shuddering breath.

"I…I fear that, in the moment, too much emotion overwhelmed us both, Mr. Hardacre." She was still breathless. "I hold myself equally to blame."

He shook his head slowly, refusing to allow her to take responsibility for his actions. She paused, as though about to say more.

Instead, she glanced at the writing box and then back to him.

"I shall leave you the box. It contains your notes to Constance. They belong to you."

Chapter Nine

THE WRITING BOX didn't fit completely in his creel, large though the basket was. One end stuck out so the lid wouldn't close and the sharp edge banged against Adam's side as he stalked back to the village. Fitting he should have a bruise close on his ribs, a proxy for the ache in his heart.

Shit.

Tearing open scars of his past wasn't a complication he was expecting when he woke up this morning.

Poor Miss Collins.

Poor Miss Collins, like *hell.*

He'd *dealt* with this years ago, he told himself. Constance was a youthful summertime infatuation he fondly remembered, and what her old man did to him, he'd managed to shrug off after a while as the actions of a father protective of his daughter.

But now, having learned the true aftermath of their affair…*damn!*

He punted a loose stone in the road as hard as he possibly could. It was all well and good for the estimable Olivia Collins to lay no blame at his feet. If she didn't want him to feel bad, she could have just not told him and kept it to herself. But she had, because she was a decent woman who simply wanted to tell the truth.

So…if it wasn't for him, Constance might still be alive. Well, what could he possibly do about it now?

And he'd kissed Miss Collins. He got so caught up in the poor governess' romantic tragedy that he forgot himself and kissed her.

He kicked another stone for good measure.

THE BLACK MOOD had not abated by the time he reached the inn.

"Fishin' bad today, Mister Hardacre?" Will asked as he wiped down the tables in the dining room.

"Yeah," Adam answered, keeping his body between Will and the bulging creel. "I'm a better sailor than angler."

"Well that'll be no good if ye're wantin' to get work – fishin' is about all there is to do around here."

"Then I'm just going to have to practice more." Adam shifted the weight of the basket strap on his shoulder and headed for the stairs.

Will called him back. "There's a man who's waitin' to see ye. *Mabm* insisted he sit in our parlor."

"Did he give his name? Has he been waiting long?"

Adam received a shake of the head in answer to both questions. "But he did look like a gentleman."

He sighed. "Tell Polly I'll be down as soon as I've cleaned up."

The man must be important if Polly invited him into her parlor, thought Adam. To the best of his knowledge, it was only ever used for high days and holy days – even then, she demanded the curtains always remained closed as not to fade the red woolen rug she had insisted had come all the way from Persia. As a consequence, the room was in permanent semi-darkness.

THE SETTLE BENCH on which the stranger sat in the gloom was high-backed carved oak with low squat tapestry cushions on the seat. Polished black boots stretched out toward the fire and, on a delicately proportioned drop-side Pembroke table, the fire illuminated a half-consumed glass of beer and the remains of a slice of cake.

Having entered the room silently, Adam ensured the door closed with a noise to draw the man from his fireside contemplations. The stranger rose to his feet.

He was aged in his forties, by Adam's estimation. Close-cropped black hair showed flecks of hair gone white. His nose was prominent but balanced by full lips. He was a man still in his prime, large in frame but not gone to fat, although that could change with any large amount of inactivity.

"You have me at a disadvantage, sir. I wasn't expecting any visitors."

"Forgive this unannounced call, Hardacre. My name is Major Seth Wilkinson, *retired*."

Adam observed the twist of the lips on the last word.

"Royal Marines?"

Wilkinson confirmed it with a nod.

"I wish to offer my sincere commiserations for your treatment at the hands of the promotions board. Those men are damned fools not to see your worth."

Adam inclined his head to accept the compliment and found a wingback chair in dark blue damask. At that moment, there was a brief knock. Polly entered with a small beer and a slice of the cake – a buttery, raisin-filled *hevva* cake.

After she left, Adam sat and gestured that his visitor do the same.

"I had no idea that the misfortune of one petty officer would become such a topic of conversation, Major," he said before wetting his throat with a mouthful of the malty brew.

"Well, you are not the first and you certainly won't be the last. Hide-bound adherence to class will always disadvantage the talented. A civilization can't advance on such a notion."

A cold spot grew at the base of Adam's skull, a warning. "Then what is one to do?" he asked. "We saw what upending the social order did in France; thousands of people dead…"

Wilkinson picked up his own glass. "One might equally argue that many millions more are freed from feudal enslavement. One might say

England could benefit from such a revolution."

The statement hung in the air as the major drank. The only sounds were the pop and crackle of the fire and the faint noises of the kitchen beyond. Adam could see he was being watched closely. His every word, every expression was being categorized and analyzed by the man before him.

Adam thought, then discarded, several responses before deciding on caution.

"A man might think such a remark treasonous," he answered at length.

"And another man might think such a remark is the very essence of patriotism. You see, Mr. Hardacre – one man's meat is another man's poison. It is time to think long and hard about the things we once considered most self-evident."

Adam smiled – he hoped convincingly. "That's a fascinating philosophical discussion, to be sure, but I am a simple man of simple tastes and it's generally my preference to get straight to the point."

Wilkinson conceded with a raise of his ale once more. He drained the contents and put the glass back on the table.

"Your talents were wasted in the Royal Navy, but they could be more usefully employed elsewhere – to a greater good, if you will. Would that be something of interest to you?"

"It might be." Adam took another mouthful of beer. "But I don't plan to commit myself to anything until I know what it's all about. I was pressed into service once. I won't let it happen again."

Wilkinson stood and fished out a card from his waistcoat pocket. "And we wouldn't expect you to."

Adam stood and accepted the card.

The Society for Public Reform. It was a benign sounding name – something of the sort that earnest bluestockings might attend.

"We meet at The Blue Anchor in Falmouth. Join us next Wednesday evening. You might find it of interest."

OLIVIA SPENT THE rest of the day ignoring the diary and letters from St. Thomas' Hospital sitting on her bedside table. Even to glance at them reminded her of the disastrous interview with Adam Hardacre.

What must he *think* of her? A poor lovelorn governess so caught up in a long ago romance that she throws herself into his arms, imagining herself in the place of the tragic heroine? No wonder he bid a hasty retreat.

As Hardacre himself said, it *was* twenty years ago. Why did she possibly imagine that he'd want to know?

Because the child may still live.

Wouldn't a man want to know *that* at least?

Perhaps not. There were plenty of men who sowed their oats without a moment's pause for the progeny that might be produced. Why should Adam Hardacre be any different? And he'd been a sailor. And sailors had a *reputation*.

And if it was none of his business, then it was *damned* certain that it was none of hers.

"Damn, damn, damn." Olivia rarely said the word aloud, but being alone in the house gave her license.

She returned to the letters and stared at the dried and yellowed paper.

As pathetic as it was, she could not let it go. She had to follow this tragic tale through to the end.

She pulled out a piece of stationery from a compendium and filled her pen with ink.

To the Superintendent
St. Thomas' Hospital

Dear Sir,

I write in earnest hope that you might be able to assist with infor-

mation regarding the fate of a young woman who was in your establishment's care some time past.

In early January of 1784, a young lady of quality, Constance Marie Denton, from Ponsnowyth outside of Truro, came into your care. She was five months with child and remained in your charge there to give birth to a boy on the twelfth of May, 1784.

I have a letter in my keeping from a nurse named M. Plowright, who writes to the family to give the sad news of Constance's death from childbed fever. Her letter I have transcribed in its entirety in the hopes that some record will be found of both the location of Miss Denton's final resting place and of the fate of her son.

Should such information be available, I will receive it gladly in care of...

Care of whom? Olivia lifted her pen from the page. What address should she put? She could find her new post halfway across England. There was only one reliable person she knew, and it would strengthen her claim if she used it.

...the solicitor of Miss Denton's family

Mr. Peter Fitzgerald
3a Lemon Mews Rd,
Truro
Cornwall

Olivia picked up another piece of paper. She addressed it and folded it into an envelope to seal it, then put it to join five other letters – three answers to employment opportunities and two to agencies – one in London, the other in Manchester.

She would post them from Truro tomorrow.

And why not? Mr. Fitzgerald had extended his services to her as well. She would take him up on it. He had an interest in her, of that she was in no doubt – and, if the truth be told, she gained a small thrill in knowing that a gentleman would do her a favor just because he liked her.

It made her aware as a woman – of herself, *for* herself – not for the role or position she held.

So, too, did Adam Hardacre's kiss make her aware of herself as a woman.

She touched the pen to her lips, emulating the press of his lips on hers and closed her eyes to capture the memory of the feel of his arms around her. Would a kiss from Mr. Fitzgerald feel the same? She was quite sure it wouldn't, although she had no evidence for it.

She placed the pen back into its holder with a sigh. The silence of the house settled its oppressive weight on her once more.

I've done all I can, Constance, please leave me in peace.

THE MORNING DAWNED overcast. Olivia decided to risk the walk to the inn to catch the coach to Truro, rather than wait for it to pass by the end of the Kenstec Manor. She was in sight of the Trellows' tavern when the heavens opened.

If she stopped to open her small umbrella, she would have been wet through, so Olivia clutched her leather reticule close to her chest and ran the last few yards. By a miracle, the door opened as she approached. Olivia ran straight inside.

"Thank you," she said to the unseen doorman while she attempted to wipe down the worst of the drops from her cloak.

"The pleasure is mine, Miss Collins."

The flush started instantly. "It was very good of you to do so, Mr. Hardacre."

She ventured a look up at him. He was dressed for town, dark blue breeches, a white shirt and matching blue jacket that was tailored for his broad shoulders and trim waist. Hazel eyes watched her fuss with her maroon cloak while she contemplated the idea of sitting for two hours or more beside the man who had besieged her dreams last night.

She opened her reticule to make sure her letters were dry. The sooner she secured herself a new position and had something more productive to do with her days, the better.

Olivia listened to the long, drawn out sigh from the man beside her.

"It's going to be a long trip if you don't speak to me," he said.

"I should think that after yesterday, you'd hardly entertain the idea of speaking to *me* at all." Yes, her voice was priggish and peevish – two characteristics Olivia detested hearing from women – least of all herself.

Hardacre laughed, a sound of genuine mirth, and her heart warmed a little at it. He didn't hate her after all.

"Perhaps we should stick to safe topics."

"Like the weather?" she asked, allowing a smile to play on her face. "And how *is* the weather today, Mr. Hardacre?"

With great exaggeration, Adam peered around her at the open door through which they could see the steady fall of rain.

"It's wet, Miss Collins."

The tension broke, like a long-anticipated summer storm.

Through the open door, Olivia heard the sound of the coach approaching. She looked outside and wondered how she might avoid the rain crossing to the carriage.

"Miss Collins..."

She turned back and those hazel eyes held her fixed once more.

"Please, call me Olivia," she insisted.

He acknowledged the regard with a nod of head.

"Olivia? I want to apologize for my behavior yesterday. I had always hoped...imagined...that Constance had gone on to live a full life. So to learn that our summer was..." Adam halted. He shook his head as though abandoning the thought. "Anyway, thanks to you, she won't be forgotten and, for that, I'm grateful."

Before Olivia could respond, Jory and Will appeared at the front door wearing oilskin coats and brandishing large umbrellas.

"We got a couple of these," said Jory, "but there's a lot of water on the ground. I'm not sure how ye're goin' to keep the hem of yer dress dry, Miss Olivia."

"I have an idea," Hardacre answered.

Before Olivia could draw breath, she found herself swept up and into his arms. Adam strode toward the door with her as though she weighed nothing.

"Mr. Hardacre! Adam! What on earth are you doing?" she gasped.

"Keeping your skirts dry. Jory and Will can use the umbrellas over us. Now, put your arms around my neck. I'm going to take this at a run."

Will Trellow whooped with delight.

Before she could utter a word of protest, Adam had steadied himself and waited for Will and Jory to form the escort, umbrellas held aloft like some kind of exotic honor guard. Olivia held on to his shoulders, tucking herself close to his chest to avoid any splashes or collision with the coachman who waited until just the last moment to open the door. The coach lurched with their inward momentum and the horses shifted to steady themselves. The door closed behind them just as quickly and Olivia found herself gently deposited on the seat.

Adam laughed. So did Olivia and she waved through the glass at the grinning faces of both Will and Jory as the coachman climbed aboard.

The carriage jolted forward. Olivia reached for the leather grab strap to steady herself and smiled easily at the man seated opposite her. She picked up her furled umbrella and, with a regal set to her chin, tapped Adam once on each shoulder.

"I dub thee, Sir Walter Raleigh," she said. "My knight protector!"

Chapter Ten

A KNIGHT…ADAM RATHER liked the sound of that.

Not a modern knighthood – where they seemed to award such things to every Tom, Dick, or Harry who wrote a pleasing poem or pranced on a stage – but rather a prize won on the field of honor.

He also rather liked the look Olivia gave him although he was hard pressed to describe it.

She smiled and laughed with him, at ease in his company although he could give her a hundred reasons why she should not be. Moreover, she treated him as an equal, not a glorified servant.

And she was considerate. Adam was beginning to feel like a bit of a cad to have ever suspected her motives.

Due to the inclement weather, the coach made a slow pace but steady. No one waited at the exposed byways and the next stop before Truro was Devoran. They had the coach to themselves for more than an hour.

To his surprise, the conversation flowed freely. He struggled to recall a time he'd ever felt so at ease in the company of a woman. He learned about Olivia's childhood as the youngest child and only daughter of a merchant in Yorkshire and her earliest memories of the dales. She painted a beautiful picture of the moors, the windswept hills, and the stone cottages; she spoke of the lines of low stone walls crisscrossing a verdant landscape, the stark ruins of nearby Bolton Abbey.

He could not match her prowess for imagery but he did his best, describing life aboard the *Andromeda*, the feeling of exhilaration as a mighty ship with nearly a thousand souls aboard rode the monstrous swell of a storm-tossed sea; the bond and camaraderie of men who sailed into battle together in the full knowledge they might be killed on the morrow.

And damn if she didn't *still* pretend to be interested when he described how he and the other ship's carpenters managed to repair a major break to a mizzenmast while in the heat of battle. Olivia had asked ever more detailed questions, as though she were trying to create the experience in her own mind.

Why on earth would a woman be interested in such a thing?

Doubt nagged at him again, but Adam tamped it down as the coach pulled into Truro. The rain was clearing and they disembarked under the portico.

Olivia was finishing an amusing story about her misadventure on horseback while accompanying her charge, when he heard a call.

"Miss Collins!"

Adam turned to see a distinguished man raise his hat in greeting. It was Olivia's previous visitor, likely the Denton's solicitor – yes, he'd confirmed the man's identify from Polly who knew everything about everyone.

Perhaps Ridgeway ought to approach *her* for his espionage games.

"Mr. Fitzgerald," said Olivia. "What an unexpected surprise. I had thought to stop by your office in the afternoon."

"Then I'm glad to have saved you the trouble and met you here."

Adam watched the man, observed him closely, but most of all waiting for the solicitor to acknowledge *his* presence. He did not.

Fitzgerald took another step forward, in fact; a not-so subtle attempt to cut him out. And since Olivia hadn't dismissed his presence, Adam planned to stay right where he was. *Right* where was.

Olivia glanced his way and took a step to the side to include him in their little circle.

"Mr. Fitzgerald, I don't believe you're acquainted with Petty Officer Hardacre. Mr. Hardacre, this is Mr. Fitzgerald, the Denton family solicitor."

He felt the older man's evaluation.

"Mr. Hardacre recently retired and has returned to Ponsnowyth," Olivia added.

Adam took up the conversation. "Family connections bring me home. I'm looking to purchase in the area. Miss Collins was kind enough to recommend you."

Adam had the advantage of seeing the faces of both Olivia and Fitzgerald as he spoke. His fabricated story of Olivia's recommendation for business seemed to have the desired effect. The solicitor seemed mollified by the explanation; he visibly relaxed. *That* was interesting in itself. Whether it was acknowledged or not, the middle-aged man felt some *proprietorial* claim over the governess.

Olivia, on the other hand, had covered her surprise well.

Fitzgerald pulled out a card.

"I'd be happy to advise you, sir. Just make an appointment with my clerk, but not today," he said with a nod of his head toward Olivia. "My day is fully occupied."

Adam didn't miss the set of Olivia's mouth change for a moment, as if to suggest that her monopoly of Fitzgerald's time was news to her.

"I shouldn't want to intrude on business, Mr. Fitzgerald," she said.

"Your visit is the highlight of the day, my dear," he said. "Did you bring the copies of the household receipts we worked through together yesterday?"

Adam heard the slight emphasis the man placed on the word "together."

Olivia retrieved a sheaf of documents from her leather bag and presented them to him.

"I shouldn't like to detain such an important man," she said sweetly. "I have plenty to occupy my morning. Perhaps Mr. Hardacre would like to join us at the White Hart to dine at two?"

Adam was tempted to accept, just to see whether Fitzgerald would lose his well-disguised temper, but that would hardly be fair to Olivia. So he paused just long enough to make the man believe he *was* considering it before shaking his head.

"Thank you for the kind offer, Miss Olivia, but sadly I have pressing engagements of my own today. Another time, perhaps."

He bowed to her, pleased to see a sparkle of amusement in her eyes. He acknowledged Fitzgerald with a nod of his head and headed away down Quay Street.

Adam continued nonchalantly along the rain-soaked street, keeping his senses attuned. He was under the impression that Fitzgerald watched for a good long moment. He'd not yet gotten a sense of the man and realized his opinion was clouded by disdain for Fitzgerald's interest in Olivia.

He shrugged. While a pissing match might be amusing, it could only serve to be a distraction. And he could not afford distractions.

Adam went to the stable yard to chase down recommendations on purchasing a horse. Having his own transportation may prove useful and, besides, he didn't entirely create a fiction from whole cloth. He *would* be interested in putting down roots after so long at sea. Somewhere on the water; a place by the river at Flushing, perhaps, that would give him easy access to the sea?

Having made the arrangement to view some horses over the next week, he headed toward Charteris House. One of the problems with his little daydream of a cottage, and a bit of land of his own, was that it came with the desire to settle down, to marry…Polly was right.

He shook his head. No, *not* for him. A life like that was for *other* men.

He made his way via the map door up to the top floor. Ridgeway was there reading through dispatches. Bassett, and two other men to whom he had not been previously introduced, were poring over a large mapping table. A glance at it revealed detailed coastlines of France and England, and the Channel that separated them. One of the cartographers was filling in details of Guernsey and Jersey.

"Hardacre, I didn't expect to see you again so soon." Ridgeway got to his feet. "Are you settling in?"

He decided to get straight to business. "I've been approached."

"Have you now?" Ridgeway's blue eyes lit up. "Bassett, come join us. Take a seat and tell me everything from the beginning. Bassett will take it down."

SIR DANIEL WAS thorough in his interrogation. Adam had always prided himself on his attention to detail but, even so, it wasn't until he was thoroughly questioned that he appreciated how much more attention he needed to pay.

Did Major Wilkinson have any scars? What were the make of his boots? Did he wear a watch chain? Did he have an accent? If so, from which county?

"No detail is too small to be discarded," Ridgeway told him.

Adam took to the lesson as he had done with everything else. He was not so proud – or so old – as to believe he could no longer be taught something.

"You've done well," said Ridgeway. "My recommendation is that you don't report here for a good few days after your meeting with the *Society* in Falmouth. They've reached out to you, but they'll be watching you carefully. Give them no reason to be suspicious."

Adam stood to attention when Ridgeway got to his feet. The chains of command are not easily broken.

"Is there anything else we can provide you with?"

Adam started to shake his head then paused.

"Spit it out, man."

"It has nothing to do with the business at hand..."

Ridgeway shrugged his shoulders. "Ask anyway."

"I need some information from St. Thomas' Hospital in London. It's about a woman who was an inmate there twenty years ago."

"Why?"

The question was direct and obvious, but it still caught Adam by surprise.

"It's a personal matter."

The clear blue eyes regarded him with silent censure. "A matter which happened twenty years ago...a criminal matter?"

"Not unless siring a bastard child on the squire's daughter is a hanging offense."

"Twenty years ago?"

Hardacre nodded.

"Why the concern now?"

"Because I've only just been apprised of the fact."

"By whom?"

He hesitated in answering; to do so would involve Olivia.

Ridgeway lowered himself back into his seat and Adam felt similarly obliged.

"We all have a past, Hardacre, that's why we're here – so you'll get no judgment from me. But skeletons have a nasty way of dancing out of the closet at the most inconvenient times. It won't have been the first time that a nice piece of blackmail has brought a good man to heel. This is *not* a game. I will not be blindsided or have our operation here compromised. And you can start by giving me the name of the woman who told you."

"What makes you think it's a woman? I never said such a thing."

"True. But it usually is."

OLIVIA SKIMMED THE address on the envelope.

St. Thomas' Hospital
Westminster Bridge Road
Lambeth

She slid the envelopes across the bench along with the coins to pay for her postage and fought a twinge of conscience. None of this was her business. She had no right to meddle in the lives of her social betters. Having uncovered the mystery, she ought to bury it and be satisfied enough with establishing what happened to the mysterious Constance, and yet if she did not remember, then *who* would?

The rain had cleared and the clouds which had brought the morning downpour were breaking up by the time she came to the corner of King and St. Nicholas Streets. She paused as a horse and dray laden with furniture blocked the crossways while two men from the department store opened the delivery gates wide.

A large sign swung into view.

Furnishings ~ Removalists and storage ~ Land and house sales registered Monthly.

Kenstec House would be one of those properties registered. The removalists from *Criddle and Sons* had already been through the house once and many of the finest pieces were gone to storage until Mistress Denton called for them.

Even now, the thought she might have to leave Ponsnowyth or even Cornwall itself was something that was not quite real. Was she afraid of adventure? She had known no one when she first arrived to teach Miss Denton and yet she had managed to survive.

And she would again. Who was to say she would not fall in love with another part of the country just as much? If she was wise and continued to save, she might be able to retire with a small cottage and a pension when she was fifty.

Inwardly, she shook her head. None of that would happen if she just stood there.

SOON, THE ROAD was clear and she still hesitated. There was still plenty of time. She'd only just sent off her applications. It could be weeks – perhaps even a month or two – before she received a new posting. It would be time enough then to think about leaving Cornwall.

She needed a distraction – something to take her mind off Constance. And Adam.

Olivia spied a bookstore ahead and went in. The owner was delighted to show her the latest releases. She picked one up by Elizabeth Gunning with the intriguing title called *The War-office*, and another by her favorite author, Mary Meeke, *A Tale of Mystery, or Celina*.

"Are you sure I can't tempt you to buy one more," asked the shopkeeper, "just unpacked this morning."

He held up the title, *The Unexpected Legacy* by Rachel Hunter.

She hesitated over the expense – the book was seven shillings and sixpence, and the two volumes in her hand already came to seven.

"Go on, Miss. Hours of pleasure in each one – forget your troubles, explore the world in the comfort of your armchair."

The man's sales pitch proved irresistible.

PETER FITZGERALD WAS a very punctual man. He was already waiting for her at the front of his office. As they walked toward the park by the river, he took a glance at the brown paper-wrapped package under her arm.

"A productive day's shopping, my dear?" he inquired.

"The bookseller had a new shipment and he was quite persuasive," she said.

"Edifying works, I trust. I certainly hope you're not one of these unserious young women who throw away good money on those dreadful gothic titles." The tease in his tone belied the censoriousness of his words.

Olivia treated the mocking in the spirit in which it was apparently to be taken.

"A lady never reveals her secrets – certainly not to confirm a suspicion that may diminish her in the eyes of a gentleman."

"It heartens me to know my opinion is something you regard."

It was a statement that could mean exactly what was meant on the face of it and yet there was something else in his tone that suggested the words could have greater meaning.

Perhaps changing the subject would be better.

"May I presume to ask a question?" she asked.

"It would be a pleasure to answer it."

"I take it the business of settling the squire's estate has been concluded."

"All the creditors have accepted terms pending the sale of the house."

"Then I was wondering about the probity of me remaining at Kenstec."

"I hope you don't feel too isolated there on your own. I didn't think about that; I should have been more considerate—"

Olivia raised a hand. "Please don't misunderstand me. Truly, I don't mind staying at the house. But with it soon to have a new owner, and my own plans as yet so uncertain, I feel it may be best if I leave Kenstec and take up rooms with Mrs. Trellow."

"It that where you met Mr. Hardacre?"

She frowned. What an odd question to ask.

"It is, as it happens."

Fitzgerald came to a stop by a park bench under the shade of a large tree. He paused a moment before speaking.

"Miss Collins, a man in my time of life has seen something of the world, and he knows what he wishes in a helpmeet."

She felt the butterflies in her stomach let loose.

"Over the past six months, you have been a source of great support and comfort, not just to the Widow Denton and her daughter, but also to me. And during this time, I have come to a deep respect and admiration—"

"Mr. Fitzgerald–" she interrupted, but he continued on.

"—We get on, so we shouldn't be too much of an imposition on each other–"

Despite the shade of the tree under which they stood, Olivia felt a furnace blast of heat course through her. She managed to cleave the tongue from the roof of her mouth and prise her jaws open enough to speak.

"Am I to understand correctly, Mr. Fitzgerald, that you are proposing *marriage*?"

He looked at her speculatively. "Would it be so intolerable to you? You've stated previously your reluctance to leave Cornwall, and I certainly would be saddened to see you leave. Marriage would provide a measure of certainty for both of us."

Olivia sunk down on the bench.

"You have given this a great deal of thought, Mr. Fitzgerald, and—"

"—*Peter*, please."

She closed her eyes and inhaled slowly, giving her brain a chance to catch up with her still hammering heart. She was reluctant call him by his given name. To accede to that level of informality might give him hope that his tender feelings were returned. And they were not...

She felt him sit beside her and opened her eyes. She allowed him to take her hand and bring it to his lips.

"Your delicacy of feelings does you credit, my dear. Although neither of us is in the first bloom of youth, surely you must have considered your future? Perhaps even entertained the notion of marriage?"

"I am deeply flattered, sir, and humbled, that an important man such as yourself has given me and my circumstances such a great deal of thought. But I cannot give you any type of answer that would please you."

She watched his face carefully, looking for revelatory signs that might indicate his thoughts, while she tried to gather her scattered ruminations and assemble them into some kind of order.

"I understand," he said.

She let out a breath, retrieved her hand and kept it in her lap.

"Miss Olivia," he continued, making the presumption of using her given name. "Rather than refuse me out of hand, may I extract another promise? Consider my offer for one month before you give me your final answer."

That she *could* do. It would give her time to properly organize her thoughts. And besides, it would also take at least that long to receive any offers of a new governess position.

"Yes," she said. Her reply brightened the face of the middle-aged bachelor. "I promise to give your kind proposal serious consideration. You will have my answer at the end of this summer."

Chapter Eleven

ADAM HADN'T MEANT to spy – and the irony of the observation was not lost on him.

None of it had been deliberate. It was just that he happened to spot Olivia and the solicitor entering the park, just as he had left the tavern. It had been idle curiosity, that's all.

And besides, the three of them *were* heading in vaguely the same direction. Olivia and Fitzgerald appeared to be in earnest conversation. Adam might even have abandoned his watch over them if not for the distinct impression that Olivia was about to faint.

Even from the distance of thirty yards, he could see the color leach from her face and the heavy way she sat down on the park bench. He'd got no further than ten paces closer when he witnessed Fitzgerald pick up her hand and kiss it.

It turned his stomach. Adam turned on his heel.

He'd headed smartly in the opposite direction and spent the rest of the afternoon pondering his visceral reaction to the scene, and the answer made him laugh out loud when it came to him.

He was jealous...proprietorial even. All because he saw a woman he had kissed fervently just a few days ago being kissed on the hand by another man. It was plainly absurd, especially considering the things he'd seen over the years in the ports of South America, but that's what it felt like in the bottom of his gut.

He returned to the coaching house for the five o'clock coach in time to see Fitzgerald helping Olivia up into the carriage.

The fine afternoon had tempted other visitors into town and they were now going back to their homes, so the return coach was full. It ruled out the opportunity for further conversation with Olivia.

Adam acknowledged the solicitor with a nod of his head as he, too, embarked, the last to climb on board.

Olivia sat diagonally opposite by the door on the far side of the coach. She was looking out of the window on that side and did not see him get on. An elderly couple sat beside her, the husband seated opposite Adam. Next to him were two children, a boy and a girl aged about nine, squeezed in the middle, with their rather harried-looking mother sitting opposite Olivia.

When the coach started to move, Adam glanced out of his window. Fitzgerald remained there on the curb and offered a tentative wave. Not to him, he was sure.

Adam glanced back into the coach and could see Olivia's attention remained fixed out of the opposite window. She had missed Fitzgerald's farewell entirely. In profile, she looked pensive. Perhaps what Adam had witnessed was a lovers' spat, not an assignation.

He closed his eyes. He was a fool for allowing himself to become distracted. And fools get themselves killed, even under the most benign circumstances. No, his mission was clear.

Adam had a meeting in two days' time in Falmouth with Major Wilkinson and his *Society*. If he *was* being observed by a third party in the interim, he hoped they'd all die of boredom.

He settled a plain-wrapped package, the size of a large book, on his lap. He'd been given it by Bassett and told to open it in private when he returned to Ponsnowyth. No amount of good-natured pressing would force the man to reveal its contents.

The journey home was slower than the one on the way out, this time having disembarking passengers and their baggage at every stop. Eventually, it was only he and Olivia alone in the coach, a mile out of

Ponsnowyth.

For the first time since departing Truro, she abandoned her vigil at the window. Adam feigned interest in the view from the window on his side, but watched her misty reflection in the glass as she straightened in the seat. She glanced his way. He wondered if she would speak to him.

After a moment, Adam stretched his arms above his head until his hands touched the carriage roof.

"A profitable day in town?"

Olivia's eyes widened. Adam nodded to the parcels on her lap.

"Oh...yes." She shook her head. "It was a very interesting day. I'm pleased the rain cleared."

"So, we're back to just talking about the weather?"

He watched her begin to pull her face into a glare before she regathered her temper.

"I am open to any other suitable subjects for discussion. The food at the White Hart is excellent. I can highly recommend it."

"That's good to know."

"I see *you* did not leave Truro empty handed."

Adam regarded the package from Bassett now on the empty seat beside him.

"It arrived today; a gift from Aunt *Runella*."

"You never mentioned an aunt this morning."

That was because Aunt Runella didn't exist. That was the code name for Sir Daniel Ridgeway. Adam had burst out laughing when he learned it, but Ridgeway had not.

"I don't recall giving an exact accounting of my family tree, either," he told Olivia. "Aunt Runella, if you must know, is a maiden aunt who never married because she was a woman with a face like a boxer and possessed of a sour disposition. Somehow, I became a favorite of hers."

That was enough to satiate his companion's curiosity on the subject.

"Look, I know it's not the White Hart, but would you consider dining with me at the Angler's Arms this evening and do me the honor of allowing me to escort you home afterwards?"

Olivia visibly relaxed. The tension in her bearing ever since they left Truro disappeared and, indeed, if he was not mistaken, there was a renewed sparkle in her eye.

"I was already planning to take a meal there so I suppose it would be no hardship to share a table with you," she said with the barest hint of a smile, and Adam relaxed, too.

THE SUN CAST long slanted rays of golden lights across the fields and through the cluster of buildings that made up the village of Ponsnowyth. He assisted Olivia down from the coach and accepted a squeeze of his hand. He even managed get a proper smile out of her as she entered the inn.

"There you are, you old salt! I've been waiting hours for you!"

Adam turned to see Harold Bickmore approach. He shook his friend's hand with vigor.

"Good to see you. I thought the *Andromeda* had put out to sea days ago!"

"Not until next week – so they've extended furlough for another few days."

"That's unusual, isn't it?"

"Word among the executive officers is that we're to await special orders."

Adam raised his eyebrows, silently inviting further elucidation.

Harold grinned. "I'd be shot if I revealed the Navy's secrets to a civilian."

Adam slapped his shoulder and urged, "Perhaps a few drinks will loosen your tongue."

"Let's put it to the test, eh? I'll tell you what *I* know if you tell me what *you* know?"

Adam squeezed the parcel in his hand reflexively.

"Know about what?" he asked, keeping his voice jovial.

"First of all about that lovely young lady I saw you with."

Adam grinned and led the way toward the inn. "A gentleman never tells."

"Ah! You never were an officer and a gentleman."

Once, the dig would have bothered him greatly. Perhaps, it still should, but he couldn't muster the energy for it. His lack of reaction hadn't gone unnoticed. Harold regarded him with a puzzled expression for a brief moment.

"For that insult," said Adam firmly, "you're buying drinks."

He excused himself to go upstairs. After closing and locking the door, Adam carefully unwrapped the parcel. A slim volume sat on top of a box that was wrapped in a cloth.

Adam set that aside to open the box. He let out a low whistle.

The box contained two pistols and their accoutrements – powder flask, flints, a cleaning fluid tin, reamer, and a bullet mold. The ram and the screwdriver handle were made of ivory, as was the stopper on the wooden powder flask which had been nicely carved into the head of a hunting dog.

He pulled out one of the pistols. It was not some elaborately decorated piece. It was made for business. He thumbed back the hammer to cock it. The action was firm. He pulled the hammer back further to release it and eased it back into place slowly to prevent damage to the flint.

Adam ran his fingers over the engraved steel on either side of the action. Then he held the pistol up, sighting along it. The weapon was excellent, the epitome of the gunsmith's art. He turned it around and looked down the barrel, observed the rifling inside the bore.

Deadly but accurate; designed to wound more than the pride of a duelist. He understood immediately the message implicit in *Aunt*

Runella's gift. He set the pistol back into the fitted case with its companion. While he considered where to store his prize, he examined the small booklet.

It contained two sets of semaphore signals – one in English, the other in French – helpfully translated since Adam's command of the language was limited to ordering food and swearing. Of the two gifts from "Aunt Runella," the code book was the more valuable.

He would need more time to study it. He'd prefer to master the signals from memory rather than having to rely on keeping the book on him.

For now, he stowed the pistol box beneath his bed. He looked around the room for a place for the code book. Constance's writing box leapt out at him. He opened it and pulled out the drawers, knowing there was space available behind them. He inserted the book and returned the drawers, pleased to see them sitting flush.

He fashioned a primitive key from a small piece of wire in his kit and worked the writing box's simple lock until the bolt slid home. It was a skill his father had taught him. People were always happy to part with a shilling or two for the trouble of unlocking an object rather than breaking it open.

Adam slid the writing box, lock-side to the back, into the base of the wardrobe. With its plain back, it looked like a part of the wardrobe itself and, with a pair of dress boots in front of it, it disappeared altogether.

When he returned downstairs, he found Harold at a table with Polly and Olivia. The two women were listening to him intently, then they burst out laughing.

Olivia threw her head back, a grin on her face. He caught a flash of white teeth and the pale column of her neck, and his breath caught.

She was beautiful. Too bad she belonged to someone else.

OLIVIA LAUGHED AT Lieutenant Bickmore's humorous tale of a slight misadventure aboard the *Andromeda* involving him and Adam Hardacre. Then she spied Hardacre himself at the bottom of the stairs and their eyes met.

For some reason, she could not look away.

He's a good man. The best never to have been promoted to officer.

Bickmore's bitterly delivered words had surprised her at first. It was clear that the young lieutenant admired his older but subordinate shipmate.

Still, Adam drew no closer, so she smiled at him, hoping that would be invitation enough to join them. She got the impression he was a solitary soul, used to being on his own, even when surrounded by hundreds of people. She could identify with that – although not all of it was by choice.

Harold shifted in his seat.

"Ah, there he is!" the lieutenant announced. "You were gone so long, I thought you were making yourself pretty for the ladies here!"

Polly giggled and blushed as if she were a debutant and not a married woman approaching her fifth decade. Adam didn't seem to take offense at his friend's ribbing.

The innkeeper's wife rose from the table, and gestured Adam to take her seat. Bickmore rose also, his perfect manners second nature.

"It's time for me to get back to the kitchen and finish makin' tonight's meal before the hordes come in. *Stargazy pie* it is tonight," she said.

"I remember the first time I saw a Stargazy pie," said Olivia. "I couldn't stop staring at the pilchard heads poking out of the crust. I thought their beady eyes were reproving me every time I cut a slice."

"So how did you overcome your fear?" Adam jumped in before Harold could make a remark. As much as he liked his friend, he did have a habit of monopolizing the attention of attractive women.

Not this time.

"I was hungry," she said dryly. "And once I'd tasted it, I decided that, dead-eyed stare or not, no pilchard was going to come between me and a hearty meal."

She hesitated a moment, suddenly unsure of what to say next. She glanced to Lieutenant Bickmore. "The lieutenant here was kind enough to keep me and Polly entertained with stories of life aboard your ship."

The two men exchanged a look. After a second, Adam responded. "Don't believe half of them, and that half you do intend to believe will be full of exaggeration, no doubt."

Harold laughed. That was one of the things Olivia liked about the lieutenant. He seemed to be as happy being the butt of jokes as much as he was prepared to have a tease of others.

She rose from the table. Adam and Harold did likewise.

"Forgive me, gentlemen, while I rest and repair for an hour before dinner. It's been quite a long day. Are you staying for dinner, lieutenant?"

"If I won't be too much of an imposition."

Adam gave an exaggerated roll of his eyes and folded his arms.

"You're *always* an imposition, you pup, but I put up with you anyway," he said, but leavened the words with a grin of his own.

ADAM WATCHED OLIVIA leave. He couldn't help but like her even more after seeing her reaction to how he and Harold behaved together. Olivia had brothers, so that could be the reason she was at ease with their banter. In his experience, few women appreciated the push and shove of male relationships.

Of course they were rough with one another. Onboard ship, their very lives depended on it. A man needed to be tough. He needed to know his weaknesses and overcome them – and sometimes it took another man to reveal them to him.

"Shall we take a stroll?" suggested Harold, interrupting his reflections.

There was something in the simple words that suggested something more than just a pre-dinner constitutional.

Outside, the sun had dipped down behind the trees and hills, giving the sky a lilac hue. Lavender-colored shadows cast before them.

He let Harold set the pace, a slow unhurried amble past the mudflats on which small fishing boats were beached until the rising tide made them usable once more. Adam had felt like that for some years – able but marooned. It had fueled his resentment, and more than once had him butting heads with his commander.

Now he had purpose.

"So what has you in the mopes?" he asked his friend.

Harold's shoulders straightened, but he didn't answer.

"Go on, you *tuss*, spit it out."

"I'm thinking of resigning my commission."

Adam accepted the declaration with a mere raise of his eyebrow. They carried on walking in silence a few more yards. Harold wanted to talk, but he *didn't* want to talk.

"Why would you want to do that?"

More silence. Adam stifled his impatience and waited.

"It's not just me, you know," Harold said after a while. "And it's not just the lower ranks either. You have a lot of friends on the *Andromeda* still. You'd be welcomed back, you know."

"But only as a bosun."

Harold shrugged, and Adam continued the struggle to keep his patience. But it was wearing thin.

"I can't be that much beloved," Adam offered, "otherwise Captain Sinclair would have sent to see me – and he hasn't."

More yards fell behind them in silence. Their shadows disappeared as the sky deepened to an inky blue.

"Sometimes I wonder whether it's all worth it, you know." Harold continued to speak his thoughts aloud. "Whether England should just leave Europe well enough alone, and then again I think of England and her empire. That's something to be proud of."

Harold stopped at a crossroads. He propped himself up on a stile in a roadside fence.

"Look, I'll tell you the real reason I came here tonight. I need your advice."

Ah-ha! That was beginning to make more sense, Adam thought.

"I've been approached by some kind of correspondence society."

Adam felt a chill that had nothing to do with the approaching night. "Really? Who?"

"They call themselves *The Society for Public Reform.*"

Chapter Twelve

ADAM WAS RELIEVED his friend was looking down because he was certain he'd failed to hide his surprise.

"*The Society For Public Reform* – sounds harmless enough," Adam shrugged as casually as he could. "Is it some charity your mother is trying to get you to support – a widows and orphans' fund, perhaps?"

"I fear they may be Radicals."

"Oh dear, *that* kind of correspondence society…your father would certainly not approve. Do you have any proof they're not just do-gooders?"

Harold shook his head.

"I was invited to one of their meetings by someone who called himself Wilkinson. He gave me a card."

"Did you go?" Adam asked.

"No. They've not had the meeting yet. It's this Wednesday evening in Falmouth."

Adam huffed a long, drawn out sigh. It was one thing to be asked to spy – another thing to involve a friend. And if this group was as he thought, then Harold could find himself tangled up in something he hadn't bargained on. Something ruinous. Something *deadly*.

"I didn't want to say anything," Adam said, at length, "but I've been approached by them, too."

In the growing darkness, he heard, rather than saw, Harold's surprise in the form of a slight intake of breath. "The same man by the sounds of it."

"I suppose we *did* make a bit of a fuss at the Admiralty."

Adam began to retrace their way back to the inn.

Harold fell into step. "Are you going to go?"

"I wasn't, but now I suppose I'll have to, if for nothing else than to keep you out of trouble. You've got your family's reputation to think about. *I* have nothing to lose."

Harold sighed. "Thanks, mate," he said.

They walked on a few yards before Harold laughed. "Well, now that I've unburdened my soul, you can answer another question for me."

Adam didn't answer. It was invitation enough.

"Tell me how you met that lovely Miss Collins creature. She's not a local girl."

"She's been in the area ten years. She was governess to Squire Denton's daughter."

"Not the same squire who got you impressed?"

"The very same squire, but different wife and different daughter by the time Olivia came along. In any event, the whole family is gone. The old man's dead and the widow and daughter have left for London. Olivia tells me the house is going to be sold."

He waited to see if Harold challenged him on the use of the governess' first name. He did not, apparently distracted by the thought of Kenstec being for sale.

"Is it now? Perhaps we should take a look."

Adam burst out laughing. "I don't know what they're paying Navy lieutenants these days, but I can tell you it'll cost way above what *you* could afford."

Harold was unperturbed. "You forget, I have a legacy from my grandmother and will be coming into a portion from both my mother and father. And I dare say *you* have a tidy sum from the Navy – we could form a corporation and buy it together."

Adam snorted.

"No, don't laugh! It's been done before – and just think on it, when was the last time you ever did anything just for the hell of it?"

The light from the inn ahead beckoned, welcoming them.

"And besides, it would be a fine opportunity to spend some time in the company of the lovely *Olivia...*"

Adam wrinkled his nose. The familiarity had not gone unnoticed after all, but he would not give Harold the satisfaction of thinking there was more to the relationship with Olivia than just friendship.

Memories of their kiss still lingered. He tamped down the thought, grateful his face could not be seen in the dark.

SURELY IT WAS more than just sheer stubbornness that caused Olivia to refuse Jory and Polly's suggestion to stay the night at inn. Not that she wasn't grateful for the couple's concern for her, but the more she pondered her circumstances, Olivia decided that a penny saved was a penny earned.

She'd been profligate with her book purchases today, although she couldn't regret the acquisition. With her extra duty to the Dentons discharged, and no prospect yet for work, she would be better saving *any* penny from this point on. And it would not be fair to impose herself upon Jory and Polly, even at their insistence, if it prevented them letting a room for a fee they had given to her at no charge.

Besides, Olivia decided, she wanted to sleep in her own bed – well, the bed that had been hers for ten years.

And now here was Adam Hardacre insisting on walking her home. Even if she did have a mind to refuse him, she had a feeling he would pig-headedly ignore her wishes and do it anyway.

It was easier to give in.

As they paced through the dark, a breeze had sprung up and on it she smelled the rich damp smell from the estuary. Clouds, thick and full, were outlined in gold, backlit by the moon as they scudded across the night sky. She and Adam climbed the hill on which Kenstec House was set.

With him at her side, Olivia paused as they reached the top of the rise. She looked back toward Ponsnowyth.

"I love the view at this point," she said. "You can always see down to the sea and, on a clear day, you can even see Falmouth. It had never occurred to me to look back at night 'til now. I shall miss it when I leave."

Out to sea, the clouds were even larger and fuller, and one glowed for a brief moment, illuminated by lightning. There was an electrical storm out to sea. It explained the odd, damp earth smell from the estuary that always presaged a cloudburst. In her mind, she said a quick prayer for those out there. A quickening breeze also told her it would be upon them before too long.

"What would you do if you didn't have to leave?"

Adam's question surprised her. For one small moment, she had forgotten he was there, distracted by the growing tempest out on the black horizon.

"I daren't let myself even think it," she whispered. "You know better than most about the importance of earning a living."

Fleetingly, she thought of Peter Fitzgerald's offer of marriage. What a dry and passionless proposal it had been. But did she want any different? An ardent avowal of passion and adoration would have been equally unwelcome. At least the suggestion was pragmatic, even businesslike.

Amiable companions.

Call her a romantic, but the wedding vows did say "*love*, honor and obey." Could she consider entering a lifelong union without being in love first? If she accepted, would she grow to love Peter Fitzgerald?

She didn't think so.

She turned and walked on, and Adam fell easily into step with her. She and her silent companion continued another four hundred yards until she spotted the stone entrance pillars that marked the drive to Kenstec House like sentinels.

Lightning flashed closer overhead and, after five paces, thunder rolled. She increased her pace, familiar with the fast moving storms that battered the Cornish coast.

Kenstec House loomed out of the landscape and the moon emerged briefly from behind the clouds to shine on the small tower turret that extended above the southwest corner of the original roofline.

It was an unusual addition to the roofline of what was a typical old English manor house. Below stairs, gossip had it that Squire Denton and his second bride had seen ones similar on their honeymoon in Italy and, in a fit of ardor for his new wife, vowed to build one for their home. Construction had only gotten as far as completing the walls and access to the roof. Plans for a cupola ended as their arguments began and the love between them ended.

To the best of Olivia's knowledge, no one had ever stood on the top of the tower and looked out to sea. On a night like this, it would be a spectacle to behold.

Soon, she and Adam were at the kitchen door. Olivia pulled out the large iron key from her leather bag. Adam took it from her hand, unlocked the door and stepped in ahead of her.

"We'll have to light the fire, I'm afraid," she said, following him into the almost black room illuminated sporadically by flashes of lightning. "There's a tinderbox and fire steel on the mantelpiece."

Adam set quickly and efficiently to work setting and lighting a fire in the stove. Once the tinder had brought flame to a few small pieces of wood, he used a spill to light the lamp Olivia held out to him. In a few moments, the kitchen was bathed in the lamp's warm yellow glow. The fire grew in the grate.

"Thank you for the escort home," Olivia said. "May I offer you tea? I'm afraid I have nothing stronger."

She lit a couple more lamps and the kitchen seemed more welcoming than it had been before. With another soul in the house, Kenstec's ghosts receded into the shadows.

Then a thought occurred to her. Adam must feel some of the ghosts here as well.

"Has much changed?" she asked, lifting the kettle and swirling it about to gauge the amount of water she had filled it with before leaving the house that morning.

Adam looked about and shook his head. "I wouldn't know. I was never in this room. I only came to the house a few times. Mistress Denton – the first mistress – would hold a Christmas party for the village children but we saw no more than the entrance hall. Perhaps you'd like to give us a tour."

"Us?"

"I mentioned to Lieutenant Bickmore that the manor was for sale. He is entertaining a fantasy of purchasing it. Would you mind indulging him?"

Olivia pulled two battered tin mugs from a shelf along with a small tea chest and set them on the kitchen table. She reached for the teapot. It was an old brown salt glazed earthenware pot relegated for the servants' use. It was chipped in places so the clay showed through.

"I'm sure that will be all right. But prepare to be disappointed. Much of the furniture is either in London, or in storage to be sold at Criddle and Sons."

She excused herself to take a lamp up to her room where she left it with the wick turned low. By the time she returned to the kitchen, the wind had picked up some more. A flash of lightning filled the windows. A moment later, thunder rumbled overhead.

The wind blowing through gaps in old stone and ill-fitting windows moaned and echoed through the house.

Adam cast his eyes to the ceiling suspiciously.

"Looking for ghosts? I'd always heard sailors were superstitious folk," she teased.

"Spend enough time at sea and you'll have cause to be," he said. Then he added with an exaggerated sigh, "You would have been wiser to take up Polly's offer to stay at the Arms. No, it's not spooks and specters that concern me. It's real two legged intruders I suggest you be worried about."

Steam billowed from the kettle. Olivia took a tea cloth from a drawer. She lifted the kettle from the stove, crossed to the table, and filled the teapot. Black pekoe aromatics filled the room.

"What is there to steal? Everything of value has gone with Mistress Caroline and Miss Lydia. Besides, I refuse to live in fear. Life is too short to think about what might be. I'll only be in the house for another few weeks at most. I've already written to several agencies about a new position, so you needn't worry about me."

"What if I choose to worry about you?"

"Then I thank you for your consideration. Sugar?"

As she prepared to pour the tea, the sound of the approaching rain rose like the trampling hooves of galloping horses, growing louder with each second until it was beating down right overhead. Olivia felt Adam's presence behind her. He stood close enough that she could feel his breath on her neck.

Would he kiss her again? She decided if he did, she would not stop him.

Her heart started beating double time and her body reacted with an awareness of his warmth and scent of pine and a faint odor of rum. She remembered the passionate kisses in the woods, and wet her lips in memory of it.

She shivered and turned around.

Adam's hazel eyes searched hers.

He raised his hand to her cheek and stroked it. He did nothing more than that. But it seemed to touch a nerve that went all the way through her chest through her stomach and settle lower.

"I want to know that it is you I will kiss, Olivia. Not a ghost."

Her lips parted of their own accord. Then she tasted his on hers.

She shifted on her feet and he took her into a full embrace, his lips not once leaving hers. She reveled in each new sensation his lips and tongue taught her. Then his mouth fell to the side of her neck. How could one pressing of his lips there cause gooseflesh to run all through her body and leave tingling in her toes?

His hands on her back were spread wide, crushing her to him; her breasts pressed against the hard planes of his chest. Words from Constance's diary recalled themselves to her as she described her own body's reaction to Adam's lovemaking.

But he had been but a boy then, as inexperienced as Constance had been. The Adam who held her now was a man who seemed to know every point to touch that would break down her reserve and send desire like quicksilver along every nerve. She wound her arms around his neck and kissed him as ardently as he did her.

He gave open-mouthed kisses across her face, down her neck. His fingers ran through her hair, held her to him firmly.

"You're wrong, Olivia," he whispered in her ear, the eddies of his breath breathing desire into every part of her body. "There's plenty here to steal…" – his lips touched the lobe of her ear – "…to plunder."

She closed her eyes and gave in to the pleasure. When would she ever feel its like again? After years of putting herself second to the needs and wishes of her charge, to her employer, to her station, why should she not have *passion*, to give herself fully to the needs of her body? She was not a girl, no ingénue – Olivia Collins was a woman full grown. She knew what she wanted, but not how to ask for it.

And yet there *was* a ghost. Constance stood at the edge of Olivia's consciousness and urged her on to reckless abandon.

Olivia did not seek permission. She touched Adam however and wherever she desired – the broad expanse of his back over the soft linen of his shirt warmed by his body, his neck, and his thick sandy-blond hair.

Then Adam's hands quested lower as did his lips, branding her collarbone, before she was lifted into his arms. The rain pounded outside.

She gasped.

"Where is your room? Upstairs?"

She nodded, afraid to speak.

He carried her through the servants' entrance, up two flights of stairs through a house now lit almost constantly by flashes of lightning. Although he'd not asked for directions, he came unerringly, as if by instinct, to her bedroom door. He lowered her gently to her feet. She stepped through the threshold into the subdued light of the room.

She waited to see what he would do next.

He took two steps in, swung the door closed behind him, and pulled out the key from the lock inside the door. She stood immobile. Adam Hardacre advanced, looking like a cat stalking its prey, his light-colored eyes mesmerizing her. The sensible part of her screamed to move, to tell him to go and to abandon this foolhardy venture; but she did not, could not.

He now stood within a hand-span of her. She trembled. He leaned in to give her a chaste kiss on the cheek.

"Stopping now is a cost to us both," he said, voice low, only just audible above the rain. "Not stopping would be a price greater still."

Chapter Thirteen

DEAR GOD, WAS *he going to make the same mistake again?*

No.

At the thought, the urgent rush of blood in his groin eased a bit, and the clamoring of the cautious part of his brain ceased.

How could he do to Olivia what he had unwittingly done to Constance a lifetime ago?

He risked another kiss. This time on the lips. It was returned in equal measure. He'd seen men who had been thrall to the opiates used to dull the pain of their battle injuries. Long after the wounds had healed, they had to be weaned off the stuff.

Lust, passion, desire – call it what you like – was just as potent.

He placed the key in her shaking hand, closing her fingers around it, stroking their smooth skin.

"Lock yourself in here, Olivia. Lock yourself away from me tonight."

He backed up a half-step.

"You can't go," she said. "The storm…"

Adam groaned and bowed his head. The low lamplight illuminated the tattoo on his hand, reminding him of who he was. "I may not be considered much of a gentleman by some, so trust me when I say it is taking almost all the chivalry I possess to leave you here."

"But–"

He put a finger to her lips. She would overcome his resolve with a single word – her eyes already articulated it, and his body wanted that promise fulfilled.

He backed toward the door. Olivia followed in silence.

"Is the study still furnished?"

She nodded.

"With a couch?"

Another nod.

"Then that will do me for tonight or until the storm passes."

Her eyes shimmered with tears. Regret? Shame? Adam swallowed against a tightness in his throat. By God, what a cad he was. He would have made love to a woman who he knew was otherwise spoken for.

"Forgive me…" Her voice, husky and raw, was very nearly the undoing of him. He kissed her to silence, tasting the salt of her tears.

"There is nothing to beg pardon for – not from me. It's just not our time, Olivia. Not yet."

The furrow of her brow gladdened him in some perverse way. She cared to some degree. He took her hand with the key, their eyes meeting. Together, they felt for the lock. He left her hand there. Now he found himself in the hall.

"Sweet dreams, darling."

He closed the door and waited. A moment later, he heard the sound of the key and then the bolt sliding home above the torrential rain and the howling wind outside.

Adam descended the servant's stairs into the kitchen once more. Perhaps he shouldn't stay at all. Olivia Collins was a respectable woman with a reputation to uphold.

He opened the back door and was hit immediately by a gale force wind. He steadied his footing just as he had done a thousand times before on the rolling deck of a ship. The damp and chill cooled his blood. Enough for him to think.

Then he felt it; the hair at the back of his neck lifted. A jagged run of lighting struck beyond the hill, nearly blinding him with its intensity, followed by an intense *cra-ack!* and a clap of thunder so loud his ears rang with it.

The demonic, howling wind intensified, bringing even heavier rain with it.

He closed the door against the gale. *Damn*. Now he could not only not leave, but the front of his shirt and trousers were damp as well.

If he dried his clothes and left early enough, no one would be the wiser that he'd spent the night at Kenstec with the young woman. Well, Polly would know. Jory, too. Gossips though they were, he knew they wouldn't say anything about this. He opened the door to the stove and inspected the orange glow of the coals. He stirred them with a poker until they reignited.

He thought he heard a sound and glanced up at the ceiling as if he could see through the floors. He listened hard over the rain to hear if Olivia moved about the house.

Nothing but the raging of the storm.

Adam loosened the lacings of his shirt and pulled it over his head to lay it over the back of a kitchen chair and set it before the stove to dry. He took off his boots, then made quick work of the buttons of the front fall of his breeches.

The chill air aroused gooseflesh across his body.

He slipped his boots back on, shrugged into his coat and buttoned it up. He ventured out of the kitchen into the passage beyond, finding his way out to the entrance hall off which he assumed the study would lie. It was damned cold out here, as well as damned *odd*.

Once he'd been in awe of the "big house" on the hill. In his boyhood, it had seemed to be as large and as grand as a palace. But it was smaller than he remembered, diminished by the lack of furniture. Over the rain, he heard a sound again and beneath a closed door glowed a sliver of light.

He approached cautiously and listened a moment. There was no sound of rummaging for valuables. Adam glanced down to make sure he was more or less modest. He opened the door cautiously, so as not to alarm the person he suspected was behind it.

Lightning illuminated the room. He spied two folded blankets on a chaise lounge of powder blue velvet. At the fireplace, Olivia knelt, coaxing small flames from the new fire she'd set. The windows rattled with the accompanying thunder.

"You needn't have gone to the trouble," he said.

"It's no trouble," she replied without looking back. "I couldn't sleep anyway."

"The storm?"

Olivia glanced at him and nodded before returning her attention to the fire where mean, thin wisps of smoke rose.

"Here, let me help with that."

Olivia got to her feet, letting him take her place by the fire. She had changed out of her day gown and instead wore a buttoned flannel wrapper hiding her figure beneath swathes of blue tartan fabric. She was subdued, cautious. Was she afraid of storms, or of him?

While he concentrated on the fire, he listened to her move about the room. He heard the sound of her shaking out the blankets. If he turned, he would be sure to see a bed being made up for him.

"When Lydia was very small, she was afraid of storms," said Olivia softly. "She would climb into my bed and I would make up stories about brave sailors and clever smugglers until she fell asleep."

Adam smiled at her recollection. The fire caught firmly at last. Flickering flames of orange and yellow burned merrily in the grate. He got to his feet.

"Would you like *me* to tell you stories of brave sailors?"

Olivia cocked her head as if considering his offer.

"Just the stories of one brave sailor will be sufficient." She picked up one of the blankets, wrapped herself in it and sat in a green leather wingback chair large enough to tuck herself fully into, feet drawn up beneath her. "What was the worst storm you've ever encountered?"

Adam pondered for a moment; not the question, but whether Olivia wouldn't be more comfortable on the chaise. No. If he asked her, she might take flight. And he'd rather have her company than not.

The French doors that led out into the garden rattled as though the wind itself was trying to force its way in like a burglar. The top and bottom bolts held firm as they must have done in such storms many times before.

He sat on the chaise and covered his lap with the blanket – for her modesty, rather than his. From this position, he could see the firelight flickering over half of her face, the rest in shadow and a single pale hand, holding her blanket together.

He recalled a storm much worse than this.

"There was a December tempest so fierce it was said it rivaled the Great Storm of 1703. I had just been promoted to carpenter on the *Icarus* when it blew in," he began.

"We'd sheltered at Falmouth with a dozen other ships and battened down the hatches, but the seas battered our moorings. The captain made the decision to put out to sea before the storm grew worse, fearing if we remained where we were, we'd be dashed to pieces."

Adam sat back along the chaise.

"There was no time to recall the full crew. The *Icarus'* full complement was two hundred men, so we short-sailed out into the Channel against the wind and rode the anchors for as long as we could before they started to drag and we lost them completely. For the first and only time in my life, I was seasick."

He turned his head to see if Olivia still listened or whether he'd bored her to sleep. But there she was, with her eyes open.

"Go on," she whispered. "Tell me more about the brave sailor of the *Icarus*."

He flashed her a smile in return and continued.

"It was also the first time I really thought of a ship as being alive, not just the way she moves when under sail but, in rough weather like this, a ship will talk to you – she groans, squeaks, and screams…oh yes, she'll talk to you if you let her."

Adam slid onto his back and closed his eyes, allowing his body to relax and drift toward Morpheus as he related the tale.

Swamped by massive seas, the *Icarus* had started taking on water. He was manning one of the pumps below when he was ordered to the stern to help with repairs to the damaged steering gear. On the way there, the ship was hit broadside by a wave. He had stumbled backwards and fell down into the lower hold which was filling with water. He was winded by his tumble onto the ballast but otherwise unhurt.

The ship lurched once again. A piece of waterlogged old timber among the dredged ballast rolled on top of him, trapping him alone in the bowels of the ship. Behind closed lids, Adam recalled that night as clear in his mind as if it were yesterday.

As water lapped around his face, mortal terror and panic rose out of him like demons – he had shouted uselessly for help, unable to be heard above the storm around them. The ship took on more water and began to list. The ballast shifted once again. He took one large breath before plunging beneath the water to scramble out from underneath the timber and on to the top of the dislodged ballast. He picked up a rock and began pounding the floor above him with all his might until his frantic cries were answered. A nearby hatch opened and he was hauled out.

The *Icarus* survived, as did most of the crew – though three had been lost overboard. They certainly fared better than those whose ships had remained in Falmouth. A dozen men died. Three ships sank at their moorings, with many more badly damaged.

He opened a heavy eye to observe Olivia asleep in the chair by the fire.

Allowing himself to drift off, he considered the real significance of that experience in his own young life. From that day on, Adam had vowed to live every moment as if it were to be his last. He grasped every opportunity offered to him and sought out just as many that were not offered. No more would Adam allow his life be dictated by those around him.

He would be master of his destiny.

OLIVIA STARTED AWAKE at the sound of the study mantel clock chiming six. She was no longer in the chair, but rather lying on the chaise lounge, blankets tucked around her. Outside, the finches that lived in the hedges close to the house were calling out to one another.

She frowned. How did she get here? She'd fallen asleep in the chair across the way. And it was now empty.

"Adam?"

She pulled the blankets aside. She was still dressed in the nightrail and wrapper from the night before. The kitchen, too, was deserted except for hot coals in the stove, a small glass jar filled with hastily picked wildflowers, and a note.

You learn to know the pilot in the storm
– Seneca

Seneca? The Roman poet? How did a humble carpenter-boy-turned-sailor learn about the ancients?

She placed the note onto the table and ran her fingers over the flowers, still fresh with dew. What a mystery Adam Hardacre had proven himself to be.

His kisses were arousing and his conversation illuminating. There was water already in the refilled kettle. She set it on the stove to boil after refueling the fire within. The two tea cups from last night were washed and back on the shelf beside the tea caddy.

Surely you must have considered your future? Perhaps even entertained the notion of marriage?

Peter Fitzgerald had asked these questions speaking of a marriage of companionship, not of love. She recalled Adam's kiss last night and tried to imagine it from the solicitor. She could not. In fact, the very notion of him kissing her on the lips was decidedly unappealing.

If Adam had not proven himself to be a gentleman and master of himself, then she was under no illusion where last night would have ended. She would have welcomed it – welcomed *him* into her bed.

What did that say about *her*? Peter Fitzgerald had made a perfectly respectable offer of marriage. Adam Hardacre had made no such promises – it was ridiculous to believe the thought had ever crossed his mind.

A choice between a passionless future and a passion with no future.

Perhaps this was a test.

Olivia prepared the teapot and returned to the kitchen dresser. She opened the bread tin and cut two generous slices, covering them with butter and damson preserve.

At the table, she poured the hot water in the teapot and stirred it.

That *must* be it – a divine test of her resolve. She had been perfectly content to apply for another governess post four months ago and nothing of significance had changed since. She was a grown woman of twenty-eight, for crying out loud, it wouldn't take too many years before she was a confirmed spinster.

The very best thing she could do was remove herself from such a Faustian bargain.

She carried her breakfast back up to her bedroom and threw the heavy damask curtains open wide, filling her small quarters with light.

She washed and dressed with alacrity before dragging her old trunk out from under the bed. It was made of timber and covered with green painted canvas held together with wide leather bands. It was scuffed, but in serviceable condition. She opened the lid to air it out then pulled out a sachet of dried lavender from her dresser drawer and dropped it in the bottom.

She would begin packing her belongings today.

Chapter Fourteen

ADAM HAD BEEN in The Blue Anchor for more than an hour nursing the same pint of beer. He observed the tide of drinkers and diners with an apparent indifference when, in reality, he worked hard to remember as many faces as possible.

How many of the *Society's* fellow travelers were here? He supposed he'd have to wait to find out. Harold had yet to join them. He was on duty until six o'clock, and it was not yet seven.

It was hard to know exactly who or what he was supposed to be looking for. There were some he recognized from the *Andromeda*, others were vaguely familiar from other smaller ships in the harbor.

"Hardacre?"

The man in front of him looked rough, sporting on his chin several days of dark growth not so far gone as to yet call it a beard. Longish dark hair fell on his forehead.

"Who's asking?"

"A friend."

"My friends already know who I am."

The man curled his lip into a sneer and leaned in. "I know who *ye* are, all right? And I don't particularly care which way we play this. If ye've been given an invitation, then ye're to follow me."

Interesting, Adam thought, they're very cautious.

"Follow you where?"

"Wherever I damned well go."

"And if I refuse?"

"Then me and a few mates will be by to make sure ye forget yer own name, let alone any meetin'."

Adam locked eyes with the man and slowly rose from the table. He was taller, but the man before him was built like an ox. Adam had already decided how he was going to play this. If Wilkinson had him pegged as a trouble-making malcontent, then he would give him one. Appearing too eager would only serve to arouse suspicions.

"I'm waiting for someone."

"Ye don't have to worry about him, Hardacre. He'll be along in his own good time."

The man turned on his heel and walked toward the door. Adam waited a beat, then followed, skirting around the patrons who milled at the bar.

Outside, the light had softened to a pale purple. Adam fell into step with the man as he marched up the hill toward the Packet Quays where some of the wealthy shipping owners had built their homes to overlook the harbor.

"If we're friends now, I ought to know your name."

All Adam received in return was a grunt.

As they crossed one of the streets, Adam felt himself grabbed from behind. He struggled hard against Grunt and his unseen associate when another man came in from the side and shoved a canvas sack over his head. The men secured his hands.

"Calm yerself, Hardacre, ye're still among friends," said Grunt, sounding a lot more companionable than he did in the pub. "We just have to be cautious like."

The three men took turns for a moment in shoving him along and turning him about, as though he were a ball in some game. By the time they finished, he had no idea where he was, precisely, nor how far they had gone. After about ten minutes, Adam could see light through the loose weave of the Hessian bag and heard the sound of a door opening.

"Hardacre," Grunt announced on his behalf. An unseen hand shoved him hard in the center of his back. Adam stumbled forward. He gritted his teeth as two firm hands clasped his shoulders, propelling him down a carpeted hallway and into a room where, from what he could hear, a group of men gathered.

At last, the bag was pulled away. Adam was momentarily blinded by the brightly-lit room.

He seemed to be in some kind of library or private gentlemen's club. Bookshelves accounted for three walls. There was a smattering of leather seats clustered around a fireplace, but the dominant feature in the room was a large, round mahogany dining table that might seat twelve. Now, however, no more than half a dozen men were in the room, including the three who had "accompanied" him. Behind him, hands worked to release the knot of the leather thong that bound his wrists together.

Unsurprisingly, Major Wilkinson sat at the end of the table. Adam experienced the odd feeling of being back before the Naval Board. He resisted the urge to stand to attention. Instead, he rubbed the red weal on his wrist where he had been tied.

"I was expecting a meeting of bluestockings," said Adam. "You gentlemen play a bit rough."

"It's because this is not a game, Hardacre," Wilkinson answered with no small measure of condescension. "Now, sit down and have a drink. Brandy will be acceptable, won't it? Or is whiskey more to your taste?"

Adam raised an eyebrow and took the nearest seat. Brandy had been near impossible to get since the outbreak of war. Whiskey, too – especially the high quality ones from Cork. They were extremely hard to come by.

Both things hinted at connections with both France and Ireland.

"Whiskey," Adam answered and a moment later one was placed to his right.

"You'll have to forgive our unorthodox methods. Prime Minister Pitt has spies everywhere and I'm sure we have better things to do than swing at the end of a hangman's noose, right gentlemen? Don't misunderstand me, Hardacre. We are all patriots here to a man. But we will not obey a mad king or his tyrannical Prime Minister."

Wilkinson's impassioned words were met by quiet affirmations by those present. Adam looked around at all of them. These men did not seem like fanatics. They seemed sober and earnest.

Wilkinson continued. "We will not stand by and see men fight in a war for which there is no just cause. Good men; hard working men whose hands are callused by true labor. Good men like you who have been made to suffer indignity, refused a commission that was rightfully yours for no other reason than you weren't born into the 'right' social class."

As the man spoke, something stirred within Adam, a vestige of resentment, the bitter taste of humiliation he bore for eight long years watching the promotion of men younger and less skilled than himself. His right hand squeezed the glass in it. His bosun's tattoo stood out starkly.

Adam downed the amber liquid and welcomed the fire in his throat that added fuel to the roiling in his gut.

The role of malcontent seemed made for him and he determined he had a few choice curses for Sir Daniel-*Bloody*-Ridgeway when he next saw him.

"What can be done of it?" he asked. "Your pretty words and sympathy won't restore my years or persuade the Royal Navy of their error. My background may be humble, but I'm not a stupid man. The revolution in France starved and slaughtered thousands. What for? They got rid of a king and got an Emperor instead. What makes you think this band of merry men can do better?"

Wilkinson's lip lifted a fraction.

"That's more than you need to know."

Adam set the glass down heavily and shook his head slowly.

"No. Not enough for me to put my neck on the line."

"Then let's put it like this, Hardacre – plans are well advanced to usher in a new era that the Radicals have only caught a glimpse of. We have men the length and breadth of the country ready to rise up. You're not the only man who has much to gain in this."

"To usher in a Heaven on Earth? I'm not buying it."

"Then what will you buy?"

Adam focused his attention on the grain of the timber of the table. *His* mission had been clear – uncover specific information about a secondary plot to invade England, and identify the ringleader.

"A revolution of the type you allude to would need a vast amount of money and organization – more than any individual possesses," stated Adam. He looked up to see Wilkinson straighten in his seat. "Everyone knows Napoleon has his forces massed at Calais. England waits hour by hour for the invasion to begin. Whoever you're working for is going to need detailed information about our fleet – numbers of men, orders, tonnage, logistics – and that's information you're only going to get from a man on the inside."

"*Men* on the inside, Mr. Hardacre," Wilkinson responded. "That's why we approached you. You're obviously very astute but I'm not sure you appreciate how your *resignation* was received by the men of the lower ranks, and not only aboard your own ship. Word gets about and, from what I hear, ordinary seamen and merchantmen from Penzance to Portsmouth have declared you a hero. These men will talk to you – and gladly – as a friend and a former colleague."

Adam fixed Wilkinson in the eye. "All right. I can get you your information," he said. Wilkinson smiled. "But I want in on the planning." The smile faded a little.

"Really?"

"Why not? I spent twenty years of my life in the Navy – I know how they all think, sailor and officer alike. I've done my time as a lackey. I won't be yours."

The man's face firmed to the expression of a man trying not to become angry.

"And your price?"

"A thousand pounds."

One of the two other men at the table – hitherto silent – sucked in air over his teeth.

"In *gold*."

"Is that *all*, Mr. Hardacre?" Wilkinson asked, more with amusement than amazement.

"It's enough to buy a house and a couple of fishing boats for my retirement."

"Sounds reasonable," Wilkinson shrugged.

Adam smirked. It might sound reasonable to Wilkinson but not to the other men in the room, he would wager.

"And one more thing – when the French come, tell them I want to be left the hell alone."

"That, too, sounds acceptable." Wilkinson leaned fully back in his chair, looking more at ease than at any other time during this interview. "But in order to earn your fee, you will have to demonstrate the quality of your information."

"What is it you want to know?"

Wilkinson slid an envelope toward him.

"The details are in there, along with twenty pounds. Start with the private dockyards in Plymouth. Find out everything you can. On receipt of your personally delivered, comprehensive report, the balance of the first installment of one hundred pounds is yours. You will then be given a second assignment. On the successful execution of that, you will be invited to join our inner circle."

The major rose to his feet and extended his hand. Adam did likewise. The two men shared a firm handshake.

"We'll meet again in a fortnight's time."

"Where?"

"Are you still staying at the inn at Ponsnowyth?"

Adam confirmed he was with a quick nod.

"You'll receive word there."

A man of about Adam's age, but with reddish hair, had been standing at the fireplace throughout the meeting. Now, he tugged on the bell pull. A moment later, Grunt entered.

"Our guest is ready to leave," the man at the fireplace said. Adam detected a lilt to his voice but he spoke too few words to guess at his accent.

Grunt held up the Hessian mask and leather ties, and approached. Adam shoved him away angrily.

"Try to put that thing on me again and I'll *slit* your throat!"

Grunt bared his teeth and looked ready to charge at him when Wilkinson intervened.

"Put them down, Dunbar. Our guest will be leaving through the front door."

Adam bared his teeth right back at the thug and stepped around him to follow a footman to the door. Out on the street, he turned and looked up at the building, a typical Georgian townhouse, third along in a terrace of perhaps ten or eleven homes, all flat fronted with chimney stacks at each party wall, three chimney pots per stack. He didn't linger.

Turning back to the street, Adam looked left and right as if deciding which direction to go in. He went right, the furthest distance to a cross street. He counted the houses as he went. Just as he turned right, Adam glanced back to see if he was being followed yet. He'd bet a crown that he would be trailed from a distance to be sure he left the area. Dunbar was probably waiting at the front door until he reached the end of the block.

That was why he'd chosen the furthest cross street.

Two steps into the street and out of sight of the front door, he suddenly changed pace, hurrying as fast as he could without his rushing footsteps giving the game away. At the back of the terrace, he turned right again and slipped into the darkest shadows of a hedgerow behind the end townhouse.

He waited and, finally, his followers arrived.

"Damn..." Grunt – correction, *Dunbar* – grumbled to his companion. "Lost him." Adam was mere feet away. He remained perfectly still. The two men stood at the corner. "I don't trust the bastard."

"Just because he brought you down a peg? Don't be daft. Anyway, he's not lurking around here. Once he gets his bearings, he'll probably go down to the pub."

Dunbar grunted again. The two men turned and went back the way they came.

Adam waited until they were gone then made his way along the back of the terrace, counting the houses again until he reached the back garden of the house he'd been in.

He hunched low in a break in the hedgerow and pulled out his pocket spyglass to train on the house. He could see only one window lit. It wasn't late – no more than nine o'clock – ten at the outside. Adam guessed if he visited the house by day, he would find it unoccupied. There were many such residences on the Quay whose owners might be absent for months at a time.

Nevertheless, he made note of the location.

ADAM ENTERED THE tavern hungry and thirsty, and a little bit annoyed to see Harold just sitting there, chatting up one of the barmaids.

He sent the young woman on her way with a barely polite request for a meal and a pint.

"Where the hell did you get to?" he asked. Harold had the good grace to look sheepish. That was something at least.

"Yes, well, the more I thought about it, the more it didn't seem right. I know people are angry and want reform, but if the Admiralty got wind of one of their officers having Radical tendencies then it'd be the end of my career."

Adam's anger receded like the tide.

"I suppose you're right."

There was silence between the two men as a fresh plate of bread and another of roast beef and gravy was set before Adam. An ale quickly followed. He didn't stand on ceremony. Adam started on his meal with gusto.

And he knew Harold had read his mood right because his friend waited until the better portion of it was consumed before he spoke.

"So, did *you* go?"

Adam chewed meditatively over a large piece of bread and considered his answer. Should he take his friend into his confidence?

If he was worried about conventional Radical correspondence societies who spoke of nothing more than the "common sense" of the workers, then the young lieutenant ought to be spared from tonight's call to out-and-out treason.

"I did," Adam finally admitted. "You'd have detested every minute of it. Pontificating blowhards to a man – and the women who were there were fat and ugly."

Harold mock shuddered.

"Then you've done me a good service, indeed. Perhaps, I can do you one in return."

"Like what?"

"Give you an excuse to see the rather fetching governess all on her lonesome at Kenstec House again."

"What makes you think I have a special interest in Olivia Collins?"

Harold shrugged. "Well, maybe I'm wrong. Perhaps, it is *she* who has taken a fancy, although I can't imagine what she'd see in an old man like you. At any rate, I've set my heart on buying Kenstec and retiring as a county squire. I think it would suit me and I'd need a governess."

Adam was beginning to grow tired of the conversation.

"You're not married and you don't have children; why would you need a governess?"

Harold didn't immediately respond, so Adam looked up from mopping up gravy from his now empty plate to look directly into his friend's eyes. They were full of mischief. Adam gave him a sour look.

"Leave the poor woman alone."

"I can't think of any good reason why I should."

"Perhaps you would like me to give you some?"

"And thus our conversation returns full circle," Harold said, ill-disguising his triumph. "Admit to me you've taken a shine to the woman and I promise not to tease you any further."

"I will not."

"Then, in that case, you won't have any objections if I take up the pursuit of her? These lonely spinster governesses are just waiting for any man to make love to them."

Adam refused to analyze the feeling welling up him – it was good enough to simply call it annoyance.

"You'd be wasting your time," he replied, putting enough gravity in his voice to alert a sober man that he was about to cross a line.

"Ah-ha!"

And it would appear that Harold wasn't sober *enough*.

"*Ah-ha* nothing," said Adam through gritted teeth. "She'd see through you in a heartbeat."

Harold paid no attention. "We'll see which of us is receiving her favors before too long."

Chapter Fifteen

It was a funny thing about friends, even the best ones. Not seeing Harold for a week had restored Adam's humor exceedingly well.

He had spent five days in Plymouth and intended to return there Monday morning following a trip into Truro to report to Ridgeway. And, before he left, he had extracted a promise from Olivia that she would be attending next Saturday's dance at Ponsnowyth.

So when a certain young lieutenant arrived to the Angler's Arms that afternoon in a single-horse drawn tilbury wearing the civilian clothes of a young buck, Adam had no animosity. He simply shook his head and laughed.

"Ready?" Harold called "You didn't think I'd forget about going house hunting, did you?"

Adam swung up beside his friend and sat on the padded leather seat. Harold snapped the reins and the handsome black horse took off at a brisk trot.

"I can't believe you still want to do this."

"Why not?" asked Harold, "You told me Miss Olivia thought the idea amusing. We can amuse her in person and see if the young lady might be persuaded to join us for a turn about the countryside."

"Sitting where? There's barely enough room for the two of us in this thing."

"Your lap, perhaps?"

"Don't be crude."

Harold gave him a sideways glance; Adam glared back. There were times he forgot how much younger and less mature his once *commanding* officer was.

"I had no idea it was like that, old man."

Adam grunted a noncommittal reply and the teasing stopped.

"I had the cook from the tavern at Falmouth prepare a picnic repast," Harold offered. "If every stick of furniture is gone out of the old place, we can dine on the lawn."

THE HORSE MADE short work of the trip to Kenstec House.

Harold brought the tilbury to a stop and stood up at the reins. He gave a low whistle. "Nice view from here. I imagine it's better from the third story."

Adam said nothing. He scanned the windows, looking for the one that was Olivia's bedroom.

The front door opened and Olivia swept down the half a dozen stone steps as though she was lady of the manor.

"Gentlemen, so good of you to call. You'll have to forgive the informality but I'm the only one in residence."

She shared a quick glance at Adam, but it was Harold who was first to jump down, take her hand, and offer a sweeping bow.

"Miss Olivia, you look more radiant than the morn," he said.

"I suspect you are so profligate with your compliments, Lieutenant, it would be wise not to believe a word of them."

Adam climbed down feeling smug, the initial prick of jealousy soothed by Olivia's words. He glanced back to Harold. "Why don't you go see to the horse? The stables are around the side. There's a good chap."

Harold moved off with nod of his head and a look in his eye that suggested Adam should be prepared for some kind of good-natured retaliation.

He went one better than his friend. He lifted Olivia's hand to his lips and kissed it – slowly. He was close enough to see her eyes widen a moment.

Harold was right. He *was* staking a claim of sorts. So what of it? Why shouldn't he? He and Olivia shared a bond that only the two of them knew about – the knowledge of Constance. For now, he preferred to keep it that way.

How strange that after twenty years, Constance should be the one to bring them together. He wanted to be alone with Olivia again, to know her thoroughly, to uncover every secret, to know why she blushed as she did now.

Adam felt a low level of arousal grow. Perhaps having Harold as a chaperone was no bad thing.

"Thank you for the flowers."

His memory of the night of the storm and the morning after felt as fresh as yesterday. Now, he cursed Harold as a chaperone.

"I'm sorry I had to leave, but you looked as though you were sleeping peacefully."

His spirits lifted along with her smile.

"You're a considerate man in every way, Adam."

"You haven't gotten to know me yet."

Olivia laughed and he found himself grinning along with her.

She accepted his arm and they moved toward the house.

"How was your visit to Plymouth?"

"Very productive."

Half a truth is often a great lie.

Adam wasn't sure where he'd heard the aphorism but it served now. He'd made no secret of his trip to Plymouth, but the story he had told was his desire to see if his skills and experience would make him suitable to find work alongside a naval architect. That had been Ridgeway's recommendation, and it was ideal for his clandestine work.

To Wilkinson and his men, Adam felt no pang of conscience to spin the most outrageous fabrications – as long as they served the purpose and the untruths did not tell on his face. He'd prepared himself for it, practiced telling the lies in the mirror until *he* was convinced by the face he saw before him. That was easy.

With Olivia, however – and the Trellows, too, for that matter – he walked a narrower line. He offered them the truth of what he was doing, but not the why.

They waited at the front door for Harold to return from stabling the horse. He arrived struggling with a large wicker basket.

"Miss Olivia, I think the first stop of our tour should be the kitchen!"

OLIVIA FELT LIKE a girl again enjoying a carefree summer with her two mischievous brothers. She was at ease in Adam and Harold's company in a way she had never felt with Mr. Fitzgerald. Harold's flirtatiousness was amusing and not to be taken seriously. Adam was becoming dear to her in a way she had never dreamed possible.

And since they both knew it could only last until the end of summer, her heart was safe.

The lieutenant insisted on exploring every corner of the house as though he were, indeed, inspecting it thoroughly for purchase. He admired the study and its French doors opening onto the garden. Then, he waxed lyrical about the proportions of the dining room with its white-painted timber wainscoting and the red and gold damask wallpaper that reached up to the ceiling. Only the faintest marks betrayed the prior location of various paintings and furniture pieces.

Adam said little but remained at her side as Harold dictated the pace of their exploration. Eventually, it took them to the top floor. A landing featured a butler's pantry at one end and servants' rooms to the north end of the building. Access to the other end of the floor was blocked by a wall in which was set a single locked door.

"What's behind here, Miss Olivia?" Harold asked. "If there are three servants' rooms on this side, then there must be equivalent space on the other side. Wouldn't you agree, Adam?"

"It makes sense to me. It also brings us close to an addition to Kenstec that I'm curious about."

"Ah, you mean Squire Denton's folly," said Olivia. She smiled at having both men's attention.

"'Tis a sad story of how soon the marriage of the squire and his second bride soured."

On arriving at Kenstec House, the housekeeper and the butler had taken Olivia aside privately and enumerated all the things she should *not* ask about, nor question, if she wished to retain her new appointment.

One of them was to never, *ever* ask about the folly. The second, to never, *ever* ask about the first Mistress of Kenstec. The third, stay out of the way of the squire when his temper was up.

What lay behind their warnings was pieced together over the years from the occasional unguarded comment from one of the older servants or from the raised voices of the master and mistress behind the closed doors of the drawing room or bedroom.

"The squire's second marriage was quick and unexpected," Olivia explained. "Caroline Denton was many years her husband's junior but, by all accounts, was pleased with her match. They honeymooned in Italy where they saw cupolas on the roofs of villas that offered the most outstanding views."

In the telling, Olivia found herself drawn to Adam's hazel eyes.

"In a fit of generosity to his new wife, the squire promised to create her such a thing. He hired workmen to raise up a tower, but the project only lasted as long as the passion, and not long at that," she explained.

"He cancelled the order for the cupola roof and ordered the builders to make the work waterproof – then told them their services were no longer needed. Their last task was to wall off this section leaving just a door. That was fifteen years ago. I have to confess, in my ten years at Kenstec, I've never been beyond this locked door."

"Then," announced Harold Bickmore, looking as impish as a school boy, "we must rectify the situation immediately, Miss Collins!"

Adam turned the knob and leaned on the door. Indeed, it was locked. "Is there a key?"

"Not that I know of."

"Then we'll break the door down or pick the lock," said Harold. He saw the look of alarm on Olivia's face. "I jest, of course. Perhaps the master key – surely that would work?"

"Well, I suppose we could try," Olivia answered. "I don't know if this lock is the same as the rest in the house."

She fished out the key from the pocket inside her skirts. The key would not turn.

"Are there any other keys in the house?" Adam asked.

"Mr. Fitzgerald took the full set of household keys with him, but I found one in the bottom of a vase I was packing away. I didn't think anything of it, since it didn't work on the other locks. I will have to go back downstairs for it."

She retrieved the key from a small decorative casket that sat on the mantel over the fireplace in her room. She handed it to Adam on her return.

To her surprise, the key worked. The mortise lock's deadbolt retracted with a sluggish clack.

"This is rather exciting," offered Harold in an exaggerated stage whisper. "Who knows what skeletons will be revealed."

"Then I'd better go in first," Adam said, matching the tone, "because I know how frightened you are of such things." Olivia put a hand to her lips to smother the giggles.

Adam turned the handle and the door opened on stiff hinges. He stepped into the room and she and Harold followed.

SUNLIGHT FROM THE southwest made the space bright and stuffy. The front corner of what was obviously two knocked-together rooms bowed into a curve, the outward expression of which was the tower.

In the center of the circle scribed by the tower was an iron spiral staircase in aged yellowed-white that disappeared into a hole in the ceiling. The walls of the large combined room may have been painted once, but one and a half decades of sunlight from the unfurnished windows had bleached any color out.

Adam ventured in a few steps but slowed as one of the floorboards creaked.

"You'd best stay there, Miss Olivia, until we can ensure the floorboards are still solid," Harold advised.

She watched the two men circle the outside of the room and then work their way in to the staircase. They glanced at one another as if silently debating who would climb first. It was Adam. The structure groaned as it took his weight.

Harold sobered. "Careful, Adam, the stairs aren't bolted to the floor. They're only fixed up top I think."

Olivia stepped further into the room and watched Adam take each step with caution. He disappeared into the hole above. A moment later, a shaft of light filled the room and fresh air breezed in for the first time in who knew how long, bringing with it the smell of the sea and swirling the dust from the floor.

The staircase shifted slightly, suggesting Adam had stepped up onto the roof of the Kenstec House tower.

After a moment, Harold hollered, "Ahoy up there!"

There was no immediate reply. He and Olivia exchanged glances before Harold took one step upwards, then another.

The staircase rattled with additional weight. Adam reappeared and descended part way down.

"The view is majestic up here!"

"Is it safe for Miss Olivia to climb up?" Harold asked.

"It is." Adam ducked down so he could see her. "Just come up slowly. The stairs are well fixed at the top. But stay away from the edge when you come out. All that's guarding it is a decorative iron railing and it's only shin high. If you stay in the middle, you'll be fine. You're not afraid of heights, are you?"

Olivia shook her head.

Harold backed down to the bottom of the stairs and held his hand out to Olivia. "After you," he said. "You'll be quite safe between the two of us."

Olivia lifted the hem of her skirt and placed a foot on the step and tested her weight. It was solid enough. She glanced up and smiled at Adam who peered down through the three foot by three foot opening. When she drew near, he reached down to take her hand and aided her final step up onto the roof.

The wind hit her as she emerged and threatened to tug her hair from her chignon. She drew close to Adam, staying in the lee of his body. Harold joined them. He whistled. "You're right about the view."

The hatchway emerged at the very center of the tower roof, a circular space about eighteen feet in diameter encompassed by the low railing Adam had mentioned. The roof itself, which would have become the floor of an enclosed structure if a cupola had ever been installed, was covered against the weather with thickly tarred canvas.

Olivia felt a strange exhilaration at being at such a height with the open air all around. Adam lightly rested a hand on her shoulder and pointed to the southwest at a cluster of buildings near the edge of the estuary. "There's Falmouth."

The beauty of it was breathtaking. It was almost like she was on an island, what with the river Fal to her right and the Carrick Roads to her left, spilling into the Channel which met the horizon. Beyond that, close – perhaps too close – was France and all of Napoleon's forces ready to strike. She shivered.

"Cold?" Adam asked. She shook her head, not wanting to tear her eyes away from the splendor of the scenery before her.

"Look at this – a perfect view of the semaphore stations at Falmouth and Feock," said Harold, stepping confidently closer to the edge. "It's a pity we don't have a telescope. We could find out the latest news from London."

"Providing we knew what it meant. The messages are coded."

The thought of codes and signals meant little to Olivia who was more than content to take in the view. As she watched, one of the twin-masted ships broke away from the cluster of vessels by the mouth of the river and pushed its way further up the Fal. She imagined its voyage at the end of another successful run, bringing news and goods from the New World – and avoiding the French Fleet, which was not averse to taking civilian ships as well as military ones.

"Such a pity the cupola was never built. It was meant for a view such as this," she said. "I'm glad I got to see it before I leave."

"So soon?" asked Harold.

She glanced at Adam's suntanned face. *Was that a frown?*

"Not yet," she replied to Harold, "but I hope I'll be offered a post after the summer."

"Well, perhaps we can come back again for a sunset viewing if the lawyer doesn't mind us making use of the place," he said. "What's his name – Fitzsimon? Fitzgibbon? Fitzgerald?"

Olivia nodded on the last and raised a hand to shield her eyes from the sun.

"I shall ask when I next see him, but I can't imagine he'd have any objection."

"Why don't we head back downstairs?" Adam suggested. "I'd wager it's about noon and Harold here promised us a quality picnic in the garden. It looks much less windy down there."

Harold and Olivia descended the iron spiral staircase once more, its foot creaking against the floorboards. Adam closed the rooftop door and came down. Olivia shook her head, getting used to the silence again instead of the noise of the wind rushing above.

They locked the room once more and headed downstairs. The hall clock ticked the minutes while the pops and groans from the house settling gave the impression of being inside a living thing.

"You're a braver soul than me, living here on your own Miss Olivia," said Harold. "In a place like this, I can entertain the thought of restless spirits."

Chapter Sixteen

ADAM PICKED UP a pencil and tapped it restlessly on the edge of the desk. Bassett blinked owlishly from behind thick round glasses and scowled.

"Some of us are trying to work, Hardacre!"

He put the pencil down.

"How soon did you say?"

"Two weeks."

The set of the man's jaw suggested he wasn't happy with the shortened timeframe for the delivery of a set of plans for a warship that didn't actually exist.

"Just preliminary sketches will do. Here," Adam offered a sheaf of densely inked paper. "I've written down the specifications; all you have to do is draw the pretty pictures."

Bassett let out a put upon sigh and reached for the documents.

"Leave it with me but I'm *not* going to promise anything."

"He keeps saying that but he always delivers. Don't you, Bassett?" Daniel Ridgeway stood at the top of the stairs in the upper room of Charteris House. He shot Adam a grin.

Adam pulled his feet off the forger's desk and put them down to the floor.

The little man merely grunted a reply.

"I hope you have more to say to *me* than that, Mr. Bassett."

At the sound of the feminine voice, Bassett stood bolt upright like a sailor coming to attention. Adam tried hard to suppress a laugh. Then he turned and saw who the voice belonged to and found himself momentarily without words.

He, too, rose to his feet.

The woman before him was beautiful. She had the type of figure and face the artists Thomas Gainsborough and George Romney might war over the honor of immortalizing on canvas – as they had done over Emma Hamilton a decade earlier.

The lady wore a fashionable and expensive walking dress, leaf green and trimmed with white embroidery under the bust. A light mantle sat over her shoulders, the fur trim brushing against her elbows.

Bassett leapt to his feet and rushed over to her. "Your Ladyship! You grace us with your presence," he exclaimed.

The woman gifted her swain with a smile and a kiss to the forehead which made the man blush down to his boots. Adam couldn't keep in his amusement any longer. He laughed and found himself under the scrutiny of the woman's grey-green eyes as she turned to him.

Viewed more closely, Adam saw she was not as youthful as she first appeared. Her white-blonde hair – one of her most striking features – was streaked with silver-grey. Around her catlike eyes showed faint traces of lines. Adam decided she might be his age, or even slightly older.

"My dear," said Ridgeway, approaching, "let me introduce you to our latest recruit, Adam Hardacre."

Adam had forgotten Ridgeway was even in the room. And it hadn't gone unnoticed. A faint smile played around the older man's lips.

"Hardacre, you have the honor of meeting my wife, Lady Abigail. My dear – Lieutenant Adam Hardacre."

Before Adam knew what he was doing, he found himself taking

her proffered hand and bowing formally over it.

Then the thought occurred to him: Ridgeway's wife *knew* about this operation? The question must have shown itself plainly on his face because the lady answered.

"Yes, you are not mistaken, Lieutenant. I'm part of what my husband likes to term 'The King's Rogues.' I'm afraid intrigue is our family business." She leaned in conspiratorially but with clear amusement in her eyes. "You might be surprised how much a man will tell a pretty woman – especially if she is an attentive listener – and how much a woman will reveal to another if they are confidantes."

Ridgeway laughed and went to his desk. He pulled out a chair for her. She thanked him not only with words but also with a look and a smile that seemed to Adam more a private exchange between lovers than husband and wife.

Bassett, meanwhile, looked on as if about to swoon then collapsed back into his own chair as Lady Abigail sat.

She looked at Adam. "I have some news that is of interest to you, Lieutenant," she said. "I've recently returned from London after making inquiries on your behalf about the girl, Constance Denton."

Adam glanced at Ridgeway who nodded mutely to confirm he had assigned the inquiry to his wife.

"The information you received from..." Lady Abigail frowned a moment in recollection, "...Miss Olivia Collins was quite correct. Constance was delivered of a boy on the twelfth of May 1794, and she died of childbed fever ten days later, but not before giving the child a name. Christopher John Hardacre."

Adam reeled with the news. *A son!* Somewhere out there was a boy who bore his name. Indeed, if he had survived infancy, he'd be a young man of nineteen or twenty now. *Christopher John Hardacre.*

Lady Abigail continued, "I should point out that my contacts and I are not the only ones who have been inquiring into your past."

"Who?" The question came from Ridgeway, his tone serious. She addressed her answer to him. Any residue of flirtatious amusement was gone, her husky voice now sober.

"They don't know, but the request for information came from the superintendent himself who simply said he'd received a letter from a family connection."

"Do we know who?"

The lady shook her head. "I've asked my contacts to find out. It could be a relative, although twenty years is a long time to be following up on a long-lost connection. Perhaps, some article clerk is being thorough in trying to track down the remaining heirs since the squire's death."

"Then that has to be someone here in Truro. Isn't that's one of the local men, Denton's family lawyer?"

"Peter Fitzgerald," said Adam.

Two sets of eyes, one pair grey-green, the other blue, looked at him expectantly.

"I suppose it makes sense. He's the family's lawyer. I met him briefly about a month ago. Through Olivia…*Miss Collins*…I know he's dealing with probate on behalf of the family. He's an officious fellow, but harmless enough."

"Be mindful of him anyway," Ridgeway instructed.

Lady Abigail rose and so did every man in the room. She kissed her husband on the cheek.

"Will you be home early? Marie and her friend are expected back from boarding school this afternoon."

"I wouldn't miss it for the world. I've missed our *petite-fille* since she didn't come home for the Easter holidays."

Again, the Ridgeways shared a look – one of a husband and wife, of proud father and mother, and yet of lovers still. For a moment, Adam wondered if he would swoon like Bassett – *or become violently ill*, a cynical voice inside offered.

He swallowed *that* voice down.

"Is there any way of finding out what happened to the *boy*?" The question came unbidden before Adam could censor it.

He now had Ridgeway's full attention.

"Are you sure you want all that trouble?"

Adam glanced to the floor briefly. "You're right – it was so long ago. Perhaps I *am* better off believing he was adopted by a good family and is earning an honest trade somewhere."

Ridgeway gave him a look that was not without sympathy. "It's a good fantasy to have – the last thing you'd want to learn is that he was hung as a murderer at Tyburn."

The furrows between Adam's eyebrows ran deep.

"Think it likely?"

Ridgeway gave a noncommittal raise of his shoulders.

"It depends on how much like his father he was."

THE ANGLER'S ARMS barn was dressed for the *troyl.* Swags of greenery festooned the walls, studded with posies of wildflowers of white, yellow and shades of pink. Outside, a pig was roasting on a spit, the smell of which was already making Adam famished.

He had been looking forward to this event all week. Frankly, it was exhausting to be on alert all the time; mindful of every action in case one is watched, and watching everyone else around you, looking for a hint they might be a spy and a traitor.

But tonight was all about the simple pleasure of a country dance among friends, where he could give himself over to the moment without reserve. It would be like furlough.

He settled himself on the edge of an unopened barrel by a door near the back of the inn.

He noticed Will lurking around the back of the kitchen. They shared a nod. No doubt, the young man was waiting for his mother and one of her maids to leave in order to help himself to one of the *fairings,* a crisp, sweet and spicy ginger biscuit that had been left out to cool.

A moment later, the lad lunged out of sight a moment before emerging with two of the delicious morsels. Adam was surprised to find himself presented with half of the spoils.

The young man grinned at him.

"If *Mamb* catches me, I'll tell her ye were the pilferer, then I won't get a clip around the ear for it."

Adam laughed. "Don't be so sure your mother won't give me a pinch for it either, so we'd better eat these now and leave no evidence."

"William Bartholomew Trellow!"

The young man jumped and then winced at the sound of his full name being yelled in top voice by his mother.

"Make yourself scarce, Will. I'll try to delay her for as long as possible," Adam said with mock urgency.

Will didn't require a second invitation. Adam chuckled as he watched the large young man sprint down the length of the barn and nearly lose his balance skidding on loose gravel as he rounded the corner.

He heard the sound of a woman's footsteps and was conscious of the fairing in his hand, the smell of warm ginger reaching his nose. For a half-moment, he considered taking off after Will.

Instead, he turned, waiting to face his punishment like a man. But instead of seeing the thunderous face of Polly Trellow, he saw a vision of beauty. He immediately got to his feet.

Olivia smiled at him nervously and lightly brushed the back of her hand down the skirt of her cream dress embroidered with flowers of light blue, pink and green.

Adam held up the filched fairing. "Share this with me?"

Olivia shook her head. "Miss Lydia made a gift of this dress when she left and this is the first time I've worn anything so fine. I'm afraid I'll spill something and spoil it."

He took her hand, raised it to his lips, and kissed it. He loved the way her lips parted when he did that. The dress was flattering to be sure, he considered, but it was still only a dress.

"It is only the wearer who can make a piece of fabric and thread look so fine," he told her and she blushed.

As far as he was concerned, Olivia could be wearing nothing at all and still be beautiful. His mind conjured an image of that possibility. *Not helpful at this point in time*, he told himself.

He enjoyed seeing her blush as well and considered teasing her about it, but the local band of men and women with guitars, violins, flutes, and concertinas began to arrive to start setting up in their allocated corner of the barn.

Adam offered his arm to Olivia and left the musicians to a discussion about which song they should begin with.

OLIVIA WELCOMED THE arrival of the musicians. She felt the heat of her blush stain her cheeks, not simply from Adam's compliments – after all, pretty words could be had for a ha'penny – but rather, it was the look in his eyes as he said them to her.

She accepted his arm and they walked in silence onto the high street and down toward the green.

He'd only been gone for a little over a week, but she'd missed him even though she had plenty enough to do with a final packing of her belongings and moving into the inn.

Before she left Kenstec for the last time, Olivia had offered a farewell to Constance, even though folklore said ghosts only haunted the place where the spirits left their bodies.

All this week, she was struck by the sensation of time slipping through her fingers. It seemed that once the summer was over, all that would be left to her was a lifetime of bleak winter.

"How is your new job in Plymouth?" she asked. Adam was silent a moment.

"It feels good to be doing something useful again," he answered.

"I imagine it must feel strange after having been at sea for so many years."

Adam offered a winning smile. "At least I can help make the ships more resilient and more maneuverable."

"All the more important for the war effort." Olivia hadn't though anything of her answer but she was surprised to see Adam's expression harden briefly. Perhaps he *did* wish he was back on his ship. Maybe he worried about his friends still serving.

The silence between them stretched on until even the music from the band's rehearsal reached them.

"Tell me about *you*," said Adam. "Have you had any replies to the inquiry letters you sent?"

For a horrible moment, she wondered whether he knew about her letter to St. Thomas' Hospital until she realized that he was talking about her applications for a new position as governess.

"No, not yet. Perhaps, by the end of summer…" her voice trailed off. *The end of summer.* She mentally shook her head to re-gather her thoughts.

"Olivia?"

Adam was wearing that intense look once more and little pleasurable butterflies in her stomach fluttered.

"I have a question to ask—"

She was struck by the similarity – a private meeting in a park, where the result was a proposal of marriage. She held her breath.

"—Did you see Squire Denton's will?"

Olivia blinked rapidly. *The will?* "Uh, no, I didn't actually see it. But I was at the reading of it."

"Were all the beneficiaries named?"

What a strange turn this conversation was taking.

"I imagine so," she replied. "The bulk of the estate went to Miss Lydia as heir. There was a residue for Mistress Caroline, and small bequests to the butler, the housekeeper, the Ponsnowyth church, and to me."

"But to no other members of the family other than the widow and daughter?"

She frowned. "There *are* no other family members. That's one of the reasons why the house is being sold. There's no one with the Denton name left to inherit."

She watched him take in her words and waited for additional explanation but none was forthcoming. Twilight had deepened, making it difficult to see his full expression.

"Perhaps we should return," he said. "The pork smells delicious, and I find myself famished."

She nodded and started back toward the inn without waiting for Adam to offer his arm.

Olivia warred with herself.

She was annoyed, although she had no right to be. In fact, she wasn't even sure who she was annoyed at. Was it at Adam, who had taken what she thought was a romantic moment and reduced it to an interrogation on Squire Denton's will? Or was it at herself for being such a silly romantic fool in the first place?

Adam had fallen in step with her but was keeping a respectable distance between them. Her curiosity still burned deep.

"Why did you ask about the will?"

For three solid paces, his only reply was gravel crunching underfoot.

"I wanted to see if Beaufort Denton remembered his eldest daughter," he said at last.

Olivia was grateful the darkening sky hid her embarrassment. Of course, Adam would want to know whether Constance was remembered in her father's will.

She was ashamed she hadn't considered the same thing herself. Squire Denton *might* have left a bequest for a marker for Constance's final resting place. But no. Bitter to the end, the squire had cast off his daughter as completely as a worn out pair of shoes and abandoned her mortal remains to an unmarked grave.

But there was more than just Constance. There was her son.

Their *son.*

Perhaps, it was Adam's way of asking whether the child survived infancy. She chanced a glance his way. He was walking at her side, eyes ahead but thoughts a thousand miles away, no doubt.

She thought of the letter she had sent to the superintendent of St. Thomas' Hospital. Should she tell him of it? Would he hate her for meddling in something that was no business of hers?

Chapter Seventeen

HALF A LIE is better than a full lie.

Adam repeated the phrase several times to himself on the walk back to the barn but it didn't make him feel any better.

He wished there were no secrets between them, but Olivia had put him on the spot with her question. Let her believe it was Constance he thought about, not the boy who was their child.

He hoped for Olivia's sake that reuniting him with the writing box and delivering news of Constance's sad passing had been enough, and she didn't think to dig further. If there was someone else poking into his past, the last thing he wanted was for Olivia to start asking questions, too, and attracting the attention of the wrong kind of people.

He chanced a glance in her direction. She was withdrawn. Did she think he was still in love with Constance?

Before them the barn was ablaze with light, alive with the laughter of villagers who, for one evening, would put all their cares aside and celebrate. The thought appealed to him greatly and, tonight, he planned to be one of those merry souls.

Tonight, he vowed, Olivia would be left in no doubt that his past was in the past.

Where it belonged.

And his future? To hell with that – he had no more control over that than he did the weather.

Eat, drink and be merry! For tomorrow we may die!

The smell of roasting pork and the sound of the band rehearsing a lively reel was more than enough to banish any worries.

He took Olivia's hand and steered her around the group of people lining up around the spit, guiding her inside the inn where he claimed a corner bench. He retained a hold of her hand.

"You said you feared a spill on your dress, so I thought you might want to dine in here, instead of risking the benches outside."

Adam watched her expression change from confusion to surprise then gratitude.

"You're a *good* man, Adam Hardacre," she said in a low voice.

Her words warmed him from within. He squeezed her hand, then brought it to his lips before rising from the table with a promise to be back with their food.

He could get used to this, Adam thought as he joined the end of the spit serving line. A quiet life in the country with a wife who loved him, to be given "this day, our daily bread."

He picked up two plates and smiled at the Angler's Arms maid who placed a generous slab of bread on each. Out of newfound habit, Adam looked at the faces around him. Some he knew, but not too many. It seemed that the Trellows' dance attracted everyone within fifteen miles of Ponsnowyth.

The line moved slowly toward the freshly-roasted meat. Then he saw a face that caused him to pause before it disappeared in the crowd. Adam searched for the black hair and the figure of middle height until he was nudged in the back by a man behind him who nodded ahead where a gap had opened.

He walked a few paces forward and accepted the roasted potatoes and carrots then stepped forward again to wait for the freshly-carved pork.

There! Adam could only see the man's back but it looked like Grunt – *Dunbar*, he corrected himself once again. What the hell was he doing here? Spying on him? Was there another message he was to receive? He found himself become resentful. He was off-duty tonight. Wilkinson be damned and Ridgeway, too.

"Hey, Mr. Hardacre? Adam!"

He turned to the mildly exasperated face of Will Trellow.

"Do ye be *wanting* gravy?"

By the sound of the question, Adam knew it had been asked more than once. He nodded curtly and, with the plates in hand, he walked the long way around to the inn.

And Dunbar was nowhere to be seen.

Adam shook his head. Perhaps he had imagined it.

Olivia offered him a smile and before them stood two full glasses – paler than ale, it must be cider. He placed the plates before them and picked up the glass closest to him. Cider it was.

During their meal, music for the first dance started, the sound of accordion and violin filling the night air. He watched a wistful expression cross Olivia's face and he wondered at it.

IT WASN'T ONLY the dress that was "new." This evening was new.

How dreadful to think that after ten years in Ponsnowyth, this was her first attendance at a village dance. For years, she had seen their villagers make arrangements for their regular events but had never been to one. Of course, she had helped Mistress Denton host the family's annual summer garden party, but as a governess – a model of probity, of discretion, of watchfulness over her charge and nothing more.

Squire Denton had made it clear at her first interview that he had very particular ambitions for his young daughter and allowing Lydia to mix with the common folk more than duty required was not part of it.

Olivia knew all the fashionable dances so she could drill Lydia in learning them to appear effortlessly graceful on the dance floor. The truth was, Olivia herself had only ever danced on rare occasions. And even then, those dances were only at Kenstec dinner parties when she was expected to make up the numbers to ensure an equal distribution of men and women.

But tonight, she was free of the obligations of her profession. Tonight, she could be like every other woman and dance to her heart's content.

Tonight, she wanted to dance with the man before her.

"Would you care to dance?" he asked.

Tonight, she could say yes without reserve. And she did.

Adam looked pleased by her answer. He escorted her from the table into the cool blackness of the evening as they crossed from the inn to the neighboring barn, the sound and light and warmth drawing her into a world where she finally felt she belonged.

They milled with other spectators on the edge of the floor waiting for the start of a new tune when she spotted a familiar face.

"Is that your friend over there?" she asked, nodding in the direction of the far end of the barn. Adam turned swiftly, the furrow of his brows marring his features.

Lieutenant Harold Bickmore made his way toward them.

"Good evening, Miss Olivia! I'm here to save you from letting this oaf trample your toes."

"Aren't you bit far from home?" Adam grumbled.

Harold offered a broad, mischievous wink in her direction. Olivia worked hard to suppress a grin. She'd never met two men so unalike who were still, by all accounts, friends.

"Have pity on a poor sailor! The *Andromeda* heads out to sea in three days. It might be months before I see a pretty girl again, let alone dance with one."

Olivia was too old and too experienced to have her head turned by a pretty speech, although she had to admit to a certain thrill in having one man flirt with her and another jealous of the attention.

"Will you take pity, Miss Olivia, and grant your humble servant this boon?"

"Perhaps the next dance, Lieutenant," she said. "I believe this one is taken."

She looked to Adam only to find him paying no attention, his focus somewhere amongst the crowd of revelers. Apparently feeling the weight of two sets of eyes on him, he shook his head as though to clear it.

He smiled, but it seemed to her it was a false one.

"I'm going to let you take pity on this pathetic wretch," he said with forced levity. "Let him have the first dance. I claim the second, then you'll discover what a true delight it is to dance with a real man."

The dance floor emptied. Other dancers filled their places. Olivia felt a gentle tap on her hand. She allowed Harold to escort her to the floor but when she looked back to where they had been standing, Adam had disappeared.

She lined up beside Harold, her left hand in his. The music began with all the dancers doing a hop step forward around in a circle before both hands were joined. Pairs danced around each other before the lady was handed off to her next dance partner and the steps continued.

She smiled with each new man who took her hand, but her attention was elsewhere. With every turn about her partner, she looked. Every move forward through the circle, she searched for Adam. As tall as he was, surely he couldn't disappear in the crowd. By the time the dance concluded, he was still nowhere to be seen.

"I've been wondering the same myself."

"Wondering what, Lieutenant Bickmore?"

"Harold, please," the young man said in a gently reproving voice.

She acceded to the familiarity with a nod of her head and accepted his arm. They strolled toward the refreshment table at the back.

"I'd wondered, too, where Adam went," he said. "It's just a little bit out of character."

"Why do you think that is?"

"I'm not sure. I haven't seen him much lately. But it seems something has been bothering him. Perhaps you could tell me."

Olivia found herself frowning. What exactly was he asking?

"A ginger beer, Miss Olivia?" he asked. That wasn't *the* question, but she nodded and he eased his way through the knot of people and returned with two glasses. "What I mean," he said, handing her one of the drinks, "is that *you* will have seen him more often in the past five weeks than I have."

She was still uncertain how much the two men shared with one another about personal details of their lives. Did Harold know about Constance and her death?

Olivia remained circumspect. "I know he's found work in Falmouth, so he's away for days at a time. And perhaps, we worry over nothing. No doubt, he's found himself engrossed in conversation."

"In that case, would you care for another dance?"

ADAM FOUND DUNBAR smoking a pipe on the other side of the hostelry stables.

"What the hell are you doing here?" he demanded.

Dunbar looked him up and down while he drew smoke from his long-handled clay pipe.

"This is still England, innit?" he replied, a stream of blue-grey smoke streaming from his mouth. "Don't I have the right to be wherever I wish?"

"Well, *I* object to being followed, being *spied* upon. Tell Wilkinson he can come to me himself if he has a problem. I don't answer to lackeys."

The big man snarled and lunged at him but he was too big and too slow. Adam simply side-stepped him. Dunbar stumbled forward before righting himself into a wrestler's stance.

"I'll tear ye in two!"

"Then I won't be much good to your employer, will I? Go on, get out of here." Adam swept his arm as if shooing away a dog, then he pushed his luck by getting right into Dunbar's face. "Tell Wilkinson…no, tell *his* boss – that if I catch even the *smell* of you again, the deal is off. He won't even catch a glimpse of the plans for the new Artemis-class frigate."

Up close, even in the semi-darkness, it was easy to see the man's face was puce.

It would be interesting to see how much self-control the man had, Adam thought. How far could he be pushed?

Dunbar shoved him in the chest, but Adam's legs were braced for it. He bore the assault wordlessly and stared him down.

"One day, ye're goin' to end up with a knife in yer back," said Dunbar, walking away. "Ye'd better deliver, otherwise I'll slice yer liver out – and do it gladly."

Adam counted to ten then silently followed Dunbar as far as the churchyard on the road to the village of Flushing. It could be that the man had rowed across from Falmouth, or Wilkinson had a bolthole in the newly-constructed houses on the eastern side of the river.

Adam listened to the man's trudging strike on the road while he softened his footfalls on the grass, then came to a halt. The light evening breeze carried notes from the violin.

Tempting though it was to follow further, Olivia waited for him.

Adam listened to Dunbar's booted steps become fainter and hoped he'd been forceful enough with the cur to make his message plain, not only to him but also whoever was in charge of this den of spies.

As he walked back to the inn, his first instinct was to tell Harold everything. Onboard the *Andromeda,* if he needed to go to a higher authority to get something done, Harold would be the man he spoke to.

The lieutenant had the knack of translating his plainly spoken demands into a more socially acceptable form to smooth over the sensibilities of some of the other senior officers.

But he wasn't in the Navy now. And he didn't need a go-between. All Adam needed was someone who knew him and could keep his confidences. Someone he could *trust*.

Harold came from a good family. For the sake of that name, he ought to keep him out of this, but being in two places at once was not a trick he knew. While he was in Plymouth, he couldn't keep an eye on what was happening in Falmouth.

He absently rubbed his chest through his shirt where Dunbar had shoved him. Sir Daniel Ridgeway looked like he knew what he was doing, but the man couldn't have limitless resources. Could he?

Adam entered the barn and spotted his friend at the back of the room near the drinks table nursing a half-finished pint. Adam helped himself to a glass and slaked his thirst.

"Where have you been, old man?" asked Harold. "I think Olivia was only one more dance away from demanding a search party to look for you."

She was easy to spot amongst the dancers, tall and graceful, tendrils of her glossy brown hair forming curls at the base of her neck. Her partner turned her about, and Adam caught a glimpse of her face. It glowed and her smile was bright.

She was enjoying herself. Without him.

Perhaps, that was how it should be.

"Well? Are you going to dance with the woman or not?"

"Mind your own damned business."

Harold drained his drink and set the glass on the bench a little harder than necessary. "What's gotten you into this ill-temper?"

Adam shook his head once.

Harold glanced at the dance floor and back to him, all teasing gone. "What happened outside? You don't *look* as though you got into a fight."

That's where Harold was wrong, thought Adam. There *was* a fight all right, but it was taking place between his ears – with one side demanding he tell his friend everything and the other that told him he should bear his burden alone.

The quadrille was coming to an end, and Adam found he couldn't take his eyes from Olivia. He wanted to monopolize her attention, to have her looking at him with the same amount of joy as she shared with her current dance partner.

The next dance would be his and the one after that as well. Adam squared his shoulders, ready to approach.

"I'll call on you tomorrow," he told Harold. The man nodded, accepting the answer and knowing him well enough to press no further.

He stepped toward Olivia, her eyes registering surprise instead of reproof. That was an encouraging sign.

"Please forgive my absence. I was unavoidably detained," he offered.

The animation faded from her face and reserve flooded in.

"The lady is with *me*."

For the first time, Adam looked at Olivia's dance partner.

Peter Fitzgerald did not look best pleased.

First Dunbar, then the interruption of his friend Harold, and now the Truro solicitor…

Adam wondered what gypsy had cursed him tonight.

Chapter Eighteen

OLIVIA WATCHED ADAM'S expression turn to frost and his eyes to ice. He held Peter Fitzgerald's glare for several seconds, enough for it to be pointed before he slowly faced her.

She hid a shiver.

"The choice is yours, Olivia," Adam said. "You don't have to stay with this man."

Fitzgerald's grip firmed on her arm, possessively. It was a small gesture. She doubted anyone else had noticed it. And it gave her immediate unease.

She drew in a deep breath and retrieved her arm. "Do excuse me, Mr. Fitzgerald. I wish to speak with Mr. Hardacre a moment."

Olivia waited for Adam's escort, but it seemed both men were frozen in place, immobile as they glared at one another.

She walked away, her patience exhausted. Let the two men bark and snap at each other like dogs if they wished. She had no intention of being part of a *scene*. She stepped out into the evening and a chill air caressed her shoulders and arms, stealing the heat created by dancing and her embarrassment.

A moment or two later, she heard long firm strides catch up with her. A glance revealed it to be Adam.

"I have to confess, Miss Collins, that since I met you I've discovered I have an illness."

What on earth was the man talking about? She couldn't decide whether Adam was serious or jesting, so she answered him in the same tone as he spoke to her.

"A serious one?"

"I cannot be sure. It happens every time you announce you wish to speak to me in that grave governess voice of yours. I find myself quite dyspeptic."

She pulled her evening wrapper tighter across her shoulders. A moment later, the warm weight of his jacket descended on her shoulders, warm with the scent of pine, leather, and the faintest trace of tobacco. She breathed in the comforting scent of it.

Why did things have to be so complicated?

The sound of murmured words, giggles and rustling skirts from a path by some hedgerows caused her to stop. Adam touched her elbow to draw her away toward the inn.

"And your silence is not good for my nerves either," he said. "Come on, let's find somewhere private so you can say what you need to say to me, and we can both decide if we want to salvage this evening."

He led her through into the Trellows' private living quarters.

Olivia was surprised and she had to remind herself he had known them for more years than she. They entered a pretty parlor that was so much grander than the rest of the inn. Looking about, she couldn't imagine Jory or Will feeling at ease amongst Polly's chintz and china.

Adam closed the door behind them, blocking out even the faint sounds of the music from the barn.

He didn't look dyspeptic. He looked grim.

She shrugged off the jacket and placed it over the back of a chair, then lowered herself onto the edge of a settee. Adam remained standing by the door.

"I should tell you that Mr. Fitzgerald has proposed marriage."

There. *That* cut to the heart of the matter.

For someone who did not know him, it might have appeared that

Adam didn't react at all, but Olivia saw – the working of a muscle in the jaw, the momentary firming of his lips, the deepening of his eye color.

"And you haven't accepted – or at least you're considering a refusal."

Olivia knew she possessed no such mastery of her expression.

"How–?"

"If you had, you wouldn't have invited a man to a private interview. I might not have spent time in drawing rooms, *Miss Collins,* but even I know that such a private *tête-à-tête* is potentially ruinous to the reputation of a young woman of quality."

The flush of warmth that had diminished during the walk outside returned tenfold. Olivia kept her attention on the jewel-like colors of the rug on the floor.

"I am not so young, Mr. Hardacre, and the rules of etiquette which apply to governesses is somewhat imperfect. A pragmatic offer of marriage that might stave off the penury and loneliness of elderly spinsterhood is not something to be dismissed lightly."

"Is Fitzgerald in love with you?"

The question raised a lump in Olivia's throat. She shook her head to dislodge it as much as it was an answer to the question.

"And you are not in love with him." Adam's words, a statement of simple truth, softly spoken, felt like a caress. A moment later, there *was* a caress. His large warm fingers brushed the back of her clenched hands. She forced herself to uncurl her fingers against the slight ache of their tension.

Adam was seated beside her, holding her hand.

"I still have Constance's diary," she whispered, "the one she kept during your summer together. The one she managed to keep hidden from her father though God only knows why he did not destroy it after her death. She wrote with such fervor of the love she had of you. Of how you made her feel in her heart…"

Olivia swallowed. "…And her body."

She felt Adam shift beside her, but his hand remained covering hers.

"I find myself thinking about her words and…I *feel* them myself. I know that such a grand passion would never be possible between Mr. Fitzgerald and me. He wants a companion, an aide for his practice, a practical woman to manage his home.

"And while I imagine he would want…" She squeezed her eyes shut, unable to bring herself to say the words. And that was the *heart* of her problem. She tried to imagine Peter Fitzgerald bringing such ecstasy in the bedchamber as Constance had experienced; she could not.

With Adam, however, it was all too easy to imagine.

"…I know he could not."

The mantel clock ticked away moments in the silence of the room.

"I…I don't know what to say."

The genuine uncertainty in Adam's voice tugged at her. When she looked up, his expression was open and matched his words.

"Marriage…" he continued. "I'd never considered the matter. My life was the sea and now…"

Adam's face blurred as tears filled her eyes.

"…A wife…"

Through the curtain of unshed tears, she saw him shake his head.

"I'm sorry, Olivia, but my life as it is now…I'm in no position to offer you marriage."

Oh, but that was the worst part! Olivia knew it. She accepted it. But still her body yearned for Adam's touch, to experience for herself all that Constance had written in such ardent detail.

The girl's ghost had even followed her here.

"Then there is just one favor I ask of you," she said.

Part of her demanded she resile from her desire and this course of action, and keep the words unsaid.

Her conscience laid before her the potentially disastrous consequences of part of her train of thought, but another, stronger, laid out a different case – one in which she would at least once know passion, as Constance did for one precious summer.

Then she could press it like a flower between the pages of the book of her own life. A treasured memory of a single summer.

With eyes clear, Olivia looked into Adam's. They told her of his caution.

"Make love to me," she said. Adam's eyes widened.

"Just once," she continued, "then I will leave you to your life, and you can leave me to mine."

NO! IT WOULDN'T be right!

Then his conscience was swamped and his arousal was instantaneous.

He wouldn't be a man – alive, with a pulse – if he reacted any other way, he told himself, shoving denial further and further away.

Adam would be lying if he said he hadn't imagined making love to Olivia before this. The night of the storm spent at Kenstec, for instance. He'd occasionally indulged himself since with a fantasy of what might have happened if he'd not been a gentleman that night – if he'd taken what was being freely offered.

Now the offer was being made again.

Unambiguously.

Still, the part of him that was a gentleman fought back.

"Constance is dead because we were young and didn't know any better," he said, hoping that might be answer enough for her.

Instead, he saw her resolve harden now that the initial embarrassment of making her request had faded.

"I know there are ways to pleasure each other without risk of a pregnancy," she offered.

"Do you now?"

He watched a cascade of expressions on her face as she absorbed the tone of his three words – her pupils darkened, cheeks flushed a soft pink, moist lips slightly parted. And, if he was not mistaken glancing down, the shadow of erect nipples showed through the lightweight fabric in the bodice of her gown.

"And after I've *satisfied* your curiosity, you still plan to accept Fitzgerald's proposal?"

"I have little choice," she told him – and very nearly matter-of-factly, too. "I have to live but, despite my efforts, I have not yet received an offer of further employment. By accepting Mr. Fitzgerald's proposal, I will at least have security."

"Then perhaps you should ask him instead," said Adam crisply. "Despite what you might have been told, a man actually prefers his wife to be an enthusiastic bed partner."

"So you are refusing me…" The sound of dejection in Olivia's voice nearly tore him in two.

She slowly rose to her feet. The color of her cheeks darkened from arousal to mortification, and she looked away.

"And as you should," she said. "Forgive me. Such an uncomfortable interview should best be forgotten."

She began to walk away.

No!

Adam leapt to his feet and hauled her backwards to his chest. He slowly drew a hand across her waist and stomach, pulling her close enough for her to no doubt feel the evidence of his arousal at her bottom.

His other hand drew away the hair around her neck and ear, and he whispered to her.

"Is this what you truly want, Olivia?"

The rise of gooseflesh on her arms and the drawn out sigh might have been considered answer enough, but he waited for the words.

His hand freely roamed across her body then, finding itself at her breasts, his fingers skirted the ribboned trim at the neckline, feeling the creamy white flesh rise with each shuddering intake of air.

"Do you want me to make love to you, to touch every part of you?" His fingers dipped lower into the warmth of the cleft between her breasts and still she had not answered him. He kissed her neck again and felt his arousal grow stronger – and just as quickly filled with self-loathing as he was torn between the right and the wrong.

The devil in him won.

How far could he go before Miss Governess scurried away?

His lips brushed her ear.

"What will happen, do you think, when you're in your bed with your husband, his little prick stabbing between your legs?" He felt Olivia jerk abruptly at his crudity. And well she should. Let her associate this proposal with disgust and distaste. "Will you be thinking of *me*? Will you resent the man you're wed to every time he touches you?"

His hand found her right breast and he fondled it, his fingers roughly brushing over the nipple until it hardened further. Olivia rubbed herself against him, unconsciously he thought, but it had the effect of making him fully erect.

"Tell me, Olivia," he breathed and his right hand moved lower until it reached her hip. He splayed his fingers wide until they covered the junction of her thighs. *He* was the gentleman last time. This time it would be up to her to tell him "no."

"Tell me this is what you *really* want."

"Yes." The word was long and drawn out.

He sighed inwardly with resignation. No one could say he hadn't tried.

"Then if that's what you want…"

He relaxed his hold on Olivia. Even now, she could pull from him if she wanted to and run out into the night. And he would not stop her, because just as much of him wished she would leave as wished she'd stay.

Olivia surprised him again by turning to him and winding her arms around his neck.

It was not the artful action of a coquette designing to get her way, confident in the power of her sexuality. Her embrace was raw and honest.

And he was vulnerable. Somehow, she had managed to take a piece of his heart and he didn't know if he could get it back.

Their lips met. It wasn't enough but it had to be for now.

"Harold and Fitzgerald will start searching for us if we're not back soon," he said.

It was the splash of cold water they *both* needed. Olivia stepped back and put her hands to her heated cheeks. She nodded.

"Where?"

For a moment, Adam didn't understand the question. Then he remembered his devil's bargain.

"You still have the keys to Kenstec?"

Olivia nodded.

"Then soon."

"I'll leave first," she said, picking up her cotton wrap from the floor. "It will look less suspicious that way."

Her brave smile unsettled him. She did not look like a woman anticipating the act of love. She looked as if she were facing the executioner.

He reached for his coat and caught the barest scent of honeysuckle on it. Olivia's hand had reached the doorknob.

"Are you really going to marry Fitzgerald?"

"I don't know."

Adam closed his eyes.

"Is he pressing you to set a date?"

"Yes."

A moment later, he heard her open the door into the hallway, then it close behind her.

Adam's body protested its denial, which his mind tried to mask with a fresh flush of anger. He departed the inn via the kitchen, nodding curtly to Will and one of the kitchen maids who were washing dishes.

HE RE-ENTERED THE barn by the smaller rear door just as the band of musicians returned from a break to their makeshift stage. A girl, about sixteen, turned and looked up at him hopefully. Wordlessly, he offered his hand and she accepted with a giggle.

The dance was to be a lively Scottish reel that had recently been made popular. Good. He threw himself into the fast and energetic dance, stepping higher and harder as though he were performing shipboard drills.

Tonight should have been a pleasant evening with a woman he liked, a piece of his life he could keep apart from the shadow world of spying. But even that had been taken from him. He passed Harold among the dancers who silently questioned him on his absence with a concerned look. Adam shook his head.

The reel came to an end and he found himself surrounded by women, young and old, looking for a partner to dance. He caught a glimpse of Olivia seated beside Fitzgerald who was engrossed, not with her, but in conversation with some other gentlemen.

Their eyes met. She looked miserable, hollow.

Good.

That's how *he* felt, too.

He picked the most striking young woman amongst the group, a lass in her early-twenties – small with dark hair and dusky skin who had the look of Welsh blood running through her veins. He made a fuss of her, giving an elaborate bow and kissing her hand.

The girl's friends giggled and sighed, but she did not. Instead, as the musicians struck up again, she gave him an appraising look that suggested she was experienced in more than just dancing. She flirted with him outrageously, a lingering touch when their hands met and when they slid around each other, she ensured their bodies touched.

He played along, knowing Olivia watched them. Was she jealous? A small evil imp inside him sincerely hoped she was, sitting there next to that *windsucker*. She was welcome to her life of stolid respectability, leg shackled to that self-important *tit*.

It wasn't just Adam's thwarted dick that made him irritable. Maybe it was *he* who was jealous.

His dance partner swept by once again, her breasts "accidentally" making contact with his arm.

The damnable creature between his legs raised its head hopefully.

Well, it would just have to be disappointed *twice* in one night.

Chapter Nineteen

PETER FITZGERALD HAD demanded her attention ever since she returned to the barn. She could see in his eyes he wanted to ask about her meeting, but he did not. After a short while, the solicitor became engrossed in deep conversation with some other men.

After fifteen minutes of discussion on a topic she did not know and could not contribute to, she found herself paying attention to the dancers.

One in particular.

Adam had thrown himself into every dance with an energy which belied his maturity. He had his pick of the prettiest women, and he accepted every offer. And yet, no matter how much he lavished attention on them, he looked her way often. She was not so inexperienced that she didn't know without a doubt it was a performance for her benefit.

Why? Did he hope to make her jealous? To what end?

Fitzgerald's conversation with the men showed no sign of coming to a conclusion. She picked at the fringe of her wrap.

It didn't matter what Adam's reasons were, she told herself. It couldn't change the outcome. So why should he make a fuss about it? He should be pleased – a summer flirtation with the governess with no obligation of marriage. She'd been led to believe many men would leap at such an offer.

The hour drew late and the crowd thinned. Adam's friend, Harold, had bade her goodnight about half an hour previously. Adam had disappeared soon after. Now, she waited under the portico with Fitzgerald for his horse to be saddled.

While they waited, she allowed him to kiss her hand. Fitzgerald stepped closer, as though to kiss her on the lips. She turned her face away and his lips and the hair of his neatly trimmed beard brushed against her cheek.

It was all she could do to stop herself from sighing with relief as she made out the silhouette of Will approaching with Fitzgerald's horse.

"Thank you for the pleasure of your company this evening, Olivia. I hope it's the first of many such delightful times."

She curtsied from habit.

"It is you who honor me, sir."

His expression was lightly exasperated.

"Call me *Peter*. Surely, I've earned *that* right, at least, especially since you indicated earlier that you have given my offer of marriage serious consideration."

"Yes...Peter."

"It's against my nature to press for an answer when there is a delicacy of feelings involved, but I had hoped you would have an answer for me tonight."

Will was still some distance away – still too far to use as an excuse to not respond. She had promised Fitzgerald an answer tonight and she would have to give it to him.

How she wished it was Adam Hardacre who stood before her to ask that question.

To yearn for him as she did without an attachment on his part was desperately wicked. It would be even more wicked for her to pursue it if she promised herself in marriage to another man.

To love, honor and obey...

If she was not afraid for her future, she would answer with a regretful shake of her head and tell him that, while he did her a great honor, her heart not could love him fully as he had a right to expect of his wife.

And yet, neither had Fitzgerald said he loved *her* or even indicated that he desired her as a woman. In fact, she knew he did not. Marriage was simply a tidy solution to the loose ends which had been the disposal of Squire Denton's estate and his apprehension, too, that life was passing him by.

Would it even matter to him that her heart was held by someone else?

The slow clip-clop of the horse's hooves and Will's heavy gait drew nearer.

Fitzgerald silently waited for her answer. And he deserved one. A pragmatic response to a pragmatic proposal.

Olivia forced her tongue from the roof of her mouth. "At the end of this summer, if I have not found position suitable, then I will marry you."

She held her breath, waiting for him to ask about the delay or react badly to the unenthusiastic way she had responded, although it was no more parched of sentiment than his proposal had been. But instead, he nodded thoughtfully.

"A quiet wedding in late October, what a splendid idea," he replied. "There's no need for us to make a fuss about it. Many of the prominent families will have returned to London for the Parliamentary season and I wouldn't like them to feel obliged to attend. It will be a private wedding. Inexpensive."

Will handed over the reins. Peter mounted. His horse huffed a breath.

"You have uncommon sense for a woman. It is one of your most admirable qualities," he said. Then he frowned, remembering something.

"Another reason I need a wife," he muttered, mostly to himself.

He reached into his coat pocket, withdrew a letter, and handed it down to her. "This arrived at my office a couple of days ago, and I almost forgot to give to you. Well, goodnight!"

He urged his horse into a trot, the way lit by a moon nearly approaching full. Olivia felt obliged to raise a hand, but he continued without looking back.

In the light of the inn's entrance, she looked at the letter and frowned, suddenly disquieted.

Fitzgerald pressed her to give an answer tonight when he knew that a letter addressed to her might contain an offer of employment?

She turned over the envelope and looked at the return address.

It was from St. Thomas' Hospital, London.

Olivia glanced around. Was Adam about? Should she show him the letter? She looked down at it once more. Perhaps that wasn't a good idea considering how disastrous this evening had been.

She tucked the letter into her reticule and went inside. In the dining room were several young men who were worse the wear from drink. They had made beds for themselves on tables and pushed-together benches.

Upstairs, all of the guest rooms were occupied. Timber floors creaked and occupants spoke quietly as they prepared themselves for bed. Olivia found her room and locked the door behind her.

She prepared a lamp, retrieved the letter and frowned at the seal. It was broken. She examined the front again. Her name was there at the top, but the care-of address, written in larger letters, was Peter Fitzgerald's office in Truro, headed by his name.

Perhaps it had been opened in an honest mistake.

She opened the letter.

Dear Miss Collins,

Please forgive the delay in replying to your query.

It is the sad truth that there are a-many an unfortunate girl who finds herself in our care and it took us some time to identify the per-

son after whom you inquired.

We have gone back over our records and found an entry for Constance Marie Denton which confirms the details you have already provided. And on this, I can offer little more other than the location of the cemetery in which she is buried, which was Cross Bones Graveyard.

The child delivered of her was a boy. Owing to the quality of the family and, indeed, of Miss Denton's presentation, we had no hesitation in promoting the infant to The Foundling Hospital. If records exist of the child at all, then you will find them there.

The name given to him was of his mother's own choosing – Christopher John Hardacre.

I trust I have answered your inquiry to your satisfaction.

Yours in God,
Reverend Amos Grantly

Adam's son lived!

Olivia read the letter twice over.

Christopher would be a man in his own right by now.

Lethargy fled. She found her own old small writing box and pulled out a piece of paper. She had gone as far as pulling out the stopper of her ink bottle and dipping her pen before hesitating over the page.

Once more, she was interfering in matters that were none of her business.

But Constance would want to know. The thought whispered in her ear like temptation itself.

Constance is dead.

Then Adam *has a right to know.*

Then it is up to Adam to make his own inquiries.

Christopher has a birthright.

Olivia put the pen down before she dripped ink on her beautiful gown. Her hands shook. What if Kenstec House was entailed? What if the legitimacy of Christopher's birth was no barrier to inheritance?

That would be something Peter Fitzgerald would know. If her suppositions were true, Constance's son would be a wealthy young man in his own right. But that would be lost once Kenstec was sold.

She picked up her pen and began her letter to the superintendent of The Founding Hospital.

ADAM TROD THE up the stairs and paused outside Olivia's room. A sliver of light out from under the door told him she was still awake.

His burst of anger and resentment from earlier this evening had left him feeling hollow – and, now, exhausted. His hand hesitated on the timber door.

He could knock and she might answer. And behind closed doors, he would show her the pleasure she was so determined to experience.

Images flashed through his mind in an instant, taking his fatigue with it. He would leave her wanting more, wanting *him*. It would be *he* who walked away from what they had. Adam wouldn't give Olivia the satisfaction of leaving him like an unrequited youth.

A stud to a mare.

As Constance did to you.

Aye, that was the heart of the matter, wasn't it? The thought of history repeating itself with the same tragic end sobered him.

But that was when he was a boy; some twenty years had passed like water under a bridge since then.

And yet, he warred with the notion that once more he was being *used*, by Daniel Ridgeway, by Wilkinson, and now by the woman he was beginning to care for.

Pulled toward a destiny he did not ask for.

It was long past time before he could become master of his own destiny – and that meant dealing with Wilkinson first.

He went to his room at the end of the corridor and let out a large open-mouthed yawn as he shucked off his coat. He let it fall over the back of the chair. That's when he saw it. A letter on his bed.

What the hell?

Adam looked about carefully. The window was bolted shut, just as he had left it. Nothing had been disarranged or was out of place as far as he could tell.

Was anything missing?

His stomach plummeted from a great height.

The semaphore code book.

He lunged toward his hidden writing box and pulled out the interior drawers. The slim document was there, undisturbed.

Adam dove under the bed and found his pistols, exactly where he had left them.

He leaned over one knee, bowed his head, and let out a long exhalation of breath. He thought he had been careful, but clearly not careful enough. Still, whoever had left the letter had only that objective in mind.

Dunbar? Adam didn't think the man would have the skill or subtlety to pick a lock and remain undetected. That meant Dunbar had an accomplice he hadn't identified.

Adam got to his feet and picked up the envelope. It was addressed to him in a masculine hand but it also featured the flourishes of a well-educated man.

The envelope was sealed with a few drops of wax but there was no impress mark from a ring or a seal to give a hint as to identity of the sender.

A mutual acquaintance is agreeable to a meeting once you have acquired what he seeks. The Collector is very fastidious and wants to be sure that your efforts have not been in vain.

There will be arrangements made to purchase the goods when he arrives next week. Any correspondence can be left with the Post Master's office at Truro.

– *W.*

It didn't seem like much but even *something* was better than nothing. He could give Ridgeway several things – Wilkinson called his superior The Collector. The Collector was a man who had to travel to make this meeting. Letters were being exchanged via the Post Master's office at Truro.

The Collector. There had to be more to his name than just a penchant for collecting plans for battleships.

Adam put the letter aside. He wouldn't be in Truro again for another week at least. He'd been leaving for Plymouth each Sunday afternoon. The only way to swiftly get a message to Ridgeway was through the semaphore towers – so he'd better master the code book.

He retrieved it and read until the noises in the inn had quieted and his eyeballs felt like grit. He closed his eyes and let them water before looking blearily at the notebook once more.

Tomorrow. After some sleep. And to help him get a good night's sleep, he'd better take some extra precautions.

He rummaged in his footlocker for lengths of rope. He tied one end of a length to the handle of the door and the other around the iron legs of the washstand. It would provide enough resistance to deter a casual intruder and make enough noise to alert him to real danger.

He sliced two more lengths and deftly looped and knotted them into two pairs of cuffs, arrangements that looked like butterfly wings and could be used to restrain a man quickly, before stuffing them into his coat pocket that hung within reaching distance. His knife he placed between the mattress and the bed frame – just in case.

Before he extinguished the lamp, Adam jammed open the window a half-inch to let the early summer evening cool remove the stuffiness from the room and stripped down to a linen shirt before climbing into bed.

He rolled onto to his back and felt for the hilt of the knife in one last act of reassurance before he closed his eyes.

The elaborate preparation for his own security tonight was a good enough reason to keep his distance from Olivia. Adam suspected the *Society* would not hesitate in using her if it would bring him to heel. The thought of Dunbar within a thousand feet of her revolted him.

In the half-conscious state between wakefulness and dreaming, Adam was struck by a revelation – another reason why he had been angry at Olivia tonight. It hadn't been just jealousy or the fear of circumstances repeating. It was the fact that *she* thought one night of passion would be enough to sustain her in a loveless marriage or, more to the point, that she was considering such a marriage at all.

She was worth more than that; deserved more than that, and yet he could do nothing about it.

He drifted off to sleep half-aroused by a fantasy of seducing Olivia into realizing her worth.

Chapter Twenty

"OLIVIA, MY DEAR! This is a most unexpected pleasure!"

Olivia allowed Peter Fitzgerald to take her hands and kiss her on each cheek in the continental manner.

"What brings you to town this morning?"

She offered a smile and held up her shopping – a sketchbook and a tin of pencils. And prepared to tell her untruth.

"I thought I'd occupy my time this summer by writing a history of Kenstec House," she said, making the well-practiced lie sound as natural as she could. "The new owner might be interested in it or, if not, Reverend Fuller from the church at Ponsnowyth might accept it as a gift. In fact, I'm going to see him tomorrow to see how far back I can trace mentions of the Denton family in the parish records."

"That sounds like an admirable project." Fitzgerald released her hands and returned to his desk.

"I was hoping to ask a favor of you."

When he raised his eyes to hers once again, she offered him an uncertain smile.

"Anything in my power to grant you, my dear," he said. "If it would make you feel even more kindly disposed toward me."

She forced herself to brighten her smile. Everything she knew about playing the coquette was learned by watching Lydia Denton and her friends. So far, it seemed to be working.

"Your law firm is one of the oldest in Truro, is it not?"

Fitzgerald all but preened himself with pride. "The founding partner had the honor of serving King Charles II during the Civil War."

"Then there would be records of Kenstec here, would there not?"

"I imagine so, but I'd only have a limited number. As you can imagine, record keeping in years gone by was not as diligent as it is today."

She struggled to keep the disappointment from her face. Apparently, she was not successful.

"My dear, cheer yourself," he said. "My clerk had to prepare documentation before the house could be listed for sale – perhaps what you seek is in there."

His words were enough to ignite a flicker of a hope in her breast.

"May I? That is, could I be allowed to see them? I don't wish to pry into the Dentons' affairs but anything about the house..." Olivia watched Fitzgerald's expression carefully to make sure she didn't overstep some boundary of propriety, but she needn't have worried – a bright smile spread across his face, making him look much younger than his fifty years.

Indeed, Peter Fitzgerald might even be called handsome, but there was nothing that stirred within her for him, not as it did when Adam looked at her.

"It is a wish I'm delighted to grant, and will gladly admit it is for a selfish reason. I get to spend more time with you."

Heat filled her cheeks, which gave the man the wrong impression entirely, and her conscience scolded her. She shoved that still small voice down as far as she could.

Fitzgerald picked up a pair of pince-nez and looked at her expectantly.

"However, as much as I'd love to spend the day with you, my dear, I do have business I need to attend to."

He indicated the papers before him.

Olivia shook her head to clear it. "Oh, yes, of course, forgive me."

He gave a short nod, and his expression settled back into that of the aloof solicitor.

"I'll have Foskett search the records and uncover everything we have," he said, brisk and businesslike. "I'll even ask him to make inquiries to examine the old ecclesiastical records if you like. Those records we have here can be ready for you after lunch; the ones archived at St Mary's may take a few weeks."

With the matter apparently settled in his mind, he put on his spectacles and started examining the documents before him.

"You're very kind, *Peter*."

Olivia wondered whether he even heard her. She quietly left his office and nodded to his clerk, a thin and smartly dressed young man, his shirtsleeves rolled up to his elbows in deference to the warm summer morning.

By the time she had emerged from the Lemon Mews arcade, Olivia felt as though she had passed some kind of test. If she played her cards right, she would be able to find out for certain whether Christopher Hardacre had any claim on the Denton estate.

If he lived.

She made her way across the township toward the post office with the letter to the superintendent at The Foundling Hospital. All of her research would be for naught if she couldn't find out what happened to the boy.

Olivia was so caught up in her musings that she didn't see the phaeton until the driver called down to her.

"Excuse me, Miss. Are we on the right road to Kenwyn Hill?

She looked up at the two well-to-do women, mother and daughter, she presumed. The older woman held the reins in black-gloved hands. She cut a trim figure in a very fashionable riding habit of vivid blue with gold braid and frogging across the breast. A pert black hat with a tall crown and narrow brim was perched on a coiffed riot of silvery white-blonde curls.

The girl was about the same age as Lydia Denton, her old charge, and wore a less elaborate but still fetching habit of blue-green. With light brown hair and brown eyes, she did not look like her mother. Perhaps she took after her father.

Olivia bobbed a curtsy. "Not quite, Madam, the name of Kenwyn Street is misleading. You will need to go back and onto King's Street and follow the road past the post office. In fact, I was on my way there to post a letter."

"Isn't that fortunate, Marie?"

"Oui, Maman," she answered with a faintly amused smile.

"Then, you *must* ride with us," the older woman said. "Move closer to me, Marie, so there is plenty of room for Miss…"

Olivia bobbed again and reached for the step to draw herself up into the high seat. "Olivia Collins, ma'am. And I beg forgive me, but who do I have the honor of addressing?"

"I am Lady Abigail Ridgeway, and this is my daughter, Marie."

"I am honored, ma'am."

Olivia barely had the words out before the lady snapped the reins and set the two handsome, matched chestnut horses into a smart canter. The phaeton barely slowed as it rounded the corner onto King Street. Olivia clung on to the rail with one hand and held the other to her straw hat to keep it from flying off.

In half a mile, they had reached the post office. Lady Ridgeway brought the horses to a stop.

"I'm very much obliged to you, Miss Collins," the woman said crisply.

Olivia took that as a dismissal. She lowered herself down onto a mounting block and stepped back down onto the pavement.

"And one more imposition," said Lady Ridgeway, reaching for a leather satchel beneath her seat. "Be a dear and post this letter to London for me."

The woman passed it to Marie, who then passed it down to Olivia who glanced at it. It was addressed to an Aunt Priscilla who apparently lived somewhere in Mayfair. Olivia also felt the weight of two guineas pressed down into her hand.

"My Lady, you've given me too much!"

"Nonsense! You've saved Marie from climbing down and there's enough for your letter there, too."

And with another sharp snap of the reins, Lady Ridgeway's phaeton took off up King Street toward Kenwyn Hill.

Olivia watched them leave and shook her head. Lady Ridgeway was probably one of the "fast set" in her youth, she suspected.

ANOTHER LETTER REACHED Adam in Plymouth. This time delivered to his place of work by post.

Adam found Admiral John Staerk's office empty and closed the door behind him so he could read the letter in private.

> *We have received your message and The Collector is anxious to meet at your earliest convenience. Be sure to have the goods ready for inspection this Sunday. There will be a letter waiting for you at Truro Post Office with further instructions.*
>
> *– W*

Adam swallowed back a curse – then helped himself to a cigar from the rosewood box on Staerk's desk.

He moved to the fireplace to retrieve a tall twist of paper from the vase on the mantel. Making quick work with the fire steel, the spill ignited. He lit the cigar then touched the lit paper to the letter in his hand, making sure it was well alight before tossing it into the fireplace.

Adam drew deep, then exhaled out into the room, using the smoke from the cigar to mask the burning missive.

Bassett was not going to be happy.

Hell, *he* wasn't happy.

That bastard Wilkinson – or whoever was pulling his strings – had brought forward the meeting by another five days.

And Adam wasn't expected to leave Plymouth for Truro for another two days. That meant if he left at first light on Saturday morning, he might just be able to make it back to Truro before the post office closed at eight o'clock in the evening.

If he was lucky.

Otherwise, he'd have to wait until Sunday morning when the office opened at eight in the morning for a couple of hours – and *that* would leave him no time to collect the Artemis warship plans from Bassett and consult with Lord Ridgeway.

The door opened. Staerk walked in and started at seeing him by the fireplace. Adam kept his expression neutral as the spry elderly gentleman looked at him, then at his humidor, and then back to him.

The old admiral's lips thinned with displeasure, but he said nothing. Adam had to admire the man's restraint. Whatever hold or incentive Lord Ridgeway exercised over the man, it must be considerable.

Adam took one last pull from the cigar, threw it in the fire, and strolled to the door as though he owned the place.

Staerk finally showed emotion as they passed, shoulder-to-shoulder, in the doorway.

"The next time you see *Sir* Daniel," Staerk ground out, "you may pass on my compliments to his *wife*."

Adam made sure he was well away from the architect's building before he allowed himself the laughter that had been bubbling in his gut ever since he left the office.

Compliments to Ridgeway's wife, indeed!

He shook his head, reminding himself never to underestimate women. Lady Abigail in particular.

And yet, as handsome – and hypnotic – as she was, in Adam's own mind she was no comparison to Olivia.

He recalled the promise extracted from him and found himself chewing over the same dilemma. Every evening this week, he had gone to bed with a vow to break his bargain, but every morning he woke up with his resolve diminished. The logic was compelling – he wanted her as much she wanted him.

The crude words he had used to shock her had the unintended consequence of rebounding on him. The thought of Fitzgerald bedding Olivia turned his stomach. The only way to avoid that was to give Olivia a reason to refuse the lawyer – and Adam was sure the only one she would accept was marriage.

Marriage…he'd vowed years ago to avoid that state until he had attained his commission and could afford to keep a wife properly. The idea of it had never occurred to him again until the night of the dance.

Perhaps he had been too hasty in dismissing the idea of an involvement. The Ridgeways made it work – marriage and this shadow world of spying. Why couldn't he and Olivia?

Damn it. He loved her. And there – now he'd actually articulated it in his mind.

Adam lengthened his stride once he had crossed the street onto the expanse of parklands overlooking the sea that the locals of Plymouth called the Hoe. Before him, still several hundred yards away, was the Royal Citadel – a fort founded by Sir Francis Drake on behalf of his queen and home to the garrison that protected this shipbuilding town.

He could see the wooden structure that stood much higher than the walls. The semaphore arms stretched out like a headless scarecrow. Adam would use it to send a coded message to Ridgeway – perhaps they could identify the man who was to deliver his next instructions.

In his mind's eye, he could see the signal book. Adam rehearsed the code over and over again in his head.

The soldier at the guardhouse greeted his arrival with suspicion bordering on hostility.

"State your business," he demanded through the grate.

"I am on a mission of great urgency. I have a message for General Campbell from Aunt Runella."

The young man made the mistake of laughing.

Adam returned an implacable stare.

He had perfected the steely-edged voice of command long ago and it was good to finally use it with true authority.

"*Now*, soldier!"

The snap to attention was almost audible. The guard disappeared and returned a few minutes later with a mustachioed sergeant who looked less than impressed.

"The general wants to know who's delivering the message."

Adam drew a deep breath. "Aunt Hilda."

The sergeant's hair-covered mouth twitched. Adam gritted his teeth and waited for the refusal. But the man had the uncommon good sense to keep his laughter behind that tea-strainer mustache. He nodded to the guard. A moment later, Adam was admitted.

Damn Ridgeway and his stupid code names!

Chapter Twenty-One

OLIVIA SET UP her easel in the main dining room, the space now cavernous without the dining table that could seat twenty and its accompanying sideboard. Those pieces were now in London. But what could not be taken away was the magnificent marble fireplace.

On first glance, it seemed plain, made of white marble with fluted Corinthian columns rising to a plinth into which was carved the Denton coat of arms. The header of the mantel featured a rectangular piece of russet red mottled marble, as were the facing legs, which picked up the color of the painted walls.

The overmantel rose high over the chimney breast to accommodate a large mirror which reflected the light from the tall windows at the opposite end of the room.

Olivia drew herself closer and sat on a stool she'd taken from the kitchen. She began her sketch.

Yes. It was good to have something to occupy her time. At least it gave some small measure of purpose to marking the days 'til the end of summer. It gave her something to think about other than the thought of moving away – or of marriage to Fitzgerald. She wasn't sure which one she dreaded most.

But she would not, *under any circumstances*, waste any more time thinking about Adam Hardacre.

She knew he had spent all week in Plymouth. But if he decided to return, he should be back in Ponsnowyth tomorrow. Perhaps, she would see him at the church.

So much for not thinking about him.

She grabbed a pencil and started short, hard strokes for her sketch.

Olivia might not have heard the arrival of a visitor but for having the dining room window open to clear the stuffiness of the room. But as soon as she heard the jangle of a bridle and heard the rhythmic trot of a single horse outside, she went to the window.

The rider's blond hair glowed in the sunlight and her breath caught. *Adam!* She glanced down at her blue day dress. It was neither here nor there in terms of fashion, but it was cool and comfortable. Perfect for the day she had planned sketching architectural items of interest in Kenstec House. Not for receiving a visitor. *This* visitor.

She watched him deftly dismount from his bay horse. Should she call out to him? Olivia found his name caught in her throat, so she waited to see what he did.

He seemed to be looking intently at the exterior of the house, as though committing it to memory. Why was he here? There could be any number of reasons why and not one of them to do with her.

But what if he was here to see her?

The little voice tickled her ear; it sent gooseflesh running down her arms and a flush running up her chest and into her face.

Was there any hope he might have forgotten her request? Surely, he was a gentleman despite not being born to it. And she would forget she had asked for such a thing – after all, no lady of quality would…

She closed her eyes as she felt the heat of her blush grow warmer still. *He* might forget, but she could not.

A breeze up from the river cooled her cheeks and she hoped it would be enough to hide her discomfiture from her visitor. When she opened her eyes, Adam was gone, his horse abandoned and happy to graze on the lawn.

She listened to see if she could hear his booted feet echoing through the sparsely furnished house but she did not.

"Looking out for anything in particular?"

His voice came from nowhere. Olivia jumped, then clapped her hands over her mouth before she could scream.

Adam's face also wore a look of surprise in return.

"I'm sorry, I thought you heard me come in..."

Olivia recognized she was not merely surprised but in shock a split second before Adam closed the distance between them and caught her in his arms. She fought the part of herself that wanted to burst into tears, accepting the embrace and comfort he offered. She held on to him until the blood ceased roaring through her ears and she could hear the familiar sound of birds singing outside and the breeze blowing through the trees.

Adam looked down at her. His hazel eyes were grave, his expression reserved. He was waiting for her to say something. She decided on the truth.

"I've missed you."

He seemed in no hurry to release her from his embrace. Instead, he kissed the top of her head tenderly.

"I've missed you, too," he murmured.

"I was afraid after last week you might treat me with contempt."

Adam pulled back. There was no derision in his eyes, no mocking. In fact, his face was serious as she imagined hers to be.

"For being honest about your circumstances? For what you want?" he asked.

Olivia didn't trust herself to even nod.

"How much better we'd all be if everyone showed so much candor." he said. He slid his hands down her arms and took hold of her hands. "Too many of my days recently have been spent trying to discern the honest man from the charlatan, the good from the deceitful. *Your* truthfulness is the one thing I've come to depend on."

He kissed one hand, then the other, waiting for her full composure to return which she signaled with a smile.

"Come with me...to the kitchen," he clarified. "No big decisions should ever be made hastily. I brought tea."

They walked unhurriedly, hand-in-hand, down the hall into the kitchen, as though they actually were sweethearts. Perhaps she could pretend.

"I didn't expect to see you today," she said. "In fact, I wondered whether I'd ever see you again."

"I left Plymouth the day before yesterday and camped overnight outside of Saint Austell."

"You must be exhausted!"

He shrugged, unconcerned, although she saw now his eyes were dark rimmed from lack of sleep.

"I had business to conduct in Truro, then I came straight here to see you."

Adam set a filled kettle on the stove before urging her to the kitchen table. They sat and he took her hands in his once more.

"What we arranged...do you appreciate what it will mean if we become lovers? There's risk involved...to your reputation if we're discovered for one; your plans to marry Fitzgerald for another. Is that something you're prepared for?"

She opened her mouth to answer, but he touched a finger against her lips. "Don't answer yet. They're not the only risks. I believe we're half in love with each other as it is. We could walk away now and still leave with our hearts intact. But after knowing one another, loving one another, becoming as one all summer – do you really think we could part then without something of ourselves breaking?"

She closed her eyes, fearing her innermost thoughts might show in them, and took in a shuddering breath.

"Think about this carefully, Olivia," he continued softly. "Think if we fell deeper still in love and you wed Fitzgerald. What would it be like to see one another, knowing we could not be together? Or worse, what if the parting between us was bitter and you resented me for taking what should have been something you shared with your husband?"

Adam paused for a moment. "So, one final time, have you given serious thought about this?"

"'Tis better to be left than never to have been loved..." she quoted. She opened her eyes to find Adam looking puzzled. She offered him a shy, reassuring smile. "I have thought of nothing else all week...longer. I am willing, if you are willing."

She watched Adam's face carefully – the slight working of a muscle at the jaw, the movement of his eyes at things perhaps only his mind's eye could see – learning the expressions that told her as much about him as words ever could.

Once again, he raised her hand to his lips, and she allowed him to see her unguarded emotion – the want, the desire laid bare. Surely disrobing could not leave her any more naked.

Adam glanced behind him. Jets of steam rose from the kettle spout. He released her hand and rose from the table.

"We have all afternoon," he said. "Tea first."

Olivia looked down at her empty hands. She hadn't realized they were shaking.

ADAM REMOVED THE boiling kettle from the stove and poured a small amount of hot water into the pot to warm it before emptying it into the slops bucket. He used the time to give Olivia a chance to compose herself.

He needed that time, too, if he was honest.

Adam pulled out a sealed envelope from his satchel that hung over the chair, opened it carefully, and poured the black leaf within into the pot. As he filled it with water, he heard Olivia rise behind him and prepare the cups.

Although he knew *he* was far from inexperienced, he understood clearly there was a marked difference between seducing a woman, winning her into his arms and into his bed, and a half-drunk but willing tumble between himself and a tavern wench or being serviced by a well-practiced professional.

He had to confess to being nervous. He knew only too well there was something delicate and precious before him and that one clumsy misstep would see it shatter. They would both be poorer for it.

Right now, the object of his musings looked at him expectantly, waiting for him to take the lead. The smell of darkly-brewed tea reached him and he breathed it in.

"I saw an easel in the dining room," he said, picking up his cup of black tea. He watched her carefully, her moue of surprise at a conversation that had little to do with the subject they had both been thinking about.

She stirred and stirred her tea until there was a draw of current that reminded him of a whirlpool he once saw at the bottom of a waterfall.

"The Denton family has come to the end of its line and Kenstec is being sold. I thought I'd write a history. The new owner might be interested. I decided to sketch some of the features."

"May I see?"

Her eyebrows rose.

"Really?"

Adam drained his cup, rose and held out his hand.

"Really."

Olivia's cooling tea was abandoned as they strolled back to the dining room. He liked the fact that she took his hand readily.

"I've always found this fireplace beautiful," she said. "I'd only ever been in the room a dozen times when the squire was alive, but now…" She pointed to the mantel header. "Look at the figuring in the marble. You'd think it was burr walnut."

Adam drew closer. He leaned forward to brush his fingers across the cool, smooth marble. His chest pressed against her back.

"From Italy, do you think?" he whispered into her ear. He was aroused at the sound of her sigh.

"Yes. I was told the pieces arrived six months after the squire and Mistress Caroline returned from their honeymoon."

Adam placed a soft kiss on the column of her neck. He loved the slight pink flush to her cheeks. The temptation to seize her in his arms and march up to her bedroom was strong, but he fought it.

"Show me where else you've sketched."

"There's the study. Most of the pieces of furniture in that room are remaining with the house. Mistress Caroline didn't want them."

"Let's compare the room with your sketches."

He took the sketchbook from the easel and carried it under his arm. His other arm went around Olivia's waist. As they walked down the hall toward the study, his fingers traced the curve of her hip, the line of her waist to the edge of her ribs, and back down.

Olivia's left hand spread across his back and, after a moment, began an exploration of its own, rubbing the planes of his back, then lower, mimicking the actions of his own hand. He imagined making love to her in every room in the manor, bed or not, furniture or not, claiming for themselves this place which held so many bittersweet memories.

The battle became a war. His body pleaded for mercy. The still rational part of his mind refused to give in.

A slow and steady seduction, remember?

It would either kill him or cure him.

At some point between an inspection of the study and the examination of the carvings on the main staircase, the balance of power shifted.

No longer was it him alone trying to seduce. Olivia became bolder in her caresses in response to his. She was beginning to know his body – and there was still so much more for her to learn.

They paused on the first floor landing. Her room was only a few yards away. Adam looked up to the top floor.

"Have you returned to the roof? The view would make a spectacular subject."

"Not yet," she said, turning in his arms so she faced him. "I'm afraid to go up there by myself, especially in the afternoon when the wind rises."

Adam abandoned the sketchbook in a wall niche, standing it on the narrow ledge, so he could hold her in both arms. Olivia reached up, circled his neck and pressed herself closer. His mind declared defeat. He claimed her mouth savagely, with all the pent up arousal of the past half-hour.

She responded with equal fervor, giving license to his hands to roam how and where they wished.

ADAM'S SEDUCTION WAS driving her slowly mad. His light touches and gentle caresses inflamed her, but kept her wanting and he was doing it deliberately. She knew she wanted so much more and had joined him in the tease, only touching him to the equal measure of his touch, hoping he would discern what her body craved.

And now, with his mouth plundering hers, Olivia knew she was closer to what she sought. She matched him where she could, carried away by the tide of passion. Her body ruled her mind, searching for satisfaction in the difference between her body and his.

Eventually, Adam broke away from their kiss. His eyes were wild. That mouth of his, that seemed to know her outside and in, was now firmly closed, his expression dangerous. A rush of heat settled between her legs.

The tender teasing was over and he very nearly dragged her down the hall to her room. Adam shoved open the door and swept her into his arms before the door rebounded off the wall.

Before she could catch her breath, Olivia felt the bed at her back and Adam's weight beside her. She knew he watched her closely as she did him, and they found their way without words. She told him all she needed by reaching for him, a subtle pressure to the back of his head brought his lips down to her once again.

He had settled himself alongside her, his hip to hers. A hand cupped her breast through her gown while they kissed, his thumb stroking against her nipples making them sensitive. The sensation was exquisite.

"How far do you want to take this, Olivia?"

She blinked rapidly, not understanding the question at first. A second later, the meaning dawned on her. Her entire body flushed but still the words wouldn't come. Instead, she answered by reaching down to stroke the erection visible within his breeches. Adam let out a shuddering breath.

"You realize you've just sealed your fate?" he asked.

"Possibly," she answered, intoxicated with this newfound influence to bring a man larger and more powerful than herself to his knees.

"Probably..." he growled, "Certainly."

She giggled, a genuine wellspring of delight.

WITH THE LITHENESS of a cat, Adam stood up from the bed, pulling her up with him.

"Then let's do this properly."

He made short work of removing most of his own clothing. Uncomfortable though it was, he kept his trousers on while he unbuttoned the back of Olivia's day dress and untied the bow that helped give shape to the bustline.

He kissed her bare neck and shoulders, then slid his hands down her waist and further still until he gathered the hems of her dress and shift beneath it. As he rose he felt the heat of her body. He drew his knuckles over her soft skin. Olivia's hands covered his. They removed the garments together. His breathing was harsh as he battled for control. And yet, over that, he heard Olivia's shuddering breath.

She looked back at him uncertainly. He smiled to reassure her and she turned to face him. He looked everywhere. She was beautiful; she was everything. But it was the trust he saw in her brown eyes that nearly brought him undone. He rained kisses on her face, savoring the feel of her naked breasts against his skin and the light strokes of her fingers across his back sent waves of gooseflesh across it.

He released the buttons of his trousers until he stood as naked as she did, before escorting her to the bed, peeling back the blankets to expose the sheets beneath. When they were settled comfortably, he drew the top sheet over their hips. Light streamed through the upper floor window, a cooling breeze whispered through the half-opened window.

He could not recall the last time he had been so tentative with a woman – perhaps the last time had been that summer twenty years ago when he was just an adolescent. He started with a soft kiss to Olivia's lips, forcing himself to slow when all he wanted was to settle himself between her legs and find the sweetness there.

"Touch me," he whispered, trying not to make it sound like a command. "Touch me freely."

Tentative fingers stroked his biceps, then slid up his shoulders to pull him down and deepen the kiss.

At that moment, he was lost. Adam knew with a certainty that come hell or high water, he would not be letting Olivia go.

AT HIS INVITATION to touch, Olivia did so, pulling him down further for a deeper kiss until they both broke apart for air. She brushed her fingers against the hair on his chest, which was darker and more wiry than the hair on his head, and savored the feel of it moments before feeling it brush on her breasts, tickling her increasingly sensitive nipples.

She drew her hands down his arms with his body over hers. Hard, yet soft…in fact, that could be said of the man Adam Hardacre himself.

She wanted to explore him as he did her. But the wondrous feelings he aroused in her stole all her focus. She wondered at it – *everything* felt new. The soft sheets that covered half of her from view caressed her skin, arousing her almost as much as the man beside her.

She welcomed his touch everywhere – in her hair, holding her head still for yet another kiss; tracing fingers across her breasts, her belly and lower still until they reached the junction of her legs where fingers parted her folds and a thumb gently caressed that sensitive part of her bringing a craving to the surface.

Any measure of control she thought she had vanished once Adam's lips surrounded one nipple and he licked it. She clung on to him, drowning in sensation, storm-tossed, electricity crackling everywhere around her. Olivia gasped as though coming up to the surface of a raging ocean and falling into the rhythm he set with his thumb. She moved her hips restlessly along with it, aware of her building arousal, wanting more until she reached the peak of it. Sparks of electricity shot through every nerve, powerfully and fully, until she could no longer prevent a cry from leaving her lips.

Adam shifted. Olivia spread her legs to accommodate him between her legs. His tip brushed against newly sensitive flesh and she was breathless once more. Adam's face was above hers, his eyes closed in concentration, his breathing harsh.

He entered her.

She threw her head back as she felt her body accommodate him and cried out once again. He paused, resting on his forearms until they shook with the strain. The look he gave her revealed the cost of holding back.

She caressed his cheek.

"My love," she whispered.

"My a'th kar, hwegoll," he whispered.

Olivia knew enough of the traditional Cornish to translate – *I love you, my sweet.*

He moved within her, his whole body taking up the rhythm his hands had struck earlier. Her own hands roamed his chest, caressed his arms, her own body feeling the rising sensation where they joined.

Then he withdrew, finishing himself off on her belly.

Adam let out a shuddering breath and collapsed beside her, his face flat against the pillow. She could see one eye and the sheen of sweat darkening the hair at his brow.

"What you do to me, my sweet…I almost forgot myself."

I know there are ways to pleasure each other without risk of a pregnancy.

Olivia blushed; she had forgotten all about *that*, and of Constance's misfortune. She started to turn her head away when she felt Adam's fingers on her chin.

"No, none of that," he said, leaning forward to kiss her lips softly. "No shyness now."

She returned his kisses. They were tender, soothing, not intended to arouse, and she settled into his embrace, now able to savor the feel of his body next to hers, the way his fingers trailed up and down her arm. She closed her eyes.

"Thank you," she whispered. "It was everything I had hoped for and more."

"It was what you asked for, but…" he replied. The words chilled her as much as her own cooling body.

"But in the end, it's not what *you* want?" she asked, sensing his thought.

"'One time,' you said. 'Make love to me just one time.'" He rolled onto his back. "I've failed at my end of the bargain."

Adam was making no sense. She raised herself up onto an elbow and pulled the sheet over her waist but kept her eyes on his face.

"How so? Do you regret what we've done?"

"Only if you tell me to leave, your curiosity satisfied. Because I'll tell you now – it's not enough for me. I could make love to you for a thousand and one nights and it wouldn't be enough."

She squeezed her eyes shut a moment. Her heart ached with his declaration; her whole body acknowledged the same desire.

"I feel the same way."

"Then break your contract with Fitzgerald."

"I cannot."

At his long drawn out sigh of frustration, her eyes fell away from his. For a few minutes, she allowed herself the indulgence of looking at his body, tanned from years at sea, muscles made strong by physical labor, before laying back on the bed and reflected on how they found themselves.

Adam was right.

Her own desire for him was nowhere near sated, but what could she do? Hope for some miracle to come between now and the end of summer? Without marriage or work, she was lost, but *never* would she press him into making a marriage proposal that he was not willing to make.

If wishes were horses, then beggars would ride...

Instead, Olivia shook her head.

"Then we will not talk of it. After all, you are in no position to wed, and I am in no position at all," she whispered.

She waited for him to say something in reply. After a moment Olivia turned. Adam's eyes were closed, the rise and fall of his chest regular and steady, his mouth slightly open.

He had fallen asleep.

Chapter Twenty-Two

You are in no position to wed and I am in no position at all...

Adam heard the words in a half-sleep state but he was too far from the surface to answer her.

Now, he had no idea how long he slept, but he was alone, the sheets beside him cold. He might have thought making love to Olivia was a dream but for the faint smell of honeysuckle from the pillow, and the fact he was still naked.

Olivia was right; he was in no position to wed. Worse, he was in no position to even tell her why he couldn't. If there had been any doubt about that in his mind, Ridgeway had provided reasons enough.

"Play this carefully," the older man had instructed. "It's clear they don't trust you, but you've offered enough bait for them to risk it. I've seeded sufficient information back to the Admiralty that rumors of a secret warship will sound credible to any traitor they may have high up in London."

"Be careful they don't slit your throat the minute they get their hands on these," said Bassett, holding up a scrolled document.

Adam had thanked him for his concern.

"Concern? Sorry, Hardacre, but that's some of my best work there, especially forging His Majesty's seal; I don't want it ruined with blood. I might want to frame it when this business is over."

Ridgeway had shaken his head indulgently before continuing to address Adam.

"Demanding to see the mastermind has got you this far, but it's not going to get you all the way. You will have to convince them you're with them one hundred percent – but also with an eye on self-preservation.

"So watch carefully. Observe *everyone*. *The Collector*, as he calls himself, will likely say little. In fact, he may be the most unobtrusive person in the room, so watch the others. They will defer to him in some way at some point – by way of a glance or nod.

"And they'll expect you to be armed, so bring something for them to take from you – a knife will do, but not one you'd be sorry to lose. And if things go bad and you have to fight, use your wits."

Bassett smirked. "Well, he's done for then, isn't he?"

Adam had reached out quickly, his hand gripping the little forger's throat but only lightly in the spirit of the jest. Ridgeway cleared his throat and Adam let go of Bassett with a smile.

"We'll have people watching you," Ridgeway continued, "so don't worry about that. Just focus on your mission. Keep your head clear. No distractions. *None*."

Adam had given Ridgeway his full attention then. The man's piercing blue eyes pinned him to the chair.

"Meaning?"

"You know full well what I mean. Olivia Collins is off limits."

THE LIGHT THAT spilled through the window was orange; soon twilight would be upon them. *Midnight*. He had to be gone just after midnight, *and* he'd need his wits about him. Adam's stomach grumbled. He also needed a good feeding.

He dressed and went down the servant's stairs to the kitchen. Olivia was there, her back to him. Her light brown hair tumbled in soft waves down her back. He wanted to run his fingers through it. His body started to stir.

She turned slightly. Adam saw her examine something in her hand.

The bloom in his chest turned to stone.

Olivia held an envelope. On the kitchen table, his satchel was open. Beside it, a scroll tied in dark blue ribbon, its wax seal broken.

The plans for the fake battleship.

"What are you doing?" he demanded.

Olivia nearly leapt. The hand holding the envelope went to her breast and he saw it was the message that had waited for him at the post office.

"That's the second time today you've snuck up on me!" she scolded, breathless.

The lively surprise on her face then dimmed to match his dark mood.

"I...I'm sorry. I accidentally pushed your satchel over when I put my things on the table. Everything went on the floor. I was just picking it up."

Adam looked at the table again. Yes, he could see where the leg of her folded easel might have easily nudged his bag. On top of the easel was Olivia's own satchel and sketchbook. It was an innocent mistake; he didn't need to be so severe.

"I'm sorry, I didn't mean to be gruff," he said. He scrubbed his face with his hands to stifle a yawn. "I was under strict instructions to bring some important documents with me. It would be my hide if I lost them."

She visibly relaxed, his apology apparently accepted. He reached out his hand. Olivia placed the letter by the plans and accepted his embrace.

"I thought you looked tired when you arrived," she said. "How much sleep have you really had over the past few days?"

"How long was I asleep upstairs?"

"No more than a couple of hours."

"Then I've had five hours since Thursday."

He accepted a look of reproof with a grin.

"Polly always has something special on the menu for Saturday night. Why don't you see to locking up the house and I'll saddle the horse and pack everything here away," he said before bringing his lips down to hers. He was pleased to feel her respond to the kiss. He deepened it until it burned away his fatigue.

ADAM WAITED UNTIL he heard her reach the first floor landing before going over to the table. He picked up the letter and unfolded it again.

Meet at the Four Cross. Three hours after midnight.

– W

Had Olivia read it?

Dear God, he hoped not.

The mile ride back to the tavern didn't leave any time for talking and as soon as they arrived, Olivia excused herself to freshen up before dinner.

Adam lashed his satchel to beneath the bedsprings so if anyone swept under the bed, they would find nothing. The dueling pistols were secure now at his lodgings in Plymouth. When he returned to the dining room, Harold caught his attention with a wave. Adam indicated two beers from Jory who stood behind the bar before joining his friend.

"You look like shit."

"Thanks."

"Did you just ride in?"

Jory dropped two tankards on the table. Adam nodded his thanks before taking a large draught.

"A few hours ago," Adam shrugged.

Harold hesitated over his beer.

"What's on your mind?" Adam prompted.

"Last Saturday and your disappearing trick. Forgive me if it's none of my business but," Harold now whispered, "how deep are you in with the *Society?*"

Adam took another drink and frowned, pretending he didn't understand what his friend was talking about.

Apparently, Harold wasn't buying it.

"You tell me some cock-and-bull story to make me feel better about changing my mind, but you *went* to their meeting. What the hell is going *on*? Is Olivia part of it?"

Adam's frown deepened. "Why would you mention her?"

Harold shrugged, as though that was explanation enough.

The beer soured in his stomach. He shoved the glass aside. "What the *hell* are you saying?"

"Steady on!" Harold raised his hands defensively, then lowered his voice when one or two patrons looked in their direction. "You never used to be like this – secretive, furtive – and you've only been that way since you met her."

Adam closed his fist and squeezed it. The crossed anchor tattoo stood out.

"I'm your friend." Harold continued. "We've been friends ever since I was a wet behind the ears cadet who had barely earned my commission. You've been a mentor to me, a man I've always looked up to. But you've become a stranger, and I'm not the only one who says so. Other men from the *Andromeda* have said as much. If I can help, let me, but whatever you decide, you don't have to do it alone."

Adam retrieved his tankard and gripped the handle. He stared down at the remnants of the amber beneath.

"You *are* a friend," he conceded. "One of the truest I've known. I wish I could tell you what's happened over the past few months, but..."

Adam shook his head to gather his thoughts.

"You trust me, don't you, Harry?"

Harold Bickmore nodded and cautiously picked up his own mug.

"I can tell you nothing more, but your worst suspicions about *The*

Society for Public Reform are not unfounded."

The young man's dark eyes widened, reminding Adam so much of the green youth Harold was ten years ago.

"How bad is it, Adam? I mean, we've all heard rumors of Boney's spies and—"

Adam shook his head sharply. "Ask me no questions, I'll tell you no lies. But I will ask a favor of you."

"Anything. Name it."

"Be a friend to Olivia, even as you are *my* friend. If she ever comes to you in need, remember our friendship."

Harold's frown deepened. "I don't like the sound of this."

"You don't have to like it…just make that promise, will you?"

"So…it's that serious?"

Adam knew the question could be answered in more than one way. Whichever way Harold took it would be mostly right in any event. Best to leave it like that. He suspected he had already stretched the bounds of what he ought to communicate anyway.

He caught a glimpse of light brown hair and the familiar blue dress. Olivia scanned the room looking for him – he hoped. He put up a hand to attract her attention and rose to his feet. Her smile lifted the black weight that had pressed down on him during his conversation with Harold.

Harold rose also and said under his breath, "Then you have my promise, old friend."

DESPITE HIS AVOWAL of love, she still wasn't sure how Adam felt about her. She knew *her* reasons for wanting to become his lover but she was not certain of his. Now with the deed done, would he be dismissive of her? He'd certainly been out of sorts this afternoon. It would be easy to blame his ill-temper on his exhausting ride.

So she took her time entering the tavern's dining room, hesitating at the threshold. Adam was in deep conversation with his friend, Harold. Olivia started looking for other places to sit, where she would not intrude, when Adam caught her eye.

He was the most handsome man she knew. Not even Constance's florid girlish descriptions of him as a youth could do justice to him now as a grown man.

And his expression of warmth and delight on seeing her gave Olivia confidence to join him and his friend. She accepted Harold's hand.

"It's always a pleasure to see you, Miss Collins." He bowed over her hand like the naval officer he was. Olivia dropped a curtsy, then looked to Adam. His intense look ignited the banked embers of desire within her, sparking memories of that afternoon. If they were alone, she would gladly take the promise she saw in his eyes.

Adam took her hand and squeezed it, then let it go before pulling out a chair for her. She almost forgot herself and their need for discretion. Olivia masked her disappointment.

"Harold has just been telling me he's finally closer to deciding how he plans to occupy his time when he becomes a gentleman of leisure," said Adam.

The expression on Harold's face told her the statement was a lie. But to the young gentleman's credit, he recovered himself nicely.

"Well, yes, as it happens. I'm viewing a townhouse in Truro at the moment." Then the young man's face turned sly. "Father tells me I should settle down and do something useful after I leave the Navy. I might thwart his ambitions for me once more by going into politics, instead."

They all laughed. Beneath the table, she felt Adam take her hand, his fingers twining with hers.

"Now, Miss Collins," Harold continued. "I have need of a lady's opinion and I'm hoping you will oblige. It is my sister Elspeth's birthday in September and I am to remember a gift on pain of death. I know nothing of these things. May I call on you in the next week to draw on your expert eye?"

"I'd be delighted, Lieutenant. How old is your sister?"

The young man looked panicked.

"You don't know!" Adam roared with laughter. "You don't even know your own sister's age!"

Bickmore had the grace to look sheepish. "Then you understand, Miss Collins, why I need to make amends this year."

Olivia grinned and decided to put the poor man out of his misery. "I'd only be too delighted to oblige, sir."

THE EARLY PART of the evening passed just as pleasantly, as the three of them shared amusing stories, even Adam, who always seemed so serious. Later, the local blacksmith approached and persuaded Adam and Harold into playing skittles. Olivia was invited to join in a game of cribbage by the curate's wife.

By the time Jory called for last drinks, Harold had departed for Truro. Olivia was ready to retire. She stopped by the tables and had a word with those who remained before finally bidding goodnight to Adam and the group of men who continued with their game.

She ascended the stairs in the company of Polly who was taking up some fresh linens. A new guest, no doubt.

"I'm glad ye be gettin' on so well with Adam," she said. "He's a good man."

Olivia knew full well what Polly was hinting at. But this relationship, such as it was, was too new to be even spoken of, and to call the words that would conjure it into being could very well destroy it.

A noncommittal answer was all she gave the innkeeper. "He would appear so," she said.

"Does that mean ye're goin' to be stayin' in Ponsnowyth?" Polly asked, making a valiant attempt to not sound too curious.

"It's too early to say. I'll certainly stay for the summer. The earliest

I would be expected to start a new position would be in September."

Olivia paused at the door to her room and wrestled momentarily with her key. Polly continued two doors down and, before Olivia entered her room, she saw Polly look back and give her an assessing look.

She closed the door behind her, removed her shawl, and worked the buttons free from the back of her dress. She examined her face in the small oval mirror on the wardrobe door. The glass was pitted and foxed with age.

Did she look like a woman in love? In truth, she had spent just as much time in Peter Fitzgerald's company as she had in Adam Hardacre's and not once had Polly ventured an opinion of a match in *that* direction.

Polly was fond of Adam, to be sure, and had known him for many years. So perhaps it was the wishful thinking of a matchmaking romantic.

In the mirror's reflection, Olivia saw her door open. By the time she turned, the door was closed again. Adam stood before her, a finger to his lips to indicate silence.

He crossed the room in a few short steps and she was pulled into his arms.

"Polly will flay the both of us if she catches you in here," Olivia whispered. "She runs a respectable establishment."

Adam dropped kisses on her neck, his hands warm on the exposed part of her back.

"Then we'll just have to be quiet," he whispered in her ear, sending tendrils of delicious pleasure down her neck.

"You can't mean to…here, I mean…so soon after we…"

He slowed his kisses then stopped, resting his forehead against hers.

"I have to leave again for a while," he said.

"So soon?" Olivia hated herself for asking the question. It made her sound like a needy ingénue. She should be glad of it – after all, she got what she asked for. Already, her resolve was at a tipping point. If Adam stayed, it would make it harder for her to agree to marriage with Peter Fitzgerald.

She swallowed a sudden panic and forced herself to calm down.

"When?"

"A few hours from now."

"Why? What takes you away at such an hour?"

The deep shadows in the room suddenly made Adam seem dangerous, a stranger.

"No questions, Olivia, please."

"Will you return?"

"All going well, yes."

"Does it have anything to do the scroll you had with you today? What is it? Plans?"

Chapter Twenty-Three

DOES IT HAVE *anything to do the scroll you brought with you today? What is it? Plans?*

Even as the words were being spoken, Adam willed her to stop. He even gripped his jaw so tight his teeth twinged, and it was all he could do to get the words out.

"Never, *ever* ask, do you hear me?" he ground out.

Olivia's hands went to her mouth. She tried to pull out of his arms, but he couldn't let go. He *wouldn't* let go.

"I…I'm sorry, I didn't mean to pry. I…"

He crushed her to him once more to help stifle her sobbing he felt through her chest. "Oh, Olivia. One day, your curiosity may kill us both," he said hoarsely. "It's not safe to ask questions. Promise me you will never, ever speak to anyone about me or what I do."

Adam held her while he battled a maelstrom of emotions that stirred through him also – anger, fear and regret were chief among them.

He wanted the woman in his arms with a desire that nearly made him abandon his duty to King and Country – to hell with Ridgeway and that weasel Major Wilkinson. To hell with the whole bloody lot of them!

By the time Olivia had composed herself, he, too, had calmed enough to hold her by the shoulders far enough away to see her large brown eyes in a deathly pale face. Adam allowed her to see the anguish in his.

He wished he knew what words to say that would reassure her.

"One day, I *will* tell you the truth. And one day, you may actually forgive me for hiding it from you. I want you more than I've wanted any woman in my life, but my life is not my own and I can't explain to you why.

"Worse than that, I can't even ask you to wait for me."

Olivia lowered her chin and let out a shuddering breath. Adam wondered whether he'd forced her to tears once again. But when she lifted her head, her eyes were clear and the set of her jaw resolute.

"Then hold me for a while, Adam Hardacre," she said. "If we are to part, then let us part with pleasure as our final memory and not sorrow."

MIDNIGHT WAS SUPPOSED to be the witching hour, but it was the early hours of the morning which were the most dangerous. Men on watch grew drowsy. Accidents happened toward the end of the middle watch. On ship, it was least favored shift of all.

It was not much better on land either. The waning moon offered barely enough light to see more than three feet in front. Adam decided to let the horse pick its own path. He reckoned on taking an hour to traverse the three miles from Ponsnowyth up to the Four Cross, so named for the meeting of the crossroads leading to Falmouth, Truro, Redruth and Helston.

Tempted though he was to look back at the inn, he did not. There lay temptations of many different sorts.

One was the woman who invited him into her bed; second was the temptation of giving her his whole heart also. Then there was the third temptation – that of the life he could have as a former sailor with no commitments other than finding a wife and keeping a roof over their heads. And more and more, that temptation was taking the form of a pretty brown-haired governess whose doe eyes made him want to promise to give her everything.

Despite her offer of intimacy, Olivia had been more than content to lie with him on her bed in quiet communion until sleep claimed her. At least, he assumed she slept. Perhaps, she feigned sleep to avoid an awkward parting.

Adam forced himself to focus on the job ahead. He had debated the wisdom of leaving his dueling pistols in Plymouth. Instead, he carried knives. One strapped to his waist, another at his right ankle, and a third sheathed on his horse. Hung around the saddle horn was one of his looped rope wrist restraints. The other was in his pocket.

It wasn't much but it would have to do.

He approached the road from the east, his way guided by a large stone obelisk on the ridge where the roads met. It was an ancient monument, said to date to the time of the earliest Christian saints of Cornwall. It stood nine feet tall and was made of grey granite but mottled black in places by centuries of weather.

The north and south faces had been carved with sinuous plaits, from the plinth up toward the top, where the carving spread out around a hole in the stone, making it resemble some kind of ancient needle as much as a cross.

Wilkinson had chosen the rendezvous location well. The wind-swept ridge provided no obvious ambush points and clear views for miles around.

Nowhere for any of Ridgeway's men to cover him, either…

A black carriage waited beneath the cross. Adam reined in his horse to a stop a good ten yards away.

A figure emerged from the back of the carriage and approached until he was only five yards away. Adam wheeled his horse about to half-face the direction he'd come from. At the first sign of a threat, he would urge the horse back down toward the valley.

"Hardacre!"

Adam recognized Dunbar's voice. He didn't acknowledge the hail.

After all, who else would it be at three o'clock in the bloody morning?

"Wilkinson wants to see ye." The man nodded his head toward the carriage.

"Tell him to come out here."

The man grunted and started to turn back when the carriage door opened. Major Wilkinson emerged from the coach.

"Do come along, Hardacre. We have business to transact. It's too bloody cold and late to be arguing about it in the middle of the road."

Adam ignored Dunbar and, instead, spoke over his head to Wilkinson.

"Nothing doing. The minute I get off my horse, your thug here kills me and steals the plans. I want my safety guaranteed."

"You have my word as an officer and a gentleman."

Adam waited a moment, then reluctantly dismounted.

"Tie your horse to the back; we're going on a journey."

Adam's heart beat a little faster. It was risky. He would have no idea where he was going. Worse still, no one else would know either.

"Come now, The Collector is waiting."

Adam unbuckled the satchel from his saddle and swung it over his shoulder. He led the horse to the back of the carriage and secured its reins to a rail.

"I'll be takin' that from ye." Dunbar lunged toward the satchel. Adam blocked him with a forearm fend.

"The hell you are, you bracket-faced lobcock. This stays with me."

Wilkinson stepped between them before extending his arm to invite Adam into the carriage. Wilkinson entered behind him and closed the door. They were the only two inside the small brougham. The windows were covered with black velvet curtains. A small carriage lamp was the only source of illumination.

"You showed such a reluctance to being blindfolded last time we met, I thought this would be more suitable," said Wilkinson.

"Where are we going?"

"You'll see when we get there."

The major offered him a faintly amused smile before stretching out his legs. "You might as well make yourself comfortable. We'll be traveling for a while."

OLIVIA HAD WOKEN from her half-doze as Adam gently removed himself from her bed. She'd kept her eyes closed while she listened to the sound of him slipping on his coat. She felt a gentle caress on her cheek before his lips touched where his fingers had been.

Even now, five days later, the tenderness of the act was enough to bring tears to her eyes.

And yet better their parting should be like this; more eloquent than an awkward goodbye.

She drew a deep breath and pulled her distracted attention away from the window that overlooked Lemon Street.

She sat in a small room at Peter Fitzgerald's office. Before her were journals and bound ledgers, along with various plans. Fitzgerald had been as good as his word. Everything his office held on Kenstec House had been brought to her by his clerk Foskett, who told her with some enthusiasm that he had been instructed to be at her disposal.

She pulled up the short, lilac-colored floral sleeves of her day dress so they sat above her elbows and opened the first ledger. It dated from 1787 and contained a trove of information about the household expenses approved by Squire Denton. He'd been newly married to Mistress Caroline then.

Whatever his sins, it seemed Denton was prepared to spend lavish amounts of money on the comfort of his new bride – the cost was in the hundreds of pounds, and that was without factoring in the cost of building the tower.

To renovate the interior to suit the new mistress' modern taste, traditional oak paneling which had been there since the time of Elizabeth the First had been taken out of the drawing rooms. The walls were to be refinished with paint or wallpaper. Tudor windows with their myriad diamond-shapes of glass held in place by lead *cames* were replaced by large-paned sash and case frames each containing a spring balance that made it easy for the slightest built parlor maid to open and close the windows.

The ledger made a reference to house plans. Olivia scanned across the desk at the stacks of paper and bundles of scrolled documents wondering how she could reunite the two.

AFTER A FULL day scouring through dusty old tomes, she was exhausted. She gave in to the swaying motion of the Truro-to-Ponsnowyth coach and closed her tired eyes a moment.

When she reopened them, the stone entrance pillars of Kenstec House caught her attention ahead. Through the window of the coach, she watched them come closer into the view. She had not returned since *that* day there with Adam.

At this moment, she felt she was seeing the house now as a stranger to it.

Trees and hedges no long tended by gardeners were beginning to grow wild; vines rose, clinging to the stone pillars like a covetous lover. It wouldn't be too long before the entrance was overgrown. Whoever bought Kenstec would also need to be prepared to pay even more to restore it back to its splendor.

If she was truly serious about recording the manor's history, she would sketch some more aspects. But Olivia knew if she went back, it would remind her of Adam. She tried to convince herself this week was no different to other weeks when he was away in Plymouth; he would return soon.

Except it was different, and she knew it.

I was under strict instructions to bring some documents with me. It would be my hide if I lost them.

He'd made light of the scroll she had picked up off the floor, but the more she recalled his words the more ominous they became.

Under strict instructions? From whom? What *were* those documents? What had Adam gotten himself mixed up in?

Would Harold know?

She grimaced. Adam had told her to tell no one of his business and yet she had done so in the search for information about his son. And now, she entertained the thought of speaking to this friend about...*what,* exactly?

That she feared Adam had become involved in bad company? Ridiculous, to be sure. But something was wrong. She could feel it in her bones.

The coach to Ponsnowyth pulled up at the inn. It would be a few hours yet before meals were served. She would put away her notebooks before taking a stroll down to the river before supper.

She greeted Jory who was coming down the stairs. On reaching the landing, Olivia looked down the passageway. The door to Adam's room was wide open.

Her spirits brightened.

He's back!

She heard the sounds of him moving about and headed for the door.

The man who stood in the middle of the room with his back to her was not Adam.

"Who are you?" she said sharply. "What are you doing in here?"

The stocky man turned swiftly, a snarl on his face softening a little as he eyed her up and down. Clearly, he regarded her as no threat to him.

"This is Adam Hardacre's room."

"Not any more. He's movin' out."

"Moving out where? Who are you?"

"An old friend what's come to help him pack."

"Then why isn't Adam here?"

"He's on business. Hardacre asked me to fetch his things and ship them along."

"I don't believe you."

The man did not bother to introduce himself, nor did he take kindly to being questioned.

"Why didn't Lieutenant Bickmore come?"

The man grunted and ignored her, instead rummaging through the wardrobe and dropping clothes into a small trunk. She looked on in increasing fury.

"I demand that you stop now and explain yourself. Right now! I'm calling for the innkeeper."

She shouted Jory's name. Heavily booted feet took the stairs two at a time. Jory came at a clip down the corridor toward her.

"I caught this thief in Adam's room!"

The man inside the room slammed the lid of the trunk violently, his face dark.

"Tell yer *guest* here not to make unwarranted accusations."

Jory laid a hand on her shoulder.

"He's all right, Miss Olivia. He came with a letter from Adam this mornin'."

Olivia was aware of her shocked expression and she forced herself to calm down.

"This here is Dunbar," Jory continued. "He's a servant of Adam's new employer. He's all right. I've seen him around here a few times. Hails from Falmouth, don't ye."

"There or thereabouts." Dunbar grunted his agreement.

"I...*suppose*...I mean if you're vouching for him, Jory."

The innkeeper gave her a sympathetic smile. "Come on down to the parlor and have a cup of tea with me and Polly. Ye can read the letter for yerself."

Dunbar barely concealed his look of triumph. He reached for Constance's cube writing box.

No! He can't take that!

At that moment, Olivia couldn't say which "he" she meant – Dunbar or Adam.

Olivia surged forward. "Stop! That belongs to me."

"Then what's it doin' in Hardacre's room?" Dunbar's disbelief dripped like acid. "Show us yer letters in it." He arrogantly went to open it. It was locked.

She thought swiftly and lied. "I lost the key. Mr. Hardacre offered to try to open it for me."

Dunbar glanced sideways to Jory who now stood at her shoulder.

"It does belong to Miss Collins. It be a gift from her late employer. My wife was there when it was given to her."

Olivia took possession of the box, cradling it to her chest.

"Well then," said Dunbar. "Since that appears to be all, I'll be takin' my leave."

He bent down and snapped the catches on the trunk before hauling it up onto his shoulder.

"I'll pass on yer regards, shall I?" he sneered before shouldering past between her and Jory.

Olivia swallowed, her chest felt tight. Her breath came in shallow pants.

"Oh Jory, I can't believe Adam would just leave like that," she said hoarsely. "He wouldn't. Not without saying farewell in person."

"He's done it before," said the innkeeper. He went to the door and looked down the hall, where he gave a sour look to Dunbar's retreating back and then looked back to her. "When he were a lad, he disappeared for a few days. Then a letter arrived sayin' he'd joined the Navy. Broke his father's heart, it did."

"But that was different. Adam was pressed against his will by Squire Denton. You know that. And he was a boy then."

"And now he's a man of the sea." Jory replied. "Twenty years of his life and he didn't come home but twice in all that time."

Jory shook his head as though that were the end of the matter and left the room.

Olivia listened to his familiar footsteps return downstairs. She closed her eyes and rested a cheek on the cool wood. If Adam wanted his writing box, he'd have to come and get it himself.

Chapter Twenty-Four

AS FAR AS cells went, it was rather comfortable.

Adam even had a bed, a chair, and a wooden table with a washbowl and ewer at his disposal. A chamber pot sat on a shelf under the table.

It appeared to be a servant's room built into the building's rafters. The sharply-angled ceiling forced him to remain largely in the center of the room under the ridge beam when standing, lest he bang his head.

A number of small dormer windows, no more than two feet square, spilled light across the floor. If Adam lay on the floor beside them, he had a good view to the southeast where, in the mornings, he could see the shimmering glint of water – whether it was the sea or the mouths of one of the rivers, he couldn't tell.

Four of the windows had opening panels, a small-hinged window that occupied half of the aperture – enough to let air in, but not enough to squeeze through and escape. The only means of entry and exit from the room was through the tall narrow door at the end wall. It was locked.

Of course, it was.

He hoped the routine was the same today as it had been for the past three days. Sometime after the long case clock chimed the seventh hour, one of Wilkinson's men would unlock the door and escort him down for breakfast.

Surprisingly, they'd even let him keep a knife. However, he was accompanied everywhere he went in the house. Whenever he ventured out into the grounds, he was accompanied by three, all wearing pistols. He was not *exactly* a prisoner, but not a trusted guest either.

If he put his ear to the floor, he could hear the sounds of activity below. Again, if his "hosts" were predictable in their habits, the time would be about six o'clock. Someone would reactivate the chimes on the clock and the first sounds he would hear would be the strike of the quarter-hour.

Adam decided to occupy himself this morning with push-ups, which he would do until he heard the key inserted into the lock.

The satchel with the plans and other papers had been confiscated immediately and yet he hadn't been interrogated right away. For two days, he had lived on the edge of fear that they'd seen through Bassett's forgery and the next man who approached him would be his executioner. For those first two days, he'd spoken to no one. Not even Wilkinson.

Then the interrogations began. The Artemis warship plans were spread across Wilkinson's desk and pored over from stem to stern, inch by inch, line by line. Questions were asked of everything. Adam answered what he might reasonably know, replied "Dunno" to others.

The morning sun filled the room with heat and light but there was little breeze to compensate. Adam increased the pace of his push-ups, puffing out air like a pump, raising sweat across his bare back and head, dripping from the week-long beard on his face.

Yesterday he decided to push back. He'd been wearing the same clothes for five days and refused to cooperate further until someone was sent for his things.

Sure enough, at seven o'clock, the door to his room was unlocked. Adam got to his feet and waited. Dunbar opened the door and shoved a small trunk along the floor with his foot.

Wilkinson entered the room behind Dunbar.

"There ye are, Hardacre, yer own clothes, as promised."

Still keeping his eye on the two men, Adam squatted down and unlatched the trunk. There were his clothes, wrinkled where Dunbar, no doubt, had just tossed them in. He felt around and came across his leather shaving pouch, a small tortoiseshell box containing soap, and his comb.

"Nothin' missin', then?"

Yes. The writing box. He ignored Dunbar's sarcasm and rose to his feet.

"No," he answered, "that's everything."

Another man bustled past with a bucket, curls of steam rising from the hot water. He filled the ewer and left.

"Make yourself presentable," said Wilkinson. "We'll be back at the half-hour. After breakfast, I want to talk to you further about the gunning placements."

Adam kept himself at attention until the door was closed and locked before letting out a long sigh.

While the water cooled, he folded his clothes neatly, then retrieved his soap and shaving kit to begin making himself presentable.

For Dunbar to go to Ponsnowyth and back in a day meant they was no more than thirty miles away from Four Cross. That meant he was still relatively close to Truro and Falmouth – close enough, if possible, to get word to Ridgeway as soon as he had anything worth reporting.

Then there was the missing writing box. He paused a moment and put the straight razor down.

Had they held it back? He'd know soon enough if they had. Or…

Apart from himself, the only person in the world who cared about that damned box was Olivia. Was she there when Dunbar collected his clothes? Had she somehow claimed the box?

If that was the case, he hoped to God that Wilkinson and his crew didn't suddenly get it into their heads that there was something of interest in it and return for it.

Damn.

Should he have confided in Olivia more? No, he dared not; revealing as much as he had to Harold was dangerous enough. All he could hope for was that if Olivia had the box and uncovered the code book, she would be sensible enough to deliver it into Harold's hands.

Adam picked up the razor and continued shaving.

Olivia. He recalled the feel of her lips on his, the full, soft weight of her breasts in his hands.

Stop.

Adam gritted his teeth. It was *over*. There was no choice, it *had* to be over. His enterprise was too dangerous. One misstep even now and he could find himself with his throat slit or a pistol ball in his brain. And, in a couple of months, Olivia would formally accept Peter Fitzgerald's proposal of marriage.

Hell and damnation!

Adam hissed against the sting of a cut and threw the razor into the bowl in anger. He picked up a towel, touched it to his neck, and glanced at it. It spotted red. He pressed the towel against the nick for a minute until he was certain the bleeding had stopped.

No.

There was no way he would let Olivia marry that grey old fool, not if he had anything to do with it.

By the time Dunbar returned to take him downstairs, Adam had made his resolution.

If he survived this dangerous game, he would go to Ridgeway and demand he accept him with a wife, or not at all.

"ARE YOU UNWELL, my dear?"

Olivia started and looked up into the concerned eyes of Peter Fitzgerald.

"You've overtired yourself," he continued. "This project of yours to write the history of Kenstec Manor – perhaps it's too ambitious for you."

Finally, the words she wanted to say made their way to the fore.

"Please don't fuss. I am *quite* well, thank you. And I am *quite capable* of quietly reading and making notes."

Fitzgerald looked taken aback at the disproportionately severe response.

Olivia shook her head. "I'm sorry, I've not slept well over the past couple of days," she conceded. "And you're correct, I've spent far too long behind the desk. I'm going to go for a walk."

"Then I'll accompany you."

Olivia really wished he wouldn't but, after her outburst, she couldn't bring herself to refuse him.

Foskett knocked on the door.

"Excuse me, sir. Mr. Fraser is here and he insists he needs to see you on a matter of some urgency."

Fitzgerald looked torn. Olivia took the opportunity to reassure him. "You are such a dear to be considered about my health...*Peter*. I promise that some time in the fresh air will have me revived in no time."

"Well, as long as you're sure."

She even managed to give him a smile to prove it. Fitzgerald returned an uncertain grimace before leaving to see his client.

Olivia closed the journal from 1730 which marked another period of major renovation at Kenstec Manor. In truth, she had lost the taste for her project.

Foskett had been only too happy to answer her legal questions and she was given the answer she had been expecting but dreaded – an illegitimate child cannot inherit, no matter the circumstances. A babe born on the wrong side of the blanket might inherit from his mother, if she had provided for it, but, otherwise, such a child could make no claim.

She picked up her reticule and stepped out into the sunshine, starting on the half-mile walk up to the post office. It had been a mistake to involve herself with anything to do with the Hardacres. If she had left well enough alone, she wouldn't have opened up such a Pandora's Box of misery for herself.

Still, there was something about the whole affair that unsettled her beyond her own bruised feelings. No one had heard from Adam since his brusque four line letter offered by the thuggish manservant who collected his belongings – not even Adam's friend, Lieutenant Bickmore.

Olivia had asked him about it when he called upon her to accompany him to shop for his sister or, as it turned out, *sisters*. Like Jory, he shrugged off the behavior, telling her it was not out of the ordinary for Adam. Still, she suspected the lieutenant only told her that as reassurance, because there was something in his face that suggested he didn't believe it either.

One day, I will tell you the truth. And then one day, you may actually forgive me.

The writing box...in her most fanciful imaginings, she wondered whether Adam had hidden something in it before he locked it – a secret letter, a clue.

Such a pity she didn't have a key. The thought of damaging the piece to get at its contents was unconscionable. What would one have to do to pick a lock?

At the post office, two letters waited for her, both with London postmarks, but before she could examine them further, Olivia heard her name called.

"Miss Collins, it's fortunate we meet again. I was so hoping we would."

Olivia dropped a curtsy to Lady Ridgeway, but frowned, puzzled.

"You wished to speak to me, my Lady?"

"Yes, let's take a walk to the park."

The woman opened a blue and white floral parasol that matched her dress. White fringing shimmied attractively as they walked. Olivia adjusted her hat to help protect her face from the midday sun. Together they walked down King's Street and onto High Cross. Despite being a decade or more younger, Olivia found herself working hard to keep pace with the other woman's brisk clip.

Lady Abigail Ridgeway had the bearing of aristocracy, her head held high as though anything in the world was hers for the taking. She must have had men falling at her feet in her youth. Perhaps they still did, since everyone they passed either nodded or curtsied.

It was no small measure of irony that Olivia found herself at the same bench, under the same tree, where Peter Fitzgerald had proposed marriage. Lady Ridgeway pulled out a lace-trimmed handkerchief from her reticule and swept the seat before sitting down. She offered a regal incline of her head, which Olivia guessed was her invitation to sit also.

"I understand you were a governess recently in the employ of Beaufort Denton."

"That is correct, my Lady."

"And you are now unemployed?"

Olivia inwardly winced. The woman was not awkward about coming forward.

"Yes."

"Do you intend to *stay* in Cornwall?"

"I don't know. It would depend on finding a situation, and I have not yet had replies to any inquiries. Perhaps, there may be an offer in one of the letters I received today."

"Would you stay if the opportunity presented itself?"

Olivia looked directly into the woman's grey-green eyes for the first time. Was this a prelude of an offer of employment?

"Yes, I *love* Cornwall."

The look she received in return was assessing. "Just the attractive scenery, is it?"

What on earth was she to say to *that*? That she had fallen in love? And with a man whose whereabouts was currently unknown and whose actions bordered on the capricious and who knew what else?

Lady Ridgeway watched her. A smile played around lightly rouged lips. "Come now, it's more than pretty views of the sea that make one stay in Cornwall, although I have to say I find the country air and rustic charm of frank speaking most refreshing after the society of London and Bath."

Olivia was taken aback by such open mockery and found herself unable to fashion a reply that didn't call out the woman for her rudeness or make her want to respond in kind. She swallowed the words she wanted to say… the ones she only said in her mind when Mistress Caroline's friends would treat her like a servant and not a respectable governess.

"I'm not sure what to tell you, my Lady."

"Well, you're showing a little spirit, that's a start. I was beginning to wonder whether you were one of these insipid creatures I so detest."

Olivia rose to her feet. "I am most assuredly not, *and* since you prefer plain speaking, my Lady, then you will not be offended if I say that you are rude and condescending – an utter misplacement of the appellation of *lady* if there ever was one!"

The aristocrat before her merely inclined her head, as though she had simply conceded a point in tennis. The movement was matched by an upturn to her lips and a light shrug.

"I have been called worse."

She also rose to her feet.

"Do you speak French?"

Olivia answered firmly and without hesitation. "I do."

"Do you wish to marry the solicitor, Peter Fitzgerald?"

"I do *not*."

The answer was out of her mouth before Olivia thought to question why Lady Ridgeway would ask such a personal question, let alone how she would even *know* of the arrangement.

"Excellent. I think my interest in you is not misplaced," Lady Ridgeway averred.

"With respect, are you looking for a governess?"

"Good Lord, no. You've seen my daughter, Marie – far too old to need a governess. I was considering a chaperone for certain engagements."

"For yourself, or for your daughter?"

"Neither." The woman twitched a sly smile.

This was the most confusing conversation Olivia had ever had in her life.

From her reticule, Lady Ridgeway withdrew a card. She handed it to her.

"In two weeks from now, attend an interview here."

Olivia looked down at the card, black ink standing bold on the heavy white paper.

Charteris House
Truro, Cornwall.

She looked up to find Lady Ridgeway walking away, the woman not even giving her a backward glance.

Chapter Twenty-Five

TODAY MARKED A red letter day.

The plans that had been laid out across the long dining table for the past week had now been rolled up. Today, Adam was being spared the endless questions about the Artemis.

He'd been dancing on the edge of a blade as he answered the questions he rehearsed with Ridgeway in a dozen different ways. Adam made up answers to some questions they had not anticipated because he felt he'd be expected to know.

It was those answers that worried him. How many lies can a man keep straight in his head? The fewer the better was the only honest answer.

Adam looked at each man in turn. There was no one new here. All who sat around this table had also been at their first meeting in the house on Packet Quays. Of the half-dozen men, he only knew two by name – Wilkinson, who sat at the head of the table, and that violent little thug, Dunbar, who had left after bringing him downstairs.

Adam had given the rest nicknames based on a physical feature. If nothing else, it would give Ridgeway some way of identifying them.

There was Scar, a man in his forties about Adam's build with brown hair and a large scar across his cheek. It ran up into his temple.

Red was a gingery man, tall and lean with a sharp nose and a chin to match. He never said a word.

Black Angus was the very model of every angry Scotsman Adam

had ever come across – black hair, permanent scowl, and nose bent from having been broken too often in fighting.

The fourth man, he'd dubbed Pockmark. He was a stocky man with a pockmarked face. He was always the one to draw the short straw and end up in the kitchen fetching food for the others. Adam considered him a bit of a *tuss*, all things considered.

"You did well, Hardacre," Wilkinson conceded. "However, according to our contact, who is very highly connected in Westminster, there has been no discussion of appropriating funds to build such a ship."

"I don't care if they've got the money for it or not," said Adam. "I got these plans at considerable risk. Either I'm trusted and I'm in, or I'm not. And if I'm not trusted, I'll be on my way right now with my thousand pounds in gold. That was the bargain."

Wilkinson glanced around at his colleagues, looking for consensus. Adam, too, looked at each face to see if he could divine their thoughts.

"It seems we have a few things to discuss, Hardacre. If it would ease your mind, you now have the liberty of the house."

"That's something, I suppose."

Adam turned on his heel and left the dining room. He closed the door behind himself and stood waiting for the discussion to begin, but it did not. Instead, he heard the sound of a chair leg scraping on the floor and footfalls approaching the door.

He managed to round the corner into a small anteroom before the door opened and then, a moment later, close again.

Well, since he had the *liberty of the house*, he should use it. Adam turned the knob of a door before him. It turned out to be the smaller of two internal entrances into the library. He entered and made a beeline to the main double doors. They, too, were unlocked. He kept them in mind for a quick exit if he needed it.

The library appeared to be used as a storeroom. A dozen trunks in various sizes were piled neatly into four pyramids of three each. Tempting though it was to examine them, Adam decided his wisest course was to look elsewhere.

A desk in the center of the room was covered in papers. He scanned the documents quickly. They were in French – and he didn't read it. He tugged loose one of the densely scribed sheets from under the pile without examining it too closely. Whoever was working here might remember the papers on top, but may not miss one buried beneath. He folded it and slipped it into the top of his boot.

It would serve Ridgeway right if it was nothing more than a shopping list for produce.

Adam left the library and made his way across the passage to the drawing room where he opened a pair of French doors that led out into the garden.

Let's see if the "liberty of the house," also extended to the garden and the stables.

The carriage house was his first stop. The unmarked brougham was not the only vehicle being stored. A much larger landau was beside it, dusty from months of disuse. The doors featured a cartouche and monogram with the letters D and V in a foliate script.

He returned to the stable by the tack room. This time, he rummaged through satchels and found in one part of a crumpled newspaper that had been used as wrapping paper. The only thing of note was on the inside flap of another satchel – a hand inked mark that looked like clubs from a playing card.

Knowing his time was limited, Adam pulled down one of the brushes and approached the stalls. He found his horse in good condition, treated as well as the other five. The horse whickered and nodded at his approach.

He patted the horse on his neck and got to work, singing as he groomed the horse.

All in a garden green, two lovers sat at ease,
As they could scarce be seen above the leafy trees.
They lovèd lofty full, and no wronger than truly,

In the time of the year cam betwixt May and July.

Quoth he, "Most lovely maid, my troth shall ay endure,
And be not thou afraid, but rest thee still secure
That I will love thee, long as life in me shall last—

"Where the hell ye been, Hardacre?" said Pockmark.

Adam, brush in hand, looked at him. "I came here to check on my horse. I haven't broken any *rules*, have I?"

To the best of Adam's judgment, Pockmark was the mildest mannered of all Wilkinson's henchman. The man looked uncomfortable. Adam could use that to his advantage.

"Look, I'm not going to cause you any trouble," he said, keeping his hands where they could be seen and hanging the brush back on its nail. "I didn't think there'd by any harm in it."

"Maybe ye shouldn't have, but come back to the house and I won't mention it," said Pockmark almost apologetically.

Adam nodded and followed Pockmark onto the lawn between the stables and the house, but his attention was caught by a man riding at full gallop toward the house. He exchanged a glance with Pockmark who looked alarmed.

"It's Dunbar," the man muttered.

"Come on," said Adam and led a jog back to the house.

They slipped in at a side door and entered the hallway in time to see Dunbar barrel through the front doors.

"Get Wilkinson," he bellowed. "There's been a change of plans."

EVERYONE GATHERED IN the dining room. Dunbar glared in his direction. Adam glared back and joined the men at the table, a lot more cheered than he had been in days.

"What about him?" said Dunbar to Wilkinson, jerking his thumb in Adam's direction.

"You can speak in front of Hardacre." Wilkinson replied.

Dunbar grunted. "Well, I got word from another chapter of the *Society*. There's goin' to be a large movement of ships within the next two weeks, but our friend doesn't know where or when. But he has managed to get us somethin' of interest."

He pulled out a slim volume from a jacket pocket and laid it on the table with great ceremony.

"The current semaphore code book used by the Royal Navy."

Adam stiffened in his chair.

"How do you know it's the latest?" Scar asked.

"Only one way to find out," said Dunbar, giving him a level stare, "ask the man who was in the Navy most recently."

Exuding a confidence he didn't feel, Adam leaned back in his chair and gave a condescending smirk. "I was a bosun, not part of the signal corps."

Nonetheless, Adam signaled with a wave of his hand to pass the book down to him. Dunbar slid it across the polished surface of the table without grace.

After flicking through a few pages, it was as he feared – the genuine article. Just like the one Ridgeway had given him; *exactly* like the one. So, what was he to say? If he lied and said it was not, it would be too easy to check. If he said it was, what then?

Adam slid the book back up the table and rolled the dice.

"Aye, I've seen one like that in use on the *Andromeda*. But as I said, I wasn't a signaler, and I didn't sit there studying it. I couldn't say if it's latest."

"Well, it is," Dunbar responded.

"Excellent," Wilkinson announced, "then we move forward with our next assignment. The Collector has instructed us to monitor English semaphore communications for the next several weeks, and we need to do it somewhere where we can be unobtrusive. We also need sufficient elevation and privacy to send signals of our own. The Collector has advised us of a suitable location. You know it, Hardacre."

"Really?"

"Yes. It's Kenstec House."

Adam covered his alarm. How much did they know about his association with the manor – especially recently? "What would I know about that place?" he said.

Wilkinson smiled. "Aside from the fact you grew up within walking distance of it? I understand you didn't exactly endear yourself to the late owner when you were a lad. Local gossip has it he *encouraged* your decision to join the Navy."

Adam thought it best to acknowledge it. "You might say that," he offered.

Wilkinson paid the matter no further mind and pulled out two sheets of paper from a folded folio at his left hand. The first was a sketch of the west facing elevation of Kenstec, complete with an inset view of the tower turret. The second was a floor plan showing all three levels. A cold chill spread across the top of his head and down his spine.

He knew the hand of the artist. Even if he had not, the signature on the bottom right of the sketches sealed it.

In her neat governess' hand was her name – *Olivia Collins.*

"FOSKETT, HAVE YOU seen my sketchbook?"

Olivia rummaged across the table, assembling her notes on Kenstec House. Two days ago, she decided to finish the history of Kenstec after all, and started writing its history interspersing the text with pen and ink vignettes based on her larger views. Now she was ready to chronicle the construction of the tower.

The red-mopped clerk stuck his head around the door. "Your sketchbook, Miss Collins? I saw it on the desk when I left the office late on Thursday."

Fitzgerald appeared behind him. "I'm afraid its disappearance is my doing, my dear."

He explained, "I thought your sketches of Kenstec House were excellent, so I've taken the liberty of having a selection of them framed."

"Framed? They're hardly as good as all that," she said.

The solicitor looked crestfallen. "I was hoping you would be pleased with the gift. I meant to surprise you with it."

Foskett bid a discreet retreat. Olivia wished he hadn't.

Fitzgerald entered the room instead. She stood to eliminate the disadvantage of him towering over her. Somehow the thought of it made her ill at ease.

"I'm sorry to have spoiled your surprise," she said. "You are a very thoughtful man and have been very kind."

His face softened.

"I would be kinder still if you allowed it."

She couldn't help the flush rise up her face. Olivia knew she was misleading the poor man and felt ashamed of herself. But her heart lay elsewhere, and she had even begun to allow herself a tiny scintilla of hope that she could break their agreement honorably should the rather odd Lady Ridgeway be serious about offering her a position.

Now, Fitzgerald smiled hopefully and she felt even worse. She didn't like the way he looked at her with some kind of affection, as if he might be falling in love with her. Even if she never saw Adam Hardacre again, she knew her heart had gone with him. And in time, Fitzgerald would know it, too, and he would hate her for it.

With a deep breath, she fixed a smile and found that part of herself that could tease.

"Are you getting sentimental on me, Peter? That most certainly will not do."

Now it was his turn to color.

"Does the framer have all of my sketches?"

"No, I have most of the folio on my desk. I'll return it now, if it is so important to you."

She felt the mild censure in his voice and remained rooted in place as he turned on his heel and stalked back to his own office.

When he handed her the loose-leaf folio, there was a look in his eye that told her he suspected secrets were being kept. Or perhaps it was her own guilty conscience. She accepted the book and let her eyes fall away from his, keeping them downcast until she heard him leave the room.

She thought again of Lady Ridgeway. *She* was the type who'd play a game like this with ease.

Olivia Collins was a novice at it.

FOR THE REST of the morning, Olivia listened keenly to the sounds beyond her own small room in Fitzgerald's offices, dreading the idea of being alone with him. So when he announced he was going to visit a client and should not be expected to return for the rest of the day, she cursed herself for breathing a small sigh of relief.

How on earth was she to agree to the formalizing of an engagement next month if the very thought of spending time alone with her would-be fiancé filled her with unease? How could she bear to have him touch her with any intimacy when all she could think about was the desire she experienced in Adam's arms?

Her thoughts turned to the strange Lady Ridgeway. Did her salvation lie there? It certainly wasn't to be found at the post office where the letters contained only regrets that the position had already been filled. What if Lady Ridgeway made no offer of work? What was she to do then?

Olivia put down her pen, feeling the beginning of a headache building at her temples.

Since there was little more she could do on her history of Kenstec without one of the missing sketches, she decided to make a hopeful visit to the post office once again on the way to join the early afternoon coach back to Ponsnowyth.

AS THE COACH rounded the bend past the woods and into the hedgerows that marked the border of Kenstec House, Olivia shouted out for the coachman to stop.

She disembarked and remained on the side of the road until she could no longer see the coach and the plumes of dust kicked up in its wake began to settle. It was hot in the sun. She felt a bead of perspiration tickle the nape of her neck. Grasshoppers, bees, and dragonflies filled the air with sound.

The ruin in the middle of the woods beckoned her. She determined to go there and say a final goodbye to Constance, and to the tragedy which bound them together. She would pray that the poor girl's soul would find peace, and that her lost and dispossessed son had somehow made a good life for himself.

She found the overgrown path from the road without much difficulty and picked her way through, brushing past ferns and hardy wildflowers. The dappled light through the trees illuminated one of the grey stones ahead. The sound of the stream drew her on also. She was thirsty and the thought of its cold sweetness spurred her forward.

Only a few yards from the clearing, she heard male voices.

"No one comes through here, only the occasional poacher."

She knew that voice! It was Adam. But there was an edge to his tone, a harshness she'd never before heard.

"Well, they'd better be keepin' away if they know what's good for 'em." The threat by a second man was unmistakable.

Olivia moved off the path, away from them, toward the back corner of the ancient ruin. She could hide there.

At a distance, she could see Adam's face. The man he spoke to had his back to her, but the barrel of the musket he carried in his hand was more than ample proof that his threat was not an idle one.

"Why don't you go tell Wilkinson the northern boundary is clear?" said Adam. "I'll be back." He began to walk away across her line of sight. She ducked behind a half-wall in case he glanced in her direction.

"Where are ye goin'?" the other man called.

"I'm taking a piss."

Olivia heard the man grumble and the sounds of him walking away swiftly followed. Then she only heard the sound of her own breathing while she counted down a minute, hoping it was enough time for Adam to have left the clearing.

Squatters at Kenstec House? Why was Adam with them? Olivia swallowed bitterness, she could think of quite a few reasons and none of them good. She rose to her feet slowly and peered toward the clearing by the stream. There was no one to be seen.

The afternoon sun was low in the sky, blinding her retreat back to the road, but she ran for it. She would tell Jory and the others in the village.

Before another thought formed, Olivia was wrenched backwards, a large hand clamped over her mouth.

Chapter Twenty-Six

"OLIVIA! IT'S ME."

Adam's harsh whisper filled her ears. She fought an involuntary tremor by squeezing her eyes shut tight until they watered.

"I need you to be silent. I'm going to hold you until you're still and quite sure you won't scream. Agreed?"

She nodded and breathed in deeply through her nose once, then twice. Adam's hand slowly lifted itself from her mouth. She continued to take in big lungsful of air until she was sure she could stand without trembling.

"Oh hell, sweetheart, what are you doing here?" he whispered, before looking behind him toward the path that came from the house. He grabbed her hand and took her further into the thicker part of the woods where the stone from the priory was covered in moss. It was cold here, even the heat of the afternoon sun offered little comfort and light.

"What sort of trouble are you in, Adam?"

Adam's head moved a degree, as though surprised by the question.

"I saw the letter your man gave to Jory. That was *not* your writing and not your words."

He huffed out a breath of his own. "I've spent weeks wishing I could see your face and now you're here, I'm frightened for the both of us."

Olivia frowned. He continued. "The men I'm with are French

spies and English traitors. I am *not* one of them. I'm with them to discover plans for an invasion of Cornwall."

Adam drew her closer. Olivia realized she was trembling again. "You have to stay away from here. Promise me you will."

She returned his embrace, her arms around him.

"And what of you? Is there nothing I can do? Is there anyone I can call on to help you?"

He answered with kisses across her forehead and cheeks before finding her mouth. She returned his desperate passion just as ardently. Only the need for air caused her to pull her lips away.

Adam's forehead was creased.

"No one must know. It will mean my death and danger to everyone in Ponsnowyth. And worse than that, I think someone I know – I don't know who – may also be a traitor."

"What are we going to do now?"

Adam rested his forehead against hers a moment as if, by their heads touching, they could come up with a plan between them.

"Hardacre! How long does it take to piss?" an impatient voice yelled out.

Adam growled profanities under his breath before shouting back "I'll be done when I'm bloody good and ready, Dunbar. Unless you want to come over here and see what a real man looks like!"

If their situation wasn't so grave, Olivia might have been tempted to laugh at Adam's look of apology at her for his words.

"I have to go," he whispered. "This man can't catch you here."

He brought her hand to his lips as he started to back away. "The mounting block at the inn. Look about tomorrow. I'll hide a note there overnight."

Olivia nodded.

"And Constance's writing box – do you have it?"

"Yes."

"Take it straight to Charteris House in Truro. Ask to see—"

"Hardacre! Where the *hell* are ye?" The man's voice now seemed closer. Adam took off at a run to intercept him without looking back at her.

As soon as she could no longer see him through the trees, she cut through the wood to the road, not even daring to look down the driveway to Kenstec House as she made her way down to the village.

ALONE IN HER room, Olivia pulled out the writing box from where she had buried it in her trunk. For weeks, she hadn't been able to bring herself to even look at it. Now she stared at the locked wooden cube.

Take it straight to Charteris House in Truro.

Charteris House? As soon as Adam had said it she recalled the card Lady Ridgeway had given her. What had any of this to do with *her*?

She gazed at the shield-shaped escutcheon, willing it to reveal some secret. If only she had time to ask Adam about it today.

Think!

It was a plain box, made by a young country carpenter's apprentice. The lock would be simple, inexpensive as the brass escutcheon. Perhaps any key would work. She couldn't believe she hadn't tried that before. A glance told her the trunk key was too large. Since it was a carpenter's piece, perhaps the carpenter had a replacement.

She took her box and walked a couple of streets over to Mr. Trezise's house. While she sat and chatted with the lady of the house, her husband disappeared to his workshop in search of suitable keys. He soon came back with half a dozen possibilities and, on the fourth try, the candidate turned in the lock.

"There you are, Miss Olivia," he said proudly. "As good as new."

The man refused payment for the old key; his wife insisted she stay for supper. Olivia didn't have the heart to refuse the generosity and tried for the rest of the evening to keep from looking at the box as it sat on their sideboard.

Finally, alone back at the tavern, Olivia carefully lowered the writing slope and increased the wick on her lamp to better illuminate the inside of the box. There was nothing out of the ordinary here. Olivia pulled out one drawer, then another.

Then, secreted behind Constance's letters, she found another slim volume. She thumbed through it. The engraved arms of the semaphore towers flickered and moved, changing positions as she leafed through it once and twice over.

Was this what Adam was concerned with protecting?

HAD HE DONE the right thing? Adam didn't know.

As he jogged toward the clearing, the answer he came up with was no comfort at all. The moment he saw Olivia's face, he knew she could not be a participant in this ring. And now she *was* involved whether she wanted to be or not.

Did it even matter about the code book hidden in the writing box? They had their own copy now. He had no doubt it wasn't his. Wilkinson would have said if it was. No. Most worrying of all was his growing belief Peter Fitzgerald was somehow associated with the gang. That was the only explanation he could figure for them fearlessly occupying Kenstec. And he suspected Fitzgerald had been the one who'd obtained Olivia's sketches.

Telling her to go to Charteris House was a risk. But the only person he could trust to really keep her safe was Sir Daniel.

And, if he had misjudged her completely, then that would become Ridgeway's problem to deal with because Adam knew what the gang would do with him....

Dunbar stood by the stream and glared before spitting a black stream of tobacco into the clear water.

Adam ignored him as he made his way back to the house at a slightly faster clip than he would have otherwise. He wanted to be the one to volunteer to patrol the northern woods tonight. He would argue he knew the area better than any of them.

He headed up to the attic rooms and climbed up the circular staircase to the roof where Wilkinson spared him a glance before returning a telescope to his eye.

In the distance before Adam, the river Fal was as bright as burnished gold, nearly obscuring the harbor at Falmouth.

"At least the standard flag semaphores don't change," observed Wilkinson. "The *Andromeda* has been sighted a few miles off shore. She's taken some damage but is still intact. How does that make you feel, Hardacre?"

Was this some kind of test?

"I know the ship and the men who sail on her," he answered. "I know what she's capable of and I know she will have acquitted herself well."

"But she's also now the enemy."

"Be that as it may, *Major*, but a man should always have proper respect for his enemies, and I certainly don't underestimate mine."

Wilkinson shrugged, as though bored with the conversation already. He trained his glass to the east where the white-painted signal arms on top of the stone semaphore tower at Feock shone in the setting sun.

"Dunbar and I did the rounds of the estate; looks like no one has been here recently. But I want to patrol the back woods tonight. Old man Denton always used to go on about poachers."

"Do it," Wilkinson said simply before putting down the glass and scribbling a sketch of the signal.

Finding himself dismissed, Adam descended the stairs and avoided the small pile of sawn planks, rope and nails. They'd not yet been told, but he suspected they were to rig up a temporary semaphore station of their own to signal to a French ship lurking off shore.

His only hope was to get a message to Ridgeway.

Earlier that day, Adam laid claim to Olivia's room. Not being one of the grandest spaces, his choice was uncontested. He lay on the bed where they had made love just weeks before and closed his eyes.

The faint smell of her soap still lingered on the sheets, and the sight of her today in the wood made it feel like her presence was with him in the room. Tension coursed through his veins as it did every time the *Andromeda* sailed into battle.

He was not a religious man but he joined in the prayer before battle and he recalled the words which resonated with him deeply.

O let not our sins now cry against us for vengeance; but hear us thy poor servants begging mercy, and imploring thy help, and that thou wouldest be a defense unto us against the face of the enemy. Make it appear that thou art our Savior and mighty Deliverer; through Jesus Christ our Lord. Amen.

A defense unto us against the face of the enemy…never before had Adam been so close to his enemy, and Wilkinson was the most dangerous because he could turn the hearts of decent men to evil.

When Wilkinson was not on watch, the man spent his time translating Napoleon's newssheet, the grandiloquently named *Journal of Napoleon and the Virtuous Men* into English for the rest of them who did not speak French.

The major was a true believer in the cause which he took on with the zeal of a missionary. Indeed, he was adept at pointing out the faults of English law and English politics. His arguments were unarguably compelling. But Adam had heard enough of the horrors of the Reign of Terror to know the blood-soaked road to which fanaticism led.

He stared up at the ceiling until sleep claimed him.

HIS DREAMS WERE disturbing. He struggled for air in some, drowning in the sea. In others, he was too late to save Olivia from the guillotine.

When he awoke, the room was dark. The activity echoing though the house suggested it was still early evening.

He quickly set up a lamp and retrieved the stub of a pencil he'd stolen from Wilkinson a week ago. From the empty wardrobe, he tore a piece of lining paper and wrote a coded letter before slipping it down the side of his left boot. The right contained the letter in French he had stolen from the other house.

By his calculations, he had not more than half an hour before he would be missed and the distance to the village was nearly a mile. There was little margin for error.

OLIVIA STOOD IN front of the building early the next morning and looked down at the card Lady Ridgeway had given her.

Charteris House.

She tentatively entered, and the bell on the door tinkled merrily. The place looked like a chandler's and chartmakers establishment, but there was no one about.

Although Adam had told her to take the entire writing box to this place, she suspected it was the code book which was the item of real interest. She had that and Adam's letter, retrieved from the mounting block at the inn, in a large satchel.

On the stroke of nine, a dozen clocks ticked over the hour in perfect synchronization, filling the store with the sound of chimes so loud she didn't hear the shopkeeper even enter the room.

"Can I help you, Miss?"

Olivia started. She turned her back to the clocks to look at the man. He was shorter than she was by at least half a head; his thick glasses made it difficult to even know what his eye color was.

"I'm here to see someone."

"Who would that be?" the little man inquired with a doubtful expression.

She didn't know. Adam had rushed away before telling her.

But she had the card.

"Lady Ridgeway."

"Lady Ridgeway?" The man sounded surprised. He looked about as if searching for such a person. "I'm sure this is no place for a *lady*."

"She gave me a card."

The odd little man held his hand out for it, examined it in great detail, then handed it back to her.

"Yes, this *is* the place."

He blinked at her owlishly before indicating the way to the front door.

"Wait! I was also told to come here by Adam Hardacre."

At that, the man halted.

When he turned back, it seemed the shopkeeper was different somehow – taller, more alert, a lot less the absent merchant of just a moment ago.

"Please wait here a moment, Miss Collins."

The man disappeared through the door of what Olivia presumed was a stockroom before she could even ask his name or, more shockingly, how he knew *her* name. Within moments, he came back.

"Miss Collins, you are to go to the White Hart Inn at one o'clock today. You will be escorted to a private room on the first floor to dine with Sir Daniel Ridgeway and his wife, Lady Abigail. Do you have any message from Mr. Hardacre?"

"I have a letter. And a writing box."

"Thank you," said the man, looking speculatively at her satchel. "I'll relieve you of the items now."

He held out his hand.

"No! Not until I know your name; not until I know how *you* know mine."

"My name is Bassett, Miss Collins. At your service," he bowed. "And as for the rest, you must speak with Sir Daniel."

He smiled at her. "The satchel?"

She hefted the strap off her shoulder and handed it over.

OLIVIA WALKED DOWN to Fitzgerald's office thinking of the excuses she'd have to make to beg off arrangements for lunch.

He had suggested last week they should dine at his house since it would be the home they would share in the autumn. And besides, it would be a good opportunity to introduce herself to the housekeeper who could brief her on how he preferred his household to be run.

Despite the warmth of the early August day, she shuddered. A desiccated life, one she had supposed she could live with. Was future security worth that compromise to her soul? To her heart?

When she arrived, it was quiet. Foskett sat at his desk transcribing some documents. The door to Fitzgerald's office was closed.

"Is Mr. Fitzgerald not in this morning?" she inquired.

Foskett looked up from his task. "No, Miss – he asked me to convey his apologies for breaking your arrangements for the day, but he received a letter requiring him to attend some urgent business. But he did say he would call on you at Ponsnowyth tomorrow, if that would be convenient."

She thanked the clerk for the message and went into the small office where she had worked on her history of Kenstec House. She would tinker with that and count down the hours to her appointment with the mysterious Sir Daniel Ridgeway and the peculiar Lady Abigail.

Chapter Twenty-Seven

Olivia arrived just as the town hall clock struck the hour. She was shown to the private dining room. The servants had just finished laying the table and, lastly, a maid set down a silver epergne filled with the sweet scent of summer flowers.

An imposing man, seemingly as broad-shouldered as he was tall, entered the room first. His suit was of the finest cut, but not ostentatiously so. He carried himself with unmistakable authority.

Olivia dropped a curtsy. At his shoulder, before moving past him into the room, was Lady Abigail. Striking as ever, she wore a fine muslin gown, plum in color. Her white curls were held in place with a matching ribbon.

"Olivia, my dear! It *is* a pleasure to see you again. I hope you haven't been put off by all this cloak and dagger business. I confess it can be quite tiresome on occasion."

Ridgeway quirked a knowing smile that suggested his wife thought it anything *but* tiresome.

"Daniel, I wish to introduce you to a friend of mine and, it would appear, a *very* good friend of Adam Hardacre," Lady Abigail continued. "Miss Olivia Collins, this is Sir Daniel Ridgeway."

A further curtsy seemed the only appropriate response. Ridgeway bowed over her hand and sat at the head of the table. His wife sat in the place to his right. Olivia followed the lead of her hosts and sat to Ridgeway's left, with Abigail opposite. Waiters brought the first course.

When the plates were before them, Olivia could no longer contain her curiosity.

"If you will forgive me, I am not sure what interest you could possibly have in me," she said, addressing them both.

"It is your interest in our Adam Hardacre which brought you to our attention," said Ridgeway.

"*Your* Adam Hardacre?"

He ignored her question. "I'm afraid we were rather suspicious of you at first."

"Of *me*? Why?"

"Your dogged pursuit of what happened to his child, for one. You were a step ahead of us and we feared you were intending blackmail."

Olivia set down her fork before it slipped from her fingers. "You know about his son? What business is it of yours?"

Lady Abigail took up the business of responding while her husband speared a morsel of food with his fork and ate.

"It's no business of yours, either," she retorted evenly, "yet here we are, strangers united by two things. Our desire to see our Mr. Hardacre safe, and to protect England from the dictator, Bonaparte. Like it or not, you are now in a league with spies."

Olivia wiped her hands on the napkin in her lap then took a sip of chilled water. Really, she ought to be more shocked by the revelation than she was.

"Your composure does you credit," commented Ridgeway. "Not everyone we encounter is so sanguine."

Olivia took up her fork once more. "Sir Daniel, if the matter concerned me alone, you have my assurance that I would be more…taken aback. I'm merely a governess and the thought of a governess as a spy is—"

"—As ridiculous as a Lady spy?" Lady Abigail added dryly. "My dear, the very absurdity of it is its genius – take the most unlikely people you could imagine and turn them into masterful agents of espionage."

"My principal concern is Adam."

Of the two, it was Ridgeway's face that softened.

"You're in love with him," he said gently.

Fortunately, she was prevented from answering by the arrival of the second course.

When the footman left, Olivia had fashioned her answer. "All I know is he is a fine man who deserved some good to come his way but he is now surrounded by men who would kill him if they found out he was in *your* service."

"Your tender feelings are reciprocated – that's why you're here," said Lady Abigail.

Olivia looked back and forth at the pair. They appeared to finish one another's thoughts.

"Adam believes you would be safest brought into our confidence and into our protection," added Ridgeway. "There is a master traitor operating out of Falmouth. We've spent the better part of the year trying to ferret out his identity, but he's been clever.

"He's also instrumental in another plot against our country, so we needed a man on the inside. One who would quickly win the confidence of this turncoat and bring him far enough out into the open to be indentified and his threat neutralized.

"The…" Ridgeway paused. "*…scoundrel…*" – Olivia suspected that on his own, Ridgeway might have employed another epithet – "has managed to obtain a code book. The one you brought to us today in the writing box means there was only one other place where it could have come from."

Olivia wanted to ask the obvious question, "*where,*" but she knew it wouldn't be answered, even if Ridgeway knew it. That's not how this game worked, so she asked another question instead.

"What can I do to help Adam?"

"There is little any of us can do for the moment," Ridgeway answered. "Adam knows what he has to do, and he's quite capable of doing it. We're reducing a weight from his mind by keeping you safe."

"You're staying at the inn in Ponsnowyth," said Abigail. "How soon could you have your belongings ready?"

"Not long. There's not much to pack."

"Good. This evening, a coachman will collect you and your belongings. He will bring with him a note from your Aunt Runella. Obey its instructions to the letter."

Aunt Runella. Adam mentioned that name a month ago. And she was?

...a face like a boxer and possessed of a sour disposition...

Olivia glanced once more at the large, well-built peer. *Oh.*

Lady Abigail commanded her attention with a small lift of her head. Olivia suddenly had a sense that the older woman, despite the crispness of her speech, sympathized with her plight.

"I think you're being very kind," she said.

Abigail made a moue of distaste. "That's only because you don't know me well."

They continued eating their meal in silence. As coffee was served, Olivia asked the question bothering her most after Adam's safety.

"Did you find out anything more about Adam's son?"

Olivia watched the couple exchange glances. It seemed to be the silent communication of a married couple in tune with each other.

"We have people checking," said Ridgeway, as though that were enough. The expression on Lady Abigail's face told her it was not the agreement she and her husband had silently reached.

"All we can confirm thus far is that the boy...Christopher?" Ridgeway looked to his wife, not her, for confirmation, "was apprenticed as a cabin boy on a Mediterranean merchant ship in 1794."

"Wouldn't he have been rather young?"

Ridgeway shrugged. "He was tall and precocious for his age by all accounts."

The clock from the floor below struck three.

"Sir Daniel, Lady Ridgeway, I must take my leave if I am to take the next coach back to Ponsnowyth."

Ridgeway rose to his feet, took Olivia's hand, and bowed over it. "It goes without saying, of course, that you are to tell no one of our meeting today – and that is as much for Adam's sake as it is for our own."

"You have my word, Sir Daniel. And thank you…for everything."

Lady Abigail took Olivia's hand in turn and gave it a squeeze.

"Don't be so swift to thank us," she said, her eyes betraying a mischievous twinkle. "I was serious about a position, but not as a chaperone. I shall be personally testing how good your French is. We have more documents than we have translators. I plan to keep you so thoroughly occupied you will have no time to moon after *your* Adam Hardacre."

Olivia gave a tight smile in response and hoped her face did not color.

SHE EMERGED INTO the early afternoon with an air of expectation. It was as though the veil had been thrown back and she finally saw the world as it was, not as she believed it to be. Every face she saw, she gazed at in doubt.

Was *anyone* who they pretended to be? Spies! In Truro, in Falmouth, indeed in the very home she had lived in for ten years…

She walked past the coaching house on her way back to Fitzgerald's office. If she were to "disappear" for a while, she ought to take everything with her, and that included her sketchpad and history of Kenstec House.

When she walked in, Foskett was absent from his desk and, on hearing voices in Fitzgerald's office, she assumed the solicitor had returned early from his appointment and was instructing his clerk.

Olivia pulled the workroom door to nearly closed, but not quite. If she was quiet, she could be in and out of the office and Fitzgerald would never know she was there.

She gathered her materials together and was nearly done when the voices became louder and more distinct. A moment later, she heard Fitzgerald's office door open.

"Alors nous sommes d'accord, Hardacre sera emmené en France à la prochaine nouvelle lune."

Olivia started. She recognized the voice but couldn't place it.

Then we are agreed. Hardacre will be taken to France on the next new moon.

Her heart hammered in her chest, her mind screamed to her body to move, but she was rooted to the spot as she listened to Fitzgerald and this unknown Frenchman talking.

"Yes, that is the instruction," said the Frenchman. "We know there is more he can tell us with *proper* incentive."

"Good; *bon*," Fitzgerald replied in a mix of French and English. "I will deal with any loose ends, any *détailer à régler*, eh?"

"Are there any?" the Frenchman asked.

"One, but it will be of no consequence after September."

"Then that is our business concluded, *non*?"

"Yes. And thank you for the final payment. Before you go, shall we celebrate over a glass of brandy?"

For a moment, there was silence then the clink of a decanter against the rim of a glass. Another brief silence then the sound of two glasses meeting and a toast.

"Vive la Liberté!"

Olivia put her hands to her mouth to prevent a sound leaving her lips. She remained paralyzed until Fitzgerald's door swung closed once again. A burst of laughter from the men was enough to spur Olivia into motion.

She swept up her portfolio and hurried for the door.

Olivia did not stop hurrying until she was at the door of Charteris

House. It was locked. She peered through the window.

"Miss Olivia!"

Olivia nearly jumped out of her skin. She spun around to see Harold Bickmore.

"What an unexpected surprise!" he grinned. "A chandlery was not the place I expected to see you."

"Oh, Lieutenant Bickmore, I was..." she looked down at her sketchpad and the loose pages beginning to spill, "I thought someone might..."

With her composure returning, Olivia offered Harold a small smile. "You will excuse me. I really do need to see someone about this."

Harold fell into step with her as she headed toward the White Hart Inn but, before she got too far, he took her by the arm.

"Olivia, what's the matter? You're upset."

"I need to *see* someone."

"About your history of Kenstec?"

"No. About Adam."

"Why?" Harold asked swiftly, concern appearing in his eyes. "What's happened to Adam?"

Olivia clamped her lips shut but allowed Harold to lead her to the nearest tea shop. He ordered for them and remained silent while the tea was poured.

"If the truth be told," Harold offered, leaning forward to bring her into his confidence, "I'm worried about Adam, too. I shouldn't be telling you this, but there are forces here in England, indeed here in Cornwall who wish to see England defeated. There's a group called *The Society for Public Reform* who've been courting him. They heard about his poor treatment by the Royal Navy promotion board. They're Radicals, and I fear they are much, much more than that."

His concern was plainly genuine, so Olivia considered her response carefully. "I'm concerned about him, too. He...he hasn't seemed himself, and I thought…"

She took a deep breath. "These people you mentioned…are they dangerous?"

"Deadly, I fear." The gravity of his words caused her to look up at him. Harold Bickmore suddenly looked dangerous himself.

"Do you know where Adam is?" he asked.

"No, I haven't seen him for weeks." Olivia had no idea what possessed her to lie, but she forged ahead with it. "That's why I'm worried."

She forced herself to look into Harold's eyes to see if she could divine his thoughts. Did he believe her? Did he think she was hiding something from him?

"If you have a care for him at all, Olivia, you'll help me to help you," Harold said, *sotto voce*.

"How?"

He reached a hand across the table and covered hers with it.

"Tell me everything you know about Adam, everything he's told you, and everything he's done. It might be our only chance to save him."

Olivia tried to tug her hand away, but Harold held it all the more firmly.

"You *do* want to help him, don't you?"

She did want to help Adam. While she had no reason to trust the Ridgeways, Adam evidently did. Moreover, Adam had not taken Harold into his confidence and she had been told by him to speak to no one. Olivia pulled her hand away.

"I need to go now."

"The inn at Ponsnowyth?"

She confirmed it with a nod.

Harold stood. "Then I'll take you back there myself, I'll ask the innkeeper to look in Adam's room. There may be something that has been overlooked."

The hardness of his expression softened from naval officer to more like the man she met two months ago.

"Wait for me here," he said. "I have a curricle. I can get you to Ponsnowyth faster and in more comfort than the coach."

ADAM REGARDED THE three beams of timber and consulted his plans. The conversation with Wilkinson had been amusing.

They weren't planning a semaphore station but they did want to be able to signal with lamps at night to a ship out at sea using some French coding system. He assumed it would be similar to the light codes in *Howe's Signal-Book for Ships of War*. Adam had been volunteered to build it due to his carpentry skills.

He had taken only the briefest glimpse at the diagram handed over by the major before tossing it back across the table to him.

"It won't do," he said brusquely.

"Why not? What's wrong with it? It was drawn up by our friends across the channel."

"That figures," Adam replied, noting with satisfaction the little flash of annoyance in Wilkinson's eyes. "It's too flimsy. It won't last."

"It only needs to last four weeks, man."

Adam snorted. "That thing won't last four *nights*, especially if a wind catches it. And it has to be taken up and assembled each time on the roof, then taken down again straight after so it's not seen in the day. It won't stand up to much of that."

"Well, don't just criticize, Hardacre – redesign it," huffed Wilkinson. "But I need it ready in two days."

Adam had drawn up his own plan and selected additional lumber and ironmongery from a storage shed behind the stables. A dozen ship's lanterns and oil had been brought up to the room yesterday. They looked like standard Navy lanterns. On closer inspection, Adam realized they were brand new and he surmised if they hadn't been stolen from the stores down in Falmouth, it would be ironic if they'd actually bought them from the shop front at Charteris House.

The ornate iron spiral staircase had been dismantled, no more than a skeleton of iron heaped in the corner. Adam lashed a sturdy old ladder in its place, all the quicker and easier to get up to the roof. He worked alone in the tower attic room of Kenstec House which, in his present frame of mind, suited him just fine.

He hammered a hinge into place violently, while entertaining fantasies of using the hammer to bludgeon Dunbar. The man had been an insufferable arse all week, and it was taking what little restraint Adam had left to not respond to his goading.

He suspected it was Wilkinson's way of testing him, seeing how far he could be pushed. And Dunbar pushed and pushed and pushed.

And, if he was not mistaken, there were the man's booted footsteps coming up the stairs to the upper floor now. A moment later, the "insufferable arse" appeared, sour-faced and arms crossed.

Adam worked on, hefting one of the beams into place and ignoring Dunbar's critical eye.

He slipped a hammer in his belt and climbed up the ladder to fasten the upper end of the beam to the frame of the hatch. Dunbar came to the bottom of the ladder.

"What are ye doin' then?" he asked.

"Making sure this is firmly fixed."

"Don't look none-too-sturdy down here," Dunbar sneered. He kicked at the unfixed bottom of the beam and it swung out and fell onto the floor with a loud bang that echoed through the house.

Adam jumped down and rounded on the man.

"Omgyjor!"

Dunbar understood the Cornish insult well enough. His amused grunt became a growl. Adam brandished the hammer.

"Want it? Come at me!" Red-tinted murderous thoughts of fulfilling his earlier fantasy of embedding the hammer's head in Dunbar's skull filled his mind. "Come on! What are you waiting for?"

Adam, though at the limit of his self-control, was not beyond it. Oh, he knew he was acting like a madman but he'd long ago learned living among rough, violent men at sea, how to show what he was capable of if pushed too far.

He surged forward, his left hand taking Dunbar by the throat in a flash and raising the hammer to the man's temple.

The sound of men running up the stairs culminated with the arrival of Pockmark and Red. Wilkinson was right behind them.

"That's quite enough, gentlemen," he said firmly.

Adam shoved Dunbar away and pinned Wilkinson with a stare. "Put your dog on a *leash*. That bastard's getting in the way," he said.

Wilkinson nodded at Dunbar to get out. He jostled his way through the men, muttering about Adam's sanity amongst a few other choice insults.

"Our tower *will* be ready tomorrow night, won't it, Hardacre? We only have a few hours when the *Cygne* can be close enough to see our signal."

"It will be if I'm left to do my *job* and fools like Dunbar are kept out of my way."

Black Angus came barreling into the room. "Someone's coming up the drive!"

Wilkinson acknowledged the interruption with a nod. "We'll get rid of them. You," he said, pointing to Adam, "get on with your work."

Adam slammed the door behind the men. He climbed up the ladder to the tower roof to see if he could catch sight of the unwary visitor. A curricle emerged from under the trees. There appeared to be two people in it but, from this angle and with the glare of the late afternoon sun, he couldn't make out any more.

The matched pair of white horses trotted confidently up the drive.

Wilkinson emerged from the house alone and waited for the conveyance to stop.

The driver got down and Wilkinson exchanged words with him, although Adam was too far away to hear them. The man's hat made it impossible to see his face, although by the ease by which he descended from the vehicle, Adam judged he was a young man. Looking once again at the curricle, Adam saw a flash of color from a skirt and a feminine arm.

Leave, dammit! For your sake, and for the woman's with you.

He heard a raised voice momentarily. The man and Wilkinson appeared to be arguing. If this went on for much longer, Dunbar and Black Angus would be out with guns.

The postures of both men became aggressive. It seemed the newcomer wasn't going to accept "no" for an answer. Then he backed up a step or two in apparent surprise. Adam peered over the edge of the tower roof as far as he dared.

Dunbar and Black Angus were advancing, each brandishing a gun.

The curricle driver raised his hands in surrender and as he did so, raised his head. Even at this distance, the identity of the man was unmistakable.

It was Harold Bickmore.

Chapter Twenty-Eight

BY THE TIME Adam had run downstairs, Harold and his companion had been escorted inside and into the dining room.

Harold saw him. "Adam! What the hell is going on here?"

He only spared a glance at Harold. There, surrounded by the *Society*, was Olivia. Her eyes were wide, but she showed more composure than her escort.

Hell and Damnation!

One misstep would be all it would take for Adam to lose the trust of Wilkinson and after today's incident, Dunbar would look for any excuse to foment just that.

Now he really *would* have to play the part of traitor if he – not to mention Olivia and Harold – had any chance at all.

He folded his arms and looked at his old friend with regret.

"You should have left when you were told, Harold."

His friend's mouth opened in shock. Harold turned to Wilkinson. "I demand you release me and Miss Collins immediately!"

"Sadly, I cannot let that be the case," said the major. "You will have to be our guests for a few days."

"No, sirrah, I will not!" Harold pronounced.

Black Angus backhanded him. Harold stumbled a step with a gasp of pain. Adam winced inwardly. Olivia brought her hands to her mouth to suppress a cry of alarm.

"Now that *is* a pity," said Wilkinson. "I was prepared to treat you well and leave you unharmed when we all abandon England's shores in a four days' time."

What? That was news to him.

He glanced at Olivia and saw something in her eyes that told him this unexpected trip to France was *not* news to her, but she remained silent.

"Perhaps I should take Miss Collins into the kitchen, while you have words with the lieutenant there," said Adam, forcing as much nonchalance in his voice as he could.

"You know this woman?" asked Wilkinson.

Adam nodded, noting that Dunbar had said nothing *and* still carried the same gormless look on his ugly mug. If the man had noticed his interest in Olivia at the barn dance, he hadn't thought to tell Wilkinson.

"She was the governess here until the family moved to London. She was staying at the Angler's Arms while I was there. We spoke a few times."

"Then go ahead. Make her a cup of tea or something. I want to make a few things perfectly clear to your friend here. But if you're thinking of helping the lady to escape, then it will be all the worse for Lieutenant Bickmore."

Adam offered a curt nod. He fought the desire to show any particular chivalry as he ushered Olivia from the room. Safer for all of them if he remained aloof.

When the kitchen door closed behind them, she let out a sigh of relief. Adam gave her a swift embrace before stoking the fire and settling the kettle on the stove. Wilkinson had said to make tea and if anyone walked in, that's exactly what they were going to find him doing.

"We don't have long to talk," he said softly. "Tell me how you and Harold came to be here."

"I don't trust him."

He turned. Olivia sat at the kitchen bench, her shawl clutched tight about her shoulders even though it was warm.

"Why?"

"A feeling. I can't explain it."

Adam offered her a reassuring smile "I've known Harold for ten years. He's stood by me when everyone else walked away. Is that enough to give him the benefit of the doubt?"

Olivia took a deep breath and nodded.

"Then I hope he's not taking too many lumps and he keeps his trap shut about you and me. Now, tell me everything from the beginning."

In low tones, she told him about her meeting with Ridgeway and Lady Abigail, Fitzgerald's conversation with an unknown Frenchman, meeting Harold in Truro, and his insistence they stop at Kenstec House.

Adam prepared the cups while he considered what she told him. So Fitzgerald was in on it. He cursed the old snake, and prayed that once Ridgeway discovered Olivia hadn't arrived back at the inn from Truro he would begin a search. But until then, as far as Adam was concerned they were on their own.

"Here's what we're going to do," he said. "We're going to play along with them. If, for any reason, we're apart, be sure to stay with Harold or with the leader, Wilkinson. He considers himself a gentleman. Keep away from the rest of them if you can."

OLIVIA SHUDDERED BUT nodded her head to let Adam know she understood.

"I fear what will happen if Mr. Fitzgerald comes here," she said. "As soon as he sees me, he may suspect I overheard his conversation. And he'll certainly reveal how…*close* you and I are."

Adam held out his hand and gave hers a squeeze, but he didn't draw any closer.

"I suspect Fitzgerald prefers to keep himself at arm's length. The man is not a true believer, not like Wilkinson. What was he promised? Gold?"

Olivia shrugged. "I don't know. It was payment at any rate."

"I asked for a thousand pounds in gold," Adam added with a wink before bringing his attention back to the stove to check on the heating kettle.

She smiled at his attempt to lighten the mood, but she suspected Adam's confidence was chiefly for her benefit.

"The new moon is in three days' time, unless our *friends* do something soon, you'll be on the Channel at the turn of the tide. You can't let them take you to France," she said.

"I won't," he said, his back still to her. "Besides, I don't speak the bloody language."

Adam turned back with a large steaming kettle in his hand and filled the teapot. "I need to talk to Harold, but they'll have him locked away. If I convince him I'm not a traitor, we might have half a chance of breaking out of here."

Olivia let her disquiet settle. Adam would never abandon his friend, but he thought of the lieutenant more kindly than she could.

Harold's brash and self-confident nature was amusing at first but she was never quite sure whether he was mocking her. His insistence in overriding her wish to head straight to the Angler's Arms was another thing she didn't appreciate. And now after the shock of his foolhardy actions had ebbed, Olivia wondered whether it was not done on purpose.

A man burst through the door without warning. Olivia started but managed to keep her tea cup upright.

"Dunbar, you have the grace of an ox," said Adam with an exaggerated put-upon sigh.

"Watch yer mouth, ye—"

"Uh-uh, mind your language in front of the lady."

This Dunbar man looked familiar, but she didn't look at him for long. Better not to make eye contact with him.

"Wilkinson wants to see ye and the *lady*."

Wilkinson was not a man who looked like a traitor, Olivia thought. But then, neither did Peter Fitzgerald. Wilkinson looked like what he was, a retired military man; he had that air of authority. The major sat alone at the end of the table.

"Miss Collins, once again I wish to apologize for the inconvenience of keeping you here for a few days, and I will do my best to ensure your stay is comfortable under the circumstances," he said.

"Thank you, sir." She said the words but didn't mean them. Gratitude was the last thing she felt. She ought to denounce him as a traitor and call him to shame. But she did not. She took her cue from Adam. There was something to be said for being not deemed a threat to threatening people. Let Wilkinson believe she would be meekly compliant.

Behind her, Adam asked, "What happened to Bickmore?"

"I'm afraid he's not been very cooperative. We've got him tied up and locked upstairs in one of attic rooms."

"I believe the room I'm in is Miss Collins' old room. She can have it back until we're ready to move on," said Adam. "How about she waits in the study while I move out of there. She can select a book or two to read – with your permission, that is."

Wilkinson shook his head. "Very chivalrous of you, Hardacre, but one of the others will escort the woman to her quarters later. Just take her to the study and lock her in. You have work to do. Our signal station has to be ready by tomorrow evening and I don't care if you have to work all night tonight to do it."

One touch of Adam's hand to her elbow was enough to communicate his tension. She allowed him to lead her to the study without protest. She looked about at the place where she had spent hours poring over records of Kenstec House. Now that memory would be forever changed.

Adam leaned in and whispered in her ear.

"When it's safe, get the house master key – the one you used when we first explored the tower room. If it's there, take it. I'll knock on your door tonight. We'll free Harold. We can buy him some time to go and get help."

Olivia nodded. "Be safe, my love."

She watched his face soften.

"I promise."

She kept her eyes on Adam as he left the room, closing and locking the door after him from the outside.

The day had softened with the shades of twilight but there was still enough light to see without setting a lamp. She went straight to the mantel over the fireplace and found the papier-mâché box she had returned to the study when she moved out of the house.

Sure enough, the master key was still inside.

Olivia tied it in a knot in the hem of her chemise and picked a book at random before approaching the desk to examine what appeared to be a booklet, amongst other papers. Although the light was not the best, there was enough to make out that it was in French not English.

She slipped the little volume into the back of the book she had taken down. Like it or not, she was now a spy. Her act of rebellion against her captors was daring, it emboldened her.

No longer would she live her life in fear or with half-measures, she vowed.

No longer would she take the safe option if it was not the *right* one.

It was strange. For some reason, she was no longer afraid of seeing Peter Fitzgerald again. Her future was in jeopardy no matter what, so she may as well be hung for a sheep as a lamb.

ADAM WAS BONE weary but he pushed on with the construction of the rooftop signal station. If he was noisy about his work, then no one would come to check on him. Indeed, so late in the night, they'd likely appreciate it if he stopped.

He wasn't sure of the time, but looking up through the roof hatch, he could see some of the constellations in the clear summer night sky. The chill air that flooded through told him it had to be well after midnight.

He'd already had the signal tower up once and taken it down again to make adjustments. Now it worked smoothly and better than Wilkinson and his cohort deserved.

He grasped the rope that extended the center mast and pulled. Through a system of pulleys, two of the upright beams slid up a wooden rail on the fixed lower beam. When they arrived at the top, the beam notched into place. Adam changed ropes and his pulley system lifted the third beam atop the second. Then it was just a matter of going up the ladder and releasing the hinged cross beams that dropped into position like spars on a ship's mast.

Each of the three levels of spars carried hooks for three lanterns. Nine lamps in all. Adam wondered what the French codes would be.

If he were genuinely finishing now for the night, he'd fold the arms in and drop the sectioned mast down into the room out of sight, then close the hatch against the open sky. But the signal tower was going to be used tonight after all…

HE DESCENDED THE stairs with a cat-like grace. A sliver of light spilled out from under Olivia's door. He scratched at the door, not even daring anything as loud as a knock. As soon as the door opened, he slipped around and closed it behind him.

He expected to find Olivia frightened but, by contrast, her eyes were bright with excitement.

"I found something!" she whispered.

Adam fought his disquiet and approached.

"What is it?"

"It's a French code book. It was on the desk in the study. I don't think anyone has discovered it missing yet!"

"Can you read it? Are you sure it's not a translation of an English one?"

"I wouldn't know. I suppose it could be, but more than that, there are handwritten notes in the back, a list of some kind. Names and figures."

"Let me see."

Olivia handed him the book.

The list was fascinating. Even though it was in French, he recognized it as a list of ships – French and Spanish – and their *capitaines*. The figures appeared to be tonnage, numbers of crew and guns on board. There were thirty-three vessels in all.

This was a list of an *Armada*. In his head, Adam rattled through the names of all the ships of the English fleet currently on deployment. To his best of his recollection, Admiral Nelson would be lucky to muster twenty-five – twenty-seven at most.

If the Fleet was defeated, England's final line of defense went with it. Napoleon would be unstoppable; an invasion inevitable.

His stomach sank.

Ridgeway needed to see this. And *that* was an understatement. Ridgeway needed to see this as soon as possible, even if it ended any chance of maintaining a pretense that Adam was part of the *Society*.

Not a too bad option as far as he personally was concerned. If they wanted to take him to France, he knew he wouldn't live to see England again.

Well, the signal tree was intended to pass messages to a French vessel at sea each night from tomorrow, but it would make its debut tonight with a signal to Falmouth.

"Time to go," he told Olivia. "I need to get you and Harold out of here and set a lantern signal on the tower."

ADAM REMOVED A penknife from his boot and handed it to her. "Here. It's not much but it's something in a pinch."

She nodded gamely. He leaned in and kissed her on the cheek.

"I love you, Olivia. Will you marry me?"

To his delight, she grinned. "Ask me again when you get us out of here safely."

Chapter Twenty-Nine

OLIVIA CARRIED A candle and accompanied Adam up the stairs to the top floor, following him into the tower room. Gone was the spiral staircase. Instead, a ladder extended straight up on one side of the hatch and a large beam was fixed from floor to ceiling on the other. Ropes hung back down through the hatch and when she looked up through it, she saw the assembly above.

Adam showed her a set of naval lanterns in one corner of the room. "They're fueled. I need you to light them," he said, then suddenly cocked his head.

Olivia frowned, then she heard the sound, too – a creak from the tread of the stairs.

Adam waved her behind the tower room door. Between the edge of the door and the frame, she saw him stand in the doorway.

"What are ye doin', Hardacre? Way past yer bedtime, innit?" The voice, now right outside, was unfamiliar to her.

Olivia clung to the wall behind the door.

"Some of us have work to do instead of boxing the Jesuit all night," Adam retorted.

"No rest for the wicked, eh?"

"You must be an absolute angel, then."

The man laughed.

Adam spoke, "Well, don't let me keep you from *your* bed, mate."

Silence stretched on between them for several agonizing moments before the man made a noise of assent and tromped his way back downstairs.

Adam whispered to Olivia. "It's safe, it was just Pockmark."

She didn't ask but set to work lighting the lamps. Adam took the house master key and crossed the stair landing to unlock the door to Harold's cell. She heard their low voices. No more than a minute or two later, Adam returned. Harold entered the room behind him.

"For God's sake, man, let me stay and help," Harold whispered.

"Take orders from me for once," he whispered harshly at his friend. "You can help us get the lanterns up on the roof then get to the inn. Wake Jory and raise a hue and cry. Get as many armed men as possible up here as fast as you can.

"You may be approached by a broad-shouldered man in his fifties, well-spoken. Tell him you have a message from Aunt Hilda. Follow his instructions. Do exactly what he says."

"But…"

"*Don't* argue!"

She looked back at Adam and Harold. The two men faced each other like adversaries, not friends. Harold turned away from Adam to look directly at her.

"Then let me take Olivia," he said. "I can get her to safety and that's one less thing for you worry about."

Adam paused a beat before answering. "No."

Olivia felt relief, her faith in Harold was far from as firm as Adam's.

"As far as this crew is concerned, you're locked safe and tight in that room," Adam said harshly. "If you can manage to get away cleanly, they might never know you're missing until it's too late."

"So your message is more important that the safety of a lady?"

"You getting to the inn *guarantees* Olivia's safety – and mine. The message I'm sending should bring better help than Jory and a bunch of villagers with pitchforks. Come on, now. I don't have time to argue."

Harold threw them both an expression that very much looked like disgust. He helped pass just five of the lit lanterns – all Adam wanted – up through the hatch to the roof, then set off down the stairs quietly but with ill-humor.

Adam closed the tower room door behind him and locked it, then dragged over a saw horse and braced it against the door. He ascended the ladder to the roof a moment later, and Olivia followed. As she stepped out onto the roof, shouts started within the house.

Adam picked up a small length of waste timber that lay on the roof beside the hatch and handed it to Olivia. "Hold this," Adam said urgently. "Pass me the lanterns when I ask for them but otherwise stay right here and if anyone pokes their head up, hit it."

No more than a minute passed before there was a banging of fists on the tower room door, accompanied by the shouting of foul oaths erupting below.

Adam took the first of the lamps and clambered near to the top of the structure. He hung the lamp almost at its apex. Below them, the tower room door began to splinter and the shouts grew louder.

As soon as Adam had descended close enough for her to stretch up, Olivia handed him another lamp and he hung it on another part of the frame – and repeated the process for the remaining three. In the end, the shape looked like a house, four lamps roughly set in a rectangle, and one set above in the center.

Cr-ack!

The whip-like sound of a musket report reached her ears. Olivia went as far as she dared to the edge of the roof. Illuminated in the moonlight below her was Harold sprinting across the lawn.

Why was he going that way? If he had headed toward the north boundary, he would already be in the shelter of the woods.

Out there, running through the open formal gardens, he was exposed. Now she saw the man with the gun step forward, priming it for a second shot.

Cr-ack!

This time the aim was true. Olivia screamed. Harold Bickmore fell and did not rise.

Olivia looked up at Adam who was still halfway up the tower. His face was pale in the moonlight, eyes wide in shock at seeing his friend shot down. Then his head turned to face the hatchway where a man was starting to emerge.

Olivia still held the piece of lumber in her hand and she took a step back toward the hatch but her skirt snagged on the shin-high railing. She pulled it and felt fabric tear.

The man, Dunbar, clambered out onto the roof and turned toward her.

ADAM POSITIONED HIMSELF above Dunbar just as the man hauled himself upright and eyed Olivia.

He dropped from his position and pulled the man to the floor. He managed to land a couple of strong punches before Dunbar shoved him off and swung at him.

Adam saw stars before he felt the pain in his jaw. Before he could draw breath, he was hauled to his feet and punched in the gut. Winded, his legs went out from under him and he dropped to his knees.

"The lights! Get the fekkin' lamps off the tower! They're visible all the way to bloody Plymouth!"

Adam had no idea who called up from below. But surely very shortly, Black Angus or one of the others would emerge from the hatch to back up Dunbar.

"I'm goin' to make ye regret the day ye crossed me," the man growled.

Adam looked up in time to see him draw a booted foot back to kick him. Before the man could do so, Adam grabbed his other ankle and pulled. The man fell back and Adam managed to regain his own feet, still half-stunned from the blow to his jaw.

Dunbar lumbered upright and faced Adam. He began pacing toward him.

Adam stepped back a pace and felt the low iron railing at his calves. The advancing man showed no signs of stopping. Would the thug try to shove him off the roof or simply grab him and take both of them to their deaths in a blind rage?

Adam leapt upwards and managed to seize a lower spar of the signal structure just as Dunbar reached him. The thug's arms wrapped round his hips and he used his full substantial weight to try and drag him off. Adam felt the spar drop an inch or two. He prayed the hinges he'd fashioned would not give way. Worse, the whole bloody thing could topple over. Above him, the lanterns, arranged in a signal that warned of "strange ships of superior force to the fleet" – an incongruous message but the best Adam could recall from Howe's code book – swung wildly. If one fell and broke, he'd have *fire* on the roof to worry about, too.

The pain in Adam's arms and shoulders was acute as Dunbar literally swung from his body, trying to dislodge him. Then a flash of brown hair passed beneath him, Dunbar howled, and Adam's lower body was released. Adam swung himself up onto the horizontal support as he'd done numerous times to reach a spar on a ship.

Looking down, he saw Dunbar reach round and touch a blooming red patch on the side of his white shirt. Olivia had jabbed him in the side of the ribs with the penknife Adam had given her, but it might as well have been a pinprick to the big man. He spat an insult, reaching out to swat at her.

Adam crossed over the beam and used it to drop down and swing.

His booted strike to the ribs was powerful enough to send Dunbar staggering backwards. His heels struck the railing and Adam saw his terrified look. His arms wheeled wildly, but his overbalance was terminal. Dunbar fell back and disappeared over the edge of the roof without a sound, perhaps struck dumb by the realization of his fate. A moment later, Adam heard the dull thud as the man's body struck the ground.

Adam immediately rushed to Olivia's side. Despite his injuries, he held her to him just as Wilkinson himself emerged onto the roof and aimed a pistol at them.

"Have we done enough?" Olivia whispered into his shoulder.

"I hope so." He kissed her hair, willing his racing heart to slow.

Black Angus rose through the hatch and Wilkinson ordered him to take down the lanterns.

"A disappointing end, Hardacre," Wilkinson said at last. "You showed such promise. Fortunately, it doesn't change our plans. You will still be going to France – but perhaps not treated as well as you might otherwise have been."

He sidled around the roof, keeping the pistol trained on them. "One false move and I won't shoot you, Hardacre, I'll shoot the lady." Adam looked into Olivia's eyes and saw only the smallest measure of fear. She lifted her chin to show her resolve to the major. If Adam had ever been uncertain of his love for her before, such doubts were now forever banished.

"Now, get downstairs," said Wilkinson. "Miss Collins has a visitor."

As soon as they were back in the tower room below, Olivia took Adam's hand and squeezed it. Black Angus gave them a sour look and pulled them apart.

They followed Wilkinson down two flights of stairs. He led them into the study – where Peter Fitzgerald waited.

"That man is a spy," the solicitor proclaimed, pointing his finger, the sense of affront plain in his voice.

It struck Adam as absurd.

He burst out laughing. "It might surprise you to know we're *all* spies here, Fitzgerald."

The man glared at Adam, then he turned to Olivia and gave her a look of visceral contempt. "Except for her." He advanced toward her. "*She's* nothing but a *whore.*"

Fitzgerald's palm connected sharply with Olivia's cheek.

Adam threw off Pockmark's straining hands and got two paces forward before his vision turned white from a flash of pain and heat that radiated from the back of his head.

Then everything turned black.

THE PISTOL BUTT made a sickening sound as it struck. Olivia's stomach fell as Adam crumpled to the floor. The scream she wanted to release was stuck in her throat, then she found herself spun around and a short velvet hood was dragged over her head.

To further add insult to injury, she was bound, then picked up like a sack of wheat and dumped without ceremony into a carriage after a rough journey through the house over someone's shoulder. As the vehicle moved off, she heard a groan from the seat opposite. She leaned forward but was immediately shoved back into her seat.

"Don't ye worry about him, darlin'" said a man with an Irish lilt to his voice. "He'll be sleepin' for quite a while yet. Ye just worry about what The Collector has in mind for ye. He wasn't best pleased to learn ye've been sharin' yer charms with another."

Soon, it was difficult to concentrate on anything other than a growing headache and raging thirst inside the fusty hood. And, disturbingly, Adam had been silent for what seemed like hours. Without sight and landmarks, it was difficult to know how far they had traveled. She fought to tamp down panic and fell into a feverish state from lack of sleep and the physical aftermath of the night's horrors.

Olivia was jolted awake by the carriage pulling to a halt. Before she could arrange her confused thoughts, she found herself roughly tossed over some man's shoulder and carried some distance before being dropped onto a pile of canvas.

"Now you be a good girl and stay here quiet-like, eh?" said Wilkinson.

"Would you be so good as to remove the hood," she croaked. "And may I have water?"

She felt a hand on her shoulder. "We'll compromise. I'll get you water but you keep the hood on for now. Agreed?"

She nodded, feeling weariness down to her bones.

"Good girl. It will all be over soon."

As he left, Olivia heard a door slam loosely shut and she guessed that she was in some kind of shed. Her wrists and shoulders hurt from being bound and the stink of the dirty canvas on which she lay added to the sick-making discomfort of the hood. She could hear water lapping.

Whereabouts was she? And where was Adam?

When the hood was finally removed, it was not by the major, but rather Fitzgerald who then put the edge of a glazed clay pot to her lips. Cold sweet water filled her mouth and she hated herself for how pathetically grateful she felt for it.

With her arms still bound behind her, she struggled to a more comfortable seating position and looked about. She appeared to be in some kind of boat shed on a pile of old sails to the side of a slipway. Two lengths of timber, worn smooth with age, sloped steeply down the center of the shed and out under the door.

There was no one else here except Fitzgerald, and that made her nervous.

She was the subject of his full attention. If she could avoid looking into his eyes…

Olivia was not going to get the option. With three fingers under her chin, Fitzgerald lifted her head. His face was mere inches away. The closeness of it was disturbing. She wanted to close her eyes but did not. She wanted to ask where Adam was but did not.

"Eavesdroppers never hear any good of themselves," said Fitzgerald. He shook his head with apparent regret, his voice soft, even gentle without the angry denunciation of earlier. "My fondness for you was genuine, you know. We might have made a successful marriage of it."

She drew in a deep breath to speak. "Why betray your country? You have a good practice, a modest living. Many a-man would be content."

"*Content?*" he spat the word like it was a profanity. "Content to see stupid men grow rich and powerful while I bow and scrape? I was made for greater things."

"Great things are earned."

He looked at her sadly. "How can I expect you to understand? You, a mere governess…you *have* nothing and you *expect* nothing. You think me Judas, selling out Christ for thirty pieces of silver? Wars can be profitable ventures. Other have done it, so why not me?"

She had promised herself to be strong, to not show fear or to beg, but her resolve could not overcome her fear.

"I implore you, Peter, if you had any regard for me at all, let Adam go. Walk away from this. It's not too late."

Fitzgerald cupped her cheek and caressed it. Olivia let out a shaky breath.

"What would you offer me in exchange for his life? Yours?"

She swallowed and nodded. "If you guarantee Adam's freedom, yes."

Fitzgerald frowned, appearing to consider it. "If we were *wed*, you could not testify against me. There is that, I suppose."

He stood and took a few steps away. "A woman who consents to be my wife because I have the power of life and death over her lover? If I hated you, I might even do it – force your obedience, force your submission to me. I could take great delight in my cruelty. But even that wouldn't be enough, would it? It really wouldn't matter if I treated you with great cruelty or great kindness. You would always love *him*." He turned to face her. "I thought all those months ago that if I won your mind, your body would follow. How ironic that now you're offering me your body, but I will never possess your mind."

"Please, Peter, you know this is over."

"Alas, I have no choice. The rendezvous is set. I promised them Hardacre and you are here to keep him obedient."

Chapter Thirty

EVERY TIME HE closed his eyes, Adam relived the moment over again. The sharp report of the musket. Harold falling to the ground dead.

Dead because of him.

The nightmarish dreams caused by his concussion terrified him.

Constance came to him in one. She was dead because of him. She appeared and looked at him in surprise across the tumble-down wall of the ruins in the woods. She was still young but he was as old as he was now.

Olivia!

He killed her, too? No…that was Harold. He killed Harold.

What happened to Olivia?

If only his head would stop pounding.

A bucket of cold water was tossed in his face, a blessing and a curse. It woke him up at last, but it reminded him how much his goddamned body hurt.

"Wakey, wakey," announced Black Angus. "Major Wilkinson wants a wee word with you. Get to your feet."

Adam started to rise, but apparently not fast enough for the Scot, who pulled him up by the arm, tugging at his already strained muscles.

The door to the room opened. The glare of a new dawning sunrise made his eyes water. From what he could see, the Carrick or even the sea itself was a short distance away. Another man, Red, Adam suspected, shoved him in the center of his back to propel him down the short hallway into a small sitting room. By the looks of things, it was the main room of a cottage; a door with a small window led into it, led immediately outside.

Wilkinson sat on a humble timber settle, looking more grey and less commanding than Adam ever recalled seeing him. Nevertheless, the man had made himself at home. A working man's earthenware mug and a small teapot sat on a tray beside him. On a footstool were papers and a small traveling inkwell.

"Tell me what you did last night," he asked, his voice mild, perhaps even resigned. "Who were you signaling? And what is the significance of the chandler's shop at Charteris House?"

Despite his aches and pains, Adam stood to attention. "You'll get no answers until I see Miss Collins set free, unharmed."

Wilkinson thumped his fist on the arm of the settle. The tea tray rattled, but the man managed to hold his temper somewhat.

"Last night, you were in a better position to bargain," he said. "All things considered, I'm not in a mood to cooperate. The Frenchies will loosen your tongue soon enough. I've seen men go mad in their prisons, they're a living death, a horror you cannot imagine."

"Why wait for the French? Why didn't you do it last night? Your men demonstrated they were quite capable of killing an unarmed man."

Wilkinson didn't answer. No one in the room answered.

Adam's movement was so swift it took everyone by surprise, even Adam himself. Before he had even formed a coherent thought to do so, he lunged at Black Angus, seized the dirk from the scabbard at his waist, and had a startled Wilkinson by the shirt, then around the throat with the knife at his ribs.

"Where is Olivia? Bring her here!"

No one moved. Wilkinson himself made only a token resistance, but was otherwise cooperative. Adam edged him backwards toward the door.

"You're under orders to deliver me to France alive? Why? I can see why it mattered if you thought I was your agent, but now?"

Adam's mind raced for possible reasons – then it struck him in one of those moments of clarity when it is as though a thin curtain has been pulled back and what was diffuse and indistinct becomes sharp and clear.

They can't *kill me. They've been given orders.*

"Your Miss Collins is in safe hands...for now."

He shoved Wilkinson hard in the back, propelling him forward toward the settle. The man regained his feet in time to avoid falling over the footstool. Adam brandished the knife at the men in the room.

"The young woman will remain safe as long as you are cooperative, Hardacre. Mr. Fitzgerald will be seeing to her welfare."

It was like a blow to the gut. Wilkinson smiled as though he'd made a checkmate move.

"Where is she?"

Wilkinson's grin widened. He shook his head. "Just give me the knife, Hardacre. You can't get away."

Adam squeezed the dirk's handle and swiftly brought the blade to under his own neck.

"Yes, I can. So tell me where Miss Collins is or you'll have to explain why the man you went to great lengths to secure just cut his own throat."

If the situation wasn't so dire, Adam might laugh at the absurdity of his situation. Here he was, threatening to self-murder, surrounded by men who would be only too happy to attend to the task if circumstances were different.

He backed against the door and felt the knob under his free hand. So far, no one had approached him. He opened the door.

No more than half a dozen steps away, a half-dozen horsemen, their noses and mouths covered, tricorn hats pulled low on their faces, bore down on him out of nowhere.

OLIVIA HAD MANAGED to persuade Fitzgerald to free her hands and give her a few moments of privacy as she attended to her needs. While waiting for his return, she scoured the boatshed, looking for anything she might use to effect an escape. There was nothing, just discarded detritus – the head of an old iron boat hook, missing its timber pole, lengths of rotten rope, a worm-eaten oar.

Through the warped timbers of the double doors, she could see the glint of sunlight on water. It was morning. If she could get away, surely there would be a nearby farmhouse and someone to give her aid.

Where on earth was Sir Daniel? Surely when she didn't arrive back at the inn, he'd have sent someone in search. But where? Where was she? The carriage last night had traveled for hours. She might be anywhere twenty miles up or down the Cornish coast from Falmouth.

Olivia looked at the door out to the water at the far end of the shed. The promise of freedom sparkling through the gaps between the old timbers drew her closer to the little slipway. Perhaps, she could force the open the rusty lock and chain that held the doors closed. What with?

The boat hook.

She picked it up, conscious that Fitzgerald would return at any moment. The weight of the iron was awkward in her hand but it was the best she could think of.

She stepped down onto the wear-polished timbers of the slip and reached out to the chain, trying to twist the hook into a link, imagining it somehow opening up. It didn't, and she couldn't get the leverage or purchase she needed at arm's length. She looked down at the lapping water. How deep was it, how slippery were the boards beneath?

Then she noticed the gap between the bottom of the door and the slipway planks. No more than two inches, rising and falling with the lapping of the water. But how much more space was there under the door beneath the water?

There was no time to remove stockings or shoes. She stepped down the ramp until she was ankle deep, then turned sideways and, lowering herself, put one foot into the gap to gauge the water's depth. It did not reach as far as her knee. Her foot squelched in mud, but she felt sure there would be enough of a gap slide to under, even if she was momentarily submerged.

The chain that locked the side door rattled.

Fitzgerald!

It was now or never. She dropped the useless boat hook in the water with a splash, sat on the slipway timbers and plunged both feet in. She gripped the lower edge of the boat doors and began to pull and slide her body beneath them. Her skirt, weighted with water, hampered her. She warred with the panic in her breast and lowered the rest of her body into the water.

"Olivia!"

She heard Fitzgerald yell, but she was committed. With one deep breath, she squeezed her eyes shut and shoved herself beneath the water and the boathouse door.

She felt her rear sliding on mud and her nose scrape the bottom edge of the door. She let go with her right hand – and felt her left wrist grabbed by Fitzgerald who plunged onto the ramp above her.

Olivia scrambled in the water, her feet slipping in the mud, unable to get purchase or pull her arm free. She fought against the urge to open her mouth to scream underwater. Then her head popped up above the surface again inside the door as Fitzgerald tugged her back inside. She gasped for breath.

"Stupid bitch!" Fitzgerald cursed. "What the hell are you trying to do? Kill yourself?"

Fitzgerald began straining to haul her up the ramp by the one arm, fulminating as he went.

"I'll make you regret crossing me, you sow. For as long as you live, you'll regret it. But you won't live long, I promise you that, you worthless c—"

He stopped mid-curse as his heels slipped on the wet wood and he dropped with an "oof!" on his behind. They slid together back down the slipway and ended in a tangle in the water, jammed between the planks and the bottom of the door.

"Bitch!" shouted Fitzgerald.

He went to throw his arm over her, his fist clenched, aiming for her face. Olivia's right hand felt something hard in the mud below and she grasped it instinctively and swung it in Fitzgerald's direction. The man's fist struck her cheek and, simultaneously, she heard a scream, but it wasn't hers.

When her vision cleared, all she could see was red seeping between Fitzgerald's fingers as he clutched his face and neck. Blood gushed down his arms and colored the muddy water slopping around them. Still screaming in pain, Fitzgerald began to slide further into the water.

Olivia scrambled back and screamed, too. Fitzgerald looked at her. His cheek and neck were torn open where the boat hook had struck him. His eyes implored her to help as his screaming turned to a gurgling groan. Olivia screamed again for the both of them as Fitzgerald's mouth seemed to open grotesquely wider than it should and more blood spilled out.

He slumped into the water and was still.

Peter Fitzgerald was dead.

And yet he screamed…no, *she* screamed until her voice gave out and all that was left was tears. With difficulty, soaked in bloody water and caked in mud, she pushed herself backwards up the sloped boat ramp, desperate not to slip and slide back down to where Fitzgerald's body shifted with the lapping of the water.

She didn't react when the side door to the shed burst open and managed only the barest flinch when a pair of hands touched her shoulders gently.

"Olivia, sweetheart." The voice sounded it like it was miles away, a sound caught by the wind. "Look at me, my love."

She followed the voice and fell into the hazel eyes of Adam Hardacre. She was lifted and she knew he carried her, but she could not feel his arms. She felt nothing. Around about, between the boathouse and a nearby cottage, were a dozen men, all dressed in black, their faces obscured by scarves. They seemed ghostlike and unreal, like everything else.

Adam paid them no heed, so neither did she. Her eyes fell on a cart near the cottage. Bound together in the back were Wilkinson and two henchmen whose names she had never learned.

She looked back over Adam's shoulder to the boathouse where two of the black figures were about to enter. They would retrieve Fitzgerald's corpse. She squeezed her eyes shut, hoping to make the vision of the man's ruined face disappear.

Despite the heat of the summer's day, Olivia was cold, her filthy, waterlogged clothes chilling her to the core. Or was it her heart that was frozen? Why could she not feel?

One of the ghostly men approached. He pulled down his scarf and adjusted his tricorn hat.

The features of Sir Daniel Ridgeway emerged from the specter.

"How is the lady?"

"I don't know," Adam replied.

The pain and weariness in his voice pulled her from the depths.

"I'm unharmed. C-c-cold…." Her answer resulted in Ridgeway removing his cloak and sweeping it around Adam's shoulders and covering her with it also.

Up on the road, a carriage waited under the shade of some trees.

To Olivia's surprise, Lady Abigail alighted with the energy of a much younger woman, though unlike previous occasions, she was dressed simply and practically in a navy blue gown, her bright white hair pulled back and hidden under a wide scarf of the same shade of blue.

"I thought I told you to stay in the village," Ridgeway called.

"I must be getting hard of hearing," she quipped. Ridgeway gave his wife a particular look, which she ignored.

"I was perfectly safe here with this." From her pocket emerged a small flintlock pistol with a barrel no longer than three inches in length. "Come on. Let's get this bedraggled pair somewhere to recuperate. Dr. Osbourne is waiting at the house."

Adam carried Olivia up to the carriage, Ridgeway walking alongside. The older man's expression softened as his wife approached him for a kiss.

Olivia wondered at the pair. Who *were* they really? What made them how they were? She waited until Adam had placed her safely into the carriage before she looked at him. A dark shadow of beard coated his chin, the skin under his eyes was dark, made more severe by the hard, concerned set of his mouth.

Lady Abigail climbed in and closed the door. "On!" she called and the carriage jerked into motion.

For now, all Olivia could do was close her eyes and allow Lady Abigail to remove her sodden, ruined clothes and cover her in blankets. She forced her heavy lids open to see Adam slumped in the corner of the bench opposite, his eyes closed, forehead against the window glass. He sported cuts and bruises, but that appeared to be the worst.

They had much to talk about – of poor Harold, Fitzgerald, and even of Constance and Christopher.

She shook her head at Abigail's silent offer of brandy from a flask, instead leaning forward and reaching for Adam's hand. Although his eyes remained closed, Adam took her hand and squeezed it tight.

That was answer enough for now.

Chapter Thirty-One

ADAM SLEPT FOR an entire day.

When he woke, he found himself in a large house in the middle of a large estate outside of Truro. Bishop's Wood – the home of Sir Daniel and Lady Abigail. He was ravenous. The tea and pastries brought up to him were enough to slake his thirst and ease the worst of his hunger as he shaved. In the mirror, he watched the footmen behind him prepare a bath. When he was dressed, he would have breakfast proper downstairs.

The straight blade glinted in the sun shining through the window. Adam recalled the threat he'd made to Wilkinson to slit his own throat. It was a threat made in desperation. Would he have done it to save Olivia's life?

Once he had waded through the fear of mortality that all sane men have but only cowards fear, the answer was still the same.

He would have done it.

Adam knew he loved Olivia more than his own life. He loved her thoughtfulness, her compassion, and her desire to right wrongs. He admired her quick wit and bravery.

The thought of how close he came to letting her go still hurt like a punch to the gut. But now, he was certain of his feelings, ready to commit to a wife, a home…a family. This time, he would be a father in more than name only. He would be there to see his children grow. They would know him and his love.

It was the only thing he could do to honor Christopher, wherever his lost boy was – to be there for the children who came after him, the father he wished he could have been for his son.

But after this ordeal, would Olivia feel the same? He hoped that in Lady Abigail she could find a confidante and a way through the shadow-world they inhabited.

He would propose marriage again. Properly. He'd been a fool to accept Olivia's offer of intimacy without it. Never again would she be in doubt of where his heart lay.

IN THE DINING room, he found Sir Daniel filling his plate from the array of dishes from the sideboard. He was alone.

"Help yourself, old man," he replied, taking his plate to the table. "If you're looking for Miss Collins, she's asked for breakfast in her room this morning."

Adam speared a slice of ham. "I haven't seen her since…how is she?"

"Stronger than you think."

As Adam recalled the day he held her in his arms, soaked to the skin and covered with blood, his newly awakened appetite withered.

"I know she said she was unhurt…but there was so much blood."

"None of it was hers – she just has a few scratches and bruises, that's all."

He joined Ridgeway at the table and made an attempt at the potatoes and ham.

"You know, if anyone can understand the ordeal she's been through, it's Abigail," said Sir Daniel.

Adam forked a slice of ham into his mouth, keeping his attention fixed on his plate to prevent his disbelief from showing. Ridgeway *was* talking about Abigail? The *Lady* Abigail? She was the type of woman to declare mismatched gloves a monumental disaster.

Apparently, his caution wasn't enough. "You shouldn't underestimate my wife, old man. One day I'll tell you how she broke into a French lunatic asylum to rescue me."

The tone in his voice suggested Ridgeway wasn't joking and, when Adam raised his head to see, the man's expression showed no amusement.

"Don't miscalculate the strength of women, and never that of a woman in love. Your Miss Collins will be fine and, if I judge her right, she won't appreciate being coddled. But since you're on the mend, I have a few questions that need answers, so I'll arrange a horse to be saddled to take us back to Kenstec House."

OLIVIA TIED THE robe around her tightly and pressed a hand to the cloth that covered her still drying hair. She looked from the window and watched two familiar figures mount horses in the yard below. Adam was the leaner of the pair. His fair hair glinted in the sun.

She touched a finger to the window, silently hoping he might glance up and see her. He and Sir Daniel rode off without a second glance. For some strange reason, it felt like a slight.

Another presence emerged behind her. Olivia glanced back to see Lady Abigail with a soft expression on her face. It departed as the woman became aware of Olivia's attention.

"Don't worry about them. Daniel won't keep him away too long; they'll be home for supper. You can join us if you feel up to it."

Olivia moved away from the window and unwound the cloth from her hair to let it dry by the fire. As she handled it, she watched the flames highlight threads of red and gold in what she always considered dull and ordinary brown – certainly, her hair was not the attention-catching white-blonde of Lady Abigail's.

"You've yet to talk about your ordeal," said the woman. She picked up a comb and gestured for Olivia to sit.

"Perhaps I don't want to."

"But that wouldn't be the truth, would it?"

Olivia closed her eyes. She preferred the haughty Lady Abigail, the woman who embraced her own status and wealth, instead of this one who was kind and sympathetic. Too much of this kindness from her and she would fall to tears.

"I took a man's life. I could hang for it."

"No, you won't. You won't even face an inquest. Besides, Peter Fitzgerald brought his death upon himself, did he not? He attacked and almost killed you. If you had not defended yourself, what do you think might have happened to you?"

Olivia snatched the comb from Abigail's hand and wrenched it through her slowly drying hair in savage strokes in an attempt to do *anything* other than cry.

"Come now, put those tears away. There's nothing worse than self-pity. Would you rather wallow as a pathetic victim of circumstance or be the mistress of your own future alongside a good man who loves you?"

"What would you know? Living here in safety and luxury, among people who cater to your every whim?"

"Ah, anger. Excellent. A much better emotion than pity. I can use anger; I can't use pity. What is it you'd like me to tell you? That *I* had to resort to violence to save my own life – to save the life of my husband? That I know what it's like to find everything completely upended, forced to live on the edge of terror? I can if you like, but I shan't – a pissing contest is what the baser sort of *men* do."

The heat of the fire was only slightly more scalding than Abigail's censure. Olivia turned her head to comb her hair from the other side.

"Had you wounded him instead, Peter Fitzgerald would still face a traitor's death." Abigail rose from the dressing table stool. "But if you still feel you have to make penance, then do it for the living. Find something that gives your ordeal meaning. Justify the reason why

Providence decided to spare your life instead of the solicitor."

Olivia fought the words, hating Lady Abigail because she knew what she said to be the truth.

"Think about what I've said," she continued as she moved to leave the room. "There's a future to be lived if you want it. But only if you're truly as brave as you've already shown yourself capable of being."

THE EVENTS OF two evenings past seemed an age ago, but here he was, attention drawn to the dried blood on the bent iron spike that had been part of the guard rail on Kenstec's tower top. Adam hadn't realized Dunbar had stabbed himself as he fell. How odd that a certain measure of pity should arise, now that the man was dead.

He shook his head, trying to make sense of it all. Coming to the house was useful. Sparks of recollection, illuminated as though by lightning, flashed through his memory. Adam relayed all of it to Ridgeway as it came to him.

Ridgeway shook his head. "Something doesn't add up."

"I don't know what else to tell you; we've been through it twice."

"I know. The fault isn't yours. We'll go through it one more time and I'll parrot back to *you* what you've said to me. It's clear there's something I'm not seeing."

It was the last thing Adam felt like doing but he trudged down the ladder and they crossed to the attic room where Harold had been held.

"Olivia handed you the key," said Ridgeway. "While she lit the lamps, you opened this door."

Adam nodded.

"When you went in, you found him with his hands bound together. Bound behind?"

Adam shook his head. "No, in front."

Ridgeway went meticulously through each step until they were back on the roof once more.

"How long would you say it was between Lieutenant Bickmore leaving you and when you saw him being shot at?"

"No more than a minute or two, why?"

His question was ignored, and annoyance started to bubble in Adam.

"Did you see Bickmore's body after he was shot?" Ridgeway asked.

This time Adam didn't hide his irritation. "No, he was shot and he went down. After that, I was too *busy* trying to stop Dunbar from killing me and Olivia."

Ridgeway glanced over the edge to the grass below. There was a shadow in the lawn.

"Dunbar certainly left an impression anyway."

"What the *hell* are you driving at?"

"What I'm saying is Bickmore *didn't*. There was no body, no blood. We searched the house and immediate grounds and the woods surrounding for good measure in case he'd crawled away. There was no trace of the lieutenant at all."

Adam was aware he was staring down at where he'd last seen Harold, but couldn't stop himself. He shook his head slowly and, despite his head for heights, began to feel vertiginous. He returned to the hatch and looked down to the ladder into the room below. He ignored the rungs and straddled the ladder's side rails to slide to the floor below.

"You're wrong," he called back up to Ridgeway. "Your men weren't thorough enough. They've made a mistake. If Harold was injured, he could still get away and your men might have missed him."

The older man joined him. "We weren't so late getting here that we didn't round up three of Wilkinson's men in the house. If Bickmore was wounded and got away, he would have sought treatment. My men have spoken to every doctor, barber and midwife in the county.

No one has presented with a gunshot wound. And he's not lying dead anywhere around here, we've covered every inch."

"So what is it you're suggesting?" Adam had to ask the question, but he was also afraid he knew the answer. He waited for Ridgeway to give voice to niggling doubts he himself had been ignoring ever since Olivia raised them.

He *knew* what he saw when the second shot rang out. He *knew* Harold Bickmore. And yet...

"There's more, if you're ready to hear it."

Adam squeezed his eyes shut. "Go on."

"I've spoken to the captain of the *Andromeda*. It returned to port with a dozen men in the brig. They'll face a court martial for attempted mutiny at sea. At the least three of the men have told the same story about being angry at *your* treatment. They've refused to name the instigator and, since I've vouched for *you*, there's only one other man it can be."

Adam scoffed. "If you and Captain Sinclair suspected Harold, why wasn't he arrested?"

"Because Harold Bickmore hasn't been part of the Royal Navy since April. He resigned his commission the day after you quit. There's a reward for his arrest."

Ridgeway frowned at his reaction. "You didn't know, did you?"

Adam's head was still spinning despite being down off the roof. He gave Ridgeway a look of contempt and half-stumbled down the main staircase to stride out on the lawn to the spot between two garden beds where he saw Harold fall.

A few moments later, he heard Ridgeway behind him.

"*C'est la guerre*," he said.

That's war. That much French Adam *did* know.

"There's still much to learn. Both here and at the cottage we found an absolute trove of documents my wife will ask your Miss Collins to help translate for us. And we're confident Wilkinson and his gang will talk. They usually do in the end."

Ridgeway dropped a hand on Adam's shoulder. "This is as large as our victories get, Lieutenant – accept them as they come and move on."

Adam raised his head heavenwards toward the trees still in their full summer glory.

"I'll see you back in the house."

Ridgeway nodded in acknowledgement and walked away.

Adam knew he should go back to the house, too, and move forward with his life the best he could. But the fact he had so utterly mistaken about Harold made him wonder what else he was wrong about.

He recalled the years he and Harold spent at sea – as comrades-in-arms and, despite their difference in wealth and class, *friends,* too. He thought he knew the man as well as he knew himself. What did that say about Adam Hardacre's judgment? How could be possibly trust his instincts on *anything*?

His Miss Collins...Ridgeway was much more certain about that fact than he was at this particular moment.

Olivia.

He'd barely had two minutes alone with her since their ordeal.

He loved her more than life itself. It was worth the risk to open his heart and share it with another. He would ask her to marry him, if she'd have him.

And there was one more piece of his past to be resolved before he could move on, and he needed Olivia by his side to do it.

Chapter Thirty-Two

OLIVIA POLITELY DECLINED the offer of company. She needed time alone.

She wandered through the hedgerows until she reached the formal gardens. The sweet scent of gardenias drew her in. How had she never before appreciated the deep green glossy leaves and the soft and waxy folds of the flowers? And the merry pink of the carnations and the orange hues of the marigolds, too – not to mention the spring of the lawn under foot?

She was alive and safe. Adam was safe, too.

Never would she underestimate the miracle she had been given.

The gravel settled under foot as she found a path to follow which led to a lake where two white swans swam serenely, barely causing a ripple on its mirror-like surface. Across the other side of the water was a summer house. That's where she wanted to be.

The lake was large enough to row on and the Ridgeways had the means to do it. A little rowboat lay upside down on its gunwales on the little jetty, useless to her without assistance. Never mind, she saw where the path turned through the meadow grasses, and followed where it beckoned until she had reached her destination.

The arbor was freshly whitewashed and inside was a daybed covered by a canvas. She removed it to expose the cushions of purple, pinks and gold.

If she closed her eyes, she saw flashes of darkness and violence, so she kept them open and watched the bulrushes at the edge of the lake sway gently in the breeze.

The warmth of the afternoon sun touched her shoulders, warming her, reminding her that a new day was a new beginning, new every morning.

Part of a Sunday homily recalled itself.

It is of the Lord's mercies that we are not consumed, because His compassions fail not.

They are new every morning: great is Thy faithfulness.

Olivia smiled, her resolve unshakable.

Yes, she was ready for the new beginning.

Across the lake and up the path, an approaching figure caught her eye.

She remained where she was. Adam would find her. He would always find her.

ADAM WAS TOLD that Olivia had gone for a walk in the grounds, so he went in search of her.

He tried to set aside all of his questions and doubts about Harold and other members of the *Society*. Yet the feeling of betrayal was raw. Adam was a man who valued control, but he'd learned the harsh lesson that there would always be things he was powerless to prevent.

But should that stop him from living? From sharing his life and his love with Olivia?

How foolish he had been to think he could walk away from Ridgeway and his King's Rogues.

It was part of who he was now, as indelible as the tattoo on his right hand. Would Olivia accept him as he was?

He followed a gravel path through formal gardens. Hedged borders stood as battlements against the encroaching grass discharging the duty of protecting the exotic flowers within.

Adam glanced in one of the manicured garden beds as he passed and spotted a plant out of place, a weed, though he knew little of gardening to be sure.

It was nature's way of saying that order was a fleeting thing and vigilance was required to maintain it.

There was much work to do to. Fitzgerald's office had been raided by some of Ridgeway's men this morning. The trove of documents they expected to find would hopefully reveal more.

How long had Harold been involved in this conspiracy? How far did its tentacles reach? What was so important about *him* that the *Society* thought it was worth risking everything to bring him to France?

To have these answers, he would have to find Harold. And he would. By God, he would.

The only question was whether Olivia would stand at his side to do it.

Adam walked through the gate pillars which led out to the lawn beyond, the glint of water drawing him to it. Somehow, he knew Olivia would be there.

He reached the lake and walked to the end of the jetty. Across the water was a summer house and that's where Olivia was.

The doubts emerged from the depths. Did he intrude? Did she want him at all?

The woman across the lake gave him no clue.

The shortest distance was across the lake. Adam righted the small rowboat on the jetty beside him and set it in the water and retrieved the oars which had been underneath. Once settled in the boat, he pushed himself away from land and began to row.

The swans called to one another. Dogs barked in the distance. The dipping of the oars created their own music but there was no hail or acknowledgment as he made his way to his destination.

Although his thoughts were only on Olivia, Adam kept his eyes on the receding jetty, using it to guide his course.

How apt, that as he moved away from the past, his attention remained fixed on it. The jetty he could see, along with all his mistakes and regrets – Harold, Constance, Christopher…

The future he moved toward was something he could not see, but he took it on faith that it would be there, that *she* would be there at the end of it.

He tied the boat to a smaller jetty that served the summer house and approached Olivia on the large daybed cautiously.

It had been two days since their ordeal. Adam found himself searching her brown eyes for clues as to how she felt.

"It's going to be a long trip if you don't speak to me," she said.

He wondered at the words a moment until recalling that he had said the words to her one rainy day at Ponsnowyth.

God, that seemed a lifetime ago.

"I should think that after yesterday," he answered, "well, the day before yesterday – you'd hardly entertain the idea of speaking to *me* at all."

A smile emerged, telling him that he recalled the meeting correctly. Olivia shifted on her seat in silent invitation for him to join her. Adam grabbed hold of it like a drowning man.

He sat beside her, searching her face. There were bruises. A visceral rage welled. Olivia calmed him with a touch.

"They're only minor hurts, they will fade with time," she told him. "It's the ones we cannot see which concern me, like Harold."

"You know the extent of his betrayal?"

"Lady Abigail told me what Sir Daniel believes, and I had my own suspicions."

"Which I should have listened to," said Adam bitterly.

Olivia reached out and touched his hand, shaking her head as she did so. "He was your friend."

"That is why his betrayal is so bitter to me." Adam took her hand and held it. "I can't let it go, Olivia. I *have* to follow this through to the end. It means that I live the life of a spy. What that means for us, I cannot say. I never want secrets to come between us, but I can't involve you in this, not after what happened at the boat house."

Olivia returned a squeeze.

"I'm already involved, whether you like it or not," she said. Olivia move closer until their thighs touched. Adam folded her into an embrace.

"Besides, you're no longer the only spy in the family."

"*What?*"

Adam pulled back until he could see Olivia's face properly. Her expression might have been sober but for a twitch of her lips that hinted at a smile.

"Sir Daniel may have his rogues, but Lady Abigail has her league of lady spies," she said.

Adam closed his eyes and groaned. Olivia giggled.

"I love you and I know what I'm getting involved with," she whispered close to his ear. It tickled, raising a run of gooseflesh down his neck and along his arm. "I've been involved ever since that day you kissed me at the priory ruins."

He hauled her onto his lap, using his lips on her face, her neck, her hair, to reveal his heart, as he could not do in words. She returned his kisses just as ardently.

Adam held on to Olivia while he shifted his position until he lay on the daybed with the woman he loved more than life draped over him.

"Then there is only one thing left to say."

Olivia placed her hands on his shoulders, supporting her weight to look at him.

"Oh, don't tell me that you forbid me from working alongside you and the Ridgeways."

Adam ran his fingers up her sun-warmed back, through her hair. He shook his head and allowed himself to smile. Although he was confident of the answer, the question still had to be asked.

"Olivia Collins, I love you. Will you marry me?"

"Yes. Absolutely yes."

Olivia may have said more after that, but Adam was too filled with joy to take in more. He kissed her deeply. The press of her body on his waking desire. His hands roamed over her form. In the late afternoon summer sun, they found their new beginning together.

Epilogue

Early October 1804

ADAM WALKED DOWN the long hallway in dress uniform, a tricorn under his arm rather than the bosun's hat of his old rank.

The lieutenant's uniform and rank was his, but no one would know it outside these select few.

What a difference a few months made.

The commendation promised to him meant little. Adam was a man who sought only justice. He wanted his due and nothing more, but Ridgeway, walking beside him with Olivia and Abigail behind, insisted on using his favor to find out this one thing.

It was not the boardroom of the Naval Office they approached, but the library, where the records of the *Pendragon* would be made available to Adam.

The clerk rose from his seat and shook him by the hand and Ridgeway's as well.

Just four months ago, Adam had learned he was a father. He tried to imagine the man his son had grown into. How much like him would he be when – *if* – he found him? How much like Constance?

"Sir Daniel, Lieutenant Hardacre," said the clerk, a young man aged about twenty, the same age as his son. "I've drawn all the records I could find for a Christopher Hardacre and his service. I'm afraid I've come to an impasse, sirs.

"It's been no easy task getting this far. The last record we have for the person was a sign-on for wages on the *Pendragon*. I believe you already know that?"

Adam nodded.

The clerk continued, "She was a merchant ship."

"*Was*?"

"I…uh…well, perhaps you should read everything here directly, sir."

Adam took the proffered seat at the desk and willed his stomach to settle. He glanced over and saw the concerned faces of Olivia and Lady Abigail.

Sir Daniel and his wife exchanged a subtle look and withdrew from the room.

Olivia placed a hand on his shoulder.

"Do you want to be alone?" she asked.

Adam could only muster a curt shake his head. He let out an unsteady breath.

"No, it's only right that you be here. If not for you, I'd have never known of Christopher's existence at all. In a way, you gave him life as much as if you had been his own mother. If the report is…*bad*…then at least we can mourn him together."

The clerk had bookmarked several pages in the volume. The first revealed the specifications of the ship in neatly written columns of blue ink. Adam read them through, the numbers forming the shape of the vessel in his mind. It was not at all a prestigious or heavily-armed ship but good enough for a merchantman in the waters of the Mediterranean.

The next page showed the crew manifest. There were seventy-five in total and, among the last to sign on, was the tentative hand of *Christopher John Hardacre (cabin boy)*.

The details of what happened to the *Pendragon* were sketchy at best. The ship was still burning when a Spanish ship encountered it. Only a dozen lives were saved; the same number of corpses were recovered.

The survivors told of a raid by a Barbary Coast xebec which boarded them with hundreds of men. The crew fought; many died. The most valuable of their cargo was taken.

Adam paused, gathering his thoughts. Life at sea was a dangerous business. He, perhaps, knew that better than anyone. And yet, if anyone had cared about the sailors aboard the ship, that was more than a decade ago. Time had passed, the mourners gone.

Even so, Adam carried a slight flicker of hope that one ten-year-old boy had been among the survivors.

That hope extinguished as he found the list recording the twenty missing, presumed killed.

One of them was cabin boy Christopher John Hardacre.

The page before him blurred. Adam closed his eyes before his tears could fall and smear the ink.

Ponsnowyth Church
October 1804

ADAM WAS HAPPY to have arrived early at the Ponsnowyth church alone. He wanted time to reflect, to pray, though it was not normally his habit. In recent times, Adam had discovered he had a lot to be thankful for – and that required someone to give thanks to.

Now, he stood at the entrance of the church where he could see a solidly-built figure making his way across the lawn. It was Reverend Fuller in his vestments, a black Bible under his arm. He greeted Adam warmly and joked about whether or not he was a nervous groom. He assured the man he was not. There was no need to be. He was as sure of Olivia's love as she was of his. His bride would be here soon enough.

Over the next ten minutes, villagers arrived and he gladly accepted their best wishes. The pews were filled, apart from the one at the front.

Adam waited at the entrance until a carriage pulled up outside the gate. That was Sir Daniel, Lady Abigail, and his wife-to-be.

It was supposed to be bad luck to see the bride in her gown before she entered the church, and he had enough respect for some superstitions to come away from the door and make his way to the altar. But part way down, he paused.

The new brass plaque had been mounted to the wall. It stood out starkly among the rest now dulled with age.

To the memory of Constance Denton (1765-1784)
and her son Christopher, lost at sea (1784-1794).

Long after Beaufort Denton's grandiose stone weathered away to nothing and his name was forgotten, his daughter's and his grandson's memory would remain bright and alive. He and Olivia would make sure of that.

Reverend Fuller gestured him to his place at the altar. Sir Daniel and Lady Abigail walked down and took their seats just as Olivia appeared at the back of the church.

She wore a gown of sea green silk, shot with blue, the color bringing out the warmth of her skin and shade of her hair. Around her neck was a cream cameo tied with a blue ribbon. She carried a simple bouquet of Calla lilies.

Even if she had been dripping with jewels, Olivia could not have looked more beautiful to him than she did at this moment.

Right now, Adam had the world. And it was enough.

The End

Adam Hardacre will return in book two of The King's Rogues: Spyfall.

Author's Note

My amazing publisher, Kathryn Le Veque, told me that she'd like to see more stories with another hero bearing the Hardacre name.

And as it so happened, I wanted to return to the beautiful Cornish coast, which was the setting of my first novel. I came back with the concept for a new series which is *The King's Rogues* – set during the early years of the Napoleonic Wars, ten years before the *Heart of the Corsairs* series.

If you've read that series, then you'll know the hero, Kit Hardacre, knows nothing of his past. If I were to continue the Hardacre line, then I had better give him a past! And that is the origin of Adam Hardacre.

And if you're intrigued at what might happen when two such strong personalities meet, then I hope you enjoy the story *Father's Day* in the *Night of Angels* Dragonblade Publishing Christmas anthology.

While I'm introducing new friends, I thought I'd welcome back old ones, too. I can't think of anyone better to lead these Rogues than Sir Daniel and Lady Abigail Ridgeway. They have an adventure romance of their own in *Moonstone Conspiracy*, one of my earlier novels.

And my husband, Duncan, is delighted. He has been one of Lady Abigail's most vocal advocates since her first appearance as the cynical and sharp-tongued love rival in *Moonstone Obsession*.

When doing research for *The King's Rogues*, I unearthed an interesting tidbit of history about one of the many ideas floated by Napoleon to invade England. One in particular which was intriguing but abandoned due to its impracticality.

But what if it wasn't impractical if it had been approached in a different way?

That sparked my imagination – and sorry, I can't tell you what it is because it will spoil the final book in *The King's Rogues* series!

I hope you enjoy *The King's Rogues*.

Made in the USA
Columbia, SC
30 May 2020